Praise for *Cooking for Picasso*

"With lively characters and a twisting plot, Aubray's novel is a smart and satisfying tale of family, creativity, romance, and intrigue." —*Booklist*

"This touching and delectable novel invokes the breathtaking scenery of the South of France and the Côte d'Azur.... Aubray paints a beautiful story of love, art, food, and the enduring romance of the Mediterranean." —*Fodor's Travel*

"A quest for the missing Picasso worthy of Cary Grant and Audrey Hepburn ... As with any good quest, the heroine finds love along the way, too. An amuse-bouche filled with secret ingredients, covert liaisons, and hidden compartments." —*Kirkus Reviews*

"The novel alternates between Ondine's encounters with Picasso and the repercussions of that brief affair, and Céline's adventures with cooking, love, and history along the Mediterranean. The real meat in this novel is the details (both real and imagined) of Picasso's fascinating life." —*Publishers Weekly*

"What would you do if you learned your grandmother had once whipped up meals for Pablo Picasso—and received a painting, now lost, in return? Head to the Côte d'Azur to track it down and fall in love with a chef, of course. Makeup artist Céline does just that in Aubray's delicious, atmospheric novel. You'll be glad you're along for the ride." —*People* magazine (Pick for "The Best New Books")

"[A] colorful family saga ... *Cooking for Picasso* ... is a novel about how people take what seems to be worthless and make it into something priceless. Whether it's a woman who creates meaning from sad circumstances or a genius who finds his way through a fallow period to create his masterwork, the characters in Camille Aubray's debut novel illustrate how essential bad is to good, life is to death and work is to art.... [Aubray] reveals that value lies not in what you own, but in who you are." —*The Washington Post*

"Two delicious love stories held together by the bonds of family unfold through Aubray's lyrical prose as she paints a portrait of Southern France, haute cuisine and the thrilling hunt for a missing masterpiece. With the skill of an artist, she describes Picasso at a crossroads in his life."   —*RT Book Reviews*

"An entertaining getaway for art lovers and Francophiles ... The novel's descriptions of food are mouthwatering, and Picasso himself is bold and engaging, a man of outsized passions."   —*Shelf Awareness*

"Charming."   —*Muses & Visionaries*

"Aubray produces a vivid and interesting picture of Picasso and doesn't shy away from his personal entanglements."
—*Historical Novels Review*

"In this delightful journey, a woman's kitchen skills blossom while Picasso struggles with the next steps in his career."   —*BookBub*

"Romance cum mystery—full of art, family bickering, and of course, fabulous food—fully enjoyable."   —*AudioFile*

"A tasty blend of romance, mystery, French cooking, plus the hairy old painter himself. Which Girl? What Window? Read on."
—MARGARET ATWOOD, *New York Times* bestselling author of *The Handmaid's Tale,* via Twitter

"Thrilling, fast-paced, and engaging, *Cooking for Picasso* is a novel that vividly portrays the South of France. Intrigue, art, food, and deception are woven together in a tale of love and betrayal around the life and legacy of Picasso. Touching and true, this well-written narrative made me long for my mother's *coq au vin* and for the sun of Juan-les-Pins."
—JACQUES PÉPIN, chef, TV personality, author of *The Apprentice: My Life in the Kitchen*

COOKING
FOR
PICASSO

COOKING FOR PICASSO

A Novel

CAMILLE AUBRAY

BALLANTINE BOOKS | NEW YORK

2017 Ballantine Books Trade Paperback Edition

Copyright © 2016 by Camille Aubray LLC
Reading group guide copyright © 2016 by Camille Aubray LLC

Published in the United States by Ballantine Books, an imprint of Random House, a division of Penguin Random House LLC, New York.

BALLANTINE and the HOUSE colophon are registered trademarks of
Penguin Random House LLC.
RANDOM HOUSE READER'S CIRCLE & Design is a registered trademark of
Penguin Random House LLC.

Published in hardcover in the United States by Ballantine Books, an imprint of
Random House, a division of Penguin Random House LLC, in 2016.

Library of Congress Cataloging-in-Publication Data
Names: Aubray, Camille, author.
Title: Cooking for Picasso : a novel / Camille Aubray.
Description: New York : Ballantine Books, 2016.
Identifiers: LCCN 2016016922 (print) | LCCN 2016024426 (ebook) |
ISBN 9780399177668 (trade paperback) | ISBN 9780399177675 (ebook)
Subjects: LCSH: Picasso, Pablo, 1881–1973—Fiction. | Women cooks—France—Fiction. |
Cooking—France—Fiction. | Biographical fiction. | BISAC: FICTION / Historical. |
FICTION / Sagas. | FICTION / Contemporary Women.
Classification: LCC PS3602.E46 C665 2016 (print) | LCC PS3602.E46 (ebook) |
DDC 813/.6—dc23
LC record available at https://lccn.loc.gov/2016016922

Printed in the United States of America on acid-free paper

randomhousebooks.com
randomhousereaderscircle.com

2 4 6 8 9 7 5 3 1

Book design by Susan Turner

For Mom

COOKING
FOR
PICASSO

PROLOGUE

Céline at Port Vauban, the French Riviera, 2016

My mother had a Provençal proverb that she recited to me in a cheerful singsong voice when I was a child: *L'eau trouble est le gain du pêcheur sage*. She told me it meant, "In troubled waters the wise fisherman benefits." I always assumed she was reassuring me that if you persevere in difficult times you get rewarded for your efforts.

But, as with most of the things my mother told me, I've discovered another meaning to this proverb, which is to say, "When things are chaotic, and everyone else is distracted by the storm and the roiling waves, you have a unique opportunity to get what you want without being noticed."

For some reason that proverb popped into my head today when I got an e-mail from a man I barely know: *I'm docking in Port Vauban at one o'clock, but just to pick up supplies. As soon as I've reloaded, I'm casting off. So if you want to do this thing, come now. Attached is a pass-card that will allow you to come aboard.*

I'd almost given up hope of hearing from him, so I was relieved, but then I noticed in alarm that it was already noon. When I hastily told my French colleagues at the movie studio in Nice that I must skip our "wrap party" so I could deal with some personal business in Antibes, they immediately assumed that I was sneaking away for a romantic rendezvous, teasingly calling me *La Americaine mystérieuse* as I hurried to my car.

Hitting the lunchtime traffic meant battling it out with tour buses, truckers and other locals, all in a hell-bent flurry to get to their *déjeuner*. But at one slowdown where I was forced to wait, I resolutely lifted my gaze and was able to regain a measure of composure.

For, no matter how many times I see this view, I still catch my breath at the way the Riviera's intense-but-soft sun fires up every color it touches to dazzling perfection: the pomegranate-red tiled roofs on candy-colored stone houses snuggled against terraced hills; the green of dense pine that clings to the shoreline and mountains; and most of all, blue—that infinite canopy of cobalt-blue sky over my head, and a wide-open aquamarine sea lapping at the shores, each reaching out to the other until they meet in a blurry watercolor embrace at a violet-blue horizon.

Now, as I arrive at Port Vauban breathless and fearful that the ship I'm looking for has already sailed, I grab the first parking space I find.

Then I set off on foot, hurrying softly in my espadrilles past a public park, where old men sit at picnic tables under the trees, playing cards in the melon-colored light reflecting off a star-shaped stone fort, whose bastions and ramparts have for centuries stood guard over the coastline against all invaders. At the farthest end of the harbor I reach "Billionaires' Quay".

Many of the biggest yachts in the world are berthed in this exclusive enclave, and some have so many decks and such complex architecture that they look more like a space station than a boat. I squint at all the fanciful names scripted on the sides of these luxurious ships whose proud owners are well known here: an Arab prince and his many sons; a reclusive American software magnate; a flamboyant Russian oil kingpin. The air simply crackles with power and money. At the tip of the dock there's a busy helipad, and right before my eyes a nimble helicopter lands as neatly as a dragonfly.

At last I find the yacht I'm looking for—*Le Troubadour,* a triple-decker with a royal blue hull and shining gold handrails. It's so big and imposing, I'm almost afraid to go near it. The crewmen, crisply dressed in matching blue uniforms, observe me warily as I step carefully onto the *passerelle* that makes a bridge over the splashing sea, connecting land to yacht. The gangway sways slightly, while bobbing ducks and geese and an occasional swan glide beneath me unperturbed. Seagulls circle overhead, ready to dive at the first sight of a leaping fish.

I hold up my phone to show my pass-card to a tall crew member, and as he reaches for it he glances at my hand, then gives me an odd look. Following his gaze I see that my fingernails still bear traces of black and blue waterproof mascara, and my palms have a few stubborn streaks of pink, white and red. That's because I've just spent the entire morning at the movie studio steadily making up the faces of anxious actors, so that the old look younger, the young more sophisticated, the nice-looking more glamorous.

I can just imagine what I must look like to this guy: a tall, slightly frazzled female with a long auburn braid down her back, dressed in a black pantsuit; whereas most visitors here show up wearing pale, luxurious leisure garb—and a perfect St. Tropez tan the color of rosy apricot.

The man waves my pass-card under the mechanical nose of a security computer and waits until he sees a response that causes him to step aside, murmuring deferentially, *"Merci, madame, entrez, s'il vous plaît."* Nevertheless I sense that he, like his fellow crewmates surrounding me, are barely tamed beasts who'd just as easily toss me over the side of the boat if the security message told them to.

At this point I'm entrusted to the yacht's captain, an impeccable Frenchman in a dazzling white and gold uniform. With a brief nod of cool formality he leads me across the teak deck, down a spiraling staircase to a mahogany door. Reaching into his pocket he pulls out a circlet of keys, unlocks the door and pushes it open, allowing me to step inside before he withdraws, closing the door softly behind him. I hear a discreet click indicating that this room has been locked again, with me inside it.

Well, at least I made it this far. I take a deep breath, then inspect what appears to be the ship's library, kitted out like a gentleman's club, with leather and silk-covered chairs, wool Persian carpets and locked cherrywood bookshelves, all kept in pristine condition to defy the effects of salty sea air. Peering closer I see that this entire cabin has bespoke climate control, yet each display case has its own complicated thermostat and humidity indicator—so nothing can spoil the imported cigars in their humidor nor the delicate treasures kept under glass in a cabinet of curiosities. I hear a quiet metallic whirr overhead, coming from one of four motion-sensitive security cameras perched high in each corner of the room, adjusting its gaze like a bird of prey. I suppress a mad urge to make a face at the camera.

In the deep silence I'm aware that my heart is still pounding rapidly from my determined effort to get here on time. Only to be kept waiting now, by a man with the manners of a gangster?

But I've come this far and I'm not leaving until I see this through. It represents the end of a long road for me, and today I'll find out if I've made the right choices. I glance about, feeling a bit doubtful. It occurs to me now that perhaps my host has taken these precautions because he doesn't trust me, either.

The lighting in this peculiar sanctuary is low, minimal, shutting out the brilliant sun, reminding me that there *is* a dark side to the Riviera; I've heard that wealthy earls and fun-loving heiresses alike have ominously vanished without a trace from its busy streets, and the spin of a wheel in a casino can ruin you or make you famous overnight. Uneasily I recall the words of the playwright Somerset Maugham who made the Côte d'Azur his home: *A sunny place for shady people.*

Before I came to these shores I never thought of myself as a shady character; but everyone here has their multi-faceted angles, like a face in a Cubist dream; and when I first arrived, two years ago, shortly after my thirtieth birthday, I began to sense that I, too, had a trace of larceny in my soul.

As my eyes adjust to the shadows, and still mindful that every move I make is undoubtedly being watched, I gravitate toward a polished walnut bench built into the wall so that it remains unmoved by the pitch and roll of the sea. It's so much like a church pew that I sit down with the hushed, contemplative attitude of a Provençal lady who has slipped into an empty chapel to bow her head and finger her rosary beads, to ask favors of her patron saints, to pray for those she loves, and to heed her guiding spirits. Perhaps in my own way, just by being here today, I myself am practicing some kind of ancestor worship.

For, while I wait, I am thinking of my shy, secretive mother who unexpectedly set my feet on this improbable path as if she'd passed a baton to me, just as her own mother had wanted to do with her. Have I managed to fulfill their cherished hopes—or have I betrayed them?

I realize that even today I'm still looking for answers, cues, clues. As if seeking an anchor to steady me in this sea of uncertainty, I close my eyes and find myself communing yet again with my Grandmother Ondine—who was once a young girl living in a modest honey-colored house attached to a deceptively ordinary-looking café, in a small seaside town not very far from here, so many years ago.

1

Ondine at the Café Paradis, Spring 1936

A SALTY SOUTHWESTERN WIND CAME RUSHING ACROSS THE MEDITERRAnean Sea with heraldic ceremony, driving a white-capped tide against the rocks and jostling the fishing boats in the harbor of Juan-les-Pins before sweeping into the backyard of the Café Paradis, where Ondine was busy peeling her vegetables.

She'd escaped outdoors with her work on this sunny April morning because the café's kitchen was already a cauldron. A tiny backyard patio was gracefully shaded by a majestic Aleppo pine tree, and Ondine sat on a low stone wall that rimmed the tree. Wielding a confident knife, she diligently pared and sorted Provence's springtime treasures—baby carrots, peas and artichokes so tender they could be served raw, topped by thinly sliced lemons sweet enough to eat with their rinds on.

She was working briskly and a delicate sheen of sweat made her sensitive to that sudden change in the wind as it rustled significantly through the pine tree's branches. Because Ondine had been raised to believe in nature's auspicious signs and warnings, she put down her knife, closed her eyes and lifted her head to greet the breeze as it skimmed across her face with an invigorating whiff of the sea.

She seldom got a quiet moment alone like this to think her own thoughts. So when a hazy premonition of a more exciting future somewhere far away began to shape itself in her mind, she struggled to capture it, as if reaching to grasp a firefly before the light disappeared.

"Ondine!" her mother shouted from the café's kitchen. "Where *is* she? On-*dine*!"

Ondine flinched as she heard her name reverberating against the huddle of pale stone buildings. She glanced up, and saw her mother's head framed by the window like a portrait of a formidable empress. Even though it was too late for breakfast and too early for the lunch service, there was never a lull in cooking chores to do in order to meet the café's high standards.

Everyone who worked in the Café Paradis knew his role, right down to the striped cat who patrolled for any mouse foolhardy enough to come near the kitchen, and the bulldog who stood guard against tramps skulking about for an easy handout or an unlocked window. As for Ondine, who was seventeen now, her job was to do whatever her mother told her.

Madame Belange peered out the kitchen window and finally spied her daughter. "What do you think you're doing, lounging there in the garden like a pasha?"

"I'm just finishing up, *Maman*!" Ondine called, rising hastily and hoisting her vegetable basket on her hip as she hurried to the kitchen. By now the fortuitous wind had gone off on its inscrutable way without her. In its place came the usual busy odors of kitchen oil and truck fuel and wood-burning from the farmers' fields. Still, there was definitely a whiff of something special in the air today—her parents had been acting oddly all morning, murmuring to each other in hushed tones.

As she drew closer to the open kitchen window, Ondine's discerning nose picked up the first scents of the day's luncheon menu: onion-and-black-olive *tartes* called *pissaladière;* a pork stew of red wine and myrtle; and, for the fish—could it be . . . ?

She burst inside and went straight to the old black stove seething in its corner with the collected heat of decades of well-cooked meals. The fragrance wafting from a big kettle was unmistakable now.

"Bouillabaisse!" she exclaimed, wondering why her mother had

chosen this special dish—which required a half-dozen kinds of fish—instead of making a simpler and less expensive fish soup called *bour-ride*. Ondine lifted the pot's lid and inhaled rapturously. Celery, onion, garlic, tomato, fennel, pepper, parsley, thyme, bay and the distinctive orange rind used in the South of France; and something else especially rare and precious, which turned the broth to the color of gold.

"Did you use Père Jacques' saffron today?" Ondine asked, impressed.

Her busy mother glanced up and actually paused for a moment. "Yes," Madame Belange said, reaching for a tiny glass vial which she held up to the light and examined reverently. "I'm afraid it's the last of it, all except this one strand which I could not bear to lose." Mother and daughter exchanged a look of awe as they gazed at the red thread of saffron, which imparted a mysterious taste that the old monk Père Jacques described as *a kiss between fresh-mown hay and chestnut honey*.

Père Jacques had given this homegrown saffron to Ondine when she graduated from a convent boarding school in the hills above Nice. The meditative old monk who ran the abbey's kitchen was one of those rare elders that appreciated Ondine's curiosity instead of being irritated by it. Knowing that her family ran a café, he'd allowed her to escape the usual convent chores to assist him in his calm, contemplative gardens, learning his ancient secrets of cuisine.

There is nothing on earth like French saffron, he'd said proudly, showing her his field of mauve-colored crocuses which he patiently tended until two rare days in October when they bloomed. Then, all the monks pitched in to pluck the delicate red pistils—only three per flower—which, when carefully dried, became those prized red threads that Père Jacques put into glass vials. Ondine and her mother doled out these strands of saffron to make them last, using them only for special occasions, like Christmas custards and *macarons*.

"What's going on today?" Ondine asked, intrigued.

"We have an important new customer for lunch," her mother answered distractedly.

Ondine dipped a spoon to taste the *bouillabaisse*. "Mmm. Wonderful! But, it could use more pepper," she suggested.

Madame Belange shook her head and said crisply, "No, it's fine as it is. I'd rather err on the side of caution today."

Ondine felt a wave of sympathy for her mother, who, unlike Père Jacques, functioned as if on a knife's-edge, her nerves taut as she constantly battled against time, supplies and cost, with scarcely a *franc* or a moment to spare. But despite her request for help, Madame Belange kept nudging her daughter out of the way impatiently, as if it were obvious that this small, cramped kitchen didn't really have room for two grown women.

Raising a flour-dusted wrist to push aside a stray lock of hair, Madame Belange said, "*Vite, vite,* get to work!" But then she cried out warningly, "*Attention!*" as the back door was flung open by a local dairy boy who barreled in with a large crate of eggs, cheese and cream. Ondine ducked out of the way just in time.

While her mother paid the boy, Ondine unpacked his crate onto an enormous table in the center of the room. She'd been awake since dawn, first to make hot chocolate for the quick breakfast she shared with her parents, then to serve the morning customers their *brioche* and coffee. After that, she got the stocks simmering gently on the stove before she went outside to pare her vegetables; now it was time to assemble all the salads for the lunch service.

Yet apparently her mother had much more unusual plans for Ondine today.

"Just make one perfect salad, fit for our new *Patron,*" Madame Belange commanded. "And write down every ingredient we've used in today's lunch for our records." With her hip she pushed a cupboard drawer shut. "This man will be a regular customer, so we don't want to give him the same lunches again and again. Make notes, *tout de suite*—and put that convent schooling of yours to some real use!"

Ondine reached up to a shelf for one of the blank notebooks they used for such occasions—bound in butter-soft maroon leather, they'd been a gift from a stationer who ate his lunch at the café three times a week. She turned to the first page, which had a printed box framed by an illustration of bunched grapes on a twirling vine. Inside the box was a line designated for filling in a *Nom*. She imagined that this new *Patron* must be some rich banker or lawyer.

She paused. "What's his name?" she asked curiously.

Her mother waved a ladle indifferently. "Who knows? He's got money, that's all that matters!"

So Ondine simply wrote a large *P* for *Patron*. Then she turned to the next page and wrote *2 April 1936* at the top before she recorded today's meal, checking on which ingredients were used and how they were cooked. Her mother kept such records only for distinguished customers, and special events like catered meals or wedding banquets. Later she would add comments about the *Patron*'s personal preferences and how the recipe might be better tailored to him.

Madame Belange looked up from the stove and said resolutely, "All right now. Put away the notebook and let's pack up this meal!"

"Pack it?" Ondine echoed in surprise.

Her mother wore an especially sober expression. "This man has rented one of the villas at the top of the hill. Here's the address," she said, digging in her pocket for a scrap of paper and handing it to her. "You will use your bicycle to bring him his lunch every weekday."

"What am I, a donkey?" Ondine demanded indignantly. "Since when do we deliver lunch to people's houses? Who is this man, that he can't come to the café to eat his lunch like everybody else?"

Madame Belange said, "He's someone *très célèbre* from Paris. He speaks French, but I'm told he's a Spaniard. The nuns taught you Spanish at the convent, yes?"

"A little," Ondine answered warily.

"Well, it might finally come in handy." Her mother glanced around decisively. "Get me that nice striped pitcher for the wine."

"But that's your favorite!" Ondine objected. Besides, the tall, hand-painted pink-and-blue pitcher had been promised to her for her wedding trousseau—if she ever made it to the altar. Her unsentimental mother shrugged. Ondine muttered, "I hope this fancy Spaniard appreciates it."

She had to move swiftly now; the meal was coming together

quickly. They packed the lunch into an insulated metal hamper, wrapping each dish tightly in red-and-white cloths. Then Ondine went into the basement to an oaken barrel of house wine, from which she siphoned off enough white wine to fill a bladder made of pigskin which she brought upstairs. Madame Belange ordered one of the waiters to carry the hamper outside and securely clip it to the metal basket on Ondine's bicycle.

"*Alors!* Listen carefully." Her mother fixed her with a stern look. "You are to enter the *Patron*'s house from the side door, which he will leave unlocked for you. Go straight into the kitchen. Heat up the food and lay it out for him. Then leave, right away. Do not wait for him to come downstairs to eat."

Madame Belange pinched her daughter on the arm. "Do you hear me, Ondine?"

"Ouch!" Ondine protested. She'd been listening attentively and felt she didn't deserve that. But her exhausted mother sometimes just ran out of words, and punctuated the urgency of her commands with a quick slap if anyone in her kitchen asked too many questions. Madame Belange, in her own youth, had never witnessed mothers and daughters having the luxury of time to indulge in searching, philosophical chats. Children were like baby chicks whom one loved the way a mother hen did—you fed them, kept them warm, taught them how to fend for themselves, and pecked them with a nudge in the right direction whenever they wandered astray.

Madame Belange repeated, "Go in quietly, prepare the food, lay it out, and leave. Do not call out to him or make noise. Later, you'll go collect the dishes, without making a sound."

Ondine had a terrible urge to burst out laughing at these absurd orders to skulk around like a thief. But her mother was so very serious that Ondine recognized the weight of her responsibility.

"I understand, *Maman,*" she said, although her curiosity was thoroughly piqued now.

"Take the daffodils from the dining room with you. Afterwards, on your way home, stop by the market to buy new flowers for the café," her mother said in a low voice, digging into her apron pocket for a few coins. "Here." Then, with her elbow, she gave her daughter a shove. "Go!"

Ondine dutifully went through the swinging doors that led to the formal dining room, which was reserved for the night meal only. Breakfast and lunch were always served outside on the front terrace, rain or shine, since there was a sturdy white-and-grey awning that could be cranked overhead and withstood most bad weather.

The Café Paradis occupied the first floor of a limestone house that was the color of a honey praline. Ondine's family lived in the rooms above the café. The second floor had a master bedroom for her parents, and a smaller bedroom for occasional overnight lodgers. Her two older brothers once occupied that guest room, but both were killed in the Great War and now slumbered in the town cemetery, near their infant siblings who'd been lost to scarlet fever before Ondine was born. The third and topmost floor had only one slope-roofed room, originally made for servants, where Ondine had slept all her life.

She crossed the silent dining room with its gleaming hardwood floor, mahogany chairs and tables and dark-panelled walls. Opposite the bar were a gilt-edged mirror and a framed replica of a Rembrandt masterpiece painted in 1645 called *A Girl at a Window*.

"Bonjour," Ondine said to the girl in the picture for luck, as she'd done ever since she was a child.

The painting was as mysterious as the *Mona Lisa;* and indeed many art experts—including some of the café's patrons—argued over who Rembrandt's *Girl at a Window* might have been. An aristocrat, because of her gilded multi-strand necklace and the detailed trim on her blouse? A servant, because of her flushed cheeks and rolled-up sleeves? Or a whore brazenly displaying a bit of bosom as she leaned on her elbows gazing out her window?

Ondine had always loved this picture, for the model's luminous round eyes seemed to see everything, as if you, too, had caught her interest when you passed below her in the street. But now she seemed to say slyly, *I know what you dream of. Think you've got what it takes to conquer the Great World?*

Ondine made a quick check of her own image in the nearby mirror. She herself was no woman of mystery, but her skin was pale gold, her eyes a warm chestnut-brown, and from her morning exertions her cheeks and lips were pleasingly flushed. Yet the most noticeable thing about Ondine was her very long, dark hair that flowed in luxurious, silky waves. A boy once told her that these marvellously undulating twirls and curls were like punctuation marks for all the intelligent questions and lively ideas dancing in her head.

The boy was named Luc, and they had fallen in love—the first real, sweet love for both of them. He'd been orphaned when he was fourteen, which ended his schooling, so he worked hard for the fisherman who hired him; and when Luc came to the back door of the café to deliver a box of neatly laid out, glistening silvery fish, he often had a little gift for Ondine—a seashell, an Alpine strawberry plant, a painted wooden necklace that a sailor had sold him from some far-off, exotic country.

In return, Ondine sneaked food to him, usually some savory *tartelettes* made of her best pastry and whatever nourishing bits of meat and vegetables that she could find. Luc was always hungry, yet he showed his gratitude not by wolfing down what she gave him, but by eating slowly, deliberately, reverentially. Ondine loved to place food into his strong, confident hands and then watch him lift it to his eager mouth.

But her father insisted that a man must have enough money in the bank to support a woman before taking her as his bride; so sweet Luc went off to work on one of the merchant ships that came and went in the harbor at Antibes.

On the night before he sailed, Luc made a daring climb up the café's narrow wrought-iron balconies and stole into her attic bedroom for a farewell night of love. Up until then, Ondine and Luc had only traded kisses and caresses when they went for long walks at secluded spots in the woods and meadows of Parc de Vaugrenier; but on this last night, poignantly mindful that anything might happen to Luc, they clung to each other, and Ondine finally discovered what all the fuss about love was about.

Somehow, after the first surprise of the rude intimacy of it, the whole thing seemed innocent and natural and cozy. They slept sweetly until the birds woke her before dawn, and the sight of Luc lying there beside her was like finding a Christmas present on her pillow.

"I'll come back for you," he promised, kissing her tenderly before he climbed right back out her window. "Once I've made a success of myself, imagine how proud your father will be to have me for his son-in-law!" he added boldly, to bolster his courage as well as hers.

That was two years ago. Luc's early letters were short on words, and long in coming, bearing only old news because not every port of call had a postal service. Then the letters stopped entirely. Few people in the town of Juan-les-Pins believed that Luc was even alive anymore, much less coming home.

Ondine could hardly grasp the fact that he was really gone. She became so mournful that her father, who'd expected the nuns to teach his daughter obedience—not art and music and foreign languages—ordered her to forget Luc and concentrate on the more useful arts of cooking, sewing and most of all, serving. "And if we are lucky enough to find you a husband," her father said sternly, "you will use all your mind and heart to make him happy. Do you understand?"

Ondine couldn't imagine any man but Luc as her husband. Yet by now she'd learned the modest art of fake compliance, with bowed head and lowered lashes, like the image of the Madonna.

"Yes, Papa," she'd demurred.

But, just as at the convent, her inmost thoughts were still her own.

DRAWING AWAY FROM THE MIRROR now, Ondine pulled the daffodils from a vase and wrapped them in a cloth napkin to take with her to the villa.

"*Bonjour,* Papa!" she called out as she reached the front of the dining room, where sunlight spilled in narrow, angular stripes from the long windows. Her father sat alone at a corner table, counting up last night's till for today's bank deposit. Most of Ondine's childhood memories of him involved the tallying of money with his old-fashioned adding machine. He was a handsome, pleasant man who enjoyed his neighbors and customers and the hubbub of a busy life, but when he circulated among his guests at the café he kept a clear-eyed view of each table's potential for keeping the cash register full.

The café's clientele were mostly local customers since it was snuggled in a quiet enclave away from main streets and shops. But that didn't stop the occasional tourists or celebrities from "discovering" the Café Paradis whenever their French friends or a hotel concierge tipped them off; even so, such esteemed visitors tended to remain discreet, instinctively hoarding this gem to themselves.

Monsieur Belange waited for Ondine to pass directly in front of him before he looked up to say quietly, "Make everything perfect. I mustn't hear one word of complaint from this man. Understand?"

Ondine nodded soberly. "Who is he?" she whispered.

Her father shrugged his shoulders in feigned indifference. "An important artist who wants to work undisturbed, in peace and quiet, before the whole summer crowd gets here."

"What's his name?" she persisted.

"He goes by the name of Ruiz." There was something just a touch odd about the way her father said it. Ondine was astute enough to notice, and a look of doubt flickered in her eyes.

Seeing his daughter's perceptiveness, Monsieur Belange smiled and said in a low voice, "But he is known in the art world as Picasso. I tell you this because you may overhear that name in his house, yet you must never repeat it to anyone else. He doesn't want people to know he's here. He needs his privacy and will pay us well, so we ask no questions," he warned, proud to be chosen for this honor. "Above all, you must tell no tales of whatever you see in that house. No gossip is ever to come from us."

"*Oui,* Papa," she said, impressed. The name Picasso rang a dim bell; something scandalous clung to it, for even the nun who taught art had refused to discuss him. Mulling this over, Ondine stepped outside onto the triangular-shaped terrace.

"*Bonjour,* Ondine!" chorused three men who'd just arrived to claim their favorite table, where they would read the news and drink *aperitifs* while waiting for their lunch to be served precisely at twelve-thirty as it always was. They often showed up early so they could watch and comment on everyone else who came to dine.

She gave them a smile but thought, *Without fail, here they are: the Three Wise Men.* Luc had invented that nickname for these pillars of the community. The silver-haired doctor Charlot smoked long, pungent cigars; the baker Renard with his trim moustache, still a bachelor at thirty, rose so early in the morning that he was always hungry well before noon; and the black-bearded bank manager Jaubert was as pale as a vampire and liked his meat cooked so rare it was *bleu*.

Because they'd all succeeded in making more money than their neighbors, these three men were relied upon by the entire community, not only for the support that their professions provided, but for their prudent and astute counsel. Although immutable in their old-fashioned views, they were kind at heart, and never too busy to advise their neighbors on matters large and small.

But when Ondine walked past them they stopped talking, and their throaty chuckles and waggling eyebrows revealed their consensus that she was shapely and desirable. She could still feel their eyes on her as she tucked her skirt between her legs, hopped onto the bicycle and began pedaling away.

The weight of the metal hamper behind her seat made her start so slowly that at first she hardly seemed to be moving at all, just barely staying up. Gritting her teeth determinedly she pushed harder and finally got herself pedaling rhythmically with gathering force as she reached the main road with its shops and hotels.

"So this important *Patron* from Paris comes here now, just to get away from his friends!" she mused. Well, it was true that most chic tourists called spring a "dead" season, wedged between two busy ones. Winter attracted American dowagers who played cards and *roulette* with haughty Russian émigrés, whiskered German bankers and English princes. Summer brought a younger, jazzy American and English crowd who liked to swim, bake in the sun, get drunk, openly flirt with one another's wives, and defy their elders' stodgy rules and traditions.

"*Bonjour,* Ondine!" called out the postman, touching the brim of his cap as she cycled by.

Another day without a letter from Luc, she thought, waving back. Ever since Luc left, she'd kept a small suitcase under her bed so that when he returned she could elope with him if necessary. But as time passed, Ondine began to think that *she* might just go off on her own, someplace where the local gossips didn't think of her as a girl who'd been jilted. So her suitcase still contained her favorite treasures and a little purse with not nearly enough money in it. Not yet.

Skimming along the graceful curve of the harbor with its briny scent of seaweed and the hungry cries of swooping gulls, Ondine saw the fishermen returning, their nets bulging with fish whose wet scales glinted rainbow colors in the sunlight. She hadn't broken the habit of scanning the figures on the dock, looking for Luc's distinctive head with his high forehead, his tousled brown hair, and his slim but strong body. Yet she averted her eyes when she passed the seedier bars and hotels where prostitutes and thieves lured the seamen to spend their pay before they could bring it home to girls like Ondine.

"If I try to go off on my own, and my foot slips just once, I might end up like those shaggy women who hover around the wharf-side bars," she said under her breath. She hadn't been afraid with Luc by her side; he'd said, *Everyone has a bright star calling them to their destiny, but if you stop listening to your star, the voice grows dimmer over the years until you can no longer hear it.*

He'd pointed to the heavens, where two stars were so close they'd almost merged into one. *Those are ours,* he'd told her, and she felt it and believed it. But now, alone and still living in her father's house, Ondine felt more like a tin star left on an old Christmas tree that someone had forgotten to take down.

She turned off the great arc of the harbor road and pedaled up a formidable hill so steep that she almost felt in peril of tumbling backwards. Ondine normally never ventured up this exclusive street; it was flanked on both sides by villas with walls so high that you could barely glimpse a house's second-floor windows or tiled rooftop. She felt she was gliding through a secret tunnel.

When she came to the top of the hill she paused triumphantly, then gazed in awe at the view, for she'd never seen the grand sweep of the harbor from this breathtaking perspective. The sparkling sapphire sea appeared more wide open and beckoning; and the pale blue sky, dotted with puffy white clouds that looked as soft as ermine, seemed to promise a wider, limitless world.

Sighing, she turned onto a brief, sandy side road and soon came upon a villa with a white-painted wooden gate set between cream-colored walls.

"Here it is," Ondine gasped, slowing down. She hopped off her bicycle and walked it up to the gate, which was topped with a row of iron spikes shaped like arrows. She discovered that while the gate was firmly shut, it was unlocked, and the metal latch lifted easily. She pushed her bike inside, parking it just long enough to hurry back and shut the gate behind her.

Finally admitted to the inner sanctum, Ondine quietly wheeled her bicycle up to the new *Patron*'s villa—a sprawling, peach-colored two-story affair with large windows, pale blue shutters, and a terracotta-colored tiled roof. The downstairs shutters were closed, but the ones on the second floor were thrown open to admit the breeze, and a gauzy white curtain fluttered ghostlike in one.

She parked her bicycle at the side of the house, where an irregular slate path led to the kitchen door. She unhooked the hamper and clambered up a short flight of stone steps. With her free hand she turned the brass doorknob. It, too, was unlocked.

Feeling strangely excited yet apprehensive, Ondine gave the door a push.

Then she stepped over the threshold, and went inside.

2

Ondine at Picasso's Villa

THE *PATRON*'S HOUSE WAS SILENT AND COOL, FOR, BEING MADE OF STONE and stucco, it still held the chill of last night's damp spring air. The kitchen was rather rustic, with wide, irregular floorboards that creaked as Ondine crossed them, carefully carrying the heavy metal hamper to a round wooden table in the center of the room.

"*Zut!*" she grunted, glancing around to get her bearings. In the far corner was a narrow black stove with its pipe angling out a bit crazily to its chimney. An icebox stood against the opposite wall.

She threw back the lid of her food hamper. Her mother had wisely folded an apron atop everything. Ondine tied it on, then lit the stove. The *bouillabaisse* was in a compact cooking pot with a fitted lid, so she carried it straight to the stove just as it was to keep it warm on a low heat. Everything else was in various containers which she unpacked now, along with the striped pitcher.

So far Ondine had not heard a single sound from anywhere else in the villa.

Perhaps he'd gone out for a walk, or to visit somebody. It never occurred to her that anyone might be sleeping past sunrise, let alone noon. As she acquainted herself with his kitchen, Ondine saw that a swinging door led to the rest of the house. She pushed it open and peered in.

A dimly lighted dining room held an oblong table ringed by high-backed chairs, with a vase of dusty dried flowers standing rather forlornly in the center. There was a chest of drawers that served as a sideboard, decorated with a long lace runner.

"It looks as if no one has had a meal in here for a thousand years," Ondine observed with a slight feeling of panic. Where did he want his lunch served? Her mother hadn't given instructions. She did not want to presume that the *Patron* would deign to dine in the kitchen, even though it was cheerier there.

Beyond this room was a small parlor with upholstered chairs arranged around a low table before a fireplace. As Ondine darted quickly through the darkened parlor she felt like a fish swimming in deep waters, curiously flitting through a sunken ship. At the far end was an open, arched doorway leading to the front door's foyer and a stairway to the second floor.

She drifted to the foot of the stairs and cocked her ear to listen. Still not a sound from above. Was nobody home? Could he have forgotten their arrangement?

A narrow hall ran alongside the stairway and led straight to the back of the villa, where a door opened onto a fenced yard, beyond which were a neighbor's flower fields. The only other room on this main floor was a little one at the back of the house. Its door was wide open, and Ondine stepped in to see if it would serve for lunch.

It was just a narrow study with a writing table, chair, telephone, lamp. Upon the table was a Parisian newspaper, and a big brown envelope addressed to *M. Ruiz* which had already been opened. Spilling out of this pouch was a scattering of smaller envelopes addressed to *Picasso,* apparently being forwarded from Paris, a postmark which made the package look important.

Ondine suddenly understood. "He doesn't want our postman to see the name Picasso and then go blabbing all over town. And he's right; the postman is the biggest gossip in the village!" Her *Patron* had taken great pains to conceal his identity. "Who *is* this Picasso?" she wondered.

She noticed a writing pad left out on the table, bearing a note scrawled in dramatic flourishes of thick inky lines. A pen lay beside it. The letter looked unfinished, for he had not signed off with either name—Picasso or Ruiz—as if he'd grown bored with the whole undertaking.

The message was written in Spanish. Recalling what her mother had said about using her convent training, Ondine could not resist testing herself now, haltingly parsing it out. It was addressed to someone with the Spanish name of *Jaime Sabartés* and seemed to be a peculiar kind of progress report:

> *I relax at last, I am sleeping eleven or twelve hours a day. You can assure Miss Gertrude Stein that I no longer write poems. Instead, I find myself singing, which is so much more satisfying than all the other arts. Olga and her wretched divorce lawyers can't sue me for possession of half of the musical notes I sing, now can they?*
>
> *Also, I received your parcel of rags, hurrah! So now I can clean my brushes, should I ever pick them up again! But what do you think? Perhaps I will give up painting entirely for my new singing career, and I'll become a Spanish Caruso.*

"Why would he ask for rags to be sent from Paris?" Ondine mused. "What kind of man can't go out and buy rags for himself? Come to that, why doesn't he just tear up an old shirt?"

Well, this *Patron* obviously did not have a wife looking after him. In fact, he'd mentioned divorce lawyers. Nobody that Ondine knew had ever gotten a divorce; it was a mortal sin.

But surely it was a sin to snoop around, too. She returned to the dining room and realized that it had seemed unwelcoming simply because it was so dark from the closed shutters. She flung them all open, allowing the bright spring sunlight to illuminate the room. The front garden's scents breezed in, chasing away the mustiness. Now she could see that this room had its own cozy Provençal charm.

"Much better," Ondine nodded approvingly. "Good thing *Maman* told me to bring flowers," she added under her breath, removing the old, dusty ones. She filled the vase with water and added her fresh bunch of daffodils. She stepped back to survey the effect; they brightened the whole room considerably.

Just then she heard a distinct thump overhead that made her jump. The spell was broken—she was no longer an adventurous fish swimming through a sunken ship, but a delivery girl who was supposed to serve. Ondine froze, and heard more creaking—yes, someone was moving about upstairs. She waited for the sound of footsteps on the stairs. Nothing yet.

But he could come down here any minute, hungry. Perhaps he'd heard her walking around and noticed the enticing scent of the food warming on the stove, which was now wafting through the house.

Quickly she hurried back to the kitchen and carefully poured wine from the pigskin bladder into the tall pitcher she'd brought. Her mother had been clever to include it, for with its brightly painted vertical pink-and-blue stripes, it looked so cheerful in the simple dining room.

Ondine returned to the stove, lifted the lid to check the *bouillabaisse,* then carried the pot to the dining-room table and placed it on a trivet she'd found in the sideboard. The broth and the fish were to be eaten separately, so she laid out a soup dish containing slices of bread that had been dried but not toasted, over which he could ladle the broth; while the seafood had its own special plate.

Mindful of her father's warning to make everything satisfying for this Monsieur Picasso or Ruiz or whoever he was, Ondine arranged the meal's dishes in an appetizing semi-circle around the main plate so that everything was within easy reach. She found a nutcracker in the kitchen and a small wicker bowl in which she put some unshelled nuts and fresh fruit.

Now it was time for her to leave the man in peace to eat his lunch. She should go. She knew this, and yet, there was something so playful about the *Patron*'s funny little letter that it infected her own lively spirit; and when she found a blank tablet and pencil on the kitchen counter, she could not resist quickly scribbling a note, in French since he evidently read Parisian newspapers, and she wasn't confident enough to compose Spanish grammar:

We hope that this lunch meets with your approval. Please let us know if there is anything we can do to improve our service. We shall return for the dishes and will tidy up afterwards. Bon appétit.

ONDINE PROPPED THE NOTE BESIDE the fruit bowl. Then she slipped out the kitchen door, hopped on her bicycle and pedaled rapidly away from the house without a backward glance.

She loved the feeling of how much lighter the bicycle was now without the food hamper. Turning out of Monsieur Picasso's street, she steered back onto the bigger road with its high-walled villas on both sides. At the top of this steep hill with its extraordinary view, she felt a sudden thrill in that brief, suspended moment before takeoff, poised between the bright sky hanging above her and the wide sea stretching beyond the harbor below.

Then she took the plunge, coasting down, down, down the hill—yet it felt more like a wonderful upward lift, as if she'd taken flight like a bird. Picking up more speed, it seemed that her flying hair and skirt were wings that might just carry her up, up and away to the great wide world beyond.

"Hooray!" Ondine cried aloud, feeling weightless and fearless and free.

But when she arrived at the farmers' market on the other side of town to pick up new flowers as her mother instructed, she felt her spirits quickly plummet back to earth under the sharp gazes of the farmers' wives who presided over the spring harvests that their customers had eagerly awaited. The florist's stall was a riot of bright color, and the fruit and vegetables were piled high in perfect pyramids.

"*Bonjour* Ondine!" the butcher's stout wife called out, eyeing her speculatively.

"*Bonjour* Ondine!" the red-haired flower vendor chirped as Ondine pulled up to her stall.

"Where have you been on your bicycle today?" demanded the skinny fruit-seller.

"A new *Patron,*" Ondine said neutrally, nodding in the general direction of the villas. Too late, she realized that there were so few holiday renters at this time of year that any visitor was bound to be news to this gaggle of gossips.

"You mean that Spaniard at the top of the hill?" the fruit-seller said, handing Ondine a small blood-orange to eat. "I hear he's got a lady-friend down here that he sees on the weekends. But what does he do with the rest of his time?"

The florist, reaching in among her blooms to pull out the delicate daffodils that Ondine pointed to, said conspiratorially, "He's a suspicious character; no one ever sees him during the day, but my brother Rafaello says he keeps his lights burning well past midnight!" Rafaello was a policeman who patrolled the neighborhood at odd hours and, after years of seeing the darker side of human nature, habitually viewed most people as potential criminals.

"Mark my words, that new tenant is a bank robber, hiding out with his loot!" the butcher's wife agreed. "I ask you—who else rents a whole house off-season all to himself, with no family?"

The others also found voluntary solitude so incomprehensible that they quickly retreated to the *terra firma* of their usual gossip about which local girls might get engaged this spring. Sooner or later, everyone became the subject of their wagging tongues.

"Don't worry, Ondine," piped up the little *fromagère,* arranging creamy mounds of cheese in appetizing rows on a wooden board. "Your day will come to marry and have children. The wheel turns."

"The wheel turns!" the others echoed wisely.

Ondine paid for her flowers and hastily pedaled away. She knew that those women didn't really mean to be so hurtful, but all they could imagine was that Luc had met a bad end or else found another girl wherever he was. Ondine had tried not to even consider such possibilities. Now something about their pragmatic marketplace chatter had revived her doubts about her own judgment, even today.

What if the *Patron* was displeased with the note she'd just left for him? A girl like Ondine—especially while serving such an important person—simply did not speak unless spoken to; so she should never have had the audacity to write to him.

"Why did I do it?" she fretted as she reached the café. She'd even inadvertently invited him to criticize her mother's cooking if he wanted to! Her father would be furious if he found out.

But there was no time to brood. A large group of out-of-town businessmen had arrived unexpectedly and were now seated on the terrace awaiting a late lunch, and the waiters were frantically hopping to serve them all. As soon as Ondine stepped into the hot kitchen, her mother, who was reheating the soups, quickly put her to work slicing, buttering and filling fresh baguettes with cold meats, cheeses, pâté and olive *tapenade* to make the delicious variety of open-faced sandwiches called *tartines*.

Madame Belange moved with the confidence of a cook who knows that her cuisine is well prized. Only when there was a brief lull did she turn to ask briskly, "Did everything go all right at the villa?" She was satisfied with a simple nod from Ondine.

Later, when her father strode into the kitchen, he glanced at his pocket-watch and said firmly, "Ondine! Go back to collect the *Patron*'s dishes, now."

"Yes, Papa!" Ondine washed her hands, put on her jacket and hurried outside. Hopping back on her bicycle she pedaled steadily, keeping an even pace, this time arriving without being breathless.

When she entered the *Patron*'s silent kitchen everything was as she'd left it. She didn't hear any clink of silverware coming from the dining room. Cautiously she peered in.

There were only a few crumbs where the bread plate had been; and empty shells from the devoured shrimp and other shellfish. The salad and cheese were gone, too.

"He ate everything!" Ondine exclaimed softly in relief. Picasso's cloth napkin was now folded politely beside the plate, and she found this gesture somehow touching.

How lonely it was to be an artist, eating all by himself, she thought, as she carried his single plate and set of flatware back to the kitchen. Lonesome, and yet, how strangely liberating to be able to come and go as you pleased without having to explain yourself to anybody, nor listen to their reproachful opinions. Ondine could barely imagine that sort of freedom.

Lifting the lid of the cooking pot which she'd left on a trivet at the table, she exclaimed, "Ah!" for she saw that Picasso had gone back for more helpings of *bouillabaisse*. "*Maman* will be pleased."

She began packing up the dishes. The villa was even more quiet than it had been before, and Ondine sensed that the house was truly empty this time. She returned to the dining room to tidy up.

The bowl of fruit and nuts had been ploughed into. And there she discovered her note to Picasso, still propped against the fruit bowl. Not only had he read it, but beneath her scribble, right on the same page he'd written something of his own:

S'il vous plait, je voudrais plus de piment

followed by a whimsical drawing of a long, bright red pepper, after which was written:

dans votre excellente bouillabaisse.

"He'd like more peppers in our 'excellent *bouillabaisse*'," Ondine giggled with delight.

She must remember to write down his preference in the notebook when she returned to the café. She put his letter in her pocket, smiling. But just as Ondine snapped the metal hamper shut and loaded it onto the bicycle, she realized that something was missing.

"Why—where's *Maman*'s striped pitcher?"

In this unpredictable place, it had apparently vanished into thin air.

3

Ondine in the Minotaur's Labyrinth

ONDINE COULD NOT DECIDE WHICH WOULD BE WORSE—GETTING CAUGHT snooping on the *Patron,* or facing the wrath of her mother if she returned without the pink-and-blue pitcher. She decided to take a chance on this artist, and look around.

A quick tour of the kitchen cupboards made it clear she'd have to go farther afield. Nothing in the dining room or study, either. She nerved herself and called out boldly, "Hello?"

Silence. This might be her only chance to search upstairs for the missing pitcher.

Ondine took a deep breath and went up, peering cautiously through the open doorway of a very small and plain bedroom, where the pillows were rumpled and the navy coverlet cast aside.

Why would he choose to sleep in this little room like a monk? She got her answer when she moved to the next room, which was strangely devoid of a bed, yet cluttered with sketchbooks, newspapers and paint paraphernalia spread out on every available surface.

What a jumble. Helplessly she scanned the room for the striped pitcher. Nowhere in sight. In this impromptu studio, she did not know what to look at first.

"What's he done with it?" she wondered. "Maybe he broke it and threw it out?"

That seemed unlikely, so she kept looking. A blank canvas stood on an easel in the far corner. Nearby was a small table crowded with unopened pots of paint and pristine brushes. She moved toward an alcove with a skylight overhead, where a large round table was heaped with newspapers and crumpled-up sketches, all thrown randomly about. Anything could be hidden under there.

Ondine drew closer and peered at the drawings, then involuntarily exclaimed, "*Dieu!* Is *this* what he's been up to here?"

At first she averted her eyes, as if a sailor had lured her into an alleyway to show her bad pictures he'd gotten from a whorehouse. But the images were so complicated that she had to go on staring to make sense of them.

One sketch was a terrifying tangle of two naked figures—a man and a woman—locked in the violent throes of a ferocious animalistic rape that at first seemed more like a lion devouring a horse. But no, these were humans, all right—for no anatomical detail was spared, including their pubic hair and sex organs.

The female was a sweet-faced blonde with a rather long nose which prevented her from being a true beauty. She had full thighs and arms and breasts and buttocks—a sturdy, athletic-looking girl, yet she was thrown into a position of helpless submission, with her head flung back from the impact of the assault, and her round breasts and belly defenselessly upturned like fleshy melons being devoured by the man—if you could call him a man, for he was a strange, horned beast with a naked human body, his aggressive flanks and penis clearly visible. Yet, he had the head—and even the tail—of a bull; and this creature's nostrils seemed to be snorting puffs of rage.

Baffled, Ondine glanced at the other violent pictures and discovered that, although the poses varied, the model was always the same blonde woman. Ondine was relieved that the last sketch was a happier one, depicting the nude beast-man and his naked lady contentedly reclining on a sofa in repose, with wreaths on their heads and goblets of wine in their hands. Behind them was a window indicating a pleasant day outside. The couple looked sweet and companionable, a friendly satyr and his goddess wife at home, becalmed, sated and affectionate.

This drawing had been held down by a large seashell employed as a paperweight. The shell's rippling colors of peach and violet and cream were so appealing that Ondine picked it up and held it to her ear to see if she could hear the sea while she continued staring at the images, mesmerized.

"You like the Minotaur?"

A rich male voice, speaking in French with a slight Spanish accent, came from the doorway behind her. Ondine whirled about guiltily. Caught nosing around the man's work already! All the worse since her *Patron*'s career involved drawing naked ladies doing strange things with bestial men. Ondine felt her face flush with shame.

The man in the doorway looked inscrutable, lounging there with his hands in his pockets, staring intently at her with the darkest, blackest eyes she'd ever seen, his gaze so riveting that she froze like a forest animal who'd just heard a twig snap.

"*Bonjour, Patron!*" she managed to gasp, wanting to flee and yet rooted to the spot.

With his almond-shaped face, blunt nose and barrel of a chest, this man seemed like a primitive figure carved out of dark wood. *Like a savage from Africa or Polynesia*, Ondine could not help thinking, reminded of the missionary books in the convent—because it seemed as if this man belonged in animal skins and a headdress made of hawk's feathers, instead of the good-quality jacket and cap that he wore.

"*Bonjour,*" he replied, still studying her boldly. When finally he smiled, it was like warm sunlight suddenly filling the room with invigorating energy. Ondine exhaled in relief, for he looked more human now as he removed his jacket. In fact, his clothes belonged to a fairly conservative middle-aged man: open-collared shirt, pullover sweater, wool pants neatly belted.

As he drew nearer she realized that for a man, he really was terribly short, even shorter than she was. He took off his wool cap, not to tip it at her as other men might, but merely to toss on a chair with his jacket.

Absently he ran a hand over his thinning hair, which was parted on one side and combed over the top of his head; yet it was longish and floppy, indicating the freedom of an artist.

Still the *Patron* did not speak. He continued staring in a way that most people would think rude. It was almost challenging, the way he seemed to take her in—not simply her clothes and appearance, but her thoughts and feelings, too. Part of her wanted to run and hide; yet there was such intelligence and vitality in his magnetic gaze that she found herself moving toward him, as if he were the planet Jupiter and she was a new little moon caught by his gravitational pull and turned into a willing satellite.

"You are the girl from the café?" he now asked politely. His voice was cultured but slightly nasal. Although he spoke French easily, he hit his consonants harder and, to her ear, exaggerated the vowels.

"Excusez-moi, Patron," she murmured, guiltily putting the seashell back on the table. She knew that she should bow her head and not stare back at him; this was what her father and the village elders expected a woman to do when confronted by male authority.

But then she remembered the red pepper he'd drawn on his note. How could a pepper look so playful? And yet it did. Thinking about that jaunty, cartoony pepper and the friendly words underneath it, Ondine suddenly could not hold back a smile.

"I am happy to serve you. And, next time I'll remember to add more red peppers," she said.

He appeared surprised. "Oh, so you are the cook? Well, you do good work for one so young."

Ondine hadn't meant to claim credit for her mother's *bouillabaisse,* but she could see no graceful way to retract it, so instead she gestured toward his pages on the table and said shyly, "Sorry to intrude on your work."

"Do you know the story of the Minotaur?" he asked, his voice low and compelling as if reading aloud a fairy tale. "He reigns over an island. The locals sacrifice their prettiest girls from the village to service the Minotaur in his decadent villa. He can't decide if he wants to ravish them or kill them. Sometimes he does both. But he also invites poets and artists and musicians to play and sing and dance for him; everyone feasts on champagne and fish, and their orgies continue all day and night. The Minotaur rules by force over *all* the women, young and old—but they fear him, so he can never truly be loved for himself. But one Sunday, a young fisherman from the mainland will find his way through the Minotaur's labyrinth, and kill the sacred monster with a dagger."

He lunged forward at the pictures and made a thrusting move as if with a sword. "But there will always be another minotaur to replace him," he said matter-of-factly, "because all women love a monster."

Ondine was speechless, spellbound.

"Which picture is your favorite?" he asked in a gentle, soothing tone, so calm that perhaps there was something mocking in it. He reminded her of the impish boys who congregated outside school and tried to trick a girl into showing them her underpants.

He was waiting for her answer. Ondine lifted her chin defiantly. "This one," she said, as casually as if she were selecting a rose from the florist, pointing to the friendlier, domestic scenario between the Minotaur and the blonde woman resting luxurious and naked on cushions together.

"Well, you can't have the calm without the storm," Picasso teased. "What's your name?"

"Ondine," she answered.

"Ah, the water nymph! From the seas of Juan-les-Pins," he exclaimed with humor.

Something made Ondine say daringly, "Shall I address *you* as Monsieur Ruiz—or Picasso?"

"Shh!" he said playfully, putting a finger to his lips. "Both names are mine. My parents gave me the longest string of names you can imagine—to honor so many uncles and relatives! Here in town, I use Ruiz, my father's family name. But since he, too, was an artist, I sign my work with my mother's family name; and so now I am simply—" he thumped his chest and declared with mock savagery, "Picasso."

As if reminded of his purpose, he turned away from her and began sorting through the many jars and brushes and other mysterious tools that filled the tables around him. Ondine understood that it was time to leave him to his work, and she quietly slipped from the room.

Not until she reached the kitchen did she remember why she'd gone up there.

"Oh, I forgot to ask him about *Maman*'s pitcher!" she exclaimed in distress. But she certainly couldn't go bother him now. If her mother asked for it, Ondine would have to make up some excuse.

WHEN ONDINE RETURNED TO THE café, Madame Belange said briskly, "There's a party at a villa out on the *Cap*. That Parisian family with the wild daughter, she's having a birthday *fête*—and their chef needs help because one of his ovens broke down!" The kitchen table was already filling up with big trays of *hors d'oeuvres*. Ondine quickly tied on an apron. "They're sending a car to pick it up," her mother said. "Be ready to take the trays out, and make sure you show them which are hot and which are cold."

Ondine expected a chef's delivery truck, so she was startled when, a few hours later a sleek black limousine pulled up to the café. She untied her apron, smoothed her hair and dress and went staggering out with a big tray, followed by waiters carrying more trays.

The back door of the car seemed to open by itself. When Ondine peered in, she saw three young men dressed in navy and white flannel; and two women in pastel party dresses. They all had cocktail glasses in hand, and one of the men held a bottle of champagne.

"Here comes our food, *splendide*! But alas—the trunk is full of our luggage from the train!" a young man shouted, and a burst of merry laughter made it clear that they were all rather tipsy. They were several years older than Ondine, but they had the cheerful, pampered faces of milk-fed calves.

They must have come down from Paris on the luxury *Train Bleu,* and clearly for them the party had already begun—or perhaps to this exuberant crowd, life was one never-ending party.

"Come on," said another fellow enthusiastically, "we'll move the girls into the front seat, and you—what's your name? Ondine, you say? Lovely. Well, Ondine, you can pile all that food right here next to us!"

There were shrieks of laughter as the girls popped out of the car and then slid into the front seat beside the driver. Ondine carefully passed her tray to the boys in the back, then the waiters placed their stackable trays on top of hers until the whole thing nearly touched the inside of the car's roof. Ondine asked the driver, "Who should I give the instructions to? Some of these need to be warmed up."

One of the young men heard her and said, "Better come with us, *chérie,* and explain it all to our hostess." The driver jerked his head at Ondine and she had no choice but to slip into his front seat where the giggling girls were now crammed.

"Onward, sir! Here, Ondine, have some champagne," shouted the first fellow as he passed her a glass. The car lurched away so she sipped hastily, just to keep her drink from spilling. It was very good—like cool, golden sunlight in a glass. Ondine, crushed between the car door on one side and a girl's corsage on the other, felt dizzy from the mingled perfume that transformed the auto into a hothouse of orchids and gardenias. And each time the driver made a turn his passengers whooped and exaggerated the swerve, leaning chummily against one another.

"Hooray for my birthday party!" shouted one of the girls.

Her friend announced pertly, "We all know why you've dragged us down here; it's because you're in love with a boy from Nice! You should have come to *my* party in Paris last week. Jean Renoir showed up, just to persuade Coco Chanel to design costumes for his next film. Renoir insisted that, since she did the costumes for one of Cocteau's ballets, there is *no way* she can refuse *him* now. I heard Picasso painted the backdrops for that ballet, you know. I wonder if he'll do that for Renoir's film, too?"

This caused the birthday girl to squeal, "Did *Picasso* come to your party? I'd *so* like to meet him!"

"No, don't you know that nobody can find Picasso these days? He's simply disappeared. I hear he's gone to the Orient to paint geisha girls! Would you pose nude for him? *I* would!" the other girl said.

One of their escorts insisted, "Picasso's not in the Orient. I know for a fact that he's gone to Spain."

Ondine stifled a giggle. The champagne was making her wonder how they'd react if she blurted out her big secret: *Hah! Picasso is a mere stone's throw away from us this very minute!*

For the car was cruising past the steep hill that Ondine had cycled up only this afternoon. But she remained silent as they moved on, circling along the coast and then up another hill to the long, private driveway of a large white villa with an array of autos parked haphazardly near it. The limousine had barely come to a stop when one of the men jumped out and opened the front door that Ondine was leaning on.

When she tumbled out, he caught her by the elbow with impeccable good manners. "Whoops! May I have this dance?" he joked. Picking up a tray he shouted, "Come on, let's all help Ondine carry the food!" His friends took the remaining trays and the group plunged across the lawn leading to the villa, where Chinese lanterns glowed in the deepening darkness.

"Here we are!" he called out to a tall, slender older woman with alabaster skin, who came gliding across the lawn toward them, her long neck making her look like a swan. She must be the hostess, for she had a natural air of authority.

Ondine's escort declared, "*Voilà!* Where do you want this luscious food?"

The swan-woman answered, "*Mes enfants,* bring them to the kitchen." Ondine heard the tinkling of piano and violins tuning up inside the house. Still carrying her tray, she followed the young people to the terrace, where waiters were offering drinks to guests who wafted about in billowing silk and chiffon.

But now the hostess stepped in front of her, blocking her path and signalling to a waiter to take Ondine's tray away. Ondine hastily tried to explain which appetizers needed heating.

"Thank you very much," the hostess said in a firm, dismissive tone. "My chef will know what to do. Good night."

Ondine flushed as if she'd been accused of trying to steal the family silver. She had come so close to the villa that she could see through the long windows into the dining room, where a magnificent table was laid with crystal and china and glowing candlelight. The guests wafted inside, silhouetted against the light, looking just as Ondine had been taught that carefree angels moved about in heaven.

She backed away, returning to the parking area where the limousine remained, but it was empty and the driver had disappeared. Clearly she was not going home in the same style in which she'd arrived. She would have no other choice but to walk back to the café tonight.

The day had started out so promisingly and excitingly, but now, as Ondine trudged through the inky darkness of the streets, although the taste of champagne was still tingling on her tongue, she felt a certain bitterness in her heart. She even felt foolish for having hopes of a happier, better future where she might discover what kind of woman she was destined to become.

"I'll bet that, all over the world, rich and important people are just the same as this lady was tonight. So what makes me think I can go out into the Great World and be welcomed with open arms, when I've got no husband, no money and nothing to recommend me?" Ondine scornfully chided herself. "They'll never let me in, and that means my life will *never* change, no matter what I do or where I go!"

Yet as she reached the harbor, a shooting star flashed across the black sky with such dramatic beauty that Ondine caught her breath, and something new occurred to her.

"Those people at the party tonight just *wish* they could meet Picasso, and I already have! *He* didn't treat me like a gate-crasher. He liked me—he even asked my opinion of his work."

It dawned on her that perhaps today's omens meant that she did not have to venture far away in pursuit of a better destiny. Maybe, just maybe, Picasso was bringing the Great World to her doorstep, right here in Juan-les-Pins.

4

Picasso, Juan-les-Pins, Spring 1936

PABLO PICASSO WISHED HE HADN'T BOTHERED TO READ TODAY'S MAIL. IT disrupted his newfound peace of mind, which was as delicate as a young green shoot in spring. At first, when he arrived in Juan-les-Pins, the forecast was not auspicious; the weather had gone damp and chilly, making him wonder if he'd made a mistake in retreating here out of season. For awhile he'd simply slept a dozen hours each day—and that itself was a miracle, after so many sleepless nights in Paris.

Then, when he finally ran out of the provisions he'd travelled with, he put on an old coat and hat and slipped into town, roaming the small neighborhoods, enjoying the whole cloak-and-dagger drama of sneaking out of Paris and escaping here *incognito*. He gravitated to the lively, friendly Café Paradis, run by locals who seemed to know how to mind their own business. He'd ordered a good peasant stew of wild boar sausages and lentils, which warmed his blood and nourished his body and soul in a profound way, reminding him of his boyhood days in Spain. The rough red wine and the warm café seemed to wrap itself protectively around his shoulders like a blanket from his doting Italian mother.

"*This* is just what I need," Picasso told himself. "A month of it and I'll be strong as a Miura bull!"

But he also understood that his newly regained strength could so easily dissipate while tussling with those small decisions and tasks that he found so life-sapping, like the daily questions of, what to eat? What time? And where? Having to settle these Lilliputian things for himself simply exhausted him.

So when the proprietor of the Café Paradis asked if he could be of more service, Picasso impulsively made an arrangement with Monsieur Belange to have his lunches brought up to him at the villa. This would hopefully become an anchor in his daily routine, ensuring that Pablo would not waste his energy with endless domestic indecision—therefore leaving him to his privacy and his work.

Just making *that* decision had helped, because today he'd awakened earlier than usual, feeling alert and hopeful again. And, he noted, today was Thursday—always a fortuitous day for arrivals and departures, for casting out old demons and beginning new ventures.

But there in his mailbox he spied a newly delivered pouch from Paris. Letters were being forwarded—selectively—by his old friend and assistant, Sabartés, who awaited instructions on how to reply to them, so that no one would discover where Picasso had disappeared to.

At first, he threw the package on the desk in the back room. But that wouldn't work. It was sitting there just like a spider, Picasso thought. The only way to kill its fearful power was to confront it.

With a defiant flourish, he opened the parcel, bypassing the envelopes from friends, art dealers and magazine editors and galleries, all the while dreading that he'd find one particular stationery—the one from a lawyer's office, which had become so wretchedly familiar that it made his gut freeze the instant he spotted it.

"The devil!" he exclaimed. He tore it open and scanned it rapidly with growing disgust. What pit bulls his estranged Russian wife had hired! Well, he shouldn't be surprised. To marry an aristocrat was one thing. To marry a ballerina, quite another. But to marry a woman who was both! You couldn't breed a more highly strung bitch if you tried.

Yet he still respected the delicate, volatile, dark-haired Olga. He had thoroughly enjoyed being her husband, dressing up like a dandy in fine clothes with "a true lady" on his arm, whose social connections opened the doors of the best parlors in Europe for him.

"In Spain, a man can keep a wife on one side of town and a mistress on the other for years, and they'd only find out about each other at the man's funeral, when he is beyond caring," Pablo grumbled.

Not so in Paris. Discretion lasted only so long. Once his young blonde mistress became pregnant, mutual "friends" couldn't resist letting Olga know all about Marie-Thérèse. Now his wife was devoting all her time, energy and fury to winning this legal battle. How could an artist compete with that?

But divorce was out of the question because the marriage agreement he'd signed, subject to French law, required an equal division of property. And property, apparently, included art. Olga's expensive, fancy lawyers were poised to split his collection in half, like the woman in the Bible who would cut a baby in two rather than let someone else have it. They'd even gotten the judge to put a padlock on Picasso's studio in Paris.

"Imagine locking a man out of his own workplace!" he brooded, still incensed.

Olga already had possession of their son, Paulo. That should be enough for any woman. As it was, Picasso could seldom bear to sell a painting when it was done; the whole process of separation from his creations depressed him for days. What did the money-men know of that kind of pain?

No, divorce must be avoided. A legal separation was the only answer. So the bargaining had begun, and the endless torture of waiting, waiting, waiting for a settlement. On and on it went, month after ghastly month, for over a year now; and for the first time in his life, Picasso stopped painting. He was not dead in those months, but he was not really alive—more like a man tied under a swinging blade that was slowly swooshing closer and closer to him until it would finally slice him to death.

In the end, he'd simply had to get out of Paris. Today's letter from his own lawyer was at least hopeful; negotiations were now under way which might finally persuade Olga simply to separate. In return, she'd get the country house outside Paris—and there would be other financial concessions because she'd make sure that he paid a hefty price for his freedom—but the paintings, which were all that mattered, wouldn't so drastically fall under the axe, after all.

Whatever the outcome, here on the Côte d'Azur where the sun shone brightly now, a man could surely regain his vitality. As nature was casting off winter for spring, Pablo was transiting from his conventional, respectable family to the illicit new one presented to him by his angelic muse, Marie-Thérèse. He felt a certain masculine pride in their little daughter Maya, who'd been born just last year.

The ever-submissive Marie-Thérèse never complained, bless her, but now she hadn't any real hope of becoming Madame Picasso, for Olga would still be Picasso's legal wife until God and death parted them. And while Pablo enjoyed playing the doting new papa during his Sunday visits with his little second family, he could already feel the stirrings of boredom that domesticity invariably evoked.

"Women are either goddesses or doormats," he concluded after each conquest.

FORTUNATELY, AFTER A MORNING OF settling in with his new supplies, he'd found today's fine lunch from the Café Paradis awaiting him; and when he sat down to eat it, once again the food worked its magic to soothe him and make him forget all those letters. Afterwards, wanting to keep his body fit for the task ahead, he'd gone for a walk in the fields behind the house—they belonged to a gentleman farmer who grew roses and carnations—and here, in the remarkable light of the Midi, Picasso's pace became brisk and purposeful. He returned to the villa feeling ready to do what had been impossible only a week ago—to mix his paints and create anew. So it looked as if he'd made the right choice with the Café Paradis, whose cuisine was far more agreeable and soul-nourishing than the boring, restrictive diet suggested by his fussy Parisian doctor to cure his anxious stomach during this time of turmoil.

As soon as the young girl from the café left his studio, Picasso's gaze rested on the seashell she'd been holding. "What a character that Ondine is. One might believe she really is a water nymph," he mused, recalling a fairy tale that a German dealer once told him about ondines—they were magical sprites who, if they married a mortal man, would lose their immortality but gain a soul.

He glanced out the window just in time to catch a glimpse of Ondine as she was gliding away on her bicycle, with long hair fluttering like the waves of the sea itself and her skirts flowing in a circle around her, like a ship with sails flying. He watched until she reached the crest of the hill, where, for a moment, she seemed to hang there in the sky just before vanishing from sight.

"She's more like a kite on the wind," Picasso observed, moving his hand in the air in a preliminary sketch of a kite. He stepped closer to his easel. "But, she has a bit too much defiance in those eyes," he thought with a shade of disapproval.

The truth was, modern girls made him uneasy. They no longer knew how to respect and serve men as women did when he had been a boy surrounded by a doting mother, grandmother, godmother, aunts and sisters who unquestioningly accepted their God-given inferior position to men they treated as kings. All those breasts and bellies and arms and laps! That outpouring of adoration. Nothing could match nor replace it.

And so Pablo grew up believing that women of all ages were meant to sacrifice their lives to men, just as the mythic maidens were sacrificed to the Minotaur. It began with his little sister—and even now, Concepción's name still had the power to pierce his heart like the crown of thorns that wrapped itself around Christ's heart in the holy cards of his youth. For, at only seven years old Concepción had contracted diphtheria, suffering in doomed agony, fading slowly, becoming almost translucent like a ghost, right before his horrified eyes. Day after day she'd lain in bed, pale and hopeless, prompting the thirteen-year-old Picasso to kneel trembling by her side and utter a prayer that he regretted from the moment it left his lips.

"Dear God, save my sister and I will never pick up a brush to paint again!"

What devil had inspired such a terrible sacrifice? For even then, the boy Picasso's talent was indisputable. As a child he'd begun drawing even before he could speak. Everyone knew that he was destined for greatness—why, his father had quit painting and handed over his own box of paints and brushes to Pablo, in a gesture that carried as much burden of guilt as it did a vote of confidence.

Would God really expect the boy genius to give up such a gift if his sister survived, just to make good on his rash bargain? In a panic, Pablo had tried to ignore another voice that whispered demonically in his ear, "Ask God to keep your artistic destiny alive, and take your saintly sister's life as a sacrifice . . ."

For days Picasso agonized as only a young boy could, imagining that it was *his* will, and not God's, which must make this decision. He would never wish his sister dead—yet he could not help praying to be released from his promise to stop painting if she survived.

Concepción died soon after.

And that was how Pablo came to believe that no one could create without destroying something dear. Birth begat death, and in Spain the ghosts of the dead never completely went away. You learned to live with them instead of resisting them, and you avoided sentimentality, or else the servants of Death would think you were ready for him much earlier than you had to be.

Now, with civil war galloping toward Spain as inexorably as a charging bull, there was no point in going along with the trend throughout Europe of pretending that there would never be another world-wide war. Life and death were like the ebb and flow of the tide. In Barcelona, people understood this. On Sundays a young man's day began in church, but it might finish up with an afternoon visit to a brothel, where love was a mere transaction, and life a mocking challenge to outwit all rivals and enemies.

Create while you can, before the forces of death catch up with you . . .

Pablo Picasso picked up his brush.

5

Céline in New York, Christmas Eve 2013

My mother waited until I was thirty to tell me about Grandmother Ondine and Picasso. It was Christmas Eve, and I'd just flown in from Los Angeles to spend the holiday with her at her house in Westchester—one of those venerable old colonials with large, elegant windows, bordered by carefully pruned shrubbery and situated on a spacious, neat lawn dotted with ancient oak and maple trees.

It was snowing lightly when my taxi dropped me at the driveway. Mom must have been watching from a window, because the front door opened before I even got near it, and she came down the walkway without a coat over her cherry-red wool dress. She always dressed impeccably in finely made suits or dresses, pretty silk scarves and subtle, discreet jewelry; and her skin appeared youthfully radiant.

I instantly admired how good she looked and how she single-handedly maintained a modest, genuine spirit of *joie de vivre*. Yet the sight of her small figure and bright face coming down the walkway also evoked a protective instinct I've often had for her, almost as if she were the child and I her guardian. For, although Mom possessed French good taste, she wasn't haughty about it; she had a shy, meek demeanor, due to some mysterious trauma from her childhood which she once alluded to but refused to fully explain, saying only, "Grandmother Ondine and I went through some bad times before I got married. But one must take the bitter with the better." I could never get her to say anything more.

Today though, Mom was especially happy and animated. "Céline, you made it! How lovely you look with your California suntan!" she exclaimed approvingly, kissing me on first one cheek, then the other. I stooped to meet her halfway, because I was so much taller. Her eyes were dark while mine were blue; in fact all I inherited from her was her auburn-colored hair—I wore mine in a waist-length braid, while hers was cut chic and short. I liked the familiar scent of her face powder; the warmth of her soft cheeks. As we hugged, her tiny frame felt a little more delicate now, for she was in her mid-seventies.

I took off my coat and threw it around her shoulders as she said, "Oh, look at the snow! Now we'll have a white Christmas, isn't that nice? It's like powdered sugar on everything. Come in, *chérie,* let's get you some *chocolat chaud*!" Although she cooked like the Frenchwoman she was, Mom felt immensely proud of being what she considered a modern American homemaker *typique*. I was actually born in France, but my parents immediately whisked me off to New York so I'd have a thoroughly American childhood.

"Hello, Julie! Merry Christmas," called out a new neighbor from across the road, who'd just come down her own driveway to collect her mail, and perhaps to look me over, because we hadn't met.

"Merry Christmas!" Mom said, then added with pride, "This is my daughter, Céline. I told you about her—she's a makeup artist in Hollywood. This year she was nominated for an Oscar award!"

"My *team* was nominated, Mom," I muttered, embarrassed.

"Ah, at last I get to meet Céline, 'the missing link'!" the woman said, bustling across the street.

I supposed I'd been called worse. All my life I was known as the "accident", a child conceived late when nobody expected it. My mother was thrilled though, because I was her only child after two miscarriages. I had older step-siblings, Danny and Deirdre, twins from my father's first marriage. Sandy-haired and freckled, they were dead ringers for Dad. Because they were older and very mysterious as only twins can be, I worshipped them wistfully as a kid, but they viewed me as a "Frenchie" like Mom.

"How's Arthur?" the neighbor asked, and she and Mom nattered on a bit about Dad's surgery. Since I'd just been on an airplane for six hours, all I wanted to do was go inside and unwind, not stand here in cold weather that my blood wasn't used to. When my mother tried to give me back my coat, I dug into my carry-on bag for a wool jacket instead, then I waited as patiently as I could until Mom was finally able to make her excuses, and at last we went into the warm house all aglow with holiday lights.

"Mmm, it smells like Christmas in here," I said as we entered, enjoying the mingled scents of nutmeg, orange, cloves, French mulled wine, and desserts baked with sweet European butter.

Mom's place was always perfectly neat in a way that I knew my apartment would never be. For the holidays, the rooms were decorated with pine branches and maroon-and-gold ribbon; the parlor had a big tree winking with lights and *baubels* and wrapped gifts shining beneath it; and, in her large, beautiful kitchen, almost every table and countertop was laden with home-baked desserts.

"You made *Les Treize Desserts de Noël*!" I exclaimed, thrilled at the charming sight of this ancient, traditional series of Provençal home-baked sweets. Delighted by my enthusiasm, Mom proudly gave me a tour of the Thirteen Desserts of Christmas. Here was the dish of dried fruits and nuts called the "Four Beggars" to represent the four orders of monks; then a sweet, *brioche*-like cake made with orange flower water and olive oil; various meringue and candied citrus and melon confections; two kinds of nougats with pistachio and almond; also the thin, waffle-like *oreillettes,* cookies dusted with powdered sugar like the snow sifting outside; and of course, the spectacular *bûche de Noël*— a Yule Log of rolled chocolate cake with a caramel cream filling, and dark chocolate frosting which had been scraped by a fork's tines to make it resemble a hunter's newly chopped log from the forest. There was even a tiny candy Santa Claus carrying a hunter's axe poised atop this beautiful Yule Log.

"Wow, Mom, you must be exhausted!" I said, impulsively giving her a big hug of congratulations for her beautiful presentation. She purred with pleasure, stroking my cheek and then patting my back.

"Pas du tout," she said modestly with an airy wave of her hand. And suddenly I realized what was different about Mom today; she possessed the calm, confident demeanor of someone who'd been home alone peacefully cooking all week while Dad was in the hospital recuperating. Even though she loved catering to him, I could see that not having Dad at home had somehow released her, making her both relaxed and buoyant; and it looked as if she'd been secretly enjoying her newfound independence.

"Leave your suitcase in the front hall, we'll get you settled in later," she said, eagerly taking my hand and leading me to the kitchen table. She sat me down there and then poured us some hot chocolate, which she'd timed perfectly for my arrival, along with a plate of fresh apricot butter biscuits.

"Mmm, so good," I said, sipping gratefully. "Now it really *tastes* like Christmas."

She'd been beaming with the instinctive physical delight that mothers have when their children are near, but now as Mom sat beside me, her expression became more sober. "Céline," she began rather tentatively, "your father has healed from his prostate surgery, but the doctors are saying that he's still got a lot of other serious health problems with his heart and his lungs. So this got him to thinking, and he decided that we ought to update our wills. There was so much paperwork to sign! You know I'm no good with such business and legal things. But thank heavens it's all taken care of now."

This conversation was highly unusual; my mother rarely talked about money. She left the family finances entirely up to Dad and his accountants. She shopped, she had credit cards of course, but as far as I knew, she'd never in her life had to balance a checkbook, pay a bill or do her taxes.

Now she took a deep breath. And then she lowered the boom. "Your brother has been helping Dad with all the complicated insurance paperwork, so they've put everything in trust to Danny, because he understands what Dad wants and can continue taking care of it all when your father isn't around to do so anymore. Is that okay with you?" I detected a guilty tinge to her voice as she said all this in a rush, as if to get the whole thing over with as quickly as possible.

Still, it took me a moment to grasp the significance of what she was saying. "Danny's going to get *all* the money? Even what you inherited from your mom?" I said. She nodded with such a stricken look that I saw it had not been an easy thing for her to agree to, yet she hastily tried to reassure me.

"But Danny won't keep the money all for himself. He'll manage it for me and then when I'm gone, he'll take care of *all* of you; it will be divided up equally. Daddy says men have more access to information for making better business and investment decisions. 'Men trust men', he says."

My hot chocolate had gone cold right there in my cup. I'd stopped sipping it. "And what do *you* say, Mom?" I asked quietly. I knew that nobody else in the family was going to ask her this.

She looked relieved and grateful, as if I'd given her permission to voice her own opinion, and I found this painfully touching. "I thought all three of you should be in charge—with the trust split three ways. I told your father that," she admitted. "But he kept saying, 'Too many cooks in the kitchen spoil the broth.' Deirdre says she's fine with Danny being in charge, so I thought it must be all right, don't you think?" she said pleadingly. Her self-doubt was so pitiful to see but I had to answer her truthfully.

"No, I don't agree. Deirdre *would* say it's fine; the twins are always thick as thieves." In fact as a kid Danny *had* been a thief, utterly unrepentant when caught cheating in school or stealing from his own family. What bothered me most was the sneaky way he did it, skulking around the house; he just wasn't the kind of boy you turned your back on. I never understood why Mom didn't use a firmer hand with him. Nor could I let my father's sexist excuse pass. "Dad's living in the Dark Ages. These days there's a whole world full of women who run companies, make investments, do everything!" I reminded her.

My mother got that look on her face—the one she wore whenever she wanted to dodge any conflict, large or small. "Oh, he's always been a good husband and a good father, and you know he loves *all* of us!" she said hastily. "Don't worry, the will says everything will be done fairly."

"Let's hope so, Mom," I sighed. I didn't want to add to her stress, and I couldn't expect her to confront Dad now. She'd been thirty when she met my father—a tall, good-looking forty-year-old at the time, whose first wife had recently died of cancer, and he was dealing with a succession of nannies who'd all quit, saying that the twins were mean and "a pair of holy terrors".

I'd heard this from Aunt Matilda, Dad's younger sister, a retired art teacher whom he derisively called "the spinster". Aunt Matilda said he was attracted to my mother because he wanted "an old-fashioned girl, fashioned from his own rib".

But Mom described being courted by a man smitten with love-at-first-sight, and surely this was true; Dad never cheated on her or even flirted with other women, and he made certain that his wife lived the good life, always able to have whatever fine things she loved. He was a "killer" lawyer at a prestigious firm, who could also be charming, gregarious and even appear modest when the situation warranted it. Mom claimed that Dad was just like the hero of her favorite movie, *The Sound of Music*—a sort of Captain von Trapp whose stern, somewhat sinister-looking handsomeness masked the heart of a good man.

I always wanted to believe so, for when Dad was in a good mood he was affectionate to us all, scooping his special ice cream sundaes, flipping Saturday-morning pancakes, singing to us on long car drives, teaching us kids to play sports and games. He liked to tell jokes, and, among his adult friends he was considered the life of the party. People mistook his jocular act for the hallmark of a contented soul.

Only his family knew that Dad was *not* a happy man. His frequent outbursts of rage were our little secret, which we seldom discussed even among ourselves. My early attempts to engage Mom about why Dad was so angry were fairly fruitless, as she excused him by saying that his career was stressful, and this was true; his legal work for high-stakes clients involved skimming the risky edges of the law.

But recently Mom had confessed to me that, during a particularly volatile period, a doctor once told my father that he had "narcissistic tendencies" and suggested therapy. "What did Dad do?" I asked.

"He was furious. Then he went and found another doctor he liked better," Mom demurred.

We all tried to coax Dad into a happier mood with things we knew had pleased him before—his favorite songs, or sports scores, or old movies. But every evening when he came home from work, no matter what wonderful steaming dish Mom set down in front of us, our appetites died as my father, his face already thunderous, took his seat at the head of the table, searching for any inkling of failure or disloyalty in order to find a scapegoat. Then he'd explode with the pent-up fury we all dreaded.

The twins learned to deflect this by flattering Dad, pretending to be exact little replicas of him. But I watched in dismay as Mom absorbed his ridicule with a meekness that even as a child, I could see only reinforced his contemptuous attitude, which extended to whatever female friends she tried to socialize with, making it uncomfortable for her to invite any of them to her home.

And there was a joke I learned to hate which he often repeated at her expense. It was about an incident at a New Year's Eve gala when she was standing in an impossibly long line for a ladies' room. I never heard the end of the joke; all he had to do was to start to tell it, and my mother would get so embarrassed that she'd beg him to stop. He'd keep going, and even as her eyes filled with tears he'd continue, until finally stopping short of the "punch line" by telling her, *Julie, you're just too sensitive*.

As the youngest in the family witnessing all this, I'd hoped my elder siblings would stand up to him; but Dad's rage was like an oncoming tank which most people instinctively ducked away from. Yet he was the sort of forceful man who didn't respect "wimps" and you couldn't miss his smirk of disdain for people he could cow. Someone had to stare down his guns for Mom's sake. When nobody did, the sight of her defeated, slumped shoulders and tearful face became so intolerable that I had to speak up. Although Dad enjoyed some preliminary sparring, he could not bear to lose an argument. And that's why, when his shouting failed him, I was the one he hit. A whack across the face or back; a shove; a rough painful twisting of my arm or wrist—right there at the table, while the others averted their gaze.

When Dad's rage was finally spent, Mom would be off the hook. At this point he usually looked bewildered, as if he could not fathom why the rest of us found his behavior so shocking that afterwards we all pretended nothing had happened; until the next time. It was always worse when the twins were away at school, leaving Mom and me alone with him. I've never admitted this to anyone, but in a way it was my father who unwittingly helped me find my calling in life—by inspiring me to become a teenage makeup expert in order to learn how to cover up the bruises I got from him.

I left home as soon as I could free myself from his financial support, fleeing to the Yale School of Drama through tuition loans and a scholarship for a theatre degree in production design. When I couldn't find work in the theatre right away, I spent a summer assisting a top makeup man in Hollywood, and I realized I was much happier playing with pots and tubes of cosmetics. Ever since then I've been in business for myself in Los Angeles. There in Lotus Land, among possibly the most neurotic people on earth, I felt that I'd found a more understanding family.

MY MOTHER WAS PATTING MY hand now. "Any new men in your life?" she asked hopefully. I shook my head, careful to appear serene about my current circumstances. She knew of my broken engagement, and probably understood, on some level, why I'd backed out of marrying a perfectly nice stockbroker who could have given me children to dote on and a life of ease—because he was the sort of guy who had to be completely in charge of every aspect of his life, and I just couldn't bring myself to entrust one man with my entire future, as my mother had done.

Perhaps because she *did* understand all too well, she reached out and stroked my hair with a soothingly fond gesture. Then, as if she'd suddenly figured out what she could do to brighten the situation, she rose to her feet and whispered conspiratorially, "Come, I want to show you something."

Somewhat halfheartedly I followed her through the hallway to the laundry room at the back of the house, where she bent down to open a sliding door in a cupboard beneath the washer-and-dryer.

"I never noticed that cupboard before," I said. "What's it for?"

"It's just a crawl space, in case any wiring or plumbing has to be fixed or changed. But to me, it's better than a vault!" She chuckled to herself. "Oh, I guess I'm just like *my* mother, after all. Your *Grand-mère* Ondine was always so worried whenever she heard about yet another burglary on the Riviera. She *did* have her little hiding places for her valuables—and I remember a secret storage area under a closet floor, where during the wars her parents hid the café's best champagne from the German soldiers."

She leaned in to retrieve a parcel sealed in a plastic bag, then rose to her feet, clutching it to her chest like a naughty little wide-eyed girl with a secret.

"Let's go back to the kitchen where the light is good," she suggested. We returned and I watched, mystified, as Mom opened the plastic bag to remove something wrapped in blue-and-silver Christmas paper, which she now deposited into my lap. "I want you to open this Christmas gift early this year—because it really came from your grandmother, not me," she said quietly. Her eyes were bright with excitement. I tore open the wrapper, half-expecting to see some family jewels. Instead, I discovered a maroon leather-bound notebook, shaped like a ledger.

"This belonged to your Grandmother Ondine. She gave it to me the day that you were born. It's a kind of cookbook she wrote herself, with all her best recipes!" Mom announced.

"It's lovely," I replied, baffled. I absolutely hated cooking, and my mother knew it. Every Frenchwoman, no matter how wealthy, believes that she should periodically cook for her family to prove that she excels at this domestic art. Mom was a generous and gifted chef, yet my father and siblings were indifferent to food and treated her like hired help. So I guess that's why I'd always steered clear of kitchen work. It occurred to me now that my mother was offering this gift as a gentle hint that I should learn to cook and thus become a more traditional female, as a path to happiness.

"At least I can give you this—for an heirloom," Mom said apologetically, noticing my hesitation.

Considering everything she'd told me this evening, the whole thing felt like just another kick in the pants, not a gift. A consolation prize, perhaps. But when I saw the hopeful look on her face I kissed her. This treasure obviously meant a lot to her, and I did like the feel of the notebook's buttery soft leather cover. Curious, I turned to the first page, which had a printed box decorated with a border of grapevines, and inside it, at the *Date* line, was a scripted flourish in blue ink saying *Spring, 1936.*

"This is Grandmother Ondine's handwriting?" I asked, studying it closely. On the line for the *Nom,* she'd only written a letter *P.* "Who's 'P'?" I said, pointing to it. Mom hesitated, and a strange, conflicted look crossed her face. Then, visibly, she made up her mind and took the plunge.

"Oh. Picasso," she said in a low voice.

"*Picasso!* Really?" I asked, taken aback. Mom nodded, and she went on to explain how Grandmother Ondine, at age seventeen, had transported lunch from her parents' café to Picasso's villa.

"Amazing!" I responded, actually feeling goosebumps imagining the scene as I flipped through the recipes, all handwritten in French. *Bouillabaisse* and *coq au vin* and beef *miroton* and lamb *rissole.* "What else did she tell you about Picasso?" I asked, feeling all the more intrigued now.

"Nothing," Mom admitted. "She just gave me this book as a keepsake and told me to pass it on to you when you were old enough." She turned to the back of the notebook where, in a leather pocket for storing mementos, Mom had tucked an envelope that was already slit open. I saw that it was posted in 1983 from *Juan-les-Pins, France.*

"Here's a letter that Grandmother Ondine wrote to me," she explained. "On old stationery from when her parents ran the café. She kept this stationery for her own personal use years later, when she grew up and took over the café after her parents died."

Fascinated, I saw that the folded sheet of delicate white paper, deeply creased from being tucked into that envelope for so long, had an appealing black-and-grey drawing of the café professionally printed at the top of the page. The words *Café Paradis* were on the awning of its picturesque terrace.

"And here's a photo of Grandma in the kitchen of her café," Mom said, passing me a snapshot. It was a cozy moment and I noticed that Mom had used the American word *Grandma* this time. "Isn't her hair wonderful? It never went completely grey—it stayed mostly dark, right to the end of her life."

She put the picture in front of me and I peered closely at the first image I'd ever seen of Grandmother Ondine—a woman wearing a rose-colored dress, whose hair *was* very different from Mom's and mine, darker and luxuriously curly. I was immediately captivated by her vital-looking face and bright, lively eyes. She seemed like a strong, no-nonsense character.

"Grandma looks *formidable*," I said, surprised. Mom was so shy that I never imagined I had a female ancestor who ran her own business in a century when women were still struggling mightily for equal rights. Grandmother Ondine was standing in an old-fashioned kitchen; behind her was a Provençal country cupboard painted bright blue, with a tall pink-and-blue striped pitcher on it.

"Hey!" I said. "Isn't that the same pitcher you've got in *your* kitchen?" I glanced up at the shelf where it was sitting right now, always in pride of place for as long as I could remember.

"Hmm? Yes," Mom answered, still scanning the letter. "Your grandmother was sixty-four years old when she wrote this! She says business is good and she's got a nice young lawyer, Monsieur Clément, who's helping her put her affairs in order. But I got worried when I read this part about Grandma needing to see a doctor for 'some heart trouble', and having to use a cane to walk. That's when I decided I *had* to go see her in France, even though I was pregnant with you. Deirdre and Danny didn't come with us because they wanted to be with their friends that summer."

Very soberly, she replaced the note in its envelope and tucked it in the leather pocket. "I've kept it all these years because it's the only letter she ever sent me. Before then, we were a bit—estranged—ever since I left France to get married. She had wanted me to—wait."

"You and Dad eloped, right?" I said. Mom nodded guiltily. She'd always made it sound so romantic, as if Dad had swept her off her feet. Now I saw there was more to it; perhaps a serious rift with her mother. Gently I asked, "How come you never told us about Grandma Ondine and Picasso?"

Mom flushed and admitted, "She made me promise never to say his name to—" She stopped.

"Dad," I guessed. She nodded. I knew he resented Mom's few stories about her life before she met him; so whenever Mom ventured to tell one she did so hurriedly, in the manner of someone who's been chided that she's not very good at it, which evoked the very irritation in her audience that she dreaded. I am ashamed to think that we all got used to only half-listening to her.

Now she actually lowered her voice, even though we were the only two people in the house.

"There's something else I find myself thinking about a lot lately. That last day—when Grandma Ondine and I were sitting together, having a nice chat just before dinner, like you and I are doing right now—she said she had to tell me something she didn't want anyone else to hear." By now I was holding my breath, waiting. Mom said wonderingly, "Grandma told me that Picasso once gave her a picture."

"Picture?" I said, awed. "Like, a painting? Or drawing?"

"A painting, I believe. She said he gave it to her as a gift for all her good cooking. I think she wanted to tell me more—but she never finished her story because right then and there I went into labor! They had to rush me to the hospital, and, well, we never had dinner that day! You certainly surprised us all, arriving a whole month sooner than you were due," Mom went on breathlessly, lapsing into the only part of the story I knew, because it explained why I'd been born in France. So I knew what was coming.

"That's the same day Grandma Ondine had a heart attack, right?" I said softly. As a child I'd felt slightly guilty about it, as if I'd somehow inadvertently caused her death. Later, in my more mystical teenage years, I told myself that my grandmother had somehow passed the baton to me that day. So now, holding on to this elegant, leather-bound book, I felt that "baton" in my hands for the first time.

"Yes. It happened when I was at the hospital. A neighbor looked in on Grandma and called the doctor. She died at home that day—the doctor said she went quickly and didn't suffer."

We both fell silent. Mom's face was puckered with regret as she said sadly, "They kept me in the hospital for weeks because I was anemic and caught bronchitis. So your father had to deal with Grandmother Ondine's lawyer for me, to settle the estate. Grandma had everything in order, just the way she wanted it. Most of it was already in trust to me. Her French lawyer knew just what to do, and, while I was recovering, he handled the sale of her property. Everything was happening so fast. And I had *you* to care for!" I reached out and took her hand, and she squeezed mine in response.

After I absorbed this, I asked, "But—what about the Picasso painting?" She shook her head.

"I never saw it! And because Grandma made me swear that day never to tell your father about it, all I could do when I got out of the hospital was to ask the lawyer if he'd found any artwork," Mom explained, looking stymied even now. "He said he emptied every piece of furniture before he sold it, and there was nothing—no art, no safe-deposit key, no receipts or bill of sale; so he believed that if she had a painting she must have sold it quite some time ago."

"Maybe the lawyer stole the picture," I couldn't help saying.

Mom smiled and shook her head. "No, he was a nice young man, a good man."

"Could Dad have found it?" I asked. We looked at each other, both perfectly aware that my father seldom resisted a good opportunity to show off. "It's not the kind of secret he could have kept," I concluded, and Mom allowed herself a smile of agreement.

Hesitantly she added, "So, I just assumed that Grandma must have already sold the Picasso and was trying to tell me about the money, which would explain why she had quite a bit to leave me."

Our solitary moment was suddenly broken by the sound of a car pulling into the driveway.

We glanced out the window. "It's your father. In Danny's car," Mom said, in a complete change of tone, hurriedly rising. "And there's Deirdre and her family in the car right behind them, back from shopping. The twins were *so* determined to get Daddy released from the hospital in time for Christmas!" she said, automatically putting on her happy face. I felt a familiar pang of sympathy for her, seeing how hard she was trying to please everyone. Instinctively I stayed close to her as we rose to meet them.

I heard several car doors slam, and I saw from the window that the twins, now in their late forties, still looked to me just as they had when they were kids—lanky, sandy-haired, freckled, with that unspoken conspiratorial air between them—except now they were stretched into grown-ups, with children of their own. I had the same thought I always do at the holidays, which was, *Maybe now we can finally be a happy, harmonious family.* But this wish faded as my father got out of Danny's car, appearing a little more bent and grey-haired these days. As usual Dad's face looked like thunder. Something was already pissing him off.

"Please take this now," Mom said urgently, handing me back Grandmother Ondine's notebook. "Put it in your suitcase before everybody comes inside—and don't tell them that I gave it to you. After all, it's what Grandma Ondine asked me to do. But we don't want Deirdre to feel jealous."

I dutifully went and zipped up the notebook in my bag. When I returned to the kitchen, the twins and their kids were milling around, carelessly wolfing down Mom's specially prepared desserts despite her mild protests that these were supposed to be served after dinner. We all kissed and hugged, and I admired how quickly the children were growing up, yet they were still touchingly eager to be approved of by their Aunt Céline who lived in Los Angeles and knew movie stars.

Deirdre was in the parlor checking out the wrapped gifts under the tree, but now she came into the kitchen to look me over. Danny informed her, "Céline's been home with Mom all afternoon."

I watched him exchange a significant look with his twin in the telegraphic way they'd done since childhood. "Oh? What have you been doing all this time, Céline?" Deirdre asked. The sharpness of her tone surprised me. Mom glanced up at me nervously, which made me think that perhaps the twins were trying to gauge if she'd blurted out the recent "updating of the wills" to me. Apparently she wasn't supposed to tell me. If my father discovered she had, he'd be mightily displeased.

"Mom's been showing me some French recipes," I said truthfully enough, nodding at the Christmas treats. Mom was busy settling Dad into his favorite chair in the parlor, fluttering solicitously around him, seeing that he was snappish and irritable. He hated being an invalid. I noticed with concern that Dad still looked pale. Then he glanced at me appraisingly, and out of habit I felt my guts freeze.

"Still fooling around with powder puffs and lipstick out in Hollywood?" he asked.

Mom smiled proudly. "Céline was nominated for an Oscar this year, for the best makeup category—I told you that, remember?" she said encouragingly, nudging my father.

"My team and I," I said. "I worked with a guy who's been in the business for ages."

Danny said quickly, "But you didn't actually *win* the Oscar. Right?"

"Champagne, everyone!" my mother said brightly.

JUST BEFORE NEW YEAR'S, DAD had to go back into the hospital. I sat with him in his room while he was waiting to be wheeled into surgery again, and he was unexpectedly warm and friendly. He even allowed me to hold his hand awhile as we chatted about a safe topic of mutual interest—old Hollywood movies. In retrospect, I think he was scared, though he wouldn't admit it. The surgery went well, and the doctors thought his outlook was good. But later that night, his body was ultimately unable to withstand the shock of another operation. He died before dawn, before we could get back in time to say goodbye.

When I went to his hospital room to collect his things, I burst into tears at the sight of his empty bed, and his leather shaving kit that held his comb, toothbrush and razor. Despite everything, Dad had been such a brooding, dominant presence that permanent absence seemed impossible. Now all I could think was, *Where did he go?* I felt a sudden, deep sorrow for his lonely soul, which I pictured floating on a raft, drifting farther and farther away into a blackened sea, because he used to scare us on our summer vacations by swimming very far out, to show off, waving back at us and enjoying our consternation.

My mother had, I think, been bracing herself for this for some time, because she seemed calm and resigned at the funeral. Deirdre went on one of her terrifying "organizing" binges, packing up Dad's clothes and things so Mom wouldn't have to face it. Friends and neighbors swarmed around my mother, clasping her hands in theirs, murmuring their condolences, so I didn't have much time alone with her.

I had to leave right after New Year's for a movie assignment in Germany, but just before I left I told her I could stop back here in springtime to visit her again on my way home, and I asked if she'd be okay in the house alone until then, adding encouragingly, "Mom, I know it might be scary at first, but being on your own gives you a chance to think about what things *you* like to do and how *you* like to live."

She nodded, brightening. "Yes. I'll be fine. Deirdre invited me to spend a few weeks in Nevada with her, to get away from all this cold weather. So, go do your work, and I'll see you here when you come back and we'll do nice things together." She glanced over her shoulder to make sure no one was watching before she pressed a new key into my hand. "Dad had the locks changed last month," she murmured.

"See you soon," I promised. She remained standing there at the front door, blowing kisses as I waved goodbye from the cab.

*   *   *

My NIGHT FLIGHT TO GERMANY was quiet, because I'd been booked into the business-class section where most passengers were trying to sleep. The communal hush was soothing. And as we were crossing over the Atlantic Ocean in that inky darkness, I found myself drowsily wondering what had really happened to my Grandmother Ondine, that year when she and Picasso crossed paths.

6

Ondine and a Party of Three, 1936

SHORTLY BEFORE EASTER THE TELEPHONE RANG AT THE CAFÉ PARADIS, AND Ondine's ears perked up when she overheard her mother using the code name for Picasso, saying in her warmest manner, "Certainly, Monsieur Ruiz. We would be happy to accommodate you."

But when Madame Belange ended the call, her tone changed entirely. "How do you like that? He says he's got two guests coming from Paris to*day* and asks if *you* could cook lunch up at the villa!"

Ondine, recalling how she'd blundered into claiming entire credit for the *bouillabaisse,* said quickly, "Don't worry, *Maman,* I can do it."

"Well, you'll have to," her mother answered, sizing up the situation pragmatically. "We're already overstretched—it's Holy Week, for heaven's sake! Men never consider what work a holiday is. But what on earth will we serve Monsieur Ruiz's lunch party on such short notice? Your father just went over the accounts and once again says we must cut costs. I suppose we'd better keep it simple, with plenty of cold dishes."

"No!" Ondine exclaimed vehemently. At her mother's surprised look, Ondine said more quietly, "It's a special occasion, so we mustn't fail this *Patron*. His visitors are Parisian and you know how they chatter when they travel! The talk will be all up and down the Côte d'Azur if they love it or hate it."

"Then *what* will we feed them? Look in your notebook. What does he like to eat?"

Ondine sat down on the chair in the corner and quickly flipped through the pages of her careful notes. Cooking for Picasso had settled into a comfortable routine. Each time she went into his kitchen she laid out his prepared lunch while he was rustling about upstairs in his studio.

Yet, quiet as he was, the Master was clearly hard at work. The smell of paint wafted downstairs, but more than that, his intense focus and steely ambition were palpable, as if he were an unstoppable, hardworking furnace that, once fired up, could heat the entire house and illuminate every room. Ondine sensed in her very skin and bones that wonderful things were happening here.

And sure enough, she soon discovered the results, for he had the habit of scattering his paintings throughout the house—propped up against a wall here, a chair there, a table beyond—while they were still wet. *Monsieur Picasso put them out to dry, just like a woman hanging her wash,* Ondine had noted, amused.

Within a week there were four paintings in this impromptu art gallery—strange, compelling pictures in pastel Easter colors, composed of circles and triangles with eyes and noses in unexpected places; and in the backgrounds were seashell-shaped spirals and cornucopias with trees sprouting from them, everything at once celestial yet warmly earthy, an explosive burst of spring fever. In one of them she recognized the Mediterranean's pale beaches and blue sea as a backdrop for what seemed like a whimsical-looking, kite-shaped face.

When later she returned to collect the lunch dishes, she sometimes found him smoking thoughtfully in the back garden, and he would nod politely without a word, looking absorbed. He seemed to feel no compunction to thank her or to offer any other critique of the meals at all, good or bad.

The only way Ondine could get any inkling of his tastes was by studying each plate he left behind; and soon she was able to read those crumbs for very subtle distinctions, just like a soothsayer interpreting tea leaves. If Picasso had enjoyed his meal, all the dishes would be wiped clean. But if his work was going especially well, although he would eat, he'd leave behind signs of his preoccupation—his napkin fallen to the floor unnoticed, a plate of cheese and a half-eaten apple in an odd place like the small table at the foot of the stairs—indicating that he'd been impatient to return to his vision. And on a rare day when a meal was not quite to his liking, or perhaps his mood was gloomy, he politely covered the leftovers with another plate, as if to save them for someone else.

Ondine always recorded her impressions in the notebook. So now, when her mother asked about Picasso's tastes, Ondine said thoughtfully, "He liked the beef *miroton* when we made a sauce of butter, onions and vinegar; and the deep-fried *rissole* pastry filled with ground lamb and cumin; and the veal braised with carrots and turnips. He prefers more rustic, country meals instead of fancy ones with creamy sauces. He especially liked our spiced stew," she reported, shutting the notebook.

"But there's no time or supplies to make a stew!" her mother exclaimed.

"Let's see what we've got," Ondine replied, undauntedly peering into the icebox. "Well, there are some *langoustines* for an appetizer. For the main course . . . here's some garlic sausage, and a little duck *confit,* a bit of slow-cooked lamb shoulder and some roasted pork. Some beef that hasn't been cooked yet, and marrow bones, fine. I'll use the goose fat to make the crust . . ."

"That beef is for Monsieur Renard's lunch," her mother objected. "And there isn't enough of anything else that I can spare for your artist *and* his guests!"

Undeterred by the appetites of the Three Wise Men, Ondine made more discoveries. "White beans already cooked with pork rind! Here's tomatoes, carrots and onions, good . . . and a *bouquet garni.* I can make a splendid *cassoulet,*" she enthused, feeling inspired. "Then, I'll bake a special cake for dessert."

Madame Belange insisted, "But a *cassoulet* has to simmer for hours! You can't do that with beans that are already cooked."

Ondine determinedly pinned back her hair and tied on her apron. "Don't worry, *Maman*. The beans and *confit* are nearly perfect already. I've got enough time to make the beef with the aromatic vegetables before blending it with everything else. It will be more delicate for the Parisian guests; they usually prefer a lighter version of what they call 'peasant' food anyway. Remember when Isadora Duncan and her friends ate here?"

"Yes, like nervous birds pecking at their food," her mother replied, finally conceding, "All right. It's the best solution we've got. I'll find something else for Monsieur Renard to eat today. Go ahead, do it. Get as much cooked here as possible."

"Where is the *cassole*?" Ondine asked. Madame Belange handed her the special earthenware pot that was never washed but simply wiped clean after every use, because each new *cassoulet* contributed good flavors to the pot, thus "seasoning" it for the next stew.

Ondine set to work, seized with a frenzy of inspiration that was fueled by something deep inside her which had apparently lain in wait for just such a chance. This strange hidden vitality now propelled her through the risks and pinpoint timing that *gastronomie* required; she was, after all, literally playing with fire, like a high priestess making incantations over an altar—and the more dramatically the meat sizzled in the hot pan or the more dangerously the sauces threatened to boil, the more she felt her own exuberance and daring rising within her to meet the challenges.

WHEN ONDINE ENTERED PICASSO'S KITCHEN, she could hear male voices engaged in a spirited discussion in the studio upstairs. "His guests have arrived already!" she gasped, feeling her heart beating faster. Who were they? Would her menu please them? Suppose she was wrong?

Resolutely, she unpacked her hamper. She'd made a small, perfect cake for dessert—*gâteau le parisien,* a real beauty, layered with almond cream and candied fruit, crowned with meringue. Even her mother had been pleased, stepping back to admire it, saying, "This will impress."

With great pride now, Ondine enthroned it on a raised cake dish upon a small table tucked away in a corner of the kitchen. Picasso and his guests mustn't see it until it was time for dessert, she decided.

After she turned on the oven she quickly set the dining room table for three, on a pale yellow tablecloth. Then she returned to the kitchen for the real work. Carefully she cut the cooked meat—duck, pork, lamb, beef—into triangles. In the *cassole* pot she made alternate layers of the meat, then the white beans with cooked tomato, and some sliced rings of the spiced garlic sausage. She seasoned it all with freshly ground black pepper, and a violet-scented salt harvested from the marshes of the Camargue by *sauliers* who raked it by hand. Finally she topped the whole thing with bread crumbs and goose fat.

"We're doing just fine," Ondine assured herself, briskly pushing it into the oven, then scurrying to the larger kitchen table to prepare the appetizer. But she was moving too quickly now; when she whirled around she stubbed her foot on the leg of the little table where her cake sat so proudly. Stumbling, she regained her balance—but right before her horrified eyes, the cake wobbled and began to slide off its throne.

"No!" she gasped, reaching out to catch it with her bare hands, meringue and all. For a moment she had it, too—until the delicate frosting cracked, and the cake slipped right through her fingers, promptly tumbling to the floor with a soft sweet *plop!* that shattered it into a mess of frosted lumps.

At first all Ondine could do was to stare in utter disbelief at this disaster. The shame and the weight of her responsibility felt, for the first time, like more than she could handle. "This can't happen *today*!" she groaned. For a moment she wished her mother had come with her; yet she also knew what Madame Belange would say if this happened to her. *No tears! Start over, make another.*

But when Ondine glanced about wildly, taking hasty inventory of the pantry ingredients she kept here, she wailed, "I *can't* make another one! I don't have enough flour."

Fiercely she blinked away tears of frustration as she swept up the cake debris. She reviewed her supplies as if they were a jigsaw puzzle. After washing her hands, she instinctively found herself chopping butter into tiny pieces with what flour she had, adding salt and a little ice-cold water to work it—mixing, flattening, folding—until she had a pastry to press in a pan, trimming off its edges. "I'll have to skip the cheese-and-fruit platter and use it for this," she panted, reaching for a soft curd cheese to mix with sugar and egg yolks. She chopped nuts, orange peel and fruit into this filling, added raisins and brandy, then poured it all into the piecrust. Finally she made a crisscross of the trimmed pastry strips for a lattice top. Père Jacques called it *crostata di ricotta*—a sweet Easter cheesecake pie.

Breathless, Ondine checked on the appetizers, then peered into the oven at the *cassoulet*. It would be done soon and she'd be able to put the pie in. The cooking fragrances filled the air, and now a thunderous herd of hungry beasts came pounding downstairs enthusiastically.

Ondine smoothed her hair, took a deep breath and went out to greet Picasso and his guests.

Two men stood in the parlor with Picasso, arguing about his new painting which he now propped on the fireplace mantel. "Well, let's hear it!" he was saying.

His well-dressed guests had been discussing the painting in low murmurs as seriously as if they were bank executives in a meeting. There was an older man who looked to be in his sixties and moved with calm, deliberate gestures. He was tall and dapper in an immaculate suit and tie, large round black-rimmed eyeglasses, and a perfectly groomed white beard and moustache. The only bohemian aspect of his appearance was the hat which he hadn't bothered to remove, made of straw with a wide brim, slightly curled up at the edges. He doffed it now in deference to a female's presence, and as Ondine took it from him the guests gave her a frank, curious stare. She glanced back shyly, equally intrigued.

"*Merci,*" he said to her in a gentlemanly voice with a beatific smile.

He's not showy enough to be a politician, Ondine was thinking, *and not as buttoned-down as a businessman.*

Picasso, having already spotted Ondine standing in the dining room awaiting his signal to serve, had given her a broad grin. "Ah—here's my young chef!" he exclaimed now.

He appeared unusually animated, almost—could it be, a bit nervous? It made him seem vulnerable and therefore more human—like any mortal who was anxious about throwing a party for friends whose opinions mattered. *He's counting on me!* Ondine thought worriedly.

The second man now said playfully to Picasso, "So! This is the angel in your kitchen?" He was taller, thinner and younger than the others—still in his forties, surely—with a fuzzy nimbus of brown hair framing a long, poetic face and soulful eyes that gave him a dashing yet slightly fragile air. He was more luxuriously dressed than the others, in a three-piece suit with a silk pocket-handkerchief and a fresh gardenia in his buttonhole. "Ah, yes, *mademoiselle,*" he said, "I heard your angel's wings beating gently as you flitted about the house."

"Watch out for Monsieur Cocteau!" Picasso cautioned her. "He'll put you in one of his *avant-garde* films. You could end up on the other side of a looking-glass, unable to get out!"

They were behaving like schoolboys competing for the only girl in the room, Ondine observed, feeling nonplussed. Next to these tall, elegant men, Picasso was like a small, swarthy Arab sultan.

His guests recovered from the distraction of Ondine, and they returned to scrutinizing the painting on the mantel. "Come, Ondine, have a look!" Picasso exclaimed in that over-animated way.

He had never directly invited her to inspect his paintings. Surprised, she advanced toward this new canvas. *"Minotaure tirant une charette,"* said the man called Cocteau. Yes, indeed, here was a naked Minotaur—she recognized the horned, bullish head from the sketches in his studio—pulling a big wheelbarrow; but this fellow was different, for he was almost like a cartoon, with a friendly, innocent face glancing over his shoulder at his haul, which was an overflowing, mad jumble of strange items: a large painting, a ladder tilted askew, a tree that might be a potted plant . . . and a poor feminine-looking horse all twisted upside down. In the background was the familiar Mediterranean sandy beach and blue tide; but the stars in the greenish sky looked more like starfish floating in an upside-down sea.

The white-bearded man commented, "You know, this character reminds me of a junk man trundling all his possessions to another town in hope of better luck. Is it moving day for the Minotaur?"

"Exactemente!" Picasso said. But he stared broodingly at his painting. Ondine noticed that he seemed unusually respectful of this older man—was he some sort of critic or art dealer or journalist? This esteemed visitor had an aura of serenity, like a professor who was confident of his expertise.

Whereas Cocteau, the youngest one, was extremely eager to impress Picasso. "But clearly this Minotaur has murdered his mate," he offered, "so he's hauling the mare away to bury her, yes?"

Indeed, the horse's head hung prostrate from the cart, almost touching the ground, her eyes staring, her open mouth revealing teeth grimaced in pain, her legs and hoofs in the air.

Picasso snorted. "Wake up, Cocteau!" he chided with a scornful expression.

The older gentleman, looking perplexed, agreed with Cocteau, saying, *"Bien sûr,* she's dead! Her entrails are hanging out!" He pointed to thickly painted lines of red and white at the poor horse's belly.

Beneath their jocular manner lurked an air of fierce professional competitiveness, Ondine noted; an underlying tension, as if they were soccer players who each didn't want to be the one to lose the ball.

"Well? What do *you* see?" Picasso asked, turning to Ondine as if to a referee. Startled, she realized that he truly expected an answer. His other guests did, too; the older man's eyes twinkled behind his thick glasses, and the younger fellow's soft mouth dropped open in amused suspense.

Like a student who'd been singled out, she gulped and studied the horse, following the bold brushstrokes so closely that she had to tilt her head as far upside-down as she could, to see the animal right-side up. Viewed this way, she realized, the red lines coming from the mare's belly were not entrails, but the outlines of a tiny creature, also upside down, with a distinct little face—a miniature version of the mare's, with a similar long head, wide eyes and flared nostrils. Yes, of course—a tiny baby horse.

"*Comme il faut?*" the white-bearded man exclaimed, craning his neck to see upside-down, too.

Ondine blushed as she straightened herself upright again. "Go ahead, say it!" Picasso demanded.

"I don't think the mare is dead," Ondine said earnestly. "She's just given birth to a foal."

"Hooray!" shouted Picasso. "Thank heaven for the pure eyes of youth!" he added with a triumphant smirk at the other men.

"Surely this angel has a name?" queried Cocteau before he returned his gaze to the painting.

"She's my Ondine," Picasso announced. "Straight from the sea. She's come to cook you the best lunch in all of Juan-les-Pins," he boasted cheerfully.

The older man peered at her more appraisingly through his owlish eyeglasses. "You know," he said thoughtfully, "if I were to paint this *jeune,* I would make her hair purple and red, because she has both beaujolais and bordeaux in those long curly grapevines of hers!" He bowed to Ondine.

"Henri Matisse*, à votre service, mademoiselle,*" he said in the most charming way possible.

Ondine gasped. No wonder Picasso was so deferential! She'd heard diners in the café arguing about Matisse's genius for years. One customer even came in proudly carrying a Matisse painting he'd bought; a landscape of the bay of Nice in shockingly primitive strokes and colors, yet, Ondine noted at the time, magically devoid of anything ugly like telephone wires, traffic, advertisements—and people.

She felt herself curtsey in response to the artist's gallantry. But Picasso was scowling with ill-concealed jealousy now. "Well, are we going to eat, or are we going to stand here talking like ladies in a tearoom?" he said abruptly.

Henri Matisse calmly, peaceably reached out to a low table where he'd apparently left two bottles of wine with gift ribbons on their necks. He picked up one bottle and presented it to Picasso.

"*À votre santé,*" he said amicably.

Ondine reached into a drawer and handed Picasso a corkscrew. He went into the dining room to open it, and the others followed him.

Ondine slipped back into the kitchen, even more worried about this business of preparing "the best lunch" in town. Quickly she arranged the appetizers on their dishes and loaded them onto a big tray. Ready. She took a deep breath, hoisted the tray and carried it into the dining room.

Picasso and his guests stood there with filled wine glasses in hand. Now they took their seats. Ondine served *langoustines* "Ninon"— shellfish in a leek, butter and orange sauce, with a *chiffonade* of greens topped by a few edible flowers. "Ah!" the men chorused, dropping their napkins in their laps.

Back in the kitchen she became deeply absorbed at the stove with final preparations of the main course. When she re-entered the dining room to collect the empty plates, the men had resumed conversing in that low, businesslike way. Picasso did not look up at her, nor give any indication of what they'd felt about the appetizers. She hurried off to put the dishes in the sink.

"Well, they all ate every bite. They wouldn't do that if they hated it," Ondine consoled herself. "But these men are connoisseurs of the world's greatest art. They must have highly sophisticated palates, too!" Her fingers were shaking as she put the *cassoulet* and clean dishes on her tray. "Mother of God, give me deliverance!" she said under her breath.

She staggered back to the dining room with her heavy tray. This time, the men stopped talking and glanced up hungrily, their eyes following her every move as she deposited the main course in the center of the table. They continued to watch while she lifted the lid of the pot. More intense silence. Ondine raised her spoon to break the *cassoulet* crust with a ceremonial *crack!* The guests broke into applause. She almost wept with relief, carefully placing each serving before them. Then she stood quietly in the doorway to assess if anything more was needed. Picasso and Cocteau dove in heartily.

Matisse used his spoon to delicately taste the sauce. "Ah. *Superbe!*"

he sighed. *"Ondine, vous êtes une vraie artiste."* She was thrilled. No one had ever called her, or her mother, a "true artist". From the head of the table Picasso smirked at the food—not her—with pride, nodding.

Ondine said, *"Bon appétit,"* before she slipped out to check on dessert. She heard a second bottle of wine open with a loud *pop!* and soon the men's voices rose in volume, boisterously laughing and even shouting.

"Good, they're happy now," she sighed in relief as she ground the coffee beans.

But when she came into the dining room to collect the empty plates, the atmosphere had changed palpably, with a dangerous tension in the air that made her want to hide like a child behind the sofa in the parlor until the guests had gone home. Already she felt she'd been holding her breath all day.

"You've really got Herr Hitler all wrong," Cocteau was saying plaintively. "He's a pacifist at heart! And he truly has France's best interests in mind."

Picasso snorted. "He's got France's best *bridges* in mind for his bombs," he replied belligerently.

"No, no!" Cocteau insisted unwisely, as if he were confident of words he'd heard repeated a hundred times at other important luncheons. "Hitler loves France. He's a true patron of the arts."

"It remains to be seen," Matisse cautioned. "The odds are that we are all on his blacklist."

Picasso turned to Cocteau with terrifyingly piercing scorn in those coal-black eyes. "You think Hitler will let a 'degenerate' like you keep staging your pretty little films and ballets?" he said tauntingly. "He'll eat you alive for breakfast, and he'll still be hungry before noon."

Cocteau wore the shocked look of a schoolboy who'd had his knuckles rapped. Picasso saw this, but rather than let his friend off the hook, he pressed on in an even crueler tone, with the look of a bird of prey swooping on a mouse. "But if you, Jean, salute whatever flag the Nazis run up the pole, then perhaps the Führer will keep you for propaganda value, as the Daisy in his buttonhole."

Ondine caught her breath but managed not to make a sound. Even she knew what it meant when one boy called another one a Daisy, but she kept her expression neutral so that Monsieur Cocteau would not be embarrassed to have a local girl hear this. Quietly she placed her Easter cheesecake pie in the center of the table, wishing she could disappear into thin air. But she had to slice it and serve it.

Matisse broke the silence. "Now, gentlemen," he said in a soothing but firm tone as she moved around them, "let's not speak of monsters like Hitler today. The world has enough ugliness. Let us turn our thoughts, and our appetites, to the *luxe, calme et volupté* of Ondine's magnificent table."

Cocteau nodded. Picasso sat like an emperor. Ondine ducked out to make coffee, her nerves jangling. "Today they like my food. Tomorrow, who knows?" For, despite their warrior-like confidence, these artists were ultrasensitive, highly strung creatures whose mercurial moods were tricky to negotiate. She'd hate to have them turn their guns on her. Especially Picasso. He was as relentless as a bullfighter.

Cautiously she re-entered the dining room with her coffeepot. The atmosphere had changed yet again; now the men looked supremely sated from the meal, and they'd produced a secret bottle of *absinthe* while joking about mutual friends. As Ondine moved among them, pouring coffee, she saw Picasso glance at her backside and exchange a look with his guests. Matisse waggled his eyebrows.

They think I'm sleeping with Picasso, Ondine realized. And furthermore, their host was doing nothing to make them think otherwise.

"Ondine, which one of us do you suppose is the best at kissing?" Picasso asked slyly.

"I'll have to ask your wives," she answered quickly, and they all laughed uproariously.

Matisse winked at her through his owlish glasses, while Cocteau, fully recovered from tangling with Picasso, lifted one of his long fingers and waved it as if it were a conductor's baton as he sang:

"Belle Ondine, Belle Ondine,
your shoes are all a-shine.
And your flowery dress so fine."

Ondine giggled, for he had slightly altered the lyrics of a popular dance-hall tune, "Caroline". The men stomped their feet and clapped as Cocteau finished the song.

But now she was acutely aware that they were sitting at the level of her bosom, their lips just inches away; and she almost felt in peril of being seized by her hips and pulled into a man's lap so he could bury his face in her breasts. This image came so suddenly and graphically that she flushed with shame at having such strange thoughts. She returned to the kitchen, relieved to be alone.

By the time she'd cleaned up and packed her hamper onto her bicycle, the guests were gone, the sun was sinking, and the damp evening air was stealing in from the harbor. Picasso had stepped outside to see off his friends. Now he remained in the front yard, working intently on something, occasionally bending to pick up a stray branch that had fallen; but instead of throwing it away he'd attach it to the other items in his hand by twining it with string.

Ondine didn't think he noticed her as she wheeled her bike past him; yet at the last minute, he beckoned for her to come to him. She parked her bike and crossed the lawn.

"So," he said as he kept working, "you *can* cook. And now you can tell your friends you've fed three *artistes* in one day. Which of these 'geniuses' did you like better?" he asked with an ironic smile.

Ondine shrugged, unwilling to choose. Picasso exclaimed, "Certainly not Cocteau! He is talented. But he is the tail of my comet," he declared. "As for Matisse, well, he's the only other great artist of our time worth talking about, but he's too old for you, right?"

"He was very kind," Ondine demurred, secretly thrilled to think that such a master painter had expressed the desire to capture all the shades of color in her hair.

Picasso immediately guessed her thoughts. "Hah! How would he like it if I went into his house and announced that I was going to paint *his* cook?" he said belligerently. "Well, perhaps I will!"

With a sudden flourish, like a magician, he handed her the thing he'd been working on. A diamond-shaped construction of tissue-thin paper, attached to a crossbow of delicate branches and sticks, with a long tail of colorful torn rags. The paper, she saw in delight, had a wonderful abstract face painted right on it, just like his earlier canvases she'd seen this week.

"It's a kite!" she exclaimed in utter delight. "You just made a kite! It's *wonderful*!"

Picasso feigned a casual attitude, reaching into his pocket for a cigarette, watching her as she swished the kite around the lawn in a little dance of delight. "You like it?" he said. "Then keep it. You'll have to take it into the park to give it a good run," he added, as if it were a pet. He lit his cigarette, drew on it and exhaled, watching the smoke rings rise up and then disappear.

"*Merci beaucoup, Patron!*" Ondine exclaimed breathlessly.

"*Au revoir,*" he said calmly as he picked up his newspaper from the front step and then disappeared inside.

ONDINE WANTED TO GO RIGHT out and fly it, but she did not dare make a detour to the park, where someone might steal her mother's pots and pans from her bike. She decided she'd take the kite out early in the morning when fewer people would be there. Back at the café, she slipped upstairs quickly and hid it under her bed, for fear that somehow her father might confiscate it.

As she returned to the kitchen to unload her basket, her mother asked, "So? How did it go?"

"Just fine," Ondine replied, feeling suddenly weak with fatigue and relief.

Madame Belange said pragmatically, "Perhaps so. We've had no complaints."

Later that night Ondine indulged in a hot bath and finally allowed herself to relax, although it was hard at first for her nerves to "come down"; she felt like a sports car whose heart was still racing.

But when she climbed into bed and snuggled under the covers, feeling warm and silky inside, she could almost feel the presence of that kite underneath her, its face turned upward as if it could see her in her bed. Drowsily she recalled those lusty male voices singing her name all around the table.

"Mmm," she murmured, "I wonder which one of them really *is* the best kisser."

She imagined the three men insisting she test them, and she pictured herself moving from one to the other around the table, just like when she'd served the coffee. She guessed that Picasso would be a brutal kisser, and Cocteau might nibble on her ears like a deer; but Matisse might oh-so-politely lift her onto the table, push aside her skirt and savor her like a dessert, tickling her thighs with his bristly beard as he kissed her, higher and higher until he reached the rose of her sex, his connoisseur's tongue encouraging the kind of yielding that makes a woman even hungrier than a man.

"I can't choose who's best," she'd have to announce finally. "I want you all."

"*Alors!* It takes *three* mortal men to satisfy this one sea nymph!" they'd proclaim.

Lying there in the dark, breathing deeply now, Ondine hummed the song that her triumvirate of great artists had sung to her today; and with this lullaby she drifted off to a most satisfying, peaceful sleep. For the first time in many months, she'd gone to bed without thinking about Luc.

7

A Mirror for Ondine

THE INEVITABLE SPRING RAIN BEGAN SUDDENLY ONE DAY, WITH A WIND blowing so hard that the waiters had to open up the dining room at the Café Paradis and serve lunch indoors instead of on the terrace.

When the Three Wise Men arrived, they immediately began to argue over which country was responsible for sending over the winds of such bad weather—Spain, Russia or Arabia.

But at the back of the house, the weather made no difference; everyone was working hard, as usual. Ondine's mother told her, "Here, take this lunch to your artist up on the hill."

It had been nearly a week since Ondine was at Picasso's villa, for he'd notified them that he did not need his meals delivered during the long Easter holiday. Ondine assumed he had family visiting, and since he'd been vague about when he might want her to return, she'd worried that he might no longer require her services. Ondine had felt strangely mournful about such a possibility; she'd come to depend on his stimulating aura of energy, and she was eager to get to know her mysterious *Patron* better.

So now she was relieved to hear that she was needed once again. But Ondine peered out the window incredulously. The rain was coming down so hard that the birds had stopped singing, and the cat and dog ran inside looking like two wet rats who'd deserted a sinking ship.

"Bicycle up there in this weather?" she asked in disbelief. "I'll get soaked." Apparently her mother had no idea of what it was like to pedal a bicycle; she acted as if it were a horse. But Ondine's father did not own a horse or an auto.

Madame Belange continued, "The *Patron* told your father that from now on he wants you to come and cook in his kitchen as you did for his guests, and wait there for him to finish his lunch. Perhaps he finds all the coming and going too distracting. Well, he's willing to pay more to have you cook up there for him. The extra money will surely help!" she said with a small, satisfied smile.

"He wants me to be his personal chef?" Ondine asked, startled at this turn of events.

"He says it would be easier for *you*." Her mother peered at her suspiciously. "Why should he care about making your life easier? Did you complain to him?" Ondine shook her head vigorously, and her mother concluded, "Well, men are always kind to girls. Wait till you get to be my age, *then* they'll show you their true colors. *Alors!* You're going to have to really learn how to cook now. We'll do as much preparation as we can here. Better wear your blue dress—it looks more *serieuse*. Take your rain slicker with the hood. And keep your mind on your cooking. But if Monsieur Ruiz asks for something different, don't pout or try to be the boss. Just give him whatever he wants!"

"Yes, *Maman,*" Ondine said, thrilled to be treated as an adult, yet a bit scared to be heading into unknown territory.

Madame Belange studied her daughter appraisingly, then chided, "Remember, you're only a cook, not a fairy-tale princess. You've been walking around on a cloud for days—your father and our customers noticed that you've been putting on airs! Don't make fools of us with this *Patron*."

Ondine was surprised at how deeply her mother's words stung. It was true that, after the lunch party with Picasso's artist friends, she'd felt a lingering joy that gave her a new belief in her destiny. It never occurred to her that she was wearing her hope on her sleeve for the entire town to mock. She'd been out in the park regularly flying the kite Picasso gave her, too; until yesterday when a sudden gust of wind impaled it on a sharp tree branch. She brought it home, intending to mend it. But her mother threw it out, refusing to listen to Ondine's entreaties, saying, "You are no longer a child, and you have no need of broken toys."

So TODAY, AS ONDINE CYCLED cautiously on the shiny black streets, she was in no mood for any challenging ill weather. She heard the rain pelting against her oilskin hood and jacket, but it wasn't too bad until she pulled away from town and lost the shelter of its buildings. Then there was nothing shielding her from the wind that blew straight in from the sea, driving the storm clouds hard and causing sharp droplets of rain to blow sideways and splash onto her face.

Worse yet, just as Ondine reached the big steep hill to Picasso's villa, the wind suddenly blew back her hood, leaving it dangling uselessly on her back, with her head completely exposed.

"Oh, *la!*" she exclaimed. She kept her head bowed in such concentrated effort that when she made the turn onto Picasso's street she didn't see a rabbit who darted into her path until it was too late.

"*Attention,* stupid rabbit!" Ondine cried out angrily as the foolish thing froze in panic, and then, instead of hopping into the safety of the tall grass beyond the road, rushed headlong into her path.

"*Ai!*" Ondine shrieked as she swerved wildly into Picasso's driveway, where the wind had blown open his gate. Her bicycle teetered and then crashed loudly, sending her flying headlong into the gravel.

"*Merde!*" she shouted. It was the first time in her life she'd uttered that curse.

Then she remembered the food and she jumped up, retrieving her bicycle. At least the lock on the hamper had kept the meal from spilling out on the ground. Ondine parked her bike, unhooked the hamper and staggered toward the house. And now the roof chose to spill its rainy troubles on her head just as she came near.

The kitchen door squeaked open even before she reached for it, and Picasso stood there looking worried. He must have heard the crash and peered out his window, then come running down the stairs.

A cigarette was still clasped between two fingers. The other hand had fresh paint stains on it.

"Are you all right?" he asked worriedly. "Poor girl, come inside quickly. You are bleeding!"

Ondine's legs were shaking as she climbed the stone steps to the kitchen while he held the door open. He took the heavy hamper from her trembling hands and set it on the kitchen table.

"Sorry!" she gasped.

"Sit down, sit down!" Picasso said in a calm, authoritative tone, pulling out a kitchen chair for her. She took off her wet, hooded slicker, which sent rivers of water to the floor.

As she sank gratefully onto the chair Ondine realized that she had a serious gash on her right knee, from which a rather impressive amount of blood was coursing down her leg. Horrified, she pulled her dress away from the blood so it would not get stained.

"*Tiens!*" Picasso exclaimed. He left the room momentarily and she heard him rummaging in a closet. He returned with an ancient-looking first-aid kit that the landlord had probably left. From this Picasso took a bottle of disinfectant, a square of gauze and wads of cotton, and laid them on the table.

Ondine, embarrassed but fascinated, watched mutely as he pulled up another chair and sat on it, then very gently picked up her leg and put it in his lap. Her skirt was still hiked up but she did not want to draw attention to it by tugging on it. Now he reached for a cotton wad, opened the bottle and doused it. There was a strong odor of disinfectant.

"Aaah!" Ondine could not help gasping as he held the cotton against the wound.

"It hurts, doesn't it?" he said, smiling with satisfaction. "It has to hurt to do good. Hold it there and press hard to stop the bleeding." His attitude was more businesslike than sympathetic. She did as he said, determined to show him how brave she was despite the pain. He reached for a thin tea towel, held one end of it in his teeth, and, with a single swift gesture, tore it into two long, narrower strips.

Ondine was impressed by this tooth-and-claw prowess. He deposited the torn strips into her lap, then told her to remove the disinfectant wad so he could place the square patch of sterile gauze there.

"Hold that firmly," he instructed, and he wound the strips of torn tea towel around and around her leg so that they would keep the gauze in place. He tied the ends securely, then, done, he gave her thigh a brisk slap of satisfaction.

Ondine felt a tide of warmth surging in her flesh, starting from the spot where his big hands were holding her leg, as if his touch had made her blood flow right back into her veins, hot and healthy; but now the blood was rushing on heedlessly to that mysterious place between her legs which girls were supposed to ignore, until their wedding day when it became the property of their husbands. The only man who'd touched her there was Luc, that time he'd stolen into her bedroom to say goodbye. It had seemed such a sacred occasion that she hadn't felt like a sinner at the time. Here, she did.

"Feeling better now?" Picasso asked, glancing at her with his piercing, all-seeing dark eyes.

Ondine ducked her head. Did it show, the strange arousal she felt? Could he sense it?

"Too tight?" he inquired, clasping her leg and making her bend her knee to test it.

Did she imagine it, or was he deliberately holding his warm paw against the inside of her thigh, sliding his hand up just a little, just to tease, as he adjusted the bandage? Ondine was now acutely aware of the physical presence of this male creature who was sitting so close with his shirt unbuttoned.

"It's all right," she said hastily. Calmly he packed up the first-aid kit and went out again. She glanced about the kitchen to recover her bearings, and something caught her eye. Upside-down in the drainboard by the sink was her mother's long-lost pink-and-blue pitcher, looking all washed and dried!

In fact, the kitchen was suspiciously neat and tidy after a week without Ondine's care. She felt sure another woman had been here. "A man just wouldn't bother to wash up this much," she reasoned. This could be a feminine warning to Ondine: *Get off my turf, take your pitcher and stay away from my man!*

"Fine," she thought, relieved to have it back. She'd bring it home to her mother today.

Picasso returned and glanced at the metal hamper. Ondine cried out apologetically, "Oh, *Patron,* your lunch must be ruined! I'll go home and make you another one!"

He waved her off and opened the hamper, peering inside. "Let's see what we've got here," he said calmly, pulling out each item and laying it on the table. Sauce had sloshed over some containers.

"It's *coq au vin,*" Ondine wailed, then immediately struggled to get a grip on herself. She formed her apology in Spanish. *"Perdóneme para la inconveniencia,"* she murmured.

The effect of unexpectedly hearing his native tongue was immediate. Picasso's features revealed a sudden, childlike astonishment, then softened into the gentlest, warmest, most benevolent expression she'd ever seen on his extraordinary face. Clearly she had touched him.

"Don't worry, *está muy bien,"* Picasso responded. He tore off a piece of bread, dipped it in the sauce and tasted it. "Mmm. Still warm," he announced with a broad smile. He got a dish and ladle from the shelf, and filled his plate as if he were at a buffet. "Ah, the noble cock," he said with mock regret as he spooned up the meat. "When he can no longer service the hens, he gets thrown into the pot!"

He peered at Ondine interestedly. "Did you break his neck and drain his blood for the sauce yourself?" he asked eagerly.

"My mother did," she answered truthfully.

"Well, anyway, it's very good," he said with relish.

Ondine smiled uncertainly, wondering where he wanted her to wait while he ate. She normally stayed in the kitchen—but now he settled himself right here at this table instead of the dining room.

Picasso sensed her quandary. "Why don't you go upstairs and dry your hair? There's a comb and towels in the bathroom," he said with a vague wave. "Then you can look at the pictures in my studio. Women always like to have opinions about things they know nothing about. Every housewife secretly thinks she's a genius." He flicked his wrist and put his hand to his chin, miming a lady frowning critically to assess a painting. "Hmmm, it's very *interesting*," he said in a high-pitched voice, "but is it *art*?"

Ondine giggled, and, relieved by his matter-of-fact tone, she rose and went through the dining room and parlor. He had never invited her upstairs into his lair. But even before she reached it, her nostrils picked up the strong odor of wet paint. Six new canvases were propped right here on the staircase. She climbed up, pausing to view each one.

Every painting featured the same voluptuous, long-nosed blonde woman from the violent, erotic Minotaur drawings. But the attitude in these new pictures wasn't wild and savage at all. The first three were all the same pose: the model sat fully dressed in front of a vanity table with pots of powder and perfume, primping before a mirror. Her figure and demeanor were no longer that of a goddess but a plump, comfy house-wife. Picasso had put the date on each one, and the third one said: *12 avril XXXVI.*

"Easter Sunday! So, his blonde lady *was* here over the holidays!" Ondine said triumphantly.

She climbed up the steps to view the next three canvases, all close-up portraits of the same lady. But now she didn't seem maternal at all—she looked more like a schoolgirl, with a sweet, innocent expression and two doll-like circles of rouge on her cheeks. Her hair appeared more pixie-like and modern.

"He's been painting her over and over," Ondine realized with a dart of envy. One woman, in all her incarnations: housewife, schoolgirl, sexpot. Imagine being so fascinating to such a great artist!

Upstairs, the bathroom was dim inside and she could not find the light switch. But Ondine discovered a folded towel to dry her hair, and a freestanding, black-framed mirror propped by the sink. She picked it up, along with a white comb, and carried it into his studio, where there was plenty of light.

The first thing she noticed was the canvas on the easel—the very wettest, newest painting, quite different from the ones on the stairs. No more portraits, no more blonde. It was a still life: a bowl of fruit, a loaf of bread, a vase of flowers—and something so familiar with its pink-and-blue stripes that Ondine gasped.

"Why—it's *Maman*'s pitcher!" she whispered in awe.

But he'd exaggerated its height, as if the pitcher had turned into putty in Picasso's hands and he'd pulled and stretched and elongated it. Well, everything in this painting looked outlandish: the fruit bowl was crazily, precariously perched at the table's edge; the ripe, round fruit inside it resembled a woman's breasts; and the loaf of bread beneath the bowl stuck out like a man's prodigious, erect penis. A vase looking more like a wine goblet held bright flowers with pinwheel-style orange blooms springing outward like riotously overgrown jungle plants that aggressively dwarfed their container.

"Wonderful!" Ondine clapped her hands in delight. It was all so defiant, like a prank played by a child who'd rushed into a stuffy, proper sitting room, blowing a comical horn. Yet somehow he'd achieved a strange, haunting beauty that elevated even a humble pitcher to something sublime.

On a nearby table was a collection of newspaper clippings, neatly pinned together, lying atop another one of those brown envelopes from Paris. Ondine could see that these were press clippings for a great, successful gallery sale of Picasso's works, just last month. The headline proclaimed it one of the biggest events of the season, at which Picasso had made a brief appearance and was wildly applauded.

"He's as important as a prime minister or an opera singer!" Ondine observed, awed.

With other paintings stacked on the floor, and scattered drawings, pots of paint, jars of brushes, and books and newspapers scattered everywhere else, there wasn't a single surface left uncovered, even the chairs, so there was nowhere to sit. The only oasis was a slim, empty alcove designed for a narrow chest of drawers or full-length mirror. Ondine curled up on the floor there, glad to be off her sore leg.

"*Uf!* This floor is hard as stone," she grumbled, looking for a pillow. All she could find was an orange cushion, flat as a pancake, trimmed with gold-and-yellow tassels. She slipped it beneath her, took up the white comb and propped the black-framed mirror against her lap so she could peer into it.

"I look like a drowned cat," Ondine said, for her long hair was plastered against her head in a mermaid's seaweed-like spirals. She fluffed out the ringlets with the comb. Her face was flushed, her eyes wide. She put down the mirror and sighed, leaned against the wall and closed her eyes, listening to the rain. She must have dozed, because at first she didn't hear Picasso when he came in.

"No, don't get up," he commanded, studying her keenly. He picked up his sketchbook and began making rapid drawings on one page after another and another. Suddenly she understood what he was doing—he was drawing *her*! She gasped. Was this why he wanted her to stay here during lunchtime?

Although she was thrilled, Ondine felt a momentary surge of panic, recalling those violent images of the naked blonde woman being raped by the Minotaur-man, for the entire world to gawp at.

Is he going to make me pose nude like that? she wondered. His penetrating stare was like a magician's, as if he could just wave his paintbrush to make a woman's clothes fall right off her body.

But all he said was, "Put the comb on the floor and hold up the mirror as if you're looking at yourself." He had set aside the sketchbook and was moving around the room, assessing different angles.

Ondine followed him with her eyes only, not daring to move her head, even when he brandished a long strand of yellow forsythia that had been in a vase near the window, which he now draped like a crown over her bowed head. She suddenly felt utterly compliant, like a sculptor's mound of clay.

Still frowning thoughtfully, Picasso removed both of her shoes, tossed them aside, and manipulated her left foot so that the sole was flat on the floor in front of her seated body. He handled her feet as if she were his prized sculpture. Ondine felt her flesh turn softer still.

"Better," he grunted, tugging at her arm. "Hold the mirror lower. Yes, lower still, just so."

Picasso disappeared behind his easel, and she heard a few long, decisive strokes. He had a vigorous, muscular way of attacking his canvas. She hadn't realized that making paintings was such a physical activity—he was breathing noisily, harder and harder with each new effort as he sketched out the preliminary lines. In fact he was actually snorting.

Like that Minotaur, Ondine could not help thinking, *whose nostrils blow great white puffs of clouds!* Picasso *was* shaped like a bull, charging at his painting as if maddened with rage for his vision. Soon, every time he snorted, Ondine had to resist snorting with laughter out loud.

A short time later, when she dared to peek at him, his expression was like a swimmer raising his head above water to get his bearings. "No, it's not right yet," he muttered, backing away to observe it.

"Too pious," he concluded. "Undo three buttons at the top of that dress."

Ondine considered this, imagining what the final effect would be, and she decided that he was surely right; after all, she didn't want to look like a martyr on a holy card.

"Don't smile. And, you're still not sitting properly," Picasso said in exasperation. He stood with his arms folded across his chest as he thought it over quietly. Ondine waited.

"Take off your *culottes,*" he said decisively.

Ondine was startled. Then she gave him a cynical look. "Hah!" she said.

He glanced up quizzically until he realized what she thought he wanted. "Foolish girl. Do you think I'd seduce a woman with a line like that? Do as I say!" he exclaimed. "And if you don't understand what we're doing here, then you can pack up and go home. Hurry up, you're making me wait too long."

Picasso had returned to his canvas and stared at it, brooding. Ondine sensed from his tone that he really was all business. Her mother's voice popped into her mind: *If Monsieur Ruiz asks for something different, don't pout or try to be the boss. Just give him whatever he wants!*

Feeling more fascinated than frightened, she crept over to a big, battered upholstered chair that looked as if it had seen better days. Crouching behind it, Ondine reached under her dress and pulled off her underdrawers without ever lifting her skirt. It was easy enough to do, but where on earth would she put them now? In a minute he might glance up, and she did not want to hear that irritated tone again.

Quickly she tucked her *culottes* under a chair cushion, then she quietly slipped back into position in the corner on the floor, arranging her legs just as he'd instructed. She felt strangely liberated, and she *was* sitting differently, more naturally somehow, though she would never admit it to him. Yet she had a moment's panic, realizing that without underwear, her crotch in this position might be clearly visible.

There is no way on earth I will let him paint that, she thought. Then she had an idea. Casually she draped one arm across the place between her thighs. If he didn't like it, too bad. She gazed in the mirror at her moist, panting reflection. Her defiant eyes stared back at her, and told her to hold firm.

The room fell silent. Picasso glanced up, registering everything she'd just done. He looked at his wristwatch, then put down his brush with a sigh. Ondine's heart sank; he was giving up on her already!

"Silly girl," he said, shaking his head in amusement as he moved forward.

She felt the warmth of his breath as he bent over her, unstrapped his wristwatch and draped it round her right wrist, which remained poised protectively between her legs. He gave the watch a final tug, then reached for her bare left foot and firmly pushed her toes flatter on the floor. He paced backwards, step by step, critically assessing the effect. Finally, without a word he moved behind his easel and picked up his brush. She couldn't believe her ears when she heard his quick bristly wet strokes on the canvas.

He's really doing it! Ondine thought in awe. *The great Picasso is painting me, of all people!*

Ondine discovered that she'd been holding her breath. Now she let it out slowly. A new, perfect silence hung in the air over their heads like a soft cloud. The wristwatch, heavy and masculine, was still warm from his arm and she felt her own pulse throbbing against the weight of it. The watch seemed to contain all the passing minutes ticking inside it like little insects buzzing in a jar on a hot summer day.

Then one by one, each moment seemed to become released from the watch, only to hang in the air like bright wet soap bubbles, each taking its lazy time drifting off into oblivion . . . as if this strange enchanted afternoon could go on forever. Soon Ondine felt that she herself was floating inside one of these magical bubbles. Time had now expanded into an eternal tranquility composed of the most profound silence she had ever heard in her life.

Picasso remained quiet for a long while, becalmed by his own vision. Finally, he spoke.

"Femme à la montre," he grunted.

Woman with a watch. Ondine had to hide a smile of pride that someone was finally referring to her as a woman, not a girl.

She did not dare look up again. But she knew that Picasso was smiling, too.

8

Céline, Spring 2014

AFTER NEW YEAR'S AT MY MOTHER'S, I SPENT THE WINTER IN GERMANY, doing the makeup for a very scary vampire movie. We were shooting on location in an ancient castle with crenellated towers, surrounded by a dark forest straight out of *Grimm's Fairy Tales*. The nearest town was an obscure village of cobbled streets and old stone shops that looked like the illustrations on a Christmas cookie tin.

I was glad to have such a demanding makeup job—lots of bloody mouths and eyes against unworldly-white and deathly-green skin. The actors showed up in my makeup room before dawn each day, because it took so long to do their faces and hands. I was like a wild-eyed mad scientist in my white smock, surrounded by jars of brushes, paint boxes of rouge and brown contourers, purple shadows and kohl-black crayons; boxes of tissues and sponges, buckets of water and oil and soap to remove smudges and do quick changes.

"Céline, you *do* create the most terrifying ghouls in the business," the leading actress exclaimed, sitting in her chair before a brightly lit mirror, her bib tucked under her chin while staring at her own ghastly image. She widened her rouged eyes and mouth, baring her teeth and hissing, making all kinds of horrible faces with utter childlike glee. "How do you do it?"

I couldn't tell her, *I just show what I see*. Most people, when they gaze into a mirror, simply want to look younger and more conventionally attractive, so they never see their faces as I do: the incredible circles, diamonds, triangles, curves and angles that make each one so fascinatingly unique. I suppose that's why my specialty is these horror films and costume dramas, where I can freely use pencil, paint and powder to unmask both their noblest and ugliest aspects. I can look at anybody and find the monster that lurks within.

JUST AS I WAS FINISHING up in Germany, my brother, Danny, called. "Mom's gone into the hospital in Nevada," he announced. Quoting the doctors, he described it as an "episode" that may have been a series of strokes. "We tried to reach you earlier, but Deirdre had only an old phone number for you," he said, as if it were my fault somehow. "We had to go through Mom's records to find you. Don't worry; Deirdre chose good doctors for her, and a nursing home that got high ratings."

He sounded so oddly matter-of-fact about this unexpected turn. I felt truly alarmed, for my mother had been in spry, perfect health when I left her, and I'd been looking forward to our planned reunion in New York, where I intended to spend time with her doing all the mother-and-daughter things that both of us would enjoy. I'd even imagined having her stay with me awhile in California, a place that fascinated her but which she'd never been able to convince Dad to visit.

So I returned to the States and headed straight out to the care home in Nevada. As soon as I walked in the door, I was hit with that inevitable smell of disinfectant, stale coffee, sweat and medicine. Despite the staff's efforts at cheeriness with bright reception furniture and flowers, my deepest impressions as I walked down the corridors were of the sad-eyed, white-haired women nodding in wheelchairs parked in forgotten corners; old men in hospital gowns and slippers creeping down the halls with their walkers; carts stacked with trays of uneaten meals alongside laundry carts yawning with soiled linens; and world-weary attendants pretending they didn't see any of this. It was the last place I'd think of for Mom, with her impeccable standards of order and cleanliness.

When I found her room I saw that she looked tinier than ever in a bed with metal railings to keep her in place. She was heavily sedated, therefore unable to walk, eat, bathe, or go to the bathroom unassisted. She just lay there, silent and terrified, unable to speak, staring at me with those big dark eyes; but she saw that I was worried, and she raised a hand to stroke my cheek and console *me* before sinking back into sleep. So I knew she'd recognized me.

"She may improve once she's ready for rehab, but with stroke, it's hard to predict," the doctor told me. I sat with Mom for hours, murmuring soothing words and holding her delicate-boned hand. She slept a lot. I thought she looked like fine porcelain sitting on a bargain-basement shelf. When I saw the food they brought her, I had to suppress a shudder, remembering her own excellent cooking.

I spent two weeks in Nevada as Mom improved only slightly. I tried to help, but she required specialized care and still wasn't speaking. I did manage to make friends with the lady who came to shampoo Mom's hair once a week, and I got her to agree to keep an eye on my mother for me, and report any new developments which I felt instinctively that Deirdre would never tell me.

Because the twins had made it very clear that they were now in charge. They insisted on taking me out to lunch at the end of my stay, as if we were all celebrating something. They had the air of children who've been given an unexpected day off from school. Deirdre's job was managing a chain of spas in several resorts out West, while Danny worked for a bioengineering company in Boston.

Being around them shot me right back to childhood. As a kid I'd always wistfully hoped that Deirdre and I could be like other sisters I knew; but because she was much older and had her own room, there were no girlish whispers confided, no playing dolls together. Besides, the twins were an impenetrable team; my most vivid memory was when they tricked me into hiding in the laundry hamper, a place they promised would be safe if a murderer ever broke into the house.

Go on, try it, they'd said, and I did, because I was so happy that they wanted to play with me. But as soon as I was inside the hamper, they promptly sat on the lid and refused to let me out unless I came up with "the magic word". I tried every word I could think of, but none were magic enough. Finally exhausted with tears and terror, I decided to go silent and let them think I'd suffocated to death.

Céline? Céline? Deirdre had demanded in panic. I'd stayed smugly quiet, and when they jumped off the hamper, flung back the lid and scooped me out, I kept my eyes shut tight and my limbs limp. Danny laid me out on the floor and smacked me on the cheek, saying angrily, *Wake up! Come on, Céline!*

I waited excruciatingly, then, very dramatically, let my eyelids flutter open. I parted my lips and they had to bend close to hear me. *Water,* I said weakly. They were immensely grateful when I revived.

Now AS I SAT DOWN to lunch with Danny and Deirdre at a trendy health-food restaurant that they both liked, I still felt as if playing dead was the safest option. "Where are you headed now?" Deirdre asked with studied casualness, poking at her turkey and avocado salad.

"I have some work to do in L.A.; then I thought I'd go back to New York and pack a few things for Mom," I said, sipping my white wine a little too fast.

"Oh, we took care of that already," Danny replied smoothly. "Anything Mom needs is on its way here. Before she left New York, she asked us to put all her valuables in a safe-deposit box. There wasn't much; just her jewelry. What wasn't valuable was disposed of. Was there anything in particular you wanted to know about?"

I already didn't like the sound of this. So I threw them a curveball. "Sure, plenty. For instance, Mom has a striped pitcher from Grandma she's especially fond of."

They had to think for a moment. "Oh, that. We threw it out. We had all the contents assessed by a professional," Deirdre assured me. I could no longer hold back my feelings of utter disbelief.

"That was an heirloom!" I objected, glancing from one impassive face to the other in a familiar, fruitless search for a more human response. They looked impatient as they always did with what they considered mere sentiment. But I thought things were moving too fast and I said so.

Danny looked up, suddenly interested. "Why? Do you think that pitcher is valuable?"

"Mom might get better, you know. The doctors said it's not impossible. Why not let her sort things out herself when she goes home?" I said, putting down my fork, unable to eat another bite.

The twins exchanged a glance. Danny took a deep, regretful breath. "There's no point being in denial, Céline. Even if she recovers, she can't be alone anymore. You know, you weren't very helpful after Dad died, egging Mom on to be independent. She's so naïve and trusting, someone might take advantage of her. Dad knew this; that's why the house was in his name only, so when he went into the hospital he gave me permission to sell the house if he didn't survive the surgery. We already have a buyer. We got a good price."

"You sold Mom's *home* already?" I asked, astounded. "I'm sure she'd never sign off on that. We can't make these decisions behind her back! We should sit down with her and give her some other options. You know how much Mom loves her kitchen and *all* her cherished, familiar possessions—and that's so important to an older person's sense of security and identity."

Danny said coolly, "Fortunately we had that conversation with Mom before she got sick. We explained it all to her, and she agreed that it was time for her to move out of New York. In fact, she and Deirdre were going around looking at assisted-living apartments here in Nevada for her. She wanted to move out here to be closer to Deirdre and, of course, to you, since you're in California."

"She never said anything to me about moving out West," I said, feeling odd. It crossed my mind that this "episode" might have been distress caused by the twins pressuring Mom to give up her home. And if my mother had mentioned the little pep talk I gave her after Dad died—about taking time to figure out what she liked—then she surely must have felt conflicted about giving up her house in New York.

"Well, the point is, now we *have* to sell the house to pay for Mom's care," Deirdre said.

"Even if that's so, she could still live with one of us," I suggested. The twins hooted at this impossibility, as if I were being a dopey younger sister. "I don't mind having her stay with me," I said more firmly. "We can hire home care for her." Instead of considering this, they looked alarmed now.

"The doctors don't really think she's going to improve," Danny said with a finality I felt didn't quite match the prognosis. "And our lawyers—including Mom's—assure me that this is what's best for her. It's all been done properly, and it will all be in the Trustees' Report, which you'll get," he added, sounding rehearsed. "If you have any questions, I suggest you contact our lawyers."

I caught my breath in shock, as if truly seeing the twins for the first time. It finally dawned on me that they thought of Mom's money as theirs, not hers; and nothing I might say about Mom's rights or feelings would make any difference to them whatsoever. It was a dismaying, sobering revelation.

So after that lunch I packed up, returning to Los Angeles for a short assignment; and I met with my lawyer, who obtained all the documents he needed, made some phone calls, then sat me down in his office, shaking his head sadly. "What's going on?" I asked. "Why are my siblings talking like some law-and-order TV show? And how come they think they can sell Mom's house right out from under her?"

Sam sighed and said, "This sort of thing happens all the time, when it comes to wills and trusts. Look at it from the twins' point of view— they may resent your mother having replaced their own, and they probably think that you'll try to influence your mom to change her will and give you all the money."

"That is *not* what I'm after!" I said, outraged. "I only want to ensure that Mom has a real say in how she spends *her* money and where she lives. Danny and Deirdre are dead-set on keeping her all doped up in a nursing home. She's delicate and sensitive; she'll never get well being treated like that."

"Well, your parents' wills do not *quite* say what your mother told you they would. Apparently, before your dad died he got her to sign papers authorizing the twins to do exactly what they want in the event that she 'becomes incapacitated'. As long as she doesn't recover and change her mind, the twins have control. I'm afraid your relatives completely stitched up your mother legally—and you as well."

He looked at me pityingly. "Perhaps your mom didn't understand the papers she signed, or she didn't imagine they'd use them to do this to her. But she didn't leave you any money or power to fight on her behalf, so she can't really expect you to throw yourself in front of this train. Take my advice. It's not like on TV. This kind of battle could take years in court, and the twins can gut your mother's estate to defend their interests. And trust me, you don't want her to be without funds to pay for her care."

WHEN I LEFT HIS OFFICE, I retreated to my apartment in a state of shock and sorrow. I reached for my key but instead grasped something else that had been rattling around in my purse. It was the key to my mother's house that she'd pressed into my hand at Christmas.

And suddenly, every mysterious thing she'd said to me seemed to take on more significance, like when she surreptitiously gave me this key. *Dad had the locks changed last month.* I recalled the conspiratorial way Mom showed me that hiding place she had in the laundry room. She'd said, *To me, it's better than a vault! Oh, I guess I'm just like my mother, after all. Your Grand-mère Ondine . . . did have her little hiding places.*

"Why did Mom keep Grandma's notebook in there all this time, and then suddenly give it to me?" I wondered aloud. I had it with me now, because my lawyer had told me to "bring everything" pertaining to the case when I met with him. He naturally wasn't much interested in a cookbook.

But what else did she put in that hiding place? I remembered the twins saying, *What wasn't valuable was disposed of.* Yet Mom's laundry room was surely the last place they'd search; she'd probably picked it for that reason. I didn't want anything she secretly cherished to be found by some new owner of her house.

Since I was in between assignments now I decided to take some time off, and I caught a flight to New York. When I arrived at JFK Airport, I rented a car and drove to Mom's house. Nobody was around, not even that neighbor across the street. The house stood there like a candle that had been blown out. Silent. Lifeless. Wrong.

I put Mom's key in the lock and walked in. It was completely empty. As I entered the foyer I heard my footsteps echo hollowly in the utter silence. Mom's parlor and dining room looked forlorn without her carefully chosen furniture. No pictures on the walls, no curtains at the window, and the elegant area rugs were gone. She wasn't even dead yet, but already I could see that she was vanishing.

Continuing on, I averted my eyes when I passed her bedroom and realized that her bed was gone. Her closet door hung open, gaping, empty. Her vanity table, her little bottles of perfume and makeup, her pretty gold matching mirror, comb and brush set had all disappeared.

I headed for the laundry room, where the shelves that once held neatly folded towels were now bare. Inside the closet, her cleaning bottles, ironing board and iron had all been heartlessly taken away.

Not even a mousetrap left behind. If I found nothing in her secret cupboard, how would I know if it had been empty all along, or if the twins already confiscated what she'd hidden there? My heart was beating faster as, steeling myself, I crouched down beneath the washer-and-dryer with its crawl space for the electrical wires and plumbing. I reached around, feeling wires, pipes, dust.

Then I discovered another solitary plastic zip-it bag like the one she'd kept Grandma's notebook in, to protect it from the damp. I drew this parcel out. It contained a shiny, thick travel packet with photos printed on the envelope and a line that said, *Open immediately. Dated material and itinerary within.*

The packet had already been opened, and judging from the welcome letter, the whole thing had evidently been arranged months ago. Mystified, I examined the rest of its contents: a color brochure, hotel reservation, plane tickets and an itinerary, all for one of those high-end tourist packages.

This one was a cooking-class trip to the South of France, called *The Cuisine of Provence,* advertising beautiful rooms in a restored farmhouse with a big shiny modern kitchen, where tour groups could gather to learn cooking from an English chef. The attendees pictured in the brochure all looked proud and pleased, posing in groups in their white aprons.

"Why would Mom sign up for a French cooking class?" I murmured. "She could probably teach this class herself!" Furthermore, my mother was the kind of woman who seldom went anywhere without her husband, let alone took a vacation from him. I flipped over the envelope and studied it closely.

Yes, it was definitely sent to Mom, but not to her home address. Instead, beneath her name, the package was addressed *in care of* Aunt Matilda and had been sent to *her* house.

This was now beginning to make sense, in a weird sort of way. Aunt Matilda went on vacation every spring to a new culture spot in Europe. But although she was Mom's age, she was her polar opposite. Aunt Matilda was outspoken, footloose and fancy-free, financially independent. She would make a good travelling companion for Mom, and might even have helped Mom break the news to Dad that his wife wanted to take a vacation without him. Obviously Mom and Aunt Matilda had conspired to keep it a secret until the last minute. And Mom had hidden this packet here as if it were diamonds.

I was suddenly certain of one thing. My mother had definitely been planning to return to this house in New York, at the very least to pack a suitcase and meet up with Aunt Matilda to go off to France together. She wasn't the type of woman to suddenly decide to chuck it all and move to Nevada, nor to give the twins instructions to sell the house and dispose of all its contents for her, as they'd claimed. It wasn't Mom's style to let other people, even her own kin, go rifling through her possessions and make hasty decisions about them, especially when the house was holding a secret like this travel packet. She was more methodical and fastidious. And even after Dad died, she'd told me, *I'll see you here when you come back and we'll do nice things together*.

I put Mom's envelope in my purse, checked to make sure there was nothing else hidden in the cupboard, and rose to my feet. My instincts told me it was time to get out of here.

But on the way out, I paused at the kitchen. Somehow, finding this room empty was the worst; seeing it so brutally stripped of all Mom's well-organized, well-chosen possessions, like her favorite copper pans and cast-iron pots. Even her cookbooks were gone.

"Cookbooks," I said aloud. And cooking classes. I fumbled in my bag for Aunt Matilda's phone number and I called her. She picked up on the third ring.

"Hello, Céline. How nice to hear from you," she said rather warily. She still had a smoker's voice, even though she'd given up the habit years ago. I'd seen her at Dad's funeral, where conversation had been muted. Now, I told her about what was going on with the house and how Dad had given all the control to Danny. I wasn't sure where Aunt Matilda's allegiances lay. After all, Dad was her brother.

But she sighed and said, "No surprise there. My father did the same thing to *my* mom and me."

"Aunt Matilda, were you and Mom planning to go to France this month?" I asked.

She hesitated for a moment, then she said, "Yes. But she didn't tell your father, and she didn't want the twins to know, either. So there's no point in blabbing about it now."

"Look," I said, "can I come talk to you, right away?" I waited for excuses. But she surprised me.

"Sure, come on over," she said. I hurried out, locking the house behind me. When I heard the latch close it seemed to whisper, *Farewell*.

AUNT MATILDA LIVED IN AN adorable little house on a hill in Connecticut, set apart from her neighbors, on a good-sized corner property where the land rose in ridges around it and formed a natural barricade from stray dogs and curious kids.

"A spinster's nest," my father always called it. But I always thought it resembled an enchanted cottage from a fairy tale or a movie, an iconic hermit's paradise. As far as I knew, Aunt Matilda had lived here all of her adult life, quietly keeping her own counsel.

She didn't even have a doorbell; just an old-fashioned brass knocker. The front yard had a profusion of forsythia already in bloom, and the lawn was dotted here and there with white and purple crocuses. She opened her door still wearing a gardening hat and gloves. She removed them and led me to the back of her house, put a kettle on, and served little tea sandwiches. They were a bit stale, their bread curling up on the ends; and the cucumber, cream cheese and salmon tasted of refrigerator.

"I bought these today," she said ruefully. "I can't cook. That's why I signed up for this class in France. I'm getting tired of eating overpriced stale take-away that somebody else cooked without love."

I gazed at her fondly. Aunt Matilda was tall and thin, with translucent pale, freckled skin, a small button nose, and Irish blue eyes. Because she'd been gardening she was wearing a pair of old wool slacks, but they'd been of good quality and had worn out with dignity. Her men's-style shirt was striped yellow and white, tucked beneath a yellow cardigan.

"How is Julie doing?" she asked quietly. I told her what condition Mom was in, and Aunt Matilda was sympathetic; they were both in their mid-seventies. I also told her I didn't share the twins' eagerness to mothball Mom. Even before I'd finished, Aunt Matilda was nodding vigorously.

"You know," she said thoughtfully, "from what Julie's told me over the years, I think those twins knew how to manipulate her with guilt. They craved constant proof that she loved them as much as she loved you. But maybe, you were the apple of her eye anyway? And money, you know, doesn't ever really compensate for love." She paused, then added with a gleam in her eyes, "But it helps."

The kettle whistled. She made tea in a fine English china pot painted with purple flowers and gold trim, served in matching teacups and saucers. We ate at a small table tucked into a kitchen alcove, looking out big windows to her garden where birds flitted around little houses and feeders she'd arranged for them.

"But why was Dad so angry all the time?" I said in a voice that sounded plaintive even to me.

She shook her head and said, "Never understood that myself; except that some people who bluster a lot are actually kinda fearful inside. To him, every encounter with another human being was a pitched battle—and believe me when I say that he lived in utter dread of ever losing a fight, as if he'd get completely annihilated if he lost even one."

"Was it true that Dad once considered becoming a priest?" I asked, mulling this all over.

"Nah," Aunt Matilda said. "Oh, he talked about it, but I knew he never would. You see, then he'd have to play second fiddle to God." She smiled. "So, my pretty. What brings you here, really?"

"Whose idea was it to go to this cooking class?" I said in response.

"Your mother's," Aunt Matilda said without hesitating. "She read about it in a magazine, and I think she felt safe travelling with me on a pre-arranged trip. Julie had been saving up her own 'pin money' for years to be able to do this without having to ask your father to pay for it."

As I absorbed this information, I glanced at a little room beside the kitchen which functioned as a small personal library, its walls lined with built-in bookshelves, and many art books stacked on tables, no doubt from her days of teaching art to high school kids.

"Aunt Matilda," I said carefully, "do you have any information on Picasso?"

"Picasso?" she said, her tone as casual as mine. "Anything in particular you want to know?"

Yes, I want to know if my mother is just dreaming, or if Grandmother Ondine really cooked for him! I thought. But all I said aloud was, "I'd like to know what he was doing in the spring of 1936." That was the period of time I'd seen for the recipes in Grandma's notebook.

Aunt Matilda raised her eyebrows and said, "Well, that's specific, all right." She rose and went into her little library, returning with a big book. She set it down and flipped to the back. "The only biographies worth reading are the ones with good indexes. That's how you separate the men from the boys." She hummed as she turned the pages. "Do you want to know about his personal life or his art?"

"Both," I said, then added, "start with the personal."

"Okay. I'd say the 1930s were a big transitional period for Picasso," she explained, now happily going into her teacher mode. "He had this mistress, Marie-Thérèse, who'd been just a teenager, really, when he picked her up outside the Galeries Lafayette department store in Paris in 1927 and they began their secret trysts. But like a big daddy, he'd also buy her toys and take her to the circus and the amusement park! You see, if you're a genius, they don't call you a pervert," she commented slyly. "Then, in the mid-1930s, she gets pregnant. So, his Russian wife ended their marriage, and Picasso stopped painting, possibly because of the turmoil in his personal life. Here it is," she said triumphantly.

"What?" I said eagerly.

"April 1936. Apparently, in great secrecy, he went off to a town on the Côte d'Azur, called Juan-les-Pins." I got goosebumps, recognizing the name of the town where Grandmother Ondine lived.

"It was a very mysterious time for Picasso," Aunt Matilda continued, scanning the pages. "Nobody really knows what happened to him that spring—some say he was just hanging out with Marie-Thérèse and their baby. But whatever he was doing down there, suddenly, he begins painting again. And within a year, he'd create his greatest masterpiece about the Spanish Civil War—*Guernica*."

She spun the book around so I could see a photograph of Picasso in his Paris atelier during this period. "Not exactly Cary Grant," Aunt Matilda commented. "Short, with a nose like a fighter. And those scary eyes. But he had charisma, you know?"

"How old is he in that photo, do you suppose?" I asked.

"He was born in October of 1881," Aunt Matilda replied. I did some fast mental arithmetic.

"He'd have been fifty-four years old in 1936," I observed.

"And why, pray tell, is that period so important to you?" Aunt Matilda asked, pouring more tea for us both. Her gestures were casual, but her eyes were alert and birdlike.

I wasn't sure I was ready to answer that question, since Mom evidently had chosen not to tell Aunt Matilda about Grandma Ondine and Picasso. So I mumbled, "Well, I studied art before I went into theatre and makeup. I love the 1930s."

"You know," Aunt Matilda said, "it's the strangest thing. But just after Christmas, your mother came by here to have tea with me. And guess what? She asked me the same questions you asked—about Picasso. When I asked her why, she said, 'It's just something I wanted to know—for Céline.'"

For a moment we sat there so quietly that I could hear Aunt Matilda's old-fashioned wristwatch ticking on her arm. It dawned on me that Mom had wanted an art expert with her on this trip.

"Are you still planning to go?" I asked. She rose again, went to a kitchen drawer, and brought a matching packet for her tickets and itinerary, laying it on the table before me.

"Sure," she said cheerfully. "It's paid up. I go to Europe every spring. Gotta see all the art and hear all the music before I get too old to walk around. Not to mention the casinos. They sure beat the lottery and the church bingo around here." I remembered that Aunt Matilda always enjoyed playing cards with us kids whenever she came to visit. She had, I recalled, the soul of a gambler.

I reached into my purse and pulled out Mom's matching packet for the trip. "I stole it," I confessed. "I didn't want Danny and Deirdre to get their hands on it."

There was another brief silence. "It would take a little doing, I suppose," Aunt Matilda observed with a gleam of mischief in her eyes. "But I bet we could re-arrange it so you could take your mother's place. You can look around the Riviera. See what you see."

I found myself winking away tears in my eyes. "I think I'd like to do that," I said.

Because even before Aunt Matilda suggested it, the same idea had been quietly building up inside me. My mother must have summoned a lot of courage to even think of going on a trip without Dad. Perhaps all she'd wanted was to immerse herself back in the culture she'd left behind. Maybe. But on the other hand, it seemed to me that her mission must have had a bit more to it than that.

What if she was going back to visit Grandmother Ondine's world in order to take one last look around the café—just in case the painting that Picasso gave Grandma still lurked somewhere in a hiding place that nobody had discovered yet? It was a wild long shot, of course. But *if* Mom had planned to do this, then maybe she knew something that made her believe there was a distinct possibility she'd find it.

So now I pictured myself flying to France in her place to recover my grandmother's lost painting. I could even imagine auctioning it off for the enormous sums of money a Picasso can claim, enabling me to rush back home with wads of cash to wave under my lawyer's nose. *Now let's go into court and kick ass,* I'd say. And I'd get my mother out of that damned nursing home in Nevada.

It was a crazy dream, but I didn't care. These days, the things that people called sane were, I thought, often dumber than what I had in mind. "Yes," I said, more definitely now. "I'd like to go."

"Well," Aunt Matilda said briskly, "then you'd better start calling me Tilda. There are going to be some single gentlemen my age in this class, and I don't want you running about there calling me Auntie. You got that?"

"Got it," I said. We actually shook hands on the deal.

And within a week, the two of us set out to explore Grandmother Ondine's world.

9

Woman with a Watch, Ondine in 1936

THE SUN WAS GROWING HOT AND STRONG, ITS GOLDEN GAZE MAKING THE earth's breast soft and pliable. Ondine, wearing lighter clothes now, and with her legs becoming stronger from her daily cycling, felt like an Amazon as she practically flew up the hill to cook, and pose, for Picasso.

She'd gotten her mother's permission to leave the café earlier in the morning, ostensibly to give her plenty of time to prep and cook in Picasso's kitchen. Ondine had become quite efficient and thus managed to arrive at his house early enough so they could work for hours before she served his lunch.

She noticed right away that he treated her completely differently, now that she was his model and the focal point of his work, which was clearly sacred to him. Whereas earlier he'd hardly noticed her arrival, now as she pedaled into his driveway she found Picasso waiting for her like an impatient lover, standing there in the doorway, smoking and staring out for the first glimpse he could catch of her.

On good days he would give her a broad smile and a courteous nod; at other times he would turn wordlessly inside and go upstairs to his studio as if he were engulfed in a brooding dark cloud that felt dangerous. She found herself anxiously searching for a clue as to which mood he was in.

"Bonjour, Patron," Ondine said breathlessly today as he held the door open for her so that she could carry her supplies and stow them in his kitchen. He was bare-chested, wearing only black pants, and sandals with thick leather straps. He was amused by her conspiratorial attitude.

"Sneaked off early again, eh?" he commented, throwing down his cigarette on the stone steps and stubbing it out with his foot. She quickly made a pot of a Provençal herbal tea that he liked, and he carried his first cup upstairs. Pretending to be motivated by courtly chivalry, he always made her go up the steps first, but Ondine suspected that he enjoyed watching her from behind.

Sometimes while he drank his tea he liked to tell her stories about his youth—how, when he was a sixteen-year-old art student in Madrid, he'd nearly died of fever, but recovered and grew stronger by hiking into the mountains and forests of Spain with a friend, making rice and beans at campfires, sleeping in caves or shepherds' huts, or just lying on the earth's bed of scented grass and herbs. At nineteen, he was already struggling to survive in Paris, cooking his own omelettes whenever he could buy eggs, and wedging his paintings in the cracks of the walls to stave off winter's drafts. But he was always jubilantly inspired by everything he saw on Paris's streets—from exhibits of ancient African art to the windmills of Montmartre; and the masons who sang as they sawed great sharp-angled blocks of white stone that rose up like a real-life Cubist landscape. Here, among poets and prostitutes and other budding artists, Picasso made his name and found lifelong friends like Matisse.

Ondine listened, enthralled by the vivid images he conjured. Sometimes he queried her about her own life, and she felt there wasn't much to tell; but his smile and warmth were irresistible as he prodded her to sing the songs of her youth and tell him all that she knew about life in Juan-les-Pins.

However, once he was ready to work, he became focused and serious. While he prepared his paints—mixing his colors on sheets of newspaper instead of a palette—Ondine went behind a screen he'd erected for her. She changed into the same blue checked dress, which she brought with her in a bag because she didn't want her mother to see her wearing her best dress over and over. Then she took off her shoes and stockings and, even though he did not keep telling her to remove her *culottes,* she did it anyway, feeling a thrill of rebellion against all the piety she'd been raised on.

Quickly she sat down on that same thin tasseled pillow on the floor, jammed into that same corner of the room, exactly as before with the props of comb and wristwatch; and, with her dress unbuttoned, her limbs all twisted, her bare feet posed just so, she pretended to gaze at herself in the mirror.

Picasso stared at her for a long time, like a pearl-diver on a cliff about to make the leap, until something seemed to get resolved in his mind and, abruptly, he disappeared behind his easel. Sometimes when he moved around, Ondine could see the muscles rippling in his sturdy arms and broad chest; and the room filled up with the masculine, and not unappealing, scent of his sweat.

Today he was so engrossed that they worked straight through his usual lunch hour. Ondine did not dare ask if she should get up and cook. Hour after hour went by, yet he kept her there immobilized, all twisted up on that hard wooden floor until her neck and back ached so much they felt as if they were burning. Even when her stomach growled loudly, he diabolically kept on painting.

Surely he hears my poor belly crying out for mercy, Ondine thought, peering at him beseechingly. He glanced up and then put on the expression of a simpleton, pretending not to notice, but she thought she saw a look in his eyes that revealed a peculiar enjoyment of her torture.

"Stop moving your arms," he reprimanded.

She'd felt the urgent need to scratch and had tried to do so before he noticed, but he caught her even before her fingers reached the spot. *All right, I won't move,* she told herself, feeling the full demand of the itch and the torturous pleasure of ignoring it. Which was stronger, the itch, or her? She tested herself, waiting to see if by sheer force of will she could sacrifice her own physical needs for the sake of his art, and master her own desperate urges in order to please his.

He seemed unaware of her struggle, yet, just when it began to be too much, he rewarded her with his most beautiful of smiles, saying, "You know that everything you and I do together in this room is of profound importance. Every word we speak, every gesture, every *thought,* do you understand?"

So what was a small itch when posing for a masterpiece?

Finally, when she was feeling completely light-headed, Picasso put down his brush. *"Tiens!"* he exclaimed, seizing her wrist to look at his watch. "Is that the time? Let's go see what you brought me for lunch," he suggested. "Don't bother to change your clothes. We might work some more after we eat."

She followed him downstairs into the kitchen, glad that today she'd instinctively packed food which required little preparation—a country pâté, some *cornichon* pickles, a beef-and-orange *daube* she'd made last night so it would "profit", a salad dressed in vinaigrette, and a cherry tarte. She always politely set the table for one, not taking a plate for herself until he formally asked her to join him, which he usually did.

But now, to her surprise, he unpacked the meal himself. "Today *I'm* going to feed *you,* my little odalisque," he announced, seeming suddenly playful. He would not permit her to handle the food; he insisted that she sit there with her mouth hanging open—like one of the pet birds that he told her he kept in his Paris studio—while he dangled each bit of bread or food above her lips and made her go for it, one morsel at a time. A few times at the very last minute he yanked it away, laughing uproariously.

"You have the lips of a movie siren," he commented. He dipped a finger into the cherry pie, and then she felt his fingertips first on her lower lip as he colored it red, then the upper as he traced the cupid's bow. She tried to ignore the strange surge of arousal this evoked in her.

"You'd better lick it off before I do," Picasso commanded. "Slowly! Make it last."

Ondine obliged with her tongue, watching him watching her. He sighed deeply.

"What a pretty bird you are! Maybe one day I'll build a golden cage to keep you in, so that no other man can feast his eyes on you," he said, surely teasing, although he looked queerly serious when he said such strange jokey things. "I'll make you sing to me every day, but if your song doesn't please me, then I won't feed you. You'll grow so faint with hunger that you'll eat anything I give you, even the scraps no dog would touch, otherwise you'll starve."

"Just as well, I probably should go on a diet," Ondine retorted teasingly.

"No, no! Don't you dare. Girls today are too thin, they look like boys," he said scornfully. "They hardly inspire me to paint them!"

He waved his hand as if swatting away a fly. She noticed that his forearm was stained with paint. He said, "I'm very careful when I choose someone to model for me!"

Picasso's expression was sober and benevolent now, as if confiding to her his greatest secret. He was watching her closely with those inky dark eyes of his, to test her somehow, yet all he said was, "Well, let's go back to work for a while longer, all right?"

As if it were her choice; as if she, like a goddess, could decide whether his genius would be indulged today. When they ascended the stairs Ondine felt elated.

For, although she wasn't even permitted to move a muscle once she sat down in her little corner and resumed her pose, she still felt freer than her parents counting their money, and the chatterboxes in the village marketplace, and the proud Wise Men playing cards, day after day; and the girls in such a rush to get married, and the old people who never once in their life broke a rule.

Soon Ondine felt she was drifting lightly through the passing minutes like a cloud floating up into the foothills of the Alps, over the snow-capped mountains and beyond, to London and New York and all the wider world.

"Finished," Picasso said unexpectedly.

Ondine received this remark as a physical jolt. "Already?" she asked, rudely awakened from her dreams. She felt a surprising sense of panic, which was surely absurd.

"Yes, we're done with this one," he said decisively. "Oh, I'll work on it a little more myself. I may even do another variation of this. But you don't have to pose for it anymore."

She felt so utterly disappointed that she did not know what to say, and could only come up with, "I really do like working with you."

He answered her neutrally, as if he had chosen to stop listening to her heart fluttering painfully like a bird beating its wings against its cage. "I'm thinking of doing a completely new series," he replied thoughtfully, more as if he were talking to himself. "But I have a nude study in mind next."

Ondine had automatically risen to go behind the screen to change her clothes. Now she heard the hopeful tone in his voice. "What do you think?" he asked casually.

Oh, so that's what he's after, she realized. Aloud she replied, "Perhaps," imitating his careful neutrality. She was enjoying getting undressed in the same room, yet just beyond his all-seeing gaze.

"In fact, I have already seen you naked in my mind," Picasso called out. "A real man can ravish a woman with his eyes, without ever removing a stitch of her clothing. So why the fuss?"

His attitude had become so matter-of-fact that Ondine felt foolish for imagining that he was trying to seduce her. Still, she wondered guiltily, *What would Maman say?* Suppose her parents found out what she'd been up to all along here with Picasso? Perhaps she could deflect their anger if she was paid well for her modelling.

It was the first time she'd thought about wages. How much did models charge? And would he pay more for a nude? Picasso's paintings had made him a rich man, she reasoned. So his models must earn a lot, like opera singers and actresses with all their jewels and furs!

Dressed now in the skirt and blouse she'd worn cycling over here, Ondine decided it was time to ask him about her earnings. Soberly she stepped out from behind the screen and asked, "How much wages will you pay me for—*that kind* of modelling?"

Picasso was fussing with his brushes. Now he looked up sharply.

"Who put that in your mind?" he asked. "Did your mama or papa tell you to ask me that?"

Ondine flushed, for indeed, just thinking about her parents had brought her down to earth.

"They don't know a thing about this," she answered. Seeking to assure him of her sincerity, she added, "I would only want the salary you usually pay your other models." She made a broad sweep of her arm, indicating the many scattered drawings and paintings of the nude blonde woman.

"*She* doesn't do it for the money!" Picasso exclaimed, insulted. "Marie-Thérèse is a *real* woman! In all these years she never asked for 'wages'—her reward is the joy of sacrificing for, and pleasing, a great artist! Do you think just *any* woman can be the subject of a painting that hangs in the best galleries of the world? But perhaps I'll end up giving *your* pictures to the trash man."

His tone was so chilly that her own blood seemed cold, and she felt suddenly, completely worthless. He was scowling darkly, looking rougher and angrier than usual as he scanned a pile of books but apparently could not find what he wanted.

"*Merde!*" he muttered. But when he spoke again, he sounded strangely casual.

"Have you heard of the Marquis de Sade?" Ondine shook her head. "No?" he asked innocently. "A brilliant man. He lived years ago— have you never seen the ruins of his castle here in Provence, up in a town called Lacoste? He kept his servant girls in a dungeon, where he used them for his pleasure and beat them when they displeased him," he said, widening his dark eyes in exaggerated horror. "Until one day, Napoleon threw him in jail."

"Then he must have been very wicked," Ondine said decisively, instinctively fighting back.

"But that's what women want," Picasso insisted. "In fact, they are only happy when they submit entirely to a man—body, mind and soul—doing whatever he commands. Even the pain he inflicts on a woman gives her great pleasure and makes her happy, don't you agree?" He was now standing right in front of her, almost nose-to-nose, as if trying to mesmerize her into compliance and defeat.

Ondine understood his bullying tone and she didn't like it. So she stared straight back into his black eyes. "No," she said evenly.

He shrugged indifferently, abruptly turned away again and began leafing through his sketchbook, his attitude thoroughly dismissive.

Ondine didn't know whether to laugh or cry. Was this a joke or another test of some kind? Tentatively she asked, "So—do you want me to keep coming here?"

Picasso didn't bother to look up when he said offhandedly, "Oh, come back when you know how to be a *real* woman!" He sounded disdainful, as if this transformation could never happen.

Ondine felt panicked, until she seized on an idea. "Well, if you don't need me anymore, perhaps Monsieur Matisse would like me to cook and pose for him," she said innocently.

"Matisse?" Picasso bristled. "Don't be absurd! That woman Lydia is the only model he needs. You are *mine*." He spat out the words like a viper. "Do I want you to keep bringing me my lunch? Of course—do you think I'm going to stop eating and just drop dead?"

"All right," Ondine said, uncertain as to whether he'd just asked her to model again, too; but in any event, she felt a degree of triumph.

Perhaps he saw this because, as she walked past him, Picasso reached out suddenly and grabbed her arm to detain her. When he raised the flat of his other hand Ondine thought he might strike her, but she managed not to flinch. He only traced the curve of her cheeks like a sculptor. She hoped he could not feel that her skin was fearfully sensitive to his touch. Beneath his raised arm she saw the tangle of hair growing wildly in his armpit. It reminded her of his hairy Minotaur drawings.

Almost unwillingly, he gave her an amused smile. "What a troublesome feline you are. But you *do* have the head of a Roman goddess," he observed. "I can see it on an ancient coin or statue. Perhaps your ancestors came here from Capri on a boat."

Now his fingertip moved along the side of her neck, lingering at her throat before continuing downward, tracing the curve of her left breast all the way to her nipple. She could not help feeling a thrill of pleasure. But she tried to keep her expression neutral, for Ondine again had the instinctive feeling that, rather than respond or step away, she must simply stand her ground.

"Ah," Picasso said, his whole face softening now.

He's going to kiss me, she thought in wonder, in that split second

before he pressed his warm, friendly lips against hers, firmly and purposefully. She felt her own mouth go soft and pliable as his kiss lin-
gered for a brief but enticing moment. Then he drew back and surveyed
her face critically.

"Good. A young girl *should* blush when a man kisses her," he said
approvingly. "Well, go on home to your mama now."

LATER THAT NIGHT ONDINE LAY awake in her bed, feeling tumultuous
every time she recalled Picasso's deliberate, leisurely kiss. "He can't be
in love with me, can he?" she wondered. "Half the time he sounds
angry. Well, he certainly didn't like being asked to pay me wages. But
what was all that other nonsense about? Torture and slaves and that
Marquis de Sade?"

Once again she felt that Picasso had been testing her, but for what?
Clearly there was a whole world out there she knew nothing about. But
if he stopped painting her, what then? It wasn't money she really cared
about. Her increasing desire to be near him again didn't feel like love,
exactly. So she wasn't even sure what she was yearning for.

Yet somehow, in spite of his changing moods, Ondine still felt that
the answer to her future lay with Picasso. She must find a way to make
him show her how to use that key that he kept dangling in front of
her—so she could finally open a door to the more beautiful destiny that
surely awaited her, in a world where people could do as they pleased
and work only for their own satisfaction, not merely to please others.
Ondine had seen just enough of this earthly paradise to know that she
wanted it for herself.

10

Ondine and a Visitor at the Villa

THE NEXT DAY, ONDINE FELT APPREHENSIVE AS SHE CYCLED INTO PICASSO'S driveway. She wasn't sure if she was still welcome here. Yesterday he'd been so unpredictable—one minute gentle and inviting, the next indifferent, even hostile. Would he forget that he'd asked her to keep cooking for him? And what if posing without her clothes was part of the deal to keep her job here?

"I don't mind so much if *he* sees me naked," she realized with a guilty thrill. But imagine having the whole world—especially the villagers in Juan-les-Pins, like the Three Wise Men in the café—ogling pictures of her in a gallery and then making rude remarks for the rest of her life!

As Ondine stepped into Picasso's kitchen she was surprised to find him sitting right there at the table, drinking tea with a strange woman who definitely was *not* the demure blonde in his paintings. This sophisticated creature was just the opposite, with black hair swept back severely in a chic Parisian twist, and stunning black eyebrows to match. She wore rouge and blood-red lipstick, and dark smudgy eye makeup. She appeared to be in her late twenties, and was dressed in a smart suit and crisp white shirt like a man's. She had a fancy, professional camera in her lap and she was winding the film expertly.

"Ah! Come in, come in!" Picasso exclaimed with exaggerated courtesy, in a tone that struck Ondine as highly theatrical and artificial. "Dora, here is my Ondine—the *best* chef in all of Provence! In fact, this girl will one day be a great culinary *artiste*."

Dora glanced up sharply, her eyes glittering like a flash of lightning, but she said nothing and just kept staring at Ondine while continuing to wind her camera. Ondine noticed that Picasso had not bothered to explain Dora to *her*. "And what has my kitchen goddess brought me to eat today, *chère* Ondine?" Picasso asked, rubbing his hands together with exalted glee.

"I am making you a sole *à la meunière*," Ondine said, a trifle reluctant to discuss this in the presence of a stranger. Without warning, the woman raised her camera, and in a blinding flash of light she snapped a picture of Ondine. It made her feel as if she had just been publicly assaulted.

"Excellent! We'll wait in the dining room," Picasso said, rising. The woman followed him out.

Ondine set to work, but her hands trembled and tears threatened to tumble from her eyes. She winked them back ferociously. She'd brought enough food for two, but that was because Picasso usually invited her to eat with him after posing. Why should she now have to give up her lunch for this female?

"I guess I'm back to being only his cook. Well, I'll make it perfect!" Ondine grumbled, picking up two delicate fish, seasoning them with fresh pepper and dredging them in the flour which gave this dish its name—*meunière* for the miller who ground the flour. Then she browned the sole in a pan with clarified sweet butter and a tablespoon of olive oil. When they were golden on both sides, she put the fish on a platter, topped with a sauce of melted butter, lemon juice, capers and freshly chopped parsley. She was serving them with tiny new potatoes, and baby green string beans perfectly aligned with thinly sliced strips of red peppers; and a crisp white vermentino wine so young it was almost green.

When Ondine brought the tray into the dining room, Picasso and his female visitor were immersed in conversation. He leaned forward to gaze at the food on its platter, giving it a quick nod of approval, and Ondine set to work with her serving fork and knife, lifting the bones entirely off the fish in one expert maneuver before arranging the meal on individual plates.

"The world is full of hypocrites," Dora was saying. "Headlines all screaming about Herr Hitler reoccupying the Rhineland—but *still* the politicians do nothing. They all know it's a blatant violation of the Treaty of Versailles! And yet those same journalists have orgasms about the Nazis hosting the summer Olympics. An outrage, to award Germany the honor, instead of Spain!"

"The fascists have more money. They can always outbid the leftists," Picasso answered calmly.

"Yes, but where do the Nazis get all that money?" Dora said meaningfully. "Who gave Hitler enough funds to build his monster stadium— oh, how he loves stadiums, and this one's going to have a hundred thousand seats! And such sophisticated sound devices, just so that foul little man can broadcast his glory to over forty countries around the globe. The world's gone mad."

Despite the frightening things they were talking about, Ondine couldn't help noticing how lovely Dora's voice was—melodic and mesmerizing, all the more so because she radiated high intelligence and a serious mind; and she spoke with passionate conviction, as if she'd thought about it deeply and cared personally about world events. Her gaze was sharp and clear, and Picasso seemed impressed with her.

"The world's been seduced by a man of force, as it always has and always will," he replied.

Ondine could scarcely believe that a woman was discussing money and politics with a man. She certainly hoped Picasso wasn't going to ask Ondine *her* opinion on Germany. She was suddenly aware that Dora was watching her every move, not directly but out of the corners of her eyes, like a cat.

Meanwhile Picasso was watching Dora's attitude toward Ondine with a look of supreme amusement.

This woman must be a reporter, come to interview him, Ondine thought uncertainly as she returned to the kitchen. Perhaps that was why Picasso was showing off about having a Provençal chef.

She was surprised to find herself feeling strangely possessive of Picasso. She'd never been bothered by the other, blonde woman, who'd seemed more like a phantom because she hadn't directly intruded on the special, weekday solitude that Ondine had been sharing with her *Patron*.

Later, when she re-entered the room to collect the plates, Picasso and Dora had moved on to an animated discussion of Parisian artists and art dealers. He looked up only to say rather grandly, "A fine meal, Ondine. We'll have our tea in the parlor," as they rose from their chairs.

Ondine, who this afternoon was feeling like his servant for the first time, returned with a tray bearing the tea he liked and an apricot *tarte* she'd made this morning specially for him. She placed it all on the low table beside the sofa in the parlor, where Picasso was sitting with his legs crossed.

Ondine poured the tea. When Dora reached for her cup, Ondine briefly glimpsed a black-and-blue bruise on Dora's forearm. Some instinct made Ondine avert her eyes. Dora rose gracefully and moved around the parlor to view the paintings that Picasso had haphazardly placed here and there.

He drank his tea, then got up and stood beside Dora, murmuring in a playful tone, "Want to come upstairs? Last time you were here, we were so *busy,* I forgot to show you 'my latest etchings'."

Ondine, having sliced the *tarte* and put it on the dessert plates, straightened up just in time to see Picasso place a hand on one of Dora's buttocks and give it a firm squeeze.

Hastily Ondine returned to the kitchen and began washing the dinner plates as fast as she could. Why should she feel so blinded by—if not tears, then some sort of rage? She didn't realize that she was clattering the dishes with more vigor than usual and perhaps making a noticeable noise, until Picasso entered the kitchen and laid a hand on her shoulder.

"Dora can't make up her mind whether she wants to be a photographer or a painter," he said in a low, confidential voice. "She's a *professional* photographer, you see. But I have advised her to be a painter, because every photographer has a painter inside waiting to be released, anyway."

Ondine said nothing. "You know how I met Dora Maar?" he continued conversationally. "It was at a café in Paris. She was playing 'the knife game' with herself. Do you know it?"

He took Ondine's hand and placed it, palm down, on the cutting board on the kitchen counter. Then he put his own warm hand on top of hers, and separated her fingers so that there were spaces between them. He picked up one of the kitchen knives that Ondine had just washed.

"One, two, three, four, five, six!" he counted aloud gleefully while poking the knife into the board in the small spaces between their fingers, starting at the outside of the thumb and going between each finger until he reached the outside of the smallest one. Then he went back more rapidly, chanting, "Five, four, three, two, one!" Ondine gasped but refused to squeal because she sensed that that was what he wanted.

"The idea is to go faster than anyone else, without chopping off your fingers," Picasso announced when he stopped. "Dora did it wearing a glove. By the time she was done, it was stained with her blood." He sounded impressed. "I keep that bloody glove on a shelf in my studio."

Then you're both crazy, Ondine thought, but she waited quietly until he removed his hand from hers and set it free. When Ondine looked up, Dora was standing in the doorway, watching again like a black cat, but then she put her cigarette to her lips, exhaled a plume of smoke and drifted back to the parlor without having uttered a word. Picasso went out after her, and Ondine hurriedly returned to her dishes.

Presently she could hear them climbing the stairs. The house grew quiet, but soon she heard strange animal grunts and thumps and cries. Ondine paused in alarm, then realized that it was lovemaking—of a sort. There came a particularly loud, rather alarming thump—as if someone had fallen to the floor or against a wall, followed by a woman's unmistakable cry of anguish. For a moment Ondine imagined having to call Rafaello the policeman to intervene. There were more cries from both of them, but these subsided into low murmurs. Ondine picked up her hamper and slipped out the kitchen door.

As she was attaching the hamper to her bicycle, Picasso threw open a window upstairs, and Ondine could see him standing before his easel, speaking calmly to his guest. Ondine knew that stance.

"Now he's painting her," she muttered, shaking her head as she pedaled away fast. All the way home she rode with a furious, violent energy. "Who was he trying to embarrass today—Dora or me? He seems to want to make both of us miserable. But why? *Why?* And what has become of the blonde lady in his paintings?" she wondered. "Well, why should I care, anyway?"

Even to herself, she could not explain the anxious, cold feeling in the pit of her stomach. All this time while he'd been painting her he'd made her feel like the most important woman in the world, and his pleasure warmed her as if she were lying on a beach basking in pure sunlight. Now, without warning, it was as if the moon had just eclipsed the sun, blackening it out and leaving her shivering in a day as dark as night, fearing that the sun would never return to warm her up again.

11

Ondine à la Plage

ONDINE ALMOST DREADED GOING BACK TO THE VILLA ON THE FOLLOWING day. Undeniably, she was eager to cook for Picasso, to talk to him, even to pose for him—but only if they could resume being together in that companionable, quiet way she'd grown to cherish.

"I'm certainly not going to cook for that Dora woman again," she told herself stoutly. "If *she's* still there, why, I'll leave his lunch hamper on the front stoop, and he can ask *her* to serve him!" Of course, in her heart, Ondine knew she was not really in a position to refuse him anything. Her mother had said so, right at the onset of this arrangement. Feeling rather glum, Ondine set off on her bicycle.

It was an unusually hot day for this time of year. That, plus the fact that it was a Friday was causing people to spill out onto the streets with an excited, festive air, as if they could hardly wait to finish work and enjoy their weekend. The breeze that filled Ondine's lungs no longer smelled solely of fish, seaweed and salt; now it was mingled with the perfume of flowers that were already tumbling over the high walls of the villas; and Ondine could hear, all around her, the heartening chirp of joyful birds.

But when she cycled up Picasso's driveway and parked her bicycle at the side of the house, she heard an entirely different kind of twittering—from two females evidently having an argument, their agitated voices clearly wafting out of the open kitchen window.

"You have no business being here with Pablo. He's *my* man!" said the first voice, very soft and feminine, yet raised with righteous anger.

"No woman can seriously believe that she can own a man like Pablo Picasso!" scoffed the second woman in an ironical, amused tone, but one that had a sharp knife-edge to it.

Ondine, who had been about to unhook her food hamper, thought she recognized this voice as Dora Maar's and paused. She was certainly not going to burst into the kitchen and interrupt a scene like this.

"*I* am the mother of his child!" the first woman shot back proudly, as if she'd played a trump card. "It is *my* place to be with Picasso. So you can just pick yourself up and get out of here, at once!"

"Whether or not I have a child makes no difference whatsoever. It's utterly irrelevant," Dora said dismissively, as if engaged in a philosophical debate with someone she considered her intellectual inferior. "I have a perfect right to be here. It is *you* who doesn't belong with Pablo anymore!"

The soft-voiced woman must have crossed the room, for now her words grew more audible and, for a moment, Ondine could see her face as she passed by the window. Ondine recognized that distinctive nose, and the almost sleepy expression in the eyes. Yes, it was the blonde girl from all those paintings—the one Picasso had called Marie-Thérèse.

It was Ondine's first real glimpse of her, at last, so she could not help straining to see better. But even this docile, gentle woman had become moved to exasperation and indignation.

"Well, Pablo?" the blonde demanded, as she drifted out of sight again. "Why do you just stand there, so calm and *trop innocent,* as if it's all none of your concern? For heaven's sake, this situation is intolerable and you know it. So make up your mind. Which one of us stays, and which one must go?"

Ondine heard a chair scraping loudly on the floor, followed by a male snort of disgust.

"*Pah!*" Picasso responded. "*I* don't have to decide anything! I'm fine with things as they are. But how is a man to get a day's work done, with a pair of hens each pecking an eardrum? If *you* two have a problem with each other, well, then, *you'll* just have to fight it out yourselves! I'm going out for some air!"

From inside came the sound of a sudden scuffle and the shrieks of both women. Before Ondine could move away, the kitchen door was flung open, and Picasso came storming out in exasperation. Dressed only in shorts, an open shirt, and thick, rough leather sandals like shepherds wore, his nearly naked body gave off the heat and scent of his fury, as if he might breathe fire with his next word.

Ondine stood quaking, not knowing what to do. But to her astonishment, Picasso gave her a broad smile of delight. "Ah! Thank God, a sensible woman!" he exclaimed. "Well, there's no point in bringing your basket inside, Ondine; not with those two harpies in my kitchen. They'll end up flinging the food like bombs, and they're sure to tear each other's hair out before they're finished," he proclaimed with exaggerated horror. "Still, I suppose I could sell tickets to this fight."

He was performing for her benefit. With a sly look of feigned dread he added, "Just suppose my wife showed up now? She'd tear them both to shreds. You and I would have to bury their remains in the garden here." He looked as if he quite enjoyed the idea of having a bickering harem.

It occurred to Ondine that Picasso might have even staged this whole confrontation today. In fact, perhaps he'd even timed it deliberately for the moment when he knew Ondine was sure to show up. There was a strange streak of the prankster in him.

But now he was surveying the sky and fine weather, and he said impulsively, "This is no day to be stuck indoors playing referee. Let's go for a swim and have a picnic lunch! Come on, take your bicycle and follow me."

He stalked off, surprising Ondine by seeming to know a shorter route to the sea, taking a beaten-earth path through his neighbor's flower fields. She followed him uncertainly, her bicycle wobbling perilously whenever she rode over a rock half-hidden in the ground. But she managed to keep up with him as he marched on—down, down, down to the sea.

They stopped at a small cove whose beach was mostly pebbles, tucked in a pocket of pine trees flanked by stone walls for shelter. Ondine leaned her bicycle against a wall. Picasso had already taken off his shoes and shirt, but kept his shorts on. His feet were surprisingly delicate, his skin so creamy and smooth that he reminded Ondine of an ivory statuette of Buddha that she'd seen in a shop window.

Now he glared at the sea as if it were a beast that he intended to conquer, and, sticking out his chin and chest, he marched purposefully toward it. When he reached the water's edge he just kept on going, stomping into the sea until he was up to his waist.

"Well?" he called out to her, trying not to gasp from the shock of the cold. "What are you waiting for? Aren't you an ondine, a little mermaid? Don't tell me you're afraid of the sea!"

Ondine had already removed her shoes and unbuttoned her dress, but she'd hesitated at pulling off her clothes. Now she decided that the faster she got into the water the more she could protect her modesty. She yanked the dress over her head, keeping her chemise and *culottes* on, then she rushed into the water several paces away from him. As soon as she could, she dove right in.

She began swimming immediately and rapidly in order to swiftly warm up her muscles. Luc had taught her how to swim by alternately exhaling into the water and then coming up for air, while stroking and flutter-kicking steadily. She ducked under the first thrusting waves, and she swam and swam, concentrating on her breathing while blinking her eyes open and shut like a lighthouse, on-off, on-off, so that the salty sea didn't sting them too much.

Then, gasping, she turned over and came up for air, recovering her breath, lightly treading water while glancing about to get her bearings and to see how far out Picasso had gone. But she couldn't find his head bobbing among the waves.

"Where is he?" she said, bewildered. "Did he go very far?"

Squinting in the sunlight, she paddled farther out, scanning the horizon. She turned back and finally spied him near the shoreline. He was splashing determinedly in a straight line, moving parallel to the shore, keeping rather close to the beach. When he saw her he waved grandly, then made a great show of stroking methodically while turning his head above the water, first left, then right, then left and right again. Ondine dove down and swam straight toward him.

As she came closer she could see his legs underwater. At first she couldn't believe it. But as she watched she saw that he'd been standing and walking the whole time! She popped up for air and saw that he was still stroking and splashing and turning his head dramatically. Then Ondine understood.

Picasso doesn't know how to swim! He's been faking it, she realized, astonished. She swam to the other end of the cove so she wouldn't embarrass him. He climbed ashore now, and she hurried up the beach, ducking behind the trees to take off her wet underclothes and spread them on some rocks to dry in the sun. She used just the skirt of her dress to dry her torso before pulling the dress back on.

By the time she emerged from the trees, Picasso had dried himself off with the shirt he'd left on the beach. As Ondine drew near, he reached out and grabbed her arm, yanking her closer to him.

"That hair of yours is still dripping wet," he said. "I don't want your mama telling me I made you catch pneumonia." He began to vigorously rub the top of her head with his shirt, but worked more gently as he dried her long, long curls all the way out to their delicate ends.

"You're hardly more than a schoolgirl!" he teased as he rubbed her dry. "You barely know how to tie your shoes and blow your nose. Were you a good student or a bad one? Hah, I bet you were one of those little girls who know all the answers. But now, you have only questions for me. Am I right?"

Ondine unexpectedly felt flushed with an all-encompassing warmth, stimulated by his hands resting heavily on her head through the shirt, which gave off an exciting whiff of his masculine scent as it flopped around. Yet, at the same time she felt strangely overpowered, as if she could hardly breathe in his presence, as if, even here in the great outdoors, he was sucking in all the available oxygen around her.

"I was a terrible student, you know," he confided. "All I ever wanted to do was draw. Numbers and words were of no interest to me whatsoever. I tried to concentrate on the things they wanted me to learn, but when I was supposed to be adding up numbers, they just looked like bird's eyes and claws."

Having finished drying her off, he surveyed her critically. "You look good when you're wet. Good enough to eat." He sat down cross-legged on a very large, warm flat rock, closed his eyes and raised his face to the sun, looking more like a Buddha than ever, saying, "Well, what have we got for our picnic? Did you bring raw fish that we must cook over a campfire? Should I rub two sticks together?"

"No, it's a *pain de viande*—a meat loaf made of ground veal and chicken. It can be eaten hot or cold," Ondine said, unhooking the hamper and carrying it over to him. He helped her lay out the apron she always brought with her, to use as a makeshift tablecloth spread out on another flat rock.

They had to eat with their hands, and drink straight from the single half-bottle of wine she'd brought. Every time Picasso passed her the bottle, Ondine thought she could identify his salty taste on the bottle's mouth, as if she were dining with King Neptune himself.

"Your meals just get better and better," he said reflectively. "And, you are one of the few chefs whose food has never upset me. Believe me, I have a most sensitive stomach! But how does a girl who's so young know so much about cuisine?"

Ondine explained earnestly, "When I was sent to a convent school, there was an old monk called Père Jacques who cooked the meals for us as well as for his abbey. He knew I came from a café so he chose me to assist him. He taught me these 'fundamental secrets' of ancient Roman and Greek and Egyptian physicians: that, just like air, fire, earth and water, there are four elemental food properties—wet, dry, hot, cold—and all foods are a combination of these. It's not as obvious as it sounds—you see, onions are hot and *moist,* but garlic and leeks are hot and *dry*. Therefore each sauce, each spice, each choice of ingredients in a meal should be made by the chef not merely to show off, but to achieve perfect balance. There are neutral foods, too; goat meat, for instance." Picasso nodded, looking serious.

"I like goats," he said thoughtfully. "So what do you do with all this knowledge?"

Encouraged, Ondine continued, "By pairing certain foods, you avoid having too much of one element in the diet. You balance food with the seasons, too. For instance, you offset cold, wet weather with hot, dry meals like meat roasts; but on hot summer days you serve fish or meat that is poached in water. Also, you take into account a person's physical complaints; Père Jacques says that some foods are catalysts which, properly used, can make a meal easier to digest—beet sugar, for instance, and fresh milk," she concluded breathlessly.

She paused, having surprised herself by being so eager to talk. And for once, nobody had interrupted her. Such free rein for her own thoughts and feelings was new.

For Picasso listened acutely, watching her face as she became more animated with excitement over all the possibilities. When she stopped, he allowed a meditative silence. Then he nodded. "You *do* have the intelligence and sensual passion of an artist," he observed.

Ondine, still flushed with enthusiasm, realized that she'd just revealed something intimate about herself, and she suddenly felt more naked than she had when she took off her clothes to swim.

For awhile they ate in companionable silence. Then Picasso said slyly, "I believe in a balanced life, too. I don't see why I should give up one woman for another, do you? I should just cut off their heads and keep them on a shelf. Then I can talk to them whenever I like, and put them in a box when I don't. So. Which woman do *you* think won the fight back at my house?"

Ondine tried not to think about the images he'd just conjured. But he seemed to want an answer, so she considered his question seriously. Luc had never made her fight for him, but she could recall the squabbles of other girls. "Neither," she said finally. "Because if you have to fight for a man, the battle is already lost."

Picasso threw back his head with a shout of laughter, then said conspiratorially, "*Exactement!* It's going to be a 'draw'. You know something, Ondine? I *like* you."

They finished eating, and together they repacked the hamper before heading back up the beach. Picasso put his arm around her shoulders to shelter her from the wind that had whipped up, and she stayed pressed against his sturdy chest until they reached her bicycle in its sheltered spot by the wall. She went behind the trees to collect her dry clothes, slipping on her *culottes* under her dress.

Picasso pretended not to watch, but he waited for her. When she returned to her bicycle, he stepped away and said rather formally, "Well, Ondine, thank you for a pleasant lunch. See you on Monday." And with that, he headed back up to his villa alone.

12

A Proposal for Ondine

ON SUNDAYS THE CAFÉ PARADIS WAS CLOSED, AND ONDINE DROWSED IN bed much later than on weekday mornings, feeling her body slowly relax, until it was time to go downstairs and accompany her parents to the Sunday Mass. But today, as the church bell tolled, her mother surprised Ondine by coming up to her third-floor bedroom and sitting down on the edge of the bed while she still lay there.

"Ondine," Madame Belange said, a bit too casually, "wear your new blue dress to Mass today."

Ondine sat up guiltily, for no one knew that she'd been wearing her best dress over and over, posing for Picasso.

"Monsieur Renard has invited you to dine with his mother after church," her mother added.

Ondine felt a clutch of fear. Dinner with one of the Three Wise Men? "Why?" she asked.

Her mother rose, went to the armoire and took the dress from its hanger. "*What* have you been doing with this?" she demanded, shaking it out. "It looks as if you've mopped the floor with it!"

But clearly she had more important matters to discuss. "Ondine, times are not easy," she began. "Your father needs a partner to keep the café going. Monsieur Renard has lots of money. And he's very interested in investing in our café."

The dread in Ondine's stomach was now gnawing at her like a fox, but she said as offhandedly as she could, "Well, what's that got to do with me?" Madame Belange tried to suppress a look of regret.

"You need a husband. You can't live with us like a little girl forever," she replied crisply.

Ondine felt as though her mother had slapped her across the face. But she covered her wounded feelings by objecting, "*What?* He's so *old!*"

"He's only thirty, and very healthy. He can still give you children," Madame Belange said as delicately as possible. "A girl like you needs a mature husband to guide her. You'll soon see the wisdom of it."

Ondine heard a creak out in the corridor, and her father appeared in the doorway as if he'd been standing there listening all along. He seldom came up here, and now remained at the threshold as if reluctant to venture farther in. He looked fondly at her, sorrowful but resolute.

"Monsieur Renard is a fine man who will provide you with a good life," he said firmly.

"But I *can't* marry him. It would be a sin. I am engaged to Luc!" Ondine cried pleadingly.

"Luc had his chance and lost it. The church says you are no longer bound by a promise to a man who's abandoned you," her father replied more sharply. "Monsieur Renard is dependable and successful. Not only with his bakery. He has informed me that he's just bought all that farmland that supplies so much of what we need for the café. Prices will keep going up—unless we own it ourselves."

Ondine knew that her father had had his eye on the property because its owners were elderly and ready to sell. She'd seen her mother carefully counting the coins as she paid the dairy boy for all the regular deliveries of meat and vegetables. Not to mention the bread from Renard's bakery. And now this one man would own it all. Her parents called it a partnership. But to Ondine, it looked as if the baker were tightening a rope around the Café Paradis—and it felt like a hangman's noose on her neck.

"So you mustn't lose your chance with Monsieur Renard," her mother warned anxiously.

"But—I don't love him! I don't even *like* him! He's so proud and proper." Ondine looked entreatingly from one parent's face to the other. What she saw frightened her, for they were astonishingly indifferent to her tears. Apparently something else worried them more.

"You will *learn* to love him," her mother assured her. "Most mamas would jump at a chance to marry off their daughter to this man! What makes you so picky, Ondine? People already think you're too independent and headstrong. That's why so many boys your age are already betrothed to other girls."

"The boys like me the way I am!" Ondine insisted. "It's their mothers who think I'm too independent. They say that about any girl who refuses to act silly and coy."

"Well, most boys listen to their parents when they choose a girl to marry," Madame Belange explained. "You don't want to end up with no husband, no child, nothing. We only want you to be safe and cared for. Not lonely and unprotected." Ondine noticed the worried pucker in her mother's brow.

"You were born after the war, Ondine," her father said. "So you don't realize that terrible things can happen to people who don't prepare for the worst. We can't always get what we want, but we can learn to sacrifice some of our dreams to make sure our lives don't end up being nightmares."

Ondine wailed and threw herself down on her pillow. Her father sighed and waited a few moments, expecting the storm of her tears to dissolve into: *Yes, Papa*. When she did not relent, he finally threatened to send her back to the convent, saying, "And this time, young lady, it will be for keeps!"

ALL THROUGH MASS, ONDINE FERVENTLY prayed that God would strike everyone dead so she wouldn't have to eat dinner with Monsieur Fabius Renard. But as the service ended and everyone filed outside into the spring sunlight, her hopes were dashed, for there stood the baker. He was all dressed up in his best blue suit and hat, with his neat little moustache and his ash-blond hair freshly barbered, waiting for her at the sidewalk, standing self-consciously erect.

"Good God, the entire parish can see what he's got on his mind!" she murmured, aghast, stepping past the ladies of the congregation who stood on the front steps, watching and whispering.

"*Mademoiselle?*" Monsieur Renard said, tipping his hat to her in a dignified gesture before he took possession of her left elbow. He seemed so serious and attentive that Ondine felt momentarily ashamed of her feelings and unworthy of such solemnity. But even so, it was like being escorted by an overly attentive uncle. She heard her father's whispered command from behind her, saying, "Go!"

She kept her eyes lowered furiously and followed Monsieur Renard to his shiny new automobile. She had a moment of fleeting triumph when she saw the admiring faces of the gossipy ladies she'd left behind on the church steps. *At least this car shut them up,* Ondine thought grimly.

Monsieur Renard drove on silently, and the streets seemed to flutter past like the pages in a flip-it book. Ondine had never given a moment's thought as to where this man lived. With a sinking heart she tried not to think of it as her future home when he pulled up to a large house in what was once a very grand neighborhood. But the doctors and lawyers who'd lived here in the earlier part of the century had moved on, and now the neighbors were like Renard—working tradesmen who'd made enough money to afford the wide lawns and spacious rooms that wealthier people had just abandoned for more fashionable streets. "*Alors!* Home at last!" he said cheerfully as he parked, got out and opened her door.

Ondine was studying him covertly, mindful of her mother's admonition that most women would feel lucky to marry off their daughter to Renard. Yes, he was just the sort of man that mothers approved of for a son-in-law—clean, nice-looking, well-pressed, courteous— pleasant but unexciting. Pushing away her own trepidation, she tried to keep an open mind and imagine him as a good husband. When he held the car door for her she noticed that he did everything very care-fully, deliberately, in the manner of a solitary man who is outgoing in public but quite shy in more intimate situations. She felt sorry for him, wondering, *How can I ever hurt this man's feelings by saying "no" because I still only love Luc?*

For, following Renard up the long straight walkway, she'd gotten a panicked feeling that, merely by going along with him today, she was murdering and burying Luc forever. She fought off a sudden impulse to just run away as the baker unlocked his front door and escorted her into a darkened parlor.

She sensed the presence of another creature nearby; but Ondine had to wait until her eyes adjusted to the dim lighting before she glimpsed two spots of white hair—one belonged to an older lady with lace at her throat, sitting in a high-backed chair; the other to a little white dog asleep at her feet.

"Mother, this is the girl Ondine," Monsieur Renard said as if they were approaching a shrine.

The woman fixed her small bright eyes on Ondine as Renard helped his mother struggle to her feet. Ondine now remembered hav-ing heard that this lady was lame in one leg from childhood polio. Re-nard gestured to Ondine to take the lady's other arm; and together they hauled her into a gloomy dining salon across the hallway, where a tall, gawky cook was serving the dinner she'd prepared.

Once seated at the head of the table, Madame Renard slowly and deliberately removed her napkin from its silver ring. Her son took the seat at the other end, so by default Ondine took the mismatched chair at his side, understanding the situation in a flash of misery.

These two have been dining across from each other for years, she sur-mised. They were having an early Sunday meal, no doubt so that the poor woman could sleep it off for the rest of the day.

"My cook isn't as good as your *Maman,*" Monsieur Renard said qui-etly, with a slightly fastidious expression on his face. "But this will suf-fice for today." If the dull-looking servant girl overheard him she didn't seem to care. Renard bowed his head and murmured an unintelligible prayer. His mother crossed herself. Then, they ate.

Since no one spoke to her—in fact, they didn't even chat with each other—Ondine could not help silently assessing the food, out of habit from working with her mother. *He's certainly right about this meal!* she thought. The soup was made from a chicken boiled days ago, with not a single trace of meat or carrot left in it. It had been watered down, no doubt to stretch it out. Some other unfortunate bird was served as the main course, but Ondine could not identify what it had been when it was alive. The cheese course was all right, and of course the bread was fresh. But the pastry served with chamomile tea for dessert was sickeningly sweet; and this, sadly, seemed to be the only course his mother relished.

Clearly Monsieur Renard kept his household on a minuscule budget. Why? Her father had said the man was well-off. She'd seen him gamble away money at cards with the other Wise Men at the café, where he indulged in a good lunch as well. So why was he so stingy with his mother's household? Heaven only knew what this poor woman ate when she was all alone here.

Baffled, Ondine recalled an old saying she'd heard the marketplace ladies quote to one another. *If you want to see how a man will treat you once you become his wife, just watch how he treats his mother.*

The ticking clock in the parlor echoed throughout the silent house. Ondine could see the older woman's bright eyes staring at her, sizing her up yet revealing nothing. The dog had been allowed to go into the kitchen, and Ondine could hear him gnawing on his bone with pathetic gusto. It seemed to Ondine that the entire house ached with such entrenched solitude that she doubted she could ever be strong enough to break the all-encompassing loneliness of a miser.

Finally Monsieur Renard pushed back his chair with a loud, scraping sound that shattered the silence, and he helped his mother to her bedroom. When he returned he said to Ondine, "Let's go into the garden." She followed him through a primly maintained backyard to a small stone bench, where they sat down together. She'd never been this close to him before; he smelled of shaving soap, mothballs, pastry and pipe tobacco. He seemed nervous now. He spoke of the garden, and made a few mild remarks about the weather. She could not seem to catch his gaze and hold it, to connect.

Mopping his brow with his handkerchief, he finally recited what was clearly a prepared speech. "Dear Ondine," he began awkwardly, as he reached out with a moist hand that reminded her of rising bread dough.

Here it comes, she thought with mounting dread as he clasped her hand firmly. But when she stole a look at his face, it dawned on her that this moment was difficult for him, too. His attitude could hardly be called ardent; he seemed dutiful, and slightly horrified by the necessity of showing any emotion at all.

She herself was fighting off the urge to burst into tears. He did not get down on bended knee; for this she was grateful, because such a gesture would have been too mortifying to bear. Instead he assured her that his bakery was very successful. He said with bashful pride, "You'll see that my ovens are the most modern ones available! I assure you, you'll like working there with me."

Ondine suddenly understood the sort of bargain that had been struck, and now she could barely hear another word he uttered. She forced a smile to hide what she really thought, which was, *I'd be exchanging Maman's hot oven for yours and I'll spend the rest of my days in the pit of hell.* As for her nights, she tried not to envision sleeping in his bed and doing the things men wanted to do. He wasn't a bad man. He wasn't ugly, or uncouth. But he was so fastidious and parsimonious that she simply couldn't imagine him as the sort of husband who might inspire deep love, much less passion, in a girl like her.

"And so, Ondine," he finally concluded, leaning closer, "be my wife."

It sounded more like a command than a request, so Ondine remained silent. She only raised her eyes to mutely wonder, *But, do you love me?* He seemed to comprehend her message, for he looked slightly alarmed before he averted his eyes. Then in a sudden burst of resolve, Monsieur Renard put his arm around her waist and pulled her close to his stomach, as if it were something he'd seen a hero do in a movie. She saw that, compared to the rest of his body, he had a rather large belly, normally hidden by his jacket. To her further surprise, he hastily planted a slightly wet kiss on her lips. It did not say *I love you*. It was more like an embarrassed *Will this do?* Ondine found herself holding her breath until it ended.

MONSIEUR RENARD DROVE HER HOME along a more scenic route, and Ondine wore a mechanical smile so he could convince himself that the afternoon was a success. Her panic had given way to numbed fear as she gazed out the window, leaning her cheek against her gloved hand, listlessly ignoring the landscape while pretending to be enjoying the drive. *I didn't want my marriage proposal to be like this,* she thought with a flash of girlish misery. Everything felt too small and mercenary—the entire town of Juan-les-Pins, even its sea and sky, suddenly seemed crushed under a claustrophobic glass dome.

But soon they were passing Picasso's neighborhood, and Ondine sat up straight as if awakening from a bad dream. Her gaze cleared, and some relief must have illuminated her expression, for Monsieur Renard smiled at her as if she were a child who'd been roused from a drowsy Sunday nap.

"They never should have let the Americans rent these villas!" he exclaimed as he steered his car past the hill that led to Picasso's street. "It was bad enough, renting them out to the Parisians!"

Ondine said nothing, but when she saw a familiar figure on the road, she leaned forward to get a better look. Yes, it was Picasso—all dressed up in a fine suit, shirt and hat, and even a tie. He must have gone into town, and he was walking home holding himself straighter and more proudly than ever, seeming conscious of the dapper figure he cut, out on a Sunday stroll.

He's not alone! she thought, straining to get a better look. For, just behind him, a woman was pushing a baby carriage. Yes, it was that blonde with the distinctive, long nose—the one called Marie-Thérèse—but now at last Ondine could see her from head to toe instead of just her face in the window.

She was short, like Picasso, and full-figured in an athletic sort of way. She looked more Swedish or Germanic than French. And she had a blonde, cherub-faced infant in the pram, clearly her daughter.

That must be Picasso's baby! Ondine realized, fascinated. It was hard for her to imagine him as the father of an infant, when he seemed such a mischievous imp himself at times. And although the mama was dressed up in a fancy Sunday hat, she was licking an ice-cream cone like a schoolgirl, tilting her head in total concentration with a childlike expression of delight, while Picasso strutted ahead like a rooster.

"That's not his wife," Monsieur Renard said in an unexpectedly harsh, disgusted tone.

Ondine, feeling caught staring, blushed. "Who?" she asked innocently.

"Over there. That man is a Spaniard. He's been in town before, in the summertime. He's friends with that noisy American crowd that started coming here in the twenties. His wife is a Russian lady of quality, dark-haired and fine. She always liked my *millefeuille* pastry." Monsieur Renard clucked. "As for *this* affair, it's disgraceful. It won't last. Such dalliances never do. Who will marry this girl after he's finished with her? *I* could never take up with a woman who's had a child by another man," he sniffed, turning the car around the corner.

Ondine sat back as the little trio of figures grew smaller in the distance. It was somehow thrilling to finally get such a good look at Marie-Thérèse. She was not a great beauty nor a perfect goddess, just a normal, flesh-and-blood female—and, despite Renard's verdict, she looked happy. Had she triumphed over Dora-the-lady-photographer? Or did they really agree to share Picasso? Perhaps his women had no choice but to do his bidding. The rules were apparently different high up on Mount Olympus, for any girl brave enough to come close to the gods. Just seeing him renewed her courage and made Ondine feel she could once again breathe in the salty air of possibility, and find freedom from stultifying propriety.

What would the villagers in Juan-les-Pins say if they knew that Ondine herself had modelled for Picasso up at his studio? How it would shock Monsieur Renard! Ondine pondered this with some triumph. *I never actually said "Yes" to Renard's proposal,* she consoled herself. *So it doesn't really count. But let him—and everyone else in town—think whatever they want, for now.*

And so Ondine merely feigned compliance, allowing Monsieur Renard to escort her back to the café to make his joyous announcement, confirming that she and he were betrothed. Her father opened a bottle of cognac infused with orange, and they all toasted the wedding. Then her parents set the date for September. Like a sleepwalker, Ondine went through all the motions of a bride-to-be. This was possible only because she'd convinced herself that somehow, this wedding would never actually happen.

But she went to bed feeling frightened. She didn't know how to exploit one's connections with a powerful *Patron*. Marriage was the only future she'd been taught. Picasso conjured up many liberating ideas to her, yet he was not her idea of a good husband. She was not so foolish as to imagine that she could be his one true love. And being his mistress was clearly a perilous affair. He was more like an Arab with his harem, Ondine realized. How many other women did he keep back in Paris?

No, there was only one man she could ever think of as a husband. Luc was a man of his word, she consoled herself. He would come back for her and carry her away from Juan-les-Pins, like a pirate!

But, alone in her bedroom where she had lain in Luc's arms as he murmured his promises to her, Ondine found herself struggling to remember the details of his gentle face, which were becoming alarmingly distant and blurry with each passing week.

"Luc, where are you?" she whispered. Far into the silence of the night, Ondine lay awake, for the first time really wondering how she would survive without him.

13

Ondine, a Girl at a Window

IT WAS RAINING SOFTLY OUTSIDE ONDINE'S WINDOW WHEN SHE AWOKE AT dawn to find a shadowy female figure standing over her like an angel.

"Wake up, Ondine!" her mother whispered. "They've taken your father to the hospital. I'm going there now, so you will have to run the breakfast service today. Monsieur Renard has already delivered bread and *brioche,* so just make the coffee. Then for lunch, have the waiters serve cold terrines and salads. As for your artist's lunch at the villa, you can make him a quiche."

"What's the matter with Papa?" Ondine asked groggily, sitting up.

"His heart again. He was working on the receipts and bills, but then he came into the kitchen looking peculiar, and he said, 'Something is wrong—I can't see the numbers . . .' He collapsed right there on the kitchen floor. Monsieur Renard will drive me to the hospital. Listen, before you go up to the villa, you must pay the delivery boy when he comes with the eggs. Did you hear me, Ondine?"

"Yes, yes," Ondine said, awake and worried now. "Pay the boy. Where is the money for him?"

"The fourth canister on the top shelf of the pantry," her mother said hurriedly. "Get up. Now!"

She swept out of the room, and Ondine heard her footsteps rapidly going down the staircase.

The rest of the morning was a blur of breakfast service and lunch preparation. Word had already spread throughout the village that her parents were at the hospital, so the diners were prepared to be grateful for whatever they got to eat today. By the time Ondine had all the platters ready on the big kitchen table for the waiters to grab, the weather was not cooperating; it had grown so windy that they were once again going to have to close the terrace and serve lunch indoors instead.

Ondine was packing up her supplies for Picasso when the delivery boy came with eggs and butter and cream from the farm. She went into the pantry and counted the fourth ceramic canister, which was labelled *herbes* but was instead filled with coins her mother squirreled away as petty cash. The fact that she'd revealed to Ondine where the money was hidden proved the seriousness of the situation. Ondine's fingers shook as she opened it, and she dropped the canister's cork top on the floor. Hurriedly she went to pay the boy, then she returned to the pantry to put the canister exactly as her mother kept it.

When Ondine stooped to retrieve the cork top from where it had rolled under the shelves, she noticed a loose brick in the wall. She touched it, intending to push it back into place, but it fell out in her hand. There were several other loose bricks around it, and when she took them all out, she saw a deep, wide space, in which she discovered a bundle of white envelopes tied together with string. Ondine wondered just how much money her mother had been squirreling away for a rainy day. She could not resist drawing the bundle out to feel how weighty it was.

But she was startled to see that the top envelope, which had been stamped and postmarked, was not addressed to her mother—the handwriting said *Ondine*. And, it had already been opened.

"This letter was mailed to *me*!" Ondine exclaimed, stunned. "What's it doing here?" She untied the string carefully so that later she could put everything back as she'd found it.

There were five letters, every single one for Ondine, each postmarked from a different exotic port of call. Tunis. Algiers. Morocco. On closer examination the handwriting was startlingly familiar.

"Luc!" Ondine cried. She sank to the floor, allowing the letters to drop into her lap. She stared at them uncomprehendingly for several minutes before she picked up the one that had lain on top:

> *My sweet Ondine,*
> *I have seen the most wonderful and terrible things that no postcard can do justice to, so I send you my thoughts instead. The world is a bigger place with a smaller heart than we ever imagined. A sailor's life is not enriching me quickly enough to please your father. But don't worry, I will work hard, and somehow I will find a way to make our fortune . . .*

Ondine had to keep blinking away her tears in order to continue reading. She reached blindly for another letter in hope of better news. It, too, had already been opened:

> *Chère Ondine,*
> *I think of you every morning as the sun comes up. Each day I wonder—Is she ill? Is she still alive? Is she just angry with me for going away? Perhaps you feel guilty because you no longer want to wait for me? Or have you simply stopped loving me? Whatever you tell me will be all right. Only, please tell me. Love, Luc*

Her mind was whirling and her breath was coming out in short, hard gasps. "What's he talking about?" she wondered, bewildered. "Why should he accuse me of not writing to him?" She seized the other letters, and all were entreaties for her to tell him that she was alive and well, and to explain her silence. All but the last one, which said:

> *Darling Ondine,*
> *I am very sick with fever. They have called for a doctor. I will ask a friend to mail this letter. In case I never make it home, know that I*

love you forever. And please keep one small corner of your heart free
for my poor soul to come to rest. Adieu, Luc

"Luc!" she wailed in despair. She felt as if a fog had crept into the room, so thick that all sounds were muffled and she could barely make out her own voice when she whispered, "But I *did* write to him in care of his ship! Why didn't he get my letters—?"

A terrible thought crossed her mind, and she peered again into the slot in the wall, dreading what she'd find. Sure enough, farther in there was another similar packet—of her own letters to Luc. In utter disbelief, she seized them.

"But I gave all these to the postman myself. I know I did!" Ondine cried, frantically sorting the unopened envelopes. Just seeing them again made her vividly recall how she'd felt writing these letters, her hopes progressively fading with each new attempt to contact Luc. And how, each time she wrote another one and handed it to the postman, he'd glanced at it, seen that it was addressed to Luc, and shaken his head as if he thought her very silly indeed.

The answer came to her swiftly. "I gave them to the postman, but *he* must have been told not to mail them—to bring them to Papa instead. My letters never got past our café."

And all this time her parents had insisted that Luc abandoned her, while his letters—and her own—lay languishing just a few feet away from the kitchen table where Ondine worked every day. Her mother had hidden them here like a guilty secret; perhaps she thought she'd explain it to Ondine one day. Her father must have intended her to marry Monsieur Renard all along; the baker might not go into partnership with her family unless he got a young wife to work for him as part of the bargain. That must be why her father had turned Luc away. In an awful way, it was all starting to add up.

The tears that had been streaming down her cheeks had finally stopped; and now her wet face made her feel chilled.

"But how could they *do* this to me?" Ondine gasped, shocked. "And how could they be so cruel to poor Luc? He was so honest and trusting, obeying their command with his entire life!"

At first she sought to find a more humane explanation. Maybe her parents truly believed that they were protecting her from a ne'er-do-well, who, no matter how much money he earned, could never measure up to a man with such standing in the community as Renard. Perhaps if Ondine's brothers had survived the Great War and returned to take care of the business, things might have been easier for her; as it was, Ondine was her parents' only hope to obtain more financing and security. One thing was certain; they absolutely didn't want Luc around.

But now Ondine felt as if her heart were being gripped by a cold hand. She checked the envelopes again; yes, Luc's letters had stopped three months ago. There had been nothing since then. Either he'd recovered and found another girl to marry . . . or something much worse had happened.

"Murderers," she cried. "All of us. We all killed Luc, because we made him go away from everything he loved here. And for what? If we hadn't interfered, he'd be alive, as he deserves to be! Luc and I would have been married by now, maybe even have a baby, and a happy life together. But now it will *never* happen!" She clapped a hand to her mouth, having finally said aloud the very words she'd tried so hard, all this time, to not even think about.

Reality was burning away the fog of shock, and she saw her whole life under this sharp new lens. Instinctively she felt that no one must know she'd found these letters. Her parents might come down hard on her, even restrict her from leaving the house just to ensure that she got to the altar. She put the letters back exactly as they'd been. Trembling, she struggled to her feet and returned to the kitchen.

While Ondine was packing up Picasso's lunch, Dr. Charlot arrived to dine with his fellow Wise Men, and he had a reassuring message for Ondine. "Your father gave us all quite a scare! But I believe he's out of danger now. Your mother will stay with him at the hospital awhile longer, but she wanted me to tell you she'll be back here in time to run the dinner service. Don't worry, my dear, he's going to be all right." He smiled and patted her shoulder before he returned to his table. Ondine nodded mutely.

But she was seized with a wild urge to break something, to stab someone, to throw herself off a cliff, to do damage to something, anyone—just to exorcise this suffocating pain from her chest. She'd once seen a madwoman who tore her own hair and clothes. Now Ondine thought she understood why.

She carried her hamper outside, climbed aboard her bicycle and pedaled furiously, flashing past the harbor, scarcely noticing that the wind was making the sea kick up angrily with choppy waves, and the sky was filled with heavy, lowering dark clouds like ominous battleships—grey, ponderous, threatening.

When she reached the driveway of Picasso's villa, the entire sky had gone as black as night, but it was no match for her own savage mood. She saw that there was only one lighted window in the house, upstairs in his workroom. She found the kitchen door unlocked as usual. She put the hamper on the table, went to the foot of the stairs and listened. All she could hear was the low rumble of distant thunder coming in from the sea, slowly moving closer, sounding like a growling beast prowling across the sky.

Ondine did not want to set the table. She did not want to cook. She didn't want to serve anyone. She only wanted to scream at the top of her lungs and wake up the dead, shout to anyone who would listen, tell them about the grave injustice that had been done to her and Luc.

Silently she drifted up the staircase and glided like a ghost along the hallway to Picasso's workroom. She had an idea that only he could help her now.

He was not there, but tall, metallic lamps stood like giants, still turned on, burning brightly. They appeared to be the professional lighting that photographers used. The lamps had been on so long that they gave off a threatening smell of overheated metal.

"He must have worked all night," Ondine realized. "He'll burn the whole place down." She began turning off each one, careful not to touch the hot aluminum shades.

Down the street, the thunder crept steadily closer, rumbling in derision, as if the devil himself were laughing at her. Ondine turned off the last lamp; but a moment later, a sudden, blinding flash of lightning made every window in the room seem filled with fire, illuminating two paintings that were propped up in the corner where she was standing.

"That's *my* pose! God, look what he did to me!" Ondine exclaimed, gazing at the first canvas, recognizing her blue checked dress and long curly dark hair. But it was like peering into a fun-house mirror. Both eyes were stuck on one side of her face, which was attached to a long goosey neck, which in turn seemed attached at the throat to two breasts shaped like oranges that were popping out of her unbuttoned dress. Meanwhile her hands looked like claws, and her feet were like flippers. And why were her toenails and fingernails black? She didn't even wear polish!

Yet here was *Femme à la montre*—she knew it because of the mirror, the comb and wristwatch, and the crown of yellow forsythia in her hair. Aghast, she turned to look at the second painting.

"Me again. But it's no better!" she said in dismay. Same pose with her blue dress and a mirror—but the yellow flowers and the wristwatch were gone, and now there was a second figure sitting on the floor who looked like a faceless wire mannequin with the same curly hair as Ondine's.

Everything was a joke to him! He'd called her a goddess, a Greek statue. Yet how people would laugh at her if they knew she'd sat here posing for *this,* without any pay, without any thanks, hoping that Picasso would guide her to a better life.

"So he sees me as an ugly, foolish creature. Well, my life *is* a joke," she said bitterly. "I'm to be sacrificed like a lamb to Monsieur Renard. They might as well roast me in one of his ovens! No, I *won't* go to church and marry the baker! I won't be his slave. They killed Luc—but they won't own *me*."

She felt like throwing herself out the window then and there, into the storm that was raging relentlessly, and she didn't care if the wind picked her up and blew her straight out to sea. This sudden urge for self-annihilation felt so real that it frightened her. Feeling momentarily lightheaded, she swayed slightly, and looked around for a chair or something to catch hold of.

"*Zzzz-zhzz!*" A snoring noise came from down the hallway, puncturing the silence. The dark, brooding morning must have discouraged

Picasso from getting out of bed. Only a city man could indulge in the luxury of sleeping so late. Ondine marched over to the room where his snores were coming from, and peered in the open doorway.

Picasso slept peacefully in his bed, oblivious to the storm. She crept closer to the foot of the bed, then stopped and stood there, staring. He'd kicked off the covers in his sleep, like an infant, and was lying on his back naked, blissfully snoring away, his body completely exposed, right down to his wiry pubic hair, from which sprung his penis, perkily alert, like an arrow.

"Here lies the Minotaur," Ondine murmured, horrified and fascinated. "He devours all the women who enter his labyrinth. Do they die of pleasure, or agony?"

She'd never looked at a man's *zizi* before—not even Luc's when he stole into her bed; she'd only felt his friendly arousal nudging against her under the covers in the dark. Yet even with Luc's tender love, sex had involved an invasion that made her bleed.

"I may as well throw myself on the Minotaur instead of out the window, and I don't care what he does with me after this!" Ondine imagined herself impaled upon him—bloody, spent, yet somehow, triumphant. She felt a surge of something else besides rage swelling inside her, arising from all her pent-up, frustrated desires for love and independence and the power of a better destiny.

"*I* want to be the one who is rich and happy. *I* want to be the one who takes *all* the pleasure!"

Defiantly she slipped off her underdrawers beneath her dress, just as she had when she posed for him. But now she wanted to rid herself of this blue dress, too, that she'd worn so many times for Picasso—and in church for Monsieur Renard.

"You don't see me as I really am," she whispered to the slumbering figure as she unbuttoned her dress. "Nobody does!" With an outraged gesture she yanked it up over her head and hurled it to the floor.

"There. Look at me! Am I not beautiful?"

The thunder crashed directly above now, like a cannon reverberating through the house to its very foundation. It woke Picasso, and with a shocked gasp he sat up suddenly.

"Who's there?" he said in a low voice, squinting and automatically pulling up the sheets. "Ondine? Is that you? What's the matter?"

"Everything," she said, coming to the side of the bed.

"What do you want?" he asked in surprise, still trying to see her.

Ondine didn't answer but trembled as she stepped out of the shadows. He saw that she was naked, and he studied her face, assessing the situation. Then suddenly he opened his arms to her. When she rushed in, he enveloped her in an embrace that surprised her with its welcoming warmth.

"*Chère* Ondine," he murmured soothingly. "Why have you come to me now?"

"Because I want—" Ondine began, then found that she could not speak. She tried again. "I want to know ... I want to feel. I want—I want—"

"Yes, yes, I know," he said, softly stroking her hair away from her cheek. He pulled her closer to his chest, and his arms around her made her feel as if, like Zeus, he could cloak her in something that the storm could not touch. At the same time, his persistent stroking ignited a spark that unleashed the hunger seething inside her—for, having tirelessly served the appetites of so many people who came and went from the café, Ondine suddenly realized she'd been starving for love all along. Now, instead of working hard to please this man and her parents, it felt like finally somebody wanted to please her.

And although she could not say exactly how it began, she found that he was kissing her and she was kissing him, and her heart was beating faster, faster, faster, as she'd once felt when she was a child climbing up a great tree, higher and higher, her limbs growing taut with strength, her blood like a fire urging her on, and her mind dizzy with the risk—how high could she go without falling?

He was kissing her breasts as she clung to his strong neck; and to Ondine's surprise her body told her that for quite some time she'd been living in an aching state of arousal, stimulated by each visit into his world, each picture he painted—her flesh already so exquisitely pliable that she felt triumphantly indestructible as he thrust himself inside her soft wetness. Nothing could stop her now, not even when he began to withdraw while he was still hard; she only seized him hungrily and held him long enough to take what she needed for her pleasure before he, too, surrendered. And for once, her own greedy strength triumphed over everyone and everything—over anger, over sorrow, over death itself.

LATER, SHE HEARD THE RAIN, like the distant rushing of an Alpine stream pouring down from the heavens in a benediction, washing away the thunder and lightning, whispering and soothing through the trees, making them toss their heads like ladies shaking their hair dry after a day of bathing in the bright blue sea.

Ondine felt fearless now; all the rage was spent from her limbs, and her muscles and bones were relaxed and strong again. She sat up and took a folded blanket from the foot of the bed to open up and wrap around her. She liked its looseness; she did not want to be restricted by clothes yet.

She would have gotten out of bed and gone to the window to drink in the fresh air, but now Picasso stirred and gave her a smile like sunlight. Ondine experienced this perfect moment as an acute grace, so peaceful that she knew, no matter what happened afterwards, nothing could ever take it away from her. *I am alive. I am a creature to be prized. He has given me this recognition and I will take it.*

Picasso leaned close to her now and picked up a long spiral of her hair that had fallen over her forehead, gently putting it back into place with the rest of her curls.

"*Belle* Ondine," he murmured in admiration. She sighed.

"Beautiful," she repeated. For a moment she remained silent, letting the word reverberate in the air. Then, without reproach she said, "I saw the paintings you made of me."

"Ah," he commented. "Well, you don't even have to say it. I know what most women think. 'Is *that* how you see me? I don't look like that at *all*!' Am I right?" His alert dark eyes were watchful for an answer.

She mulled it over, then offered the only explanation she could honestly come up with.

"I guess it's very difficult," she said thoughtfully.

"What is?" he asked, looking wary now.

"To paint people's souls right into the flesh on their faces," she offered. "Like Rembrandt."

At first, he howled with laughter. Ondine smiled uncertainly, then shrugged.

"Humph!" he exclaimed, taken aback. "What do you know about Rembrandt?"

"I've seen a picture of his," Ondine explained. "Just a girl looking out a window."

"Oh, *that* one!" Picasso nodded.

"You've seen it, too?" she asked eagerly. "I see it every day in the café. And yet she is a mystery to me. Isn't it incredible—to make a person look real and yet so much more than ordinary?"

"You think I couldn't do it?" Picasso said abruptly, sitting upright and reaching for his clothes. "Come with me to my studio, right now."

Calmly, still partially wrapped in her blanket, she followed. The soles of her bare feet seemed to feel every grain of the wooden floor, like a healthy animal stalking through the forest.

"Go to that window where the sun is," he ordered, for indeed, the sky was clearing now. She hesitated until he said challengingly, "You want to be *my* immortal *Girl-at-a-Window,* don't you? Then pose like her, but leave your shoulders bare."

She could not resist saying, "Look, there's a rainbow out there! What perfect colors."

"Hmm," he observed gruffly, "you know, you're *not* like most females, especially when you make love. You're too . . . aggressive, like a man. A woman can be strong—but not in bed!" A faint tone of paternal disapproval crept into his voice. "You're not a virgin, are you?"

Ondine looked away defiantly and warned, "Don't spoil it." She didn't want a father or a priest lecturing her now.

"Then turn your head more this way and be still," Picasso growled, picking up his brush.

For a long while, all was quiet. Then she asked curiously, "What's Paris like?"

"Dirty and wonderful," Picasso replied, still looking preoccupied.

"If I came to Paris would you—" Ondine began, but he looked up so sharply that she said hurriedly, "—introduce me to people who run the restaurants? I want to be a great chef there."

"Everyone always wants the glory, but nobody wants to do the work," Picasso muttered. "It takes years to learn a trade, any trade. Assuming one has the talent to begin with."

"Hard work doesn't scare me. I've worked hard for *years*!" Ondine exclaimed. "Whatever I don't know, I'll learn fast. You can see that. You know I have the gift for cooking," she said, matter-of-factly.

Picasso conceded, "You do. But in Paris all the head chefs are men. They won't give a top job to a woman. Besides, a big restaurant kitchen is no place for a girl. They're full of bad men working there. They'd rape you in the basement the day you arrived. What's the matter with you? You belong *here*. Why do you want to run away from lovely Juan-les-Pins?"

"My parents are planning to marry me off to a man I can't possibly love!" Ondine cried passionately. "I must get away and cook on my own."

He stopped painting momentarily. "Listen to me," he said sternly, "Paris is no place for a sweet country girl like you. They'll eat you alive. You can't just find a job. You have to know somebody."

"I know *you*," Ondine pointed out. But she could see that he looked fairly alarmed at the idea, and clearly he had no desire whatsoever to have her turn up in Paris looking for favors. Remembering what the nuns sometimes did to place their students in positions of governesses and ladies' maids, she said softly, "Won't you at least write me a letter of recommendation, saying that I am an *artiste* in the kitchen, just as you told Miss Dora Maar? I could use that anywhere."

Picasso wore the trapped expression of a small boy ensnared by his own boasts. He returned to his canvas, muttering, "Of course, of course. I'll do it tomorrow. But don't blame *me* if you hate where you end up! Those kitchen jobs pay shit. You'll die an old, hardworking peasant unless you learn to take yourself seriously."

"What do you mean?" Ondine asked, intrigued.

"If you want something in life," Picasso said, looking hard at her now with those fearless black eyes, "you don't ask nicely and politely for it. You don't write letters. You have to kill for it."

"Kill?" Ondine echoed. "Kill who?"

"Anyone who gets in your way," Picasso answered. He saw her doubtful expression. "You think I'm wrong? Listen, every time you cook something for me, you have to kill it first. It doesn't matter if it's a carrot or a pig," he said bluntly. "You have to kill something, every day, just to live."

Ondine pondered this. She could think of people she'd like to kill. The postman, for one.

"So you might as well stay home in Juan-les-Pins," Picasso said, putting down his brush now, "and let a man do the killing for you, while you have his babies."

But Ondine smiled defiantly to herself. One thing she'd already learned today, to her surprise, was the strength of her own ravenous appetite, the discovery of her own powerful teeth and claws.

"Can I see my portrait now?" she asked, observing that he had stopped painting.

"It's not finished," Picasso said, "but yes, you may look."

Ondine padded across the floor and peered at it. "Oh!" she cried. "It *is* beautiful!"

Like the other canvases it was stretched upon wood, but this one was smaller. It was indeed *A-Girl-at-a-Window*—and it was a Picasso, but what sort of Picasso? More tender, natural, eternally human. She'd never seen him paint this way before. This girl in the picture had Ondine's face, of that there could be no doubt. Her flesh glowed with the radiance of youth, health and vitality. Her eyes were alight with curiosity, her mouth just hinting at her innermost thoughts, her hair in all its colors seeming as if every expressive strand was an echo of her spirit.

"It's so different from anything I've seen you do," she said quietly.

"Oh, well, the critics will say I've gone back to my Rose Period," Picasso said ruefully.

"What does that mean?" Ondine asked.

"Absolutely nothing," Picasso answered. "It's what they're born to do—chatter like squirrels. Then the dealers will convince some cautious businessman, who'll buy it to decorate his new house so he can tell his friends, *Here's my Picasso! Don't worry, it's not one of the ugly ones!*"

Ondine stood before the portrait, her hands clasped. "Oh, how can you bear to sell this painting to people who only want it because you're famous?" she asked softly. "If I made this I would never let anyone take it away, unless I knew that they loved it and understood what makes it beautiful."

Picasso looked truly touched. "Fine! It's yours," he said impulsively, with a sweep of his hand.

Ondine was thrilled. "Really?" she asked, awed. "I would love to have it! It would bring me luck, I am sure."

"Ah," he said sagely. "But—what *kind* of luck?"

"When will it be finished?" she asked eagerly.

"Tomorrow, perhaps," Picasso said vaguely. "And now, *chère* Ondine, I'm hungry. So, feed me!"

14

Céline and Aunt Matilda in Mougins, 2014

WHEN I AWOKE ON MY FIRST MORNING IN THE SOUTH OF FRANCE, AT FIRST I couldn't remember where I was. The windows were shuttered, the room was dark, and I was still fuddled by the time zone change.

But Aunt Matilda solved this by jumping out of her bed, thrusting her long, narrow feet into spa slippers and padding over to the window to fling open its quaint shutters. Instantly, our room was flooded with brilliant sunlight and the heady scent of flowers borne on a mild but persistent breeze.

"Mmmm," I sighed from my bed, eyes still closed, "*what* is that wonderful scent?"

"Jasmine, I believe," Aunt Matilda said, peering out to the shrubbery below. "Some of the best perfumes in the world are made from these flowers! Oh, get *up,* Céline. Look at the view!"

"I saw the view from the airport ride yesterday," I mumbled sleepily. We had been picked up by the hotel minivan and driven along the coastline before climbing high up into the hills of Mougins. "Blue sky, blue sea—no wonder they call it the *Côte d'Azur*. And no wonder Mom wanted to come back to the French Riviera! The real question is, why would she *ever* have wanted to leave it?"

"Well, it's one thing to be a tourist. It's quite another to be a local gal working and growing up here. Small towns are the same the world over," Aunt Matilda said philosophically, turning away from the window. She was wearing an old-fashioned nightgown, trimmed with lace on the collar, front and cuffs. She reminded me, dimly, of Mary Poppins. "For instance," she continued, "on the plane I was reading my Picasso book, and I found out that his housekeeper in Paris was a jasmine-picker from this very town, Mougins! You might not think jasmine smells so wonderful if you've been picking it all day. So who *wouldn't* want to work for Picasso instead?"

When I heard the name Picasso, *that* got me out of bed, for it reminded me of why I was here. I found my mother's predicament so deeply haunting and unbearable to think about, that the only way I could fight off the gnawing sadness in my gut was to stay focused on carrying out her mission for her. From my map I could see that it was about a thirty-minute drive to Juan-les-Pins, where Grandma's café was located. As soon as there was a break in the schedule I'd go there.

"You can shower first," Aunt Matilda said. "Let's not be late for our first day of class."

We hadn't met Master Chef Gilby Halliwell yet; that was going to happen today. Last night we'd been greeted by the concierge, a lanky Frenchman named Maurice who gave our class a tour of this chic Provençal boutique hotel, a *mas* or large L-shaped farmhouse whose older wing was in the final stages of renovation. We'd been given a supper of lobster and zucchini ravioli in a citrus and caper sauce, served on a terrace overlooking impeccably landscaped grounds and terraced fields.

With my first forkful of that meal I had an instant sense of our chef's talent; in fact we all stopped chattering to say the same thing: *Wow.* Gil had brightened up a local dish with a wizardly new combo of Provence's very own herbs, spices, lemons and orange peel.

During this meet-and-greet we got to know our fellow classmates, who'd all flown in from far-flung cities, all of us in varying stages of jet lag. They were very much like Aunt Matilda—elderly but vigorous, well educated, comfortably retired but still curious and eager. We were assigned rooms where we bunked two to a *chambre.* The "gentlemen" in our group were housed in the older, far wing of the *mas,* while we "ladies" were upstairs in the already-modernized bedrooms that were elegantly decorated.

"Not too shabby," Aunt Matilda had commented, looking pleased. Our room had two nice beds with red damask bedspreads, an upholstered chair covered in brocade near a desk piled with books, brochures, and a generous basket of fresh local fruit. I popped into the bathroom, which was flooded with light, and stocked with an array of small, paper-wrapped Provençal soaps and little bottles of shampoo. Two white bathrobes and spa-slipper packets were neatly laid out.

After I'd gotten dressed I felt a bit nervous at the prospect of facing down a Michelin-starred chef. My mother had taught me to have "taste" yet I knew so little about how she actually cooked such magnificent meals. For the first time I had qualms that I didn't really belong here and might look awkward. I thought it would be a good idea to do a little prep with a quick look at Grandma's recipes.

When Aunt Matilda emerged from her shower and went to the closet to select her clothes she asked, "What's that notebook you're reading? You look like a student cramming for an exam."

"That's exactly what I'm doing," I admitted sheepishly. "It's a cookbook my mother gave me. It belonged to my Grandmother Ondine. Her best recipes. She had a café in Juan-les-Pins."

Aunt Matilda crossed the room to retrieve her hairbrush, pausing to glance over my shoulder.

"Your grandmother wrote those?" she said, impressed, reading a few recipes as I turned the pages. "Then you've already got this cuisine in your blood. You'll ace it."

I was tempted to announce that Grandma had cooked all these meals for Picasso, but I held back, since obviously Mom hadn't told her about this. Aunt Matilda was distracted anyway, eager to join our group for breakfast. "Come on, kid, let's get down into that kitchen and meet the Big Cheese!" she said. "Or should I say, *Le Grand Fromage*?"

The class was assembled in a huge modernized kitchen, all chrome, steel and marble with an impressive array of multiple ovens and workstations. A buffet breakfast was laid out in a far corner, and all those early-birds had already discovered the mouth-watering croissants, *brioche* and pastry that you can only get in France. A festive, eager atmosphere permeated the place.

"Mark my words, this course won't be a picnic," warned Magda, a sturdy, cheerful woman with salt-and-pepper-colored hair, who owned a dog-breeding farm in Scotland. "My niece took Gil's professional class in London last season and had to quit halfway through. But she's lazy."

"I hear he makes grown men cry," said Joey, a balding old gentleman from Chicago who ran a catering business with his sons. There was a murmur of agreement, because we'd all seen Gil's cable TV program from several years ago, *Can YOU Stand the Heat?*, where it was clear that he didn't suffer fools in his kitchen and could be easily provoked into unleashing his fearsome temper.

"Well, they say all good chefs are half-mad," said Peter, a retired wine steward from London whom Aunt Matilda had already "taken a shine to" over sherry last night. A neat, trim Englishman, he had a full head of white hair and well-groomed white eyebrows, and was dressed in an old-fashioned navy blazer with gold nautical buttons, and light-colored flannel pants, an impeccable silk shirt and tie, and a red handkerchief in his pocket, as if he were going yachting today instead of learning how to cook.

"Heads up!" Aunt Matilda said. "Here he comes."

I saw a tall figure standing just outside the kitchen doorway. Our master chef had paused to give instructions to his kitchen crew. My classmates instinctively huddled closer together to collectively assess the man.

"Ooh, he's so good-lookin'. I don't know how I'm gonna keep my mind on the cookin'!" whispered Lola, a thin, ultra-tanned rich widow from Dallas with expensively highlighted hair and lots of gold glinting on her neck, arms and fingers.

"He's a big fella, i'nt he?" her tall, good-natured brother Ben added with some surprise.

It was true; unlike many TV personalities who turn out to be smaller and thinner than they appear onscreen, Gilby Halliwell was bigger and beefier, looking healthy and athletic in a crisp white chef's jacket and black pants. The only indication of his celebrity status was the perfect cut of his blond hair. We eyed Chef Gil—as his staff called him—with wary fascination.

My classmates had parsed many details about him over dinner last night. So now I knew that Gil, a working-class English bloke from Manchester, had overcome a troubled youth of petty crime and reform school by apprenticing with an impressive list of French chefs working in London. When he was hired by a posh hotel to update their Grill Room it soon became a trendy success, which, with his appealing goods led to a quirky little British TV show that got picked up in the States by a food channel.

But then he'd burned out just as quickly. There'd been some gossip about why he disappeared from sight for awhile—an affair with a partner's wife, lawsuits, a nervous breakdown resulting in the abrupt closing of his popular London restaurant.

The press reacted to his unexpected departure by writing him off as just another "flash in the sauté pan" as one wag put it. But two years later he surprised the culinary world with a roaring comeback, winning a Michelin star within a scant year of opening this new restaurant here in Mougins, a formidable *gastronomie* hub where the competition for great places to dine was fierce.

And, never one to rest on his laurels, Gil then announced he'd found a silent partner to help him expand this stone *mas* or farmhouse where we were staying into a fully updated hotel, which would reopen later this year. To further publicize his ambitious plans, he was offering these cooking classes.

"All right, boys and girls!" he exclaimed to us as he moved away from his staff and came into our midst. Immediately his raw energy— he practically crackled with electricity—dominated the room, and a sudden hush fell over the group. He quickly checked off everyone's name on his clipboard, formally welcoming us by asking the students about our "goals". I mumbled something about wanting to learn about my grandmother's cuisine and culture.

We had three "boys" and four "girls" enrolled in the class—ludicrous to call them that, I realized; for it occurred to me now that Chef Gil and I were the only people in this room who were under the age of seventy. He was strutting like a peacock. So damned sure of himself.

"Eyes on me, now!" he said emphatically, putting aside his clipboard and clapping his hands together like the captain of a rugby team. As if we weren't already raptly attentive! "This is the kitchen of my restaurant, *Pierrot*. Here you will learn some basic cookery—and more importantly, the local *At*-ti-tude toward food, which makes Provençal cuisine so fantastic. So now, to your battle stations!"

He gestured at a long, shiny aluminum counter in the center of the kitchen, where his staff had been quietly arranging seven bowls of eggs lined up in front of seven empty mixing bowls, seven folded aprons and seven sets of knives. "It's spring, a time of rebirth. Easter and whatnot, eh? It all begins with the egg," he said, holding up one. "Today you're going to learn the proper way to crack—and cook—eggs. Like so."

With a swift move Gil deftly demonstrated how to make a single clean crack using only one hand. "A truly *fresh* egg will break clean, and should never shatter into bits of shells," he declared, "unless you are a total screw-up. Put on your aprons. Stand at the ready. And now—get cracking!"

The large kitchen echoed with the sound of multiple eggs breaking. Anyone who giggled or chattered was sternly silenced by our master chef as he paced watchfully around the kitchen, ready to pounce on those who tried to cheat by using both hands.

He caught me as I was surreptitiously banging my egg against the side of the bowl in front of me. "Dear-oh-dear," he sighed. "You say you came here because your French *grand-mère* was a chef from this area. Well, if only poor Grandma could see you now. Do it over."

Gingerly I picked up a new egg.

"God, Céline!" Gil said in exasperation. "It's not *hard*. Just concentrate, for fuck's sake."

I was now sorry I'd told Gil anything personal in response to his cozy little questions about my "goals"; he clearly wasn't averse to using such information as a weapon. I began thinking about how I'd like to roast this rooster of a man. When one of his staff appeared in the doorway with a message for him, and Gil stepped away momentarily to listen, Aunt Matilda murmured to me, "Congratulations. You got the first F-word out of him. I knew he couldn't hold back forever."

"Big tough guy! He doesn't scare me," I said sourly. Until now I'd been so focused on my mother that I hadn't noticed I'd signed on to a cooking class with just the kind of aggressive, cocksure, in-your-face man whom I normally wanted nothing to do with. All the bluster and bullying invariably evoked residual memories of my dad.

Gil was making another sweep past my section now, and, unable to bear seeing me screw up again, he seized my hand in his big paw and manipulated my fingers as if I were his puppet, forcing me to break the egg properly. I was surprised to feel how tough and scarred his fingers were; yet they moved with the dexterity and precision of a jeweler. Miraculously the eggshell opened perfectly.

Then, as the egg slid out, he let go, like a man who's been holding on to your bicycle but now quietly releases you to pedal away on your own. The slippery egg landed with a quiet *plop!* in the copper bowl, while I still held the shell, which I could now throw away in triumph.

"Wow," I said, impressed in spite of myself.

"Wow yourself," he said with a nod. "Do it again. And again." He moved away, calling out, "Clean up your work-stations as you go, people!" So, we spent the morning making eggs. We boiled. We fried. We poached (with vinegar in the water). We scrambled, first with butter, then oil, to compare taste and texture. We flipped omelettes in the air (mine landed right on my forearm). We made eggs *fines herbes* with parsley, thyme, chives, marjoram. And we discovered an herb called borage, whose leaves had a cucumber taste and got chopped up into delicate hard-boiled-egg sandwiches. The herb's deep blue flowers were beautiful and edible.

"Medieval ladies used to float borage flowers in the wine cups of their knights, to give them courage," Gil announced with a knowing nod and a wink.

"This guy just thinks the world of himself," I muttered to Aunt Matilda.

"I like him anyway," she replied, as if she'd already assessed Gil's assets and liabilities.

Gil then announced that we were now taking a field trip to a farmers' market in Antibes. He led us outside where, in the brilliant sunlight, the gardeners were hard at work at the longer end of this L-shaped *mas,* pruning and watering all the beautiful flowers and herb shrubs that lined the curving paths along the terraced spa, pool and restaurant with its big gravel parking lot.

"This way," he said, briskly trotting us down a winding path that snaked past the oldest section of the *mas*—the shorter end of the "L"—where construction workers were doing the renovating. We could hear the shrill whine of their drills amid all the other banging and hammering.

The sight of their progress energized Gil even further, if that were possible. "The crew has to get as much work done as they can before the summer season officially begins," he explained, waving back to the construction supervisor, a man in a hard hat who was shouting at his men. "What a job it is! The previous owner was a very traditional French dairyman who lived to a ripe old age but never changed a ruddy thing around here."

We were all herded into a white van, which lurched down the great winding front drive and then around several traffic circles in Mougins, before we finally picked up the highway that took us down to the elegant coastline and the town of Cannes, where beautiful hotels faced the beaches.

"Look, there's the Carlton Hotel, where Grace Kelly and Cary Grant went to the beach in *To Catch a Thief*!" Aunt Matilda exclaimed, nudging me in the ribs with her pointy elbow, as she craned her neck and snapped pictures madly. She had popped on a big straw hat and movie-star sunglasses. The view of grand old hotels, stylish cars, palm trees, striped umbrellas, the sea nibbling at the shoreline, and a few intrepid sailboats lazily crossing the harbor all contributed to a sense of luxurious pleasure.

We zipped onward to the peninsula of Antibes that jutted out to the Mediterranean Sea. Two main towns clung to this peninsula—on the west coast lay Grandmother Ondine's hometown of Juan-les-Pins; but our destination was on the east coast, in the actual town of Antibes.

"Look alive now, and follow me!" Gil boomed as we dismounted from the van onto a busy road in a densely built town. I glanced around, trying to get my bearings. Immediately he marched us through a warren of streets that were small and narrow, even crooked, and crammed with ancient buildings and mysterious shops. "This is the 'old town' section of Antibes. We're going to market. Open your eyes, but more importantly, use your nose! Use every sense you've got. Remember, this is the land that inspired Picasso, Matisse, Goethe and Browning and even bloody Nietzsche. Now it's your turn to be inspired because *you're* cooking tonight." He continued at a breathless pace, marching us beyond the touristy shops, to an enormous iron arcade with a bustling hubbub of food stalls.

"This farmers' market is where the best chefs load up their pantries for the villas and yachts of the richest clients in the world," he proclaimed as he steered us from one awe-inspiring stand to another while jostling with savvy regulars. When we reached the fish stall, it was impressively piled high with the catches of the day.

Abruptly Gil stopped and whirled around to face us. "If you could pick only one fish dish you'd like to learn to cook while you're here, what would it be?" he demanded, rocking forward on the balls of his feet like a tennis player about to launch a serve. Most of us froze on the spot.

"Bouillabaisse," Aunt Matilda volunteered, nodding at me, having just seen this recipe in Grandma Ondine's notebook. I was glad now that I hadn't told her about Picasso; she was not by nature a secretive soul and she might have blurted it right out, here and now, to the entire class.

"Ah!" Gil exclaimed. "A true Provençal meal and definitely a challenge worth pursuing. All together now, let's hear each one of you say it, *bouillabaisse,"* he exhorted, cocking his head expectantly.

"Bweeya-base," everyone chorused hopefully.

Gil sighed mightily. "Historically speaking, there are at least forty varieties of seafood that you can use for this meal. And a proper *bouillabaisse* must contain at least five to a dozen kinds of fish."

"Golly," said Magda, looking worried for the first time.

"Say hello to a *rascasse,* the world's most venomous species of fish, which can sting you with its killer mucus," Gil announced with relish, holding up a spiky orange-and-white scorpion fish.

"You're just teasing, right?" Lola said worriedly. "Am I right?"

Gil had already moved on, selecting an assortment of more familiar, fleshy fish. "We'll do a variation on the basic Marseilles version of *bouillabaisse*. People up and down the Mediterranean all do it a bit differently," he explained enthusiastically. "The Spanish call it *sabeta* and they use more peppers."

I perked up, for he'd just echoed exactly what I'd read in Grandmother Ondine's leather-bound cookbook. Many of her recipes—all written in French of course—had notes at the end for future improvements. For the *bouillabaisse* she'd written what I'd translated as: *Nota bene: More peppers next time.*

Gil paid the fishmonger and we carried our bulging bags of food back to the parking lot, where his French kitchen assistants were lounging by the side of the van enjoying a quick smoke. At the sight of Gil they sprang to attention, stubbed out their cigarettes and expertly gathered all our bags, quickly putting the fish and other perishables into silver coolers full of bagged ice.

"Okay, class, my staff will take these fabulous groceries back to the *mas*. The bus will return here to pick you all up," Gil announced. "You may use this time to gather-ye-souvenirs-while-ye-may."

A sudden strong breeze leapt up, causing several identical banners along the road to flap and snap overhead like the sails of a boat. We all glanced up: against each flag's black backdrop was the extraordinary face of Pablo Picasso, his dark eyes looking down on us with a piercing gaze that was both compelling and unsettling. The Riviera, I knew from my guidebook, always had a Picasso exhibit somewhere. This one was called *Picasso: Between the Wars and Between the Women*.

I gazed up at his image. His balding head made his high forehead seem even higher; his nose gave him a pugnacious air, yet his lips had a curl of amusement. *You're on my turf now,* he seemed to say.

"Just don't go to the Picasso exhibit," Gil said, "because I've already booked you guys into a terrific private tour next week! But there are plenty of other museums, historic sites, a ton of shops, and most importantly—lots of brilliant cafés and bistros. So make sure you eat lunch." He began handing out euros and vouchers for our meal.

We heard a sudden roar as one of his assistants arrived on a motorcycle. The guy was young and French and had apparently driven the bike over for Gil, who seemed to expect it and went walking over to take it. Gil peered at the big wristwatch on his arm. "All right, everybody. Be back here by three o'clock sharp. Everyone got the *mas*'s number on your phones? Good. Call if you get lost. But if you miss the bus"—he drew his finger across his neck as if slitting his throat—"then you're out of the class."

He clapped his hands loudly, startling a flock of pigeons hovering hopefully. "Time's a-wasting, so get on your marks, set, and—go!" he said, tapping his wristwatch. Relieved and released, we broke off into excited clusters, not really sure where to go but feeling we ought to put visible energy into the situation. Gil had already hopped onto his fire-engine-red motorbike, and now he zoomed off.

Joey broke the ice first. "Flickin' great Ducati," he said, impressed by the bike. With his Chicago accent, it sounded more like *Duh-cawh-ti.*

"Betcha he's got a girl in town to help him work out all that energy," Lola drawled wickedly. "After all, it's *siesta* time on the Med."

"That's Spanish, dear, not French," Ben pointed out in a gentle but pained attitude.

"Sweetie, it's all the same behind the shutters, no matter whatcha call it," Lola replied, as she and Ben, and Joey and Magda, headed directly for the town and its shops.

Meanwhile Peter was giving Aunt Matilda a sly look. "Care to have a go at the casino?"

What a perfect pair, I thought as she nodded enthusiastically.

"Want to join us for lunch, Céline?" Aunt Matilda asked.

"You guys go ahead. Think I'll do a little shopping," I fibbed, feeling Picasso's eyes staring down at us, as if he were reminding me of my true purpose in coming to the Côte d'Azur.

I was still clinging to my theory about why my mother had been so keen to return to the Riviera, based on what she'd said at Christmas. Certain words of hers now resonated in my thoughts, loud and clear: *Grandma told me that Picasso once gave her a picture.* What if Mom *had* chosen this guided tour as an excuse to come back and take one last look at Grandma Ondine's café—and maybe to search for her lost Picasso painting?

A long shot, perhaps. But up and down this Blue Coast, gamblers were dealing with tougher odds than this every day. Invigorated by all the energy emanating from these surroundings, I was now ready, willing and able to take a chance for Mom.

In fact, last night I'd gone online and tracked down a shop in Antibes where I could rent a bike. Now, feeling excited, I hurried over there, hopped onto a sturdy bicycle, and rented a GPS for cyclers. It told me precisely how to cut across the peninsula of Antibes—straight to that little town on the other coast called Juan-les-Pins, where Grandmother Ondine once lived.

15

Lost in Paradise: Céline in Juan-les-Pins

"YOU HAVE REACHED YOUR DESTINATION," MY GPS ANNOUNCED AFTER leading me into the heart of Juan-les-Pins—a bustling but smaller town with jazzy clubs alongside simple, tiny eateries, all mixed in among souvenir and clothing shops, yet not far from elegant old hotels and residences. Baffled, I found a small low-walled turnaround at the end of a main road where I could park my bike and lock it on a rack.

Then I set off on foot, heading for the smaller enclaves of narrow streets, secretive and sequestered, with no visible numbers on the buildings. The stone houses were huddled together, casting a cool shade, their first-floor windows shuttered tightly against prying eyes like mine, so impenetrable that I began to worry. For all I knew, Grandma's café could have been razed to the ground.

Hastily I dug into my bag, pulled out Grandmother Ondine's notebook and consulted the letter she'd sent Mom that was tucked in a back leather flap. The words *Café Paradis* were embossed on the envelope and so was the street name, which was how I'd gotten this far. The printed drawing on the letter's stationery gave me a fairly good idea of what Grandmother Ondine's café looked like.

I took it out now and studied it more closely, noting how the trian-gular dining terrace, with its pretty striped awning saying *Café Paradis,* was angled against the charming building, making it distinctive. I walked on, and then, right around the corner, I thought perhaps I'd found it. A small neighborhood café occupied the ground floor of a honey-colored limestone house, and had a triangular terrace.

But something *was* different, I thought. Then I saw that it was because these tables had umbrellas over them, instead of that big striped awning that said *Café Paradis* on it. Still, this *could* be it.

I sat at a table and used one of Gil's vouchers to order lunch. The waiter studied it, then showed it to the maître d', who shrugged and nodded. My fellow diners looked like locals, with only a smattering of tourists. There was no menu; you got the lunch of the day, served in simple dishes of pale yellow pottery trimmed with bright blue, and little roosters and hens decorating the outer edges.

As I waited there, the dappled sunlight crept across the terrace and sneaked under my umbrella in a friendly way. The first course was a small bowl of curried mussel soup, for which I had no great expectations. But when I ate it, I couldn't help a small gasp of pleasure; I never knew a mussel could be so tender. An older man dining at the next table heard me and smiled, then returned to his newspaper.

The second course was a "blue lobster" which seemed more like a big shrimp. It came dressed in a mushroom gratin, accompanied by a row of thin *haricots verts*. I felt as if I were tasting my first string bean and my first lobster and my first mushroom. My mother had tried to tell me about this more than once. She'd said, *There is a thing called "terroir". It's the soil, water and air where the vine, vegetable, bird or animal put its feet when it grew up. If you take the same vine or seed to another country, it simply will not taste the same, under another land's sun.* I found myself wistfully wishing that Mom could be here with me to enjoy this meal.

The next plate contained a slice of duck *confit* with a sweet-and-sour orange sauce; followed by a delicate salad and a modest-looking assortment of tiny rounds of cheese, one of which was a goat's cheese wrapped in freshly ground pine nuts. I had my own little half-carafe of house wine, a chilled pale rosé with hints of peach and berry. Again and again, I felt my taste buds reawakening—after a long, Rip van Winkle–like slumber of grabbing indifferent take-out food at work. Even though Mom had cooked these recipes, the French ingredients had their own distinct character. And so this meal kept surprising me, enhanced by the atmosphere of salty sea air, a seductive sun, and wine as cool as a hidden stream.

Maybe I was gripped with gourmet delirium, or maybe the wine just went to my jet-lagged head. Whatever it was, I felt emboldened to resume my mission. I'd noticed an alleyway alongside the café, where a few deliverymen came and went, carrying boxes. As I rose to leave, something compelled me to go back there, bypassing the front entrance.

I found a cozy yard where a tiny patio was dominated by an enormous pine tree whose big twisty arms reached out so far, they embraced the whole garden; and its gnarly roots were popping out of the ground, bringing up some patio stones with it.

"Look at the size of that thing!" I marvelled. I had seen a smaller version of such a tree back at the *mas,* when the concierge gave us a tour. He'd said it was called an Aleppo pine.

A small grey cat sat on the stone wall that encircled the tree, and I paused to pet its inquisitive head. When a breeze rustled softly through the pine's boughs like a whisper, I was gripped by a strange familiarity that gave me goosebumps. Was it *déjà vu*? I'd certainly never been here before, yet there was something about that big twisty tree, the low stone wall bordering it, and the silky cat purring beside me.

Suddenly a chef flung open the back door to relieve the heat, and I heard the clatter of dishes being washed. The chef, a short, red-faced, sweaty man dressed in stained whites, was taking a cigarette break. He puffed away, gazing at the sky, until he spotted me, half-hiding behind the big tree.

"*Mademoiselle?*" he called out, looking faintly alarmed.

Quickly I went over to him and praised his excellent cooking. Then I explained that my grandmother had once cooked here in this very café. "*J'aimerais voir la cuisine de ma grand-mère,*" I said as winsomely as I could. The chef was clearly one of those guys who doesn't expect younger women to give him a second look, so he seemed immensely flattered by my interest in him and his kitchen. With a pleased shrug, he threw down his cigarette, opened the door and let me in.

The kitchen was blanketed with hot, moist air. Waiters and cooking staff rushed in and out, dodging around each other in the crowded space, which was smaller and much more modernized than I expected. There was an industrial stove and oven, and shiny open aluminum shelves all stacked with pots and pans, bowls and other cooking apparatus. I saw at a glance that there was really nothing here that could ever have belonged to Grandma Ondine. And certainly no place to hide a Picasso.

The chef ushered me out now to the front of house, a formal dining room, which, while empty of guests, had busboys already laying out white tablecloths and gleaming silverware for tonight's dinner service. *"C'est bon?"* the chef asked. I nodded and thanked him, and he disappeared back into his kitchen. Looking for an excuse to linger, I asked the bartender for an espresso from the great gold machine he had there.

Sipping my coffee, I glanced across the room at a lovely antique framed mirror in which my own image looked a bit ghostly, as if I, too, had stepped out of the past and could disappear right back into it.

When I'd first hatched this scheme back home, I'd been filled with maniacal confidence that finding Grandma's Picasso would be a simple matter of strolling into town, locating her café and casually ransacking it. Now the whole thing seemed extremely quixotic, to say the least.

But what about the upstairs rooms? I'd seen their windows from the street, decorated with wrought-iron grillwork, just like the picture on Grandma's letterhead. That would be where she'd lived. As I glanced across the dining room, the maître d' wandered into the kitchen, giving me an opportunity to get past his abandoned podium; so that was the moment when I decided it was now or never.

"Where is the ladies' room?" I asked the barman. He pointed to a red *Exit* sign at the far corner of the room. With this excuse I headed that way, where two restrooms had framed signs for *Les Dames* and *Les Messieurs*. As I'd guessed, a short nearby hallway led to a staircase, roped off by a red velvet sash with a sign hanging in the middle of it that said *Private* in three languages.

I glanced over my shoulder, then quickly stepped over the rope and climbed the stairs, my heart pounding with guilt. I paused at the second-floor landing, until I heard the heavy tread of footsteps coming up the stairs behind me. *The only way out is deeper in,* I thought. I scampered up a shorter flight of stairs to the third-floor landing just seconds before a heavyset woman appeared in the hallway below, panting from the effort of carrying something. I ducked into the attic room and froze, listening to the mechanized droning of a vacuum cleaner as the maid dragged it noisily all around the second-floor corridor. She was going to be awhile, which meant that I was trapped on the third floor.

This attic room was being used as a storage area, with old, rolled-up café umbrellas, and wicker chairs stacked in a tower. Other boxes contained extra plates, cups and saucers that looked as if they'd come from a restaurant closeout sale. There was absolutely no Picasso here, nor anything that could have belonged to Grandmother Ondine. It felt lonely, as if an altar's candle had been blown out.

Several minutes passed before the maid below switched off her machine for good and, breathing heavily, went down the stairs taking the vacuum cleaner with her. Cautiously I descended to the second floor, and dutifully peered into a small, very simple guest room: bed, table, lamp, shelves, no closet at all.

I moved on to the master bedroom, which was more opulent, containing a king-sized brass bed and a large flat TV screen mounted on the opposite wall. I kept hearing my mother's voice ringing in my ears: *Grandma did have her little hiding places for her valuables—and I remember a secret storage area under a closet floor, where during the wars her parents hid the café's best champagne from the German soldiers.*

But there wasn't any closet here. The only antique piece of furniture was a large walnut armoire. I discovered it was nearly empty, with just two pristine red terrycloth bathrobes on padded hangers; and on the shelf above were a few spare pillows and blankets. I checked carefully for any trick drawers or secret compartments, but found none.

The thought struck me that if Mom was wrong about a closet, she could have been wrong about a Picasso, too. Maybe this whole trip was just a fantasy, after all.

For in the brilliant Riviera light, it seemed as if the present day was obliterating the past; not only Grandma Ondine's world, but Mom's, too. I'd wanted so badly to rescue her that I'd pinned all my hopes on this wild quest. To my surprise, I gave a little sad gulp and my eyes welled up with tears.

It was just reality finally setting in, I concluded. Maybe I had to cross an ocean to face it.

Then I heard a loud, authoritative male voice on the stairs. I glanced around wildly. There was no other exit, so I had no choice. I ducked into the armoire, and pulled its door closed after me.

I barely made it in time. A man entered the bedroom and walked right past my hiding place with such a heavy tread that everything shook a little as he passed—including the armoire with me in it. He must have snapped on the TV, because suddenly the room was filled with loud romantic music sung in French. I thought I heard water running in the bathroom. As the minutes ticked by, I was agonizingly trying to decide if I could slip out and make a break for it.

Just as I was preparing to peek out, the door of the armoire was abruptly yanked open. Blinding sunlight poured in from behind a tall man with a big belly who stood there stark naked, dripping wet.

"La-*LA*!" he exclaimed, taking a step backward in astonishment. He was a bald fellow with a high forehead that made his face look like a fist with eyes. His large stomach was overhanging, and therefore slightly obscuring, the rest of his equipment. He hadn't even bothered to grab a towel from the bathroom; he'd simply made a beeline for the terrycloth bathrobes hanging beside me.

"*Bonjour,*" I said, idiotically handing him a robe as I hastily stepped out of the armoire.

"*Qui êtes-vous?*" He frowned suspiciously, grabbing my arm with a grip like an iron clamp. Then Mr. Naked—he still hadn't put on the damned robe yet—threw back his head and shouted, "*Au voleuse!*"

"I am *not* a thief!" I objected involuntarily. Even when I said it again in French, he shouted once more. Now the maid reappeared with a slew of restaurant workers behind her, including the maître d'. Mr. Naked had finally put on that bathrobe and he screamed at his staff what sounded like a French slang version of "*You* deal with this!" before he stomped back into the bathroom and slammed the door.

Apparently, I had just met the owner of the café. The maître d' was exclaiming into a tiny mobile phone, and although I never heard him say the word *Police,* it wasn't long before I heard the wail of sirens outside the café. Still, the whole thing had the quality of a bad dream, so I couldn't believe I was truly "in the soup"—not until the maître d' said curtly to me, "*Mademoiselle,* follow me, please."

We marched downstairs past the velvet rope, into the dining room, where two uniformed cops were waiting for *me*. "Oh, God," I said to myself, hastily reaching for my phone to call Aunt Matilda.

She didn't answer. I remembered that she was at the casino with her newfound boyfriend. She'd probably shut off her phone to save money overseas. After a moment's hesitation, I called the number Gil gave us in case we got lost. Maurice, the concierge, answered.

"I'm in trouble," I confessed. "I think I'm about to be arrested."

16

Céline and Gil in Juan-les-Pins

NOTHING CAN PREPARE YOU FOR THE TERRIFYING EXPERIENCE OF BEING accused of a crime—especially when you can't tell anyone the whole truth. *I came here to steal a Picasso, Officer.* I tried to convince the French policemen and the café owner that I'd trespassed upstairs simply to see the room where my grandmother lived. I don't think this convinced anybody, least of all Chef Gil, who showed up just in the nick of time—looking really, really pissed off.

He said he'd been in Antibes checking in with a restaurant-supply shop which was going to provide him with new uniforms for his waiters. So when Maurice frantically called him, Gil hopped onto his motorcycle and came zipping over here to do damage control, because, as Aunt Matilda later put it, "It wouldn't look so great for Gil if one of his cooking students got thrown in the clink."

He argued valiantly on my behalf. For awhile it looked pretty bad for me, since the police viewed Gil as a flashy English chef with a troublemaking girlfriend. Apparently, just a week before, a busboy from this café had been arrested for selling drugs. So the owner of the place—the naked guy who found me in his armoire—naturally assumed the worst. They even searched the rooms upstairs looking for—what? Drugs, diamonds, counterfeit money?

"They don't really think I'm some kind of drug mule, do they?" I asked, horrified.

As we argued, the cops kept making impatient gestures toward me as if ready to put me in handcuffs. But Gil persevered with calm reasoning that enticed the older cop into an animated discussion of my actions in particular and foreigners in general.

"C'est une vraie Américaine—naïve!" Gil insisted, pleading with the fat, still-damp owner of the café to be *raisonnable*. Finally the owner threw up his hands in disgust, ordering us to never set foot in his café again. The police looked as if they were still considering hauling me off in chains, and I pictured myself locked in that prison fort on an island off Cannes where the Man in the Iron Mask was sequestered.

"Come on, let's go before they change their minds," Gil hissed. We had to walk past the sidewalk terrace where curious onlookers were thronging, aiming camera phones at us as we left.

Gil quickly put on his sunglasses, looking exactly like what he was—a local celeb caught in a bad scene. He jumped on his motorcycle and I stalked off, heading for the spot where I'd parked my rented bike. I heard Gil start up his Ducati, but I didn't realize at first that he was following me.

"*Now* where do you think you're going?" he snapped when I paused to unhook my bike. The little stone cul-de-sac was like an oasis, shady, cool and calm. I put up my kickstand and wheeled my bicycle out, still breathing hard but trying to calm down as I sat on it.

"I have to get this bike back to the rental shop in Antibes," I said, not bothering to hide my irritation. Gil had a bossy attitude which was really starting to grate on me, even if he had just saved my neck.

"Hold on! Once you drop the bike in Antibes, how are you going to get back to Mougins?" he demanded, grabbing the back wheel of my bicycle as I began to pedal away, causing me to clutch at the handlebars. Immediately the whole bike lurched to one side, and my bag slipped out of the basket.

The outer compartment fell open—and out dropped Grandmother Ondine's notebook, which I'd stuffed back in there hastily after consulting it for her letter with the café's address. Now the whole thing lay open, right there on the pavement.

"Damn! Look what you've done!" I exclaimed, leaping off the bicycle and letting it crash to the ground. The wind was already tearing at the delicate pages.

Gil sprang into action and scooped it up. "What's up with you, Céline?" he asked impatiently. "My assistants were worried—they sent me a message saying everybody else got on the bus except you."

"So I'm out of the class?" I said distractedly. "Well, I assure you, I never was chef material anyway," I added with false bravado. I sat on the stone curb to assess any damage to the notebook that Gil now handed me. The envelope was still tucked in the back. I carefully checked the pages to see if any of them had come loose.

"Hoo, what's *this*?" he asked with sudden interest, snatching a runaway page from the curb. "No plans to be a chef, my ass!" He glanced over my shoulder and saw that the notebook in my lap contained other recipes. "Obviously you're writing a cookbook? Or opening a restaurant?"

"Frankly it's none of your business," I retorted.

"Hell, it's cooking and that *is* my business. Most teachers would think you've been stealing their recipes. It wouldn't be the first time that's happened to me." His eyes narrowed suspiciously as if he still half-believed that I was some sort of culinary spy. Why else would I skulk around other people's cafés?

"You *wish* these were your recipes!" I countered. "They're my grandmother's. I bet she could out-cook you any day."

"Really?" Giving me his million-wattage smile he added, "Can I have another look?" I sensed an opportunity and I took advantage of it.

"If you let me stay in the cooking class, I'll let you see these," I coaxed in my most charming, winning way. "But you must swear on your Michelin star that you won't steal them."

He held my gaze when he said meaningfully, "You promise no more wandering off the reservation? I'm not some hotel concierge who fixes parking tickets and drunk-driving arrests. Got it?"

"Yeah, sure. Fine," I said a bit stiffly. That whiff of paternalism again really grated on me.

"Right," he replied enthusiastically, sitting down beside me now. I reopened the notebook, wondering if he could possibly shed some light on it. He studied it eagerly, then turned a few more pages. "Wow," he said admiringly. "Wow-ee wow-wow." I saw a glimmer of his wolfish ambition.

"Are they good?" I asked, curious now.

"Nice. Very nice," he replied, hungrily scanning a few pages. "Traditional Provence, but with a slightly different twist here and there. Could be regional. Could just be the times your grand-mum lived in. Mmm, nice *cassoulet*. And here's a genuine *coq au vin* made with the rooster's blood to get that dark sauce—and decorated with his comb and his kidneys," he said enthusiastically.

"Yuck," I said inelegantly.

"She uses a carrot to sweeten it," he said, more to himself now, "and lots of thyme. Huh, and a sprinkle of homemade red vermouth made with Alpine herbs. That's interesting."

I closed the notebook, and Gil glanced up as if waking from a spell. "You still haven't explained what the bloody hell you were doing sneaking around upstairs in that café. What exactly were you looking for?"

"I can't tell you," I said quietly, "because it's something my mother told me in confidence. She never had a chance to come back here for—um, closure," I said, being deliberately vague now, "so I did it for her. I hope you understand."

He gave me a searching look, then said, "Okay, obviously you've got some emotional connections here. But the last thing I need right now is the local police giving me the fish-eye when I'm applying for business permits! Not to mention the bloody tourists snapping pictures on their phones so they can be the first to blab about us on the Internet before I even open the doors of my hotel."

"I'm sorry," I said, and I meant it. But I couldn't resist trying to lighten things up by adding, "I thought all publicity was good publicity."

He scowled. "Not in business circles! Investors hate notoriety. Looks too unstable. *Nothing* must jeopardize the reopening of the hotel. My employees are depending on me to succeed—and if I don't, it won't be easy for them to find other jobs. So I can't let anyone screw it up by doing something reckless or stupid," he added meaningfully.

"Okay, okay," I said. I was ready to get on a plane right now and go home.

Gil saw my discouraged look. "Brace up," he said briskly, looking at his watch. "I'll follow you to your bicycle shop and then I'll run you back home to the *mas*."

So I pedaled on the road that crossed the peninsula to Antibes, with Gil puttering on his Ducati behind me, and all that traffic roaring around us. The bike-shop people looked glad to see me, perhaps worried that I'd run off with one of their cycles since I was late. I paid them, then returned to Gil.

He gave me his helmet and started up the bike without waiting. "Right, hop on!" he shouted above the roar of the motor. I had no choice but to slide onto the bit of seat behind him, clasp my arms around his waist, and try to keep my legs safely away from any hot metal or the steaming exhaust pipe.

Hanging on to Gil's broad chest I tried not to notice that he smelled agreeably of sweat, aftershave and laundered shirt, a mingling of bergamot, citrus and spice. With a roar we took off, bypassing the main, shorter route because it was now thoroughly choked with traffic. Gil had chosen a much more scenic road that wound around the coast at the Cap d'Antibes.

It was the first time I'd really absorbed—into my flesh as well as my thoughts—that here I was, in one of the most beautiful spots on the Mediterranean, with its green hills, rocky coves, palm trees, and tucked-away beaches at the edge of the deep blue sparkling sea.

The wind that blew against my face whooshed all my troubled thoughts right out of my head. My heart felt glad for the first time in many months. And as we whirled around the curves and coves, past steep hills with half-hidden villas tucked behind tall, pastel walls, I could just picture Grandmother Ondine carrying a basket of food up these mysterious roads—just a young slip of a girl, with long, flowing dark hair spiraling in rippling tendrils—like a mermaid rising up from the sea, and bearing all sorts of wonderful things for Pablo Picasso to eat.

17

Ondine and Picasso, Antibes 1936

SUMMER WAS COMING. IT WASN'T HERE YET, BUT IT WAS ON ITS WAY, AND everyone could feel it. The villagers of Juan-les-Pins were behaving like happy animals awakening after a winter slumber, tilting their heads up to the sun, their nostrils flaring, all the better to breathe in the soft, salty, healthy, sun-warmed air, their voices giddy with the delight of casting off their woolens and no longer having to brace themselves against the wind.

Already the first of the yachting sailboats were drifting lazily across the sea. Soon, more visitors would be arriving—the rich young things looking for fun, eager to be naughty, drinking and dancing at the casinos, frolicking openly with one another's husbands at the beach. Ondine, along with the other locals, usually viewed these fair-weather guests with a mixture of scorn and wistfulness for such carefree, even careless lives. Now she found them utterly predictable.

But Ondine never knew what to expect from Picasso—or even from herself when she was with him. Two days ago, she'd been in his bed, and then posing for a portrait! Yesterday he'd greeted her warmly—with just enough of a twinkle in his eyes to let her know that she still pleased him, making her feel that she was still his goddess— and when he'd eaten his lunch he complimented her, patted her shoulder fondly. Then he became preoccupied with his mail, which he carried upstairs, deeply engrossed. "Business," was all he said to her on his way up, shaking his head with a scowl. She didn't dare ask if he'd finished her portrait. She wasn't really worried about that—nor anything else under the sun.

For, amazingly, all she felt was this new strength, even a supreme confidence, about everything. The future and her destiny, her beauty and desirability, even the benevolence of the world at large—suddenly it all seemed possible, all spread out before her, full of wonderful opportunities like a buffet from the gods. This must be what it felt like to be rich, she told herself. Yet Ondine could see that it wasn't only money that did this for you. Such a joyous surge of confidence came from feeling you knew people who understood and valued you.

It was almost like love; not the kind you had when you were a child and got a lullaby to reassure you while you remained subject to the whims of adults. No, this feeling of triumph had no guarantees of stability, no net beneath the high wire; and yet, it was your own, so it was fiercer. If you took it by the reins, it made you strong. She could sense this with an astonishing certainty.

Today, as Ondine cycled to the end of her street, her jubilant thoughts were disrupted when a farmer in a donkey cart blocked her path. The man wore an old floppy straw hat and a brown jacket whose large collar was pulled up around his ears, making his head seem sunk into his shoulders without benefit of a neck in between. The donkey was already sweating from his efforts on this warm day, and he smelled, well, very donkey-ish. Ondine wrinkled her nose, impatient for him to clear the way.

"*Allez, allez, mon ami,*" the farmer growled to his donkey in a scratchy voice.

Exasperated, Ondine stopped pedaling and waited for him to pass. But now the driver drew his wagon even nearer, leaning far over and reaching out to pinch her cheek. "Can you keep a secret, young lady?" he said in a stage whisper. Now that voice was all too familiar.

"*Patron?*" Ondine whispered back in disbelief. Picasso howled with glee.

"Well, if my disguise can fool you, it can fool anybody!" he proclaimed, waggling his eyebrows. He had an unusually festive air, like a truant schoolboy. "Today, I'm not going to work. So, throw your bicycle and your hamper in the back and hop on! We're going to Antibes for the parade of the Virgin."

Seeing him in the flesh again had a strange effect on her; she suddenly felt shy. The tumult of their lovemaking came rushing back to her now like a memory stored in her body, not her mind. She could feel herself flushing with both pleasure and embarrassment. So many other mysterious emotions came tumbling all around her that for a moment she had to steady herself.

Yet something about Picasso's over-hearty behavior today was unnerving. He still had a twinkle in his eye as his gaze roved over her approvingly. But when she hesitated he became impatient, jumped down and helped her lift the bicycle into the cart before he returned to his seat. He wasn't drunk, just cheerful and animated. His enthusiasm was so infectious that she climbed aboard. Picasso flapped the reins, and the donkey continued plodding on.

"Where did you get this cart?" Ondine asked, still bewildered by this carnival atmosphere.

"I went for a walk into Juan-les-Pins this morning and saw a farmer with it. I asked if I might borrow it. I gave him enough to buy a better donkey, but he still wants it back."

Picasso looked delighted by the whole transaction. "I do prefer to travel in disguise," he said as they took the road that cut across the peninsula. "Perhaps you should, too. Let's see if there's anything in my ragbag you can wear. A hat? Or scarf? It sounds like a religious festival. Shouldn't you wear something on your head, as if you were in church?"

Ondine glanced dubiously at the sack behind their seat. Picasso reached in and pulled out an old purple shawl. "Put that on. Yes, much better," he said, half-approvingly and half-ironically. It was all a game to him, but he was so eager to share his pleasure that she didn't want to spoil it. He just wanted to have fun today, she concluded. After all, he worked so hard and unrelentingly.

Their donkey plodded along with other carts, wagons, trucks and autos that were bustling by in the everyday business of trundling flowers, fish and vegetables from one place to another. All around them rose the pine and palm trees, like supplicants stretching their arms up, up, up to the sun. When Picasso reached the old-town section of Antibes, he fearlessly steered his stalwart donkey through the jostling crowds of pedestrians. As they drew nearer the coast, Ondine could smell the salty tang of the breeze blowing in from the sea, and soon she saw the waves rushing to the shoreline.

"Look, over there," Picasso said, pointing at a small group of fishermen and their families, led by a priest in a solemn procession down to the sea, bearing a flower-bedecked statue of the Blessed Virgin. The women on the shoreline carried small candles; the children had baskets of blossoms which they scattered on the path. At the beach, a row of seashells were filled with sand to hold lighted candles upright, marking a path down to the water's edge. The fishermen brought their statue of the Madonna right into the water, with the waves lapping against the holy figure until they reached her neck. And then the sailors hoisted her aboard a boat.

"What's it all about?" Picasso asked.

Ondine said, "They are asking the Virgin Mary and the saints to bless their boats. There is a legend that three saints who witnessed the crucifixion of Christ were chased away from the Holy Land and put out to sea to die; but miraculously their boat washed ashore in the South of France, and ever since then the saints have favored us."

"Everyone wants to believe that God chose their land as especially holy," Picasso commented. "Well, you know, God is really only another artist. He invented the giraffe, the elephant, and the cat. He has no real style. He just goes on trying other things." Ondine smiled. On a day like today, she could certainly imagine God sitting up there in his studio, just like Picasso, frowning at his newest canvas.

Picasso paused, watching the procession in silence. He reminded Ondine of a man who, upon entering a church, dips his finger in the holy-water fountain and sits in a back pew to pray or think in silence. And like such a worshipper, a short time later, he responded to some interior signal that it was time to go. He flapped the reins and, turning the cart away from the festival, he drove it farther down the coast.

Presently Picasso noticed a group of young boys playing by the wall of an old castle surrounded by tumbled stones and overgrown weeds. He slowed the donkey and leaned out to ask the children, "What is this place where you play?"

"It's a secret," one said impudently. They were local kids, barefoot and happily dirty.

"I like secrets," Picasso replied. "But they are no fun unless you tell them to someone."

The children sized him up, then shrugged. One of them said casually, "You can come with us, but you must be quiet." Picasso parked at the side of the road and tied the donkey to a nearby tree.

"Come on, let's go," he said enthusiastically. "They look like they're having much more fun than the fishermen." Ondine, who'd grown up around kids like these, could not share his enthusiasm now.

"You go," she said. "I think I'd better watch the cart and the donkey and my things." She knew perfectly well what would happen to her if she returned home without that bicycle and hamper.

Picasso had already climbed down and followed the children. Ondine got out, stretched her legs and spoke soothingly to the donkey, but she did not pet him; his coat was scraggly with patches of dried mud he'd kicked up. But he seemed to like the sound of her voice, and listened intently as she kept saying things like, "Well, who knows if Picasso will ever come back? I hope those kids aren't little thieves. They didn't look so bad. Don't you think?"

Then she realized that she was spending her afternoon talking to a donkey. Her parents would never believe it, but of course, she would never tell them. In fact, she was enjoying pretending to be a farmer's wife with her donkey; so some of Picasso's whimsy had rubbed off on her.

When eventually he returned without the kids, he exclaimed, "Well, you should have come! They took me through a hole in the wall, and what a place! It's an old Roman fort. But now it's called the Château Grimaldi. They say it belonged to some medieval clan of rich cutthroats. Someone's turned it into a museum. But the castle has seen better days. Someday I'll come back here."

Picasso climbed into the cart and continued to drive along the coast, until he reached the parking lot of another beach, a much fancier one which catered to tourists in the summertime and had a scattering of white cabanas and striped umbrellas. He pulled in, stopped, and took off his hat. So Ondine shed her shawl, too. She covered her bicycle under the tarp in the back.

"Look at all the fine autos parked here! Nobody's going to steal our things at this place," Picasso assured her as they removed their shoes and made their way across the hot sand.

Today the beach had a smattering of visitors chattering in foreign tongues—some leftover Russians from the winter, a few hardy Germans and English, some early-bird Americans. One large French family was capering at the shoreline. A group of English young adults wore identical navy wool bathing costumes that made it hard to tell the men from the women, who were fashionably thin with short, boyish haircuts, so they all looked companionably androgynous in a Peter Pan, preadolescent way.

"I used to come here, years ago," Picasso commented. "These people today are not the crowd I knew. The Murphys—the Dos Passos—the Hemingways and Fitzgeralds—I like Americans, but it got to be a circus. The stock market crash chased a lot of them away."

Ondine was already feeling a trifle uneasy, for she recognized another French family camped under linden trees. Wasn't that the butcher's wife from the farmers' market, with all her kin?

Picasso pointed toward a row of brightly painted beach huts. "Do you know what a cabana is?"

"Yes, of course," Ondine said indignantly. "It's where you go to get changed."

He put his hand on her shoulder. "Yes," he whispered, "you go into that dark place to *change*. Some people go in and change their minds. Some change themselves—men turn into women, and women turn into men. Some go in young and come out old. Most go in respectable and come out pagan. It's like a magician's booth. Go on, I'd like to see what you change into! Here's my bag. There surely must be some swimsuits in it." He gave her a playful push.

Ondine was still struggling to understand her jumbled feelings and his strange antics. But maybe a swim would clear her head. She went inside. It was really just a simple shed, with very weak light that came from a tiny window, high up, and shone a bit through cracks in the slats of the wooden walls. There was a rough bench and some hooks on one wall, with other peoples' swimsuits in various stages of dampness or dryness. Dubiously, Ondine undressed and put her clothes on a hook.

Her eyes adjusted to the darkness as she opened the bag Picasso gave her. Why, it was the ragbag from his cart. She was so busy searching for swimsuits that she didn't hear the door of the cabana open, nor the man who crept in until he put his arms around her bare waist and kissed her quickly to keep her from involuntarily exclaiming. She recognized the scent of his flesh. Picasso whispered quickly, "It's only me, your secret lover. Of course, in the dark, you can't really be sure, can you?"

His hands were on both sides of her, tracing the curve of her naked body from breasts to hips, as if sculpting a figure 8, in a way that made her involuntarily shiver. Then he cupped her breasts, one in each hand, and whispered in her ear so close it tickled, "How many lovers has Ondine had? One, two, three? More?" He sat down on the bench and drew her hips to his mouth, kissing her delicately in that hairy place.

"Tell me how many lovers you've had," he demanded, and when she did not answer, his tongue began to probe her as he reached the petals of her sex.

"Ohhh!" she gasped, flushed with pleasure but embarrassed by the intimacy of it.

"How many, besides me?" he persisted.

"Oh—only one other," she whispered.

"Are you sure?" he asked, and then his tongue was probing harder and faster now.

"Yes!" she cried out.

"Shhh!" he said. He stood up and turned her around, pushing her forward so that she had to catch both hands against the wall to steady herself. His hands continued exploring her body. "You must be very quiet no matter how much you want to shout," he murmured. "Because if you cry out, all the men will come running to rescue you. But when they see you like this, they'll all want you, too. They'll each take you, one by one. I won't be able to stop them. So you must be silent, no matter what."

Along with the splash of the sea against the shore, Ondine could indeed hear the voices and shouts of people coming and going, running across the beach all around them. More people seemed to be arriving, judging by all the noise. Voices—and feet—clattered right past them. No one called out to Ondine and Picasso, no one knocked on the door while he was kissing her. Yet strangely, each time a voice went rushing past, she felt her pleasure increasing at the very perilous nature of their privacy.

He put his hand flat on her mouth. Then he put a finger into her lips, and she found herself sucking on it, unable to hold back. "Quiet, very quiet," he repeated, his other hand squeezing her buttocks and then reaching around to stroke her belly. "The little boys who play outside, do you know what they do when they see a beautiful woman go into a cabana? They creep up at the back of it and they peer through any hole in the wall they can find. Do you suppose they can see us now?"

Then suddenly he took her hips in his hands and drew her to him, bent her forward and entered her where she was already pulsing so desperately for him, so wet that he could plunge in deep enough to make them both gasp, and once again, she came before he left her.

For several moments in the dark, they leaned against the wall together, panting hard. Finally, when he spoke, it was with some humor. "I don't feel much like swimming right now, do you?"

Ondine shook her head. She suddenly felt she could not face that crowd on the beach, for surely they'd all know exactly what had transpired, and she didn't want to see it reflected on their faces. Especially if the butcher's wife was still there. The news would be all over town to-night, that she was Picasso's—or Ruiz's—whore. How would Ondine explain that to her parents?

"Well," said Picasso teasingly, "we could go back to the feast of the Virgin."

"No!" she exclaimed, feeling guilty at the thought of all that piety.

"Yes, I want to go home and paint," he said decisively.

As they emerged from the cabana, Ondine hesitated in the door-way until she thought nobody was looking. Picasso said a bit impa-tiently, "Why do you hang back like that? Come, let's go this way."

The donkey was still waiting for them, tied under the shade of a tree, chewing on some grass. Ondine and Picasso climbed aboard, and headed back for his villa. His manner was warm and reassuring as he asked her what she'd made for lunch and searched for a good spot to stop and eat it. She smiled and nodded, feeling flushed with physical pleasure. At last they found a quiet place to pull over and eat their lunch—*tartines* of spiced ham and cheese and roasted red peppers and young arugula. Feeling expansive, Picasso praised her cooking, look-ing deeply into her eyes, enough to make her blush with pride.

The food revived her, too, and she relaxed. In fact, Ondine realized that until now she'd gone through her entire life feeling all closed up within her body; but now it was as if she'd flung her arms open and wanted to embrace all the pleasures she saw—the open sky, the warm sun, the tumbling sea, the gulls calling out to her. That feeling of invin-cibility had returned; and yet, she also felt drowsy, as if sleep were an undertow she could barely resist.

When they reached Juan-les-Pins, Picasso yawned and said, "You can get off here. I have to return this cart, and I might sleep before I work today."

She dismounted from the cart and dragged her bicycle off it. He reached out a steadying hand, then caught one of hers, kissed it gently and said, *"Adieu, Ondine."* He placed his hand under her chin for a mo-ment, smiled, and then he was on his way.

18

The Wheel Turns: Ondine and Picasso

THE NEXT DAY THE BIRDS SINGING EXULTANTLY OUTSIDE HER WINDOW seemed to be calling to Ondine to awaken and hurry, hurry to greet the day. But she rose feeling unsettled and a bit guilty about that incident in the cabana, right on the Blessed Virgin's day! How had things gone so far? She realized that all this time she'd felt quite overwhelmed—first with the challenge of cooking and pleasing her *Patron* as her parents wanted; and then finding his free-spirited orbit so liberating from everyday life.

But now that the warm weather was bringing more people out and about in the streets, she couldn't take a chance of being paraded around in public as Picasso's girl. Did he expect her to be sexually available at his beck and call, whenever he felt like taking a day off? As exciting as it was, she didn't want to end up just another jealous woman in his harem, fighting tooth and claw over a man who, she was beginning to realize, didn't really take women seriously. The only thing sacred to him was his art, which was why she'd felt safer—and more exalted—as his model.

"I'll just have to tell him, I'll be his cook and his model, but not his concubine," she resolved.

Yet outside, she could feel that everything was suddenly in full flower, with every leaf, bud, bird, animal and human bursting with the thrill of being alive. She felt her heart beating joyfully in response. She was bringing Picasso a cold asparagus salad and grilled trout; and a pastry that would melt on his tongue, served with cream and delicate Alpine strawberries—tiny, juicy and sweet as candy.

As she cycled past the harbor she detected the distinct odor of wet paint. At first she imagined it was wafting down from Picasso's house. Then she saw that it was boat paint from the brushes of workmen on the summer yachts. When at last she pushed her bicycle through Picasso's gate, she felt a strange thrill. Would he paint her today? Would she relent and let him make love to her, after all?

Then she stopped short. The front door of the villa was wide open, and there was a truck parked in the driveway. Ondine had to veer around it to get to the side door. And when she entered the kitchen, a strange woman with a towel around her head was pushing a wet mop across the floor.

"What's this? Why are you here in my kitchen? I must cook now," Ondine said sharply.

The charwoman just kept mopping, speaking only to chide Ondine when she walked across the wet floor. Ondine went into the parlor. Men were coming down the stairs carrying boxes of paintings and the big metal lights. They moved heavily, quickly, as if in a great hurry, taking everything outside. Ondine felt a surge of panic, seeing all those familiar items like old friends now vanishing from her life.

"Where is Picasso?" Ondine cried.

One of the men, a younger one, stopped momentarily and said, "Who?"

Ondine recovered enough to correct herself. "Monsieur Ruiz." The young man shrugged with a smile of regret that he could not be more helpful to a pretty girl on a warm sunny day in May. Ondine rushed up the staircase, dodging the other men. Picasso's studio was completely emptied out. Already it had reverted to being an ordinary guest bedroom, with a brand-new bed and table standing where his easel used to be. In the next room, a laundress was stripping the linens off the very mattress where Ondine and Picasso had lain. "Are you the new tenant's maid?" the laundress asked doubtfully.

"No! I am Monsieur Ruiz's chef. Didn't he leave me a letter?" Ondine asked breathlessly.

The woman shook her head. "They never say goodbye," she said dryly. "It's like the circus when it leaves town. Just more trash for *us* to clean up."

Ondine searched every room herself. All signs of Picasso had evaporated into thin air. Not even a cigarette stubbed out in an ashtray. No jaunty little painted notes for her, no letter of recommendation. She'd half-expected to find it propped up against the fruit bowl. But even that was empty.

How could he just leave like that? she wondered with a hollow ache in the pit of her stomach. A single sob escaped her as a terrible thought occurred: *Nothing wonderful will ever happen to me again.*

She felt gutted, as if he'd taken the most vital part of her away with him. "He *can't* be gone for good," she whispered. But she recalled what now seemed like warning signs during their outing yesterday: parading around where he might be recognized by the crowds despite that ridiculous disguise; his festive air, as if the circus were in town—in fact, he'd behaved just as people do at the end of their holiday when they want to get all the fun they can out of their last day. And the way he'd taken her, in that dark cabana. Most of all, the way he'd said goodbye. Gently, regretfully. *Adieu*. Not his usual *au revoir* or *à demain*. Already his absence was palpable, leaving her absolutely nothing.

She dashed outside to the open back of the truck parked in the driveway, and without hesitation she climbed in among the curious moving men, insisting on examining every box of paintings. She had seen most of them before—but now there were some drawings of a new model who appeared over and over again—the photographer-lady, Miss Dora Maar, looking like a windswept force of nature with her sharp cat's eyes and pale skin contrasting dramatically against her fashionably cut dark hair.

Would anyone ever believe that Ondine herself had known Picasso, cooked for him, loved him, posed for him? She only wanted to see one painting. The one that was hers. The one that was no longer here.

"Where is it?" she exclaimed, rushing back into the house, hoping that the moving men hadn't found her *Girl-at-a-Window* yet. She frantically searched every closet until the charwoman told her to go home. Only then did Ondine think to ask for Picasso's address in Paris, but the woman shrugged.

Ondine whirled around and rushed down the stairs to ask the moving men, but even before she reached the front door, they'd already closed up their truck, backed it out of the driveway and sped off down the hill. By the time she hopped onto her bicycle and pedaled after it, the truck had vanished.

When she returned to the café, her mother told her that a man working for Picasso had telephoned just after Ondine left, to inform her father that their services were no longer required and assuring him that they would be paid. Her father had already calculated the bill; and somehow it was this gesture that finally convinced Ondine.

Picasso was definitely gone.

19

Shock of the New: Céline in the Old Town, 2014

A FEW DAYS AFTER I NEARLY GOT MYSELF ARRESTED, I DECIDED TO TAKE Aunt Matilda into my confidence about what I'd been searching for in Grandmother Ondine's café. But I had to swear her to secrecy, because my aunt was turning out to be amazingly garrulous. Even before I could tell her my news, I learned that she'd already told the entire class—including Gil—that I had come all this way to take a cooking course for my poor mother, who was laid up in a nursing home and unable to attend.

"You told Gil that?" I exclaimed. "Why? He's a pain in the ass. He uses personal information to embarrass people." It was morning, and Aunt Matilda and I were getting dressed for class.

She said airily, "Oh, you misjudge Gil. I had a nice chat with him and he's actually a very sweet man. But you have to understand, he's under a lot of stress right now. What with all the renovations he's making—he had to borrow a 'massive' amount of money, you see— and his silent partner, who's supposed to help him pay back the loan, is making a lot of demands, and putting a lot of pressure on Gil to make sure they reopen the *mas* as a hotel on time."

I stared at her, agog. "How'd you wangle all that information out of him?"

She smiled at me a bit smugly. "He lost his mother at an early age, so he's susceptible to soothing, older gals like me. He grew up among tough kids, so he had to be tough, too. And his wife, you know, committed suicide. It wasn't his fault, of course. She was a poet," she said, as if that explained everything.

"Oh! That's awful!" I exclaimed, taken aback.

"See? Doesn't that shed new light on Gil? Sometimes people with so much tragedy in their lives are prickly and pugnacious, just to hide their extreme vulnerability," Aunt Matilda observed.

I glanced at her and said, "But I *know* he didn't tell you all those details about his wife!"

"No," she admitted, "I read it in a magazine."

I muttered, "I still don't see why you told him about Mom."

Aunt Matilda said gently, "Anyone can see how concerned you are about your mother. It's all over your face, in everything you do. I see you checking for messages all the time, looking worried." This was true. I'd been in regular contact with the hairdresser at the care home, who said Mom's progress was slow since they'd increased her meds, which the woman thought made it harder for Mom to move unassisted.

"Gil understood. See, you can't keep it all inside," Aunt Matilda was saying earnestly. "When dealing with other human beings, dearie, there has to be some give and take. Personal information is like currency. You trade something to get something. Gil told me *his* troubles, I told him yours."

"I see you didn't swap *your* troubles for his," I pointed out.

She explained, "No, because I had to set him straight about you. He was convinced that you were up to no good at that café in Juan-les-Pins." She peered at me. "So—*were* you up to no good?"

"Of course not!" I replied. And that was the point when I realized I needed her help. "Look, if I tell you what I was doing, will you absolutely *swear* that you will tell no one, no matter *what* happens?" I asked. Sensing a juicy tidbit, she nodded eagerly. So I told her about how Grandma Ondine cooked for Picasso, which of course immediately intrigued Aunt Matilda. And then I explained that maybe, just maybe, Grandma had hidden a painting for safekeeping somewhere.

I waited for her to tell me I was crazy, but her gambler instinct kicked right in. "Ahhh!" she said. "Now, that *would* be quite a find." She pondered this. "Well, in an odd way it all makes sense now. You know, when your mother asked me about Picasso, she said, 'It's just something I wanted to know—for Céline.' Maybe she hoped to find that painting for *you*—to give you your own legacy."

I couldn't help having a catch in my voice as I said, "I looked all over that café. It's not there."

But Aunt Matilda was now like a hound who'd been given the scent of her quarry. "You can't give up that easily," she said briskly. "Let me see that notebook of yours. There must be something you overlooked. Do you have any living relatives in France?" I shook my head. That much I knew for sure.

"People," she said. "Always start with people. Who do you know that knew your Grandma?"

"Besides Picasso?" I said. "Let's see. Well, the doctor who tended her. But I don't know his name. Wait, there was a lawyer. It's in Grandma's letter." Aunt Matilda's optimism was contagious, and I showed it to her. "Monsieur Gerard Clément. He executed her last will and testament." I used my phone to do a quick search on the Internet. I could find nothing, not even a website for his law firm.

"Not so unusual in France," Aunt Matilda said, undaunted. "Sometimes they have enough local business so that they don't need to advertise to the greater world." The breakfast bell sounded. We left our room for the circular staircase that led to the main level. As we hurried across the lobby she veered away from me and said, "Go on and grab me a *brioche* and *café au lait* while I find you an address."

She was heading for the front desk. I said in alarm, "You swore secrecy, remember?"

"No sweat," Aunt Matilda replied.

A few moments later she caught up with me just as our morning class was about to start, and she triumphantly handed me a slip of paper with an address and telephone number for Monsieur Gerard Clément. He apparently had an office in the "old town" section of Mougins.

"Where'd you get this?" I asked, nonplussed.

"The old-fashioned way, dear," she said, wolfing down her coffee and bun. "The phone book."

I quickly telephoned Clément, but a rather frosty receptionist told me that he was extremely busy. She said she'd give him my message; I doubted it.

"Watch it," Aunt Matilda hissed. "Here comes Gil."

By now, our class was cooking in earnest. Each day was a trial-by-fire devoted to one particular category of food: eggs, poultry, fish, meat, vegetables and beans. But some of the giddy novelty of a French culinary holiday was now giving way to the reality of *if you can't stand the heat, get out of the kitchen*.

You never knew which one of your errors would elicit a laugh or a scowl from Gil. He treated the elders gently, but I think he figured that since I was younger I was fair game, and should somehow know better, just because I had a French chef in my lineage. He once actually told me to "Please move your spoiled little American *cul* a bit faster."

"What's a 'cuh-yool'?" Lola whispered to me in her Texan drawl.

"Ass," I whispered back, indignant.

"Oooh," she said knowingly. "He likes you."

Today, as we heard Gil's animated voice out in the hallway, Aunt Matilda's pal Peter warned, "He sounds rather more aggressive than usual, if that's possible." We soon found out why. Gil entered accompanied by a slender woman dressed entirely in chef's whites, including a tall white hat.

"Class, meet Heather Bradbrook, the best pastry chef in all of London," Gil said proudly.

She was delicate-looking, with naturally white-blonde hair, green eyes and an innate serenity that seemed to calm everyone, even Gil.

"Heather has graciously agreed to be a guest chef today, to teach you all about the magic of bread-making," he said, smiling down at her from his big sporty height. His broad shoulders looked even broader with Heather standing next to him.

"They make a cute couple, don't they?" Magda the Scottish dog-lady said in a stage whisper so loud that I stepped away in embarrassment, not wanting anyone to think I'd made that comment.

"As for *pâtisserie*," Gil was saying, "this delicate-looking chef will show you how tough she really is when she demonstrates how to pound puff pastry."

One of the men—Joey from Chicago, I think—murmured that she could pound him anytime. I tried not to be shocked hearing this from a man his age, but the others were totally unfazed.

"So today, I leave you all in Heather's capable hands," Gil concluded, "but I *will* get a full report card on each of you, so behave." He bowed shortly to Heather, saying, "I'm off to my meeting."

She gave him a nod and whispered, "Good luck." Two young men from Gil's kitchen staff came barreling in, carrying enormous sacks of flour over their shoulders, and a few sizeable bags of sugar. "Okay, gather round," Heather said to the class in a pleasantly modulated voice, but with such authority that we all shut up and shuffled forward. "Bread is flour—water—salt," she chanted like a high priestess. "The magic is in the simplicity. But don't be fooled. You can't scrimp on time or effort."

A baguette dough, a puff pastry made of folded multi-layers of butter and flour, a cake made of almond flour, and cookies of ground hazelnuts. The whole experience turned out to be so unexpectedly sensual—the warm yeasty scent of bread rising, and the soft, fleshy dough yielding beneath our kneading touch. We were working so intently that I didn't even notice my mobile phone ringing in my apron pocket until Magda nudged me and said, "It's *yours,* you know!"

I wiped flour off my hands and fumbled for it. Heather did not miss the look on my face when I saw who was calling. She said calmly, "You can step outside. We're done for today anyway; I was about to call a break. This afternoon there's an outdoor tour around the farmland of the *mas*."

"Thanks," I said, yanking off my apron and going out onto the terrace for privacy.

It was Monsieur Gerard Clément. "Yes, *bien sûr,* I remember your grandmother." In his deep, melodious voice he spoke flawless English with just a hint of an elegant French accent. "What can I do for you?" he asked. I told him I needed to meet with him as it was too personal to discuss over the telephone. "I see, I see," he replied in a mild, polite tone indicating he had no idea why I was being so mysterious. "Well, I am sure that my secretary can arrange for us to meet next month—"

"Oh, no, no, it can't possibly wait that long!" I cried. "I really must see you right away."

"Ah, but you see, I leave this evening for *les vacances*," he said.

"Vacation?" I exclaimed. "Then I've *got* to meet you today! I won't *be* here when you get back. My mother—she told me that you were the only one she trusted—" I choked up, then and there.

"Please don't distress yourself," he said quickly, and I heard him rustling about as if he were consulting his calendar. "If it's really so critical, the only time I can possibly see you today is at two forty-five—"

"*Bon, merci beaucoup,*" I said quickly, wondering how I'd get there on such short notice.

"But I must warn you we'll only have fifteen minutes, because I have a meeting that starts promptly at three," he said, sounding as if he absolutely meant it.

"I'll see you at two forty-five," I promised. He gave me the address and some brief directions.

After we hung up, I told Aunt Matilda what I was up to. "Good luck," she said, crossing her fingers. I dashed upstairs to grab a cardigan and purse, then returned to the concierge desk.

"I need a map for the old town area of Mougins," I told the tall Frenchman, Maurice, who was on duty, "and, um, I need a car right away."

He sucked in his breath. "A car today will be difficult to get on such short notice," he warned mildly, as he handed me the map. Then he straightened alertly as a well-dressed man appeared in the lobby acting like a guest, helping himself to the coffee cups and urns that stood on a side table.

This surprised me, since the hotel part of the *mas* wasn't yet open to the public, just to my cooking class. Maurice took note of the man and nodded deferentially to him, all the while still talking on the phone trying to find me a car. When Maurice hung up he rather insultingly addressed the stranger before me. "Monsieur Gil is away in meetings all day, I'm afraid."

Then with a slight change in tone he turned to me. "Sorry, *mademoiselle*. No car is available."

"Look," I said, "failure is *not* an option here. I *have* to get to the old town, *now*."

The stranger meanwhile had begun scribbling on a small pad, and now he tore off a page and slid his note across the counter, not bothering to hide its contents, which said: *Gil, I still have a few issues to resolve with the contract. I'll be out of town until next week. Let's talk when I get back.*

Maurice, being more discreet, hastily put it in an envelope and swept it into a drawer.

I hurried outside, pausing to search my phone for some taxi or car rental service Maurice might have overlooked. I was so absorbed, I scarcely notice that the stranger had followed me out the door.

"You're Gil's friend?" the man asked. He didn't sound British, yet I'd noticed that Maurice had spoken to him in English. "Allow me to be of service. I'd be happy to drive you; I'm going past the old town anyway." I studied him more closely. He was about ten years older than Gil. He had the look of casual wealth—a golden suntan, some bespoke but easygoing attire in linen and cashmere, expensive russet-colored loafers, gold wristwatch and rings, longish but well-styled hair like a lion's mane, dark with a touch of grey; and the grey, alert eyes of a friendly but successful predator.

"Richard Vandervass," he said, extending a hand to shake. I took it; his skin was softer than mine, but his grip was firm. "Like the hotels," he added.

I had to think for a moment, then remembered a posh chain of very trendy, modern hotels all around the world owned by an enigmatic Dutch entrepreneur. "Any relation?" I asked jokingly.

"You might say. I own them," he said with a modest smile.

"Oh," I said, blushing. A sleek black town car pulled up, its uniformed driver steering it to a stop precisely where this guy stood in his leather loafers.

"I'm Rick, to friends of Gil's. Shall we?" he said, gesturing toward the car as the driver sprang from it with alacrity and opened the back door for him. "Just give us the address you want."

I entered the car, sliding across its plush seat. Rick sat next to me, and the driver closed the door for us before slipping back behind the wheel.

"So Gil is out today at a meeting," Rick observed amiably as we drove away. "Who with?"

I shrugged. "No idea." His relaxed demeanor was a welcome contrast to Gil's relentless energy.

"Does he do that a lot?" Rick asked with a dazzling smile. "Have a lot of meetings?"

I was so surprised by the question that all I could say was, "I couldn't say."

"How long have you known Gil?" he pursued, totally unapologetic for being nosey in the most charming way possible. I figured this was the price for getting a free ride into town.

"Just met him this month, but it feels like ages," I replied, trying to remain as noncommittal as possible. "How do *you* know him?" I countered, back on my guard again.

Rick looked surprised, then laughed. "Didn't he tell you about me? I'm Gil's partner."

"Ahh!" I said, curious now. He struck me as one of those appealingly courteous moguls who occasionally like to come down from Mount Olympus to see what regular folk think.

"Construction workers can be so unpredictable," he commented, glancing out the window as we passed the site with a crew hard at work. "Think they'll be ready in time for the hotel's grand opening?"

I shrugged. "Gil seems pretty confident," I observed, trying to shift the focus off my opinions.

"You must think me an awful nuisance." Rick's brilliant smile showed perfect teeth. For a "silent" partner he sure was pretty chatty. "But I've known Gil for a long time, seen all his ups and downs. And he's not the type to ask for help until he's really under the gun. We who care about him just want him to be successful and happy, right? Women are so much better at assessing this stuff."

I caught the driver glancing at me in his rearview mirror before he exchanged a knowing expression with Rick, so I finally understood.

They thought I was Gil's new girlfriend. Maybe they'd seen some Internet photos of my little fiasco at the Café Paradis, I surmised with a touch of guilt. A jingling sound came from a mahogany box near Rick's elbow. When I realized that the box served as a fancy charger for his phone—which was decorated rather showily with a diamond horseshoe studded with big emeralds—I managed to conceal my amusement at his ostentatious display of wealth, even when he said grandly, "Sorry, I have to take this," then proceeded to spend the entire ride talking in low monosyllables so that I couldn't follow it. I was just glad that somebody else had distracted him.

We arrived in the old town of Mougins with only minutes to my appointment time. I'd seen from my guidebook that it was laid out like a circular honeycomb of medieval streets, designed by the rulers of Genoa to keep out other invaders. Trying to get a car in there was almost out of the question. I told Rick's driver to drop me off at the corner. By then I was eager to escape. Rick stepped out of the car with me and he actually kissed my hand.

"Thanks for the ride!" I said, and I rushed off, past countless art galleries, shops, stone archways and incredibly narrow streets that spiraled inward like a seashell. When I finally spotted the law firm's door I hurried breathlessly inside to its cool, dark lobby. The receptionist, a stiff blonde girl in a grey suit, searched her calendar but could not find my name written down on her schedule.

A door across the lobby opened, and a sophisticated-looking man in his sixties peered out. When the receptionist addressed him as Monsieur Clément, I said quickly, "*Bonjour*. I'm your two forty-five."

He looked stymied until I gave him Grandma Ondine's name. Then his expression cleared and he said, "Yes, yes. Come in." I followed and he closed the heavy door behind us with a soft thud.

I took the seat opposite him across his imposing, old-fashioned desk which was topped with caramel-colored leather. "So you are the grand-daughter of Madame Ondine," he said, leaning back in his chair and looking me over from head to toe with amused interest. "I thought your grandmother was *quite* marvellous. A woman who knew exactly what she wanted." He smiled fondly to himself.

I stared at him. Was this silver-haired gentleman really the "nice young man" that Grandmother Ondine hired years ago? As if to answer my thoughts, he said gently, "Your *grand-mère* was very good to me. I was—what's the expression—'wet behind the ears' when she took me on. I was replacing a very beloved lawyer who was retiring. Some of his clients were *not* happy to have me take over the practice! *Eh bien,* now it is *I* who am the elder partner. Time passes."

His voice was pleasingly masculine with an air of natural sensuality; in fact, he was undeniably sexy. But I was eager to get past the niceties and raise the delicate question of the missing Picasso, so I replied quickly, "My grandmother—and my mother—always had the highest regard for you, too."

But this only prompted him to ask after Madame Julie's health, and I ignored the plunge of misery that such ordinary questions about my mother caused. I told him she'd been ill but was okay.

He accepted this. "And how is your father?" he asked politely. I took a deep breath.

"He's dead," I said shortly. Somehow I still couldn't believe it.

"I'm sorry," Monsieur Clément said, not particularly regretful but sympathetic, and looking quite observant, as if he'd astutely witnessed all the contradictory thoughts passing across my face.

"He was a difficult man," I acknowledged.

"Yes," he replied calmly. "I found him—aggressive. And, always angry." He sounded puzzled.

"Yeah, that's him, all right," I said, intentionally signalling that he could speak freely about Dad. "How involved did he get in the handling of my grandmother's estate?" I asked directly.

"I was well aware of Madame Ondine's—concerns—about him," Monsieur Clément said with the best of Gallic delicacy. "When she died, your father consulted with me in order to defend your mother's interests. But I must say that the man seemed reckless to me, wanting to push the limits of the law and test it. I was not comfortable with this. I made it clear that the laws of my country must be obeyed to the letter. In France, we do things carefully," he explained. "That's really all I can say."

Still watching him closely I replied, "As I said, my mother had great confidence in you. But she had just one question she felt never quite got resolved." I ignored his raised eyebrows here and plunged ahead, aware that our time was already half-gone. "Apparently there was a work of art that she believed Grandmother Ondine possessed. Mom was uncertain, after all these years, as to what became of it."

I braced myself for an exclamation of insulted outrage. But he only smiled tolerantly.

"Oh, the Picasso!" he said in amusement, reacting as a confident professional would, taking no offense and adopting a tone of mild curiosity. "Yes, your mother asked me about it recently, very quietly—she didn't want to excite your father. I assured her I'd never seen any such artwork. Even so, when your mother raised the issue I went over everything again to be sure I hadn't missed anything."

I waited. He explained, "In addition to the documents Madame Ondine left in my care, I had collected all the papers she left in the house, and everything was in perfect order. Deeds, title, official certificates. There was nothing whatsoever about the purchase or sale of a Picasso. If she ever possessed and then disposed of such a treasure, she must have done it some time ago, long before she hired me."

He'd said the name *Picasso* as if it were as grand and out of reach as the moon. Also, there was just a tinge of chauvinism in his tone, as if I were a fanciful female whose head was full of nonsense her mother told her. Now it was my turn to remain cool and unruffled, though I felt anything but serene.

"Still," I persisted, "I'd like to be absolutely sure about this."

Without a word, he rose and disappeared into an adjacent room. Agonizingly, I watched the clock on his desk—it was mounted inside a golden model ship anchored on a wooden base—mercilessly ticking the time as it flitted by. Finally he reappeared, carrying a thick file that he put on his blotter.

"Here we have every single item of her possessions," Monsieur Clément said, running his finger down the page. "Yes, it's just as I remembered. The contents of her property were sold in their entirety to the buyers. Nothing had to go to auction, nothing sold piecemeal. No artwork of *any* kind. I assure you, if Madame Ondine had such a valuable treasure in her possession, I am certain she'd have told me."

According to his clock I had a scant minute left. "May I see this list, please?" I asked.

The door opened behind me, and the receptionist peered in to say, "Your three o'clock is here."

"Yes, just a moment," he said dismissively, and she faded back into her lobby. He turned to me and said, "Come. You can take this folder into my file room and peruse it yourself. But please, leave it there on the table when you have finished." I followed him into an adjacent room that was lined with tall wooden cabinets, and in its center there was a long, narrow table with library chairs and lamps.

"Okay, great," I said, but I was feeling doubtful now. There is nothing more dispiriting than a pile of paperwork when you're pretty sure it will provide only another dead end. "By the way—that doctor who tended my grandmother when she died. Do you have a name and address for him?"

Clément said regretfully, "Alas, he died many years ago. A fine old bachelor." He turned to go.

I said, "One last question. Did anyone besides my parents go into my grandmother's house in Juan-les-Pins after she died there?"

"Juan-les-Pins?" Monsieur Clément repeated, pausing with his hand on the doorknob. "But your grandmother did not die in Juan-les-Pins."

"Didn't she live in the rooms above the café?" I demanded, startled.

"For many years, yes. But not the year she died! Goodness, no. By then she walked with a cane and had difficulty climbing stairs. She had someone drive her to the café every day, to check on the kitchen, but she rented out those rooms above the café to paying guests. No, Madame Ondine was living at a *mas* in Mougins at the time of her death. Her bedroom was on the ground floor there."

"A *mas*?" I exclaimed. Suddenly I felt as if I were standing under an avalanche. Then I realized that it was simply more pieces of the puzzle falling into place.

"Yes, a farm that supplied most everything she needed to run her café."

"What is the address of this *mas*?" I asked, certain I already knew. And sure enough, he pointed to a page with an address that matched Gil's hotel and restaurant.

"Grandma *lived* at this *mas*?" I asked. He nodded vigorously. I stammered, "Then—everything you've told me about the day she died took place in Mougins—not in Juan-les-Pins?"

"*Absolument,*" he said. "Didn't your mother remember that Madame Ondine died in Mougins?" There was just the slightest indication in his voice that if Mom could be wrong about something so basic, then she was surely mistaken about any missing Picasso artwork.

I realized that Mom hadn't actually spelled out where Grandma was living when she visited her. "It's my mistake," I said, still reeling. "Who did you sell the *mas* to when Grandmother Ondine died?"

"A dairyman who owned the farm next door; he'd had his eye on Madame Ondine's property for some time, with a view to merging it into one estate. He really only wanted the *mas* for its farmland. So he didn't live at Madame Ondine's house; he used her buildings for storage. He had no children, and his wife predeceased him. When he died the combined property was sold, I believe, to an English chef."

I sat motionless, waiting to see if he had any more bombshells to drop. But he glanced worriedly at his watch. "I'm afraid I won't be able to see you again later," he reminded me. "I hope this satisfies."

"Fine, fine," I said, now eager to get my hands on the file on the table. "*Bonnes vacances.*"

Monsieur Clément gave me a polite nod, then disappeared back into his office.

I pored over the file for an hour. It was all in French, of course, and in legalese, which made it hard to decipher. But I managed to plough through the list of all the furnishings, which was easier. It was pretty exhaustive, right down to each pot and pan in the kitchen and every flowerpot or vase.

But my mind was reeling with this stunning new perspective. If what Monsieur Clément said was true—and I believed him, because he was so straightforward, unlike Mom and her secretive, roundabout way of giving out information—then the whole story she'd told me about Grandmother Ondine giving her the notebook had occurred not at the Café Paradis, but at Gil's *mas* in Mougins, and I had simply misunderstood. There hardly seemed to be any point in investigating the café in Juan-les-Pins any further—especially since the current owner had banned me from ever darkening his doorway again.

"*That's* why Mom was so keen to take this cooking class," I said under my breath. "For years Grandma's *mas* had been under private ownership, so there was no chance that she could look for the Picasso painting. But along comes Gil with his cooking class, and suddenly the whole place becomes available for Mom to search it, one more time!"

I rested my chin in my hands, contemplating three possibilities: *One:* Grandma Ondine sold the artwork long ago and deposited the money in the bank. *Two:* Somebody—the dairyman who bought Grandma's *mas,* or even a thieving neighbor—found the Picasso and sold it, so it was long gone. *Three:* Grandma hid the Picasso and *nobody* found it, which meant it must still be somewhere at Gil's *mas,* right where I'd been sleeping and cooking, all this time. This led to a truly dire thought.

"Does this mean that, technically, the painting—if it's still hidden there—now belongs to Gil?" I gasped. Resolutely I pushed that idea out of my mind. I knew perfectly well that, if I somehow managed to find the Picasso at the *mas,* it would rightfully belong to my mother. I would just have to remove the artwork quietly, without anyone else—Gil especially—knowing that I'd found it.

20

Ondine in September, 1936

Picasso had simply vanished from the face of the earth as far as Ondine was concerned, for Paris was as far away as the moon to her. And now that Ondine no longer had an artist to cook for, her mother was keeping her on a short leash, not only cooking but waiting on tables during the busy summer season. Her father expected her to turn over her tips to him at each day's end. It was as if her parents sensed that she must be constantly watched in order to get her to the altar on her wedding day.

But as the summer months faded, no one, least of all Ondine, grasped what was actually happening to her until, just a few weeks before the wedding, she went to the dressmaker who was altering Madame Belange's bridal gown to fit Ondine. But now, in what was supposed to be just the final fitting, suddenly the gown could not be buttoned at Ondine's waist.

"I'll have to let out the seams," the dressmaker observed. There was a silence, punctured only by the sound of the scissors picking out the threads. "I'd say it's about four months," she said finally.

Ondine, standing on the tufted footstool, saw her own startled expression reflected in three mirrors around her. "It can't be true," she whispered. "I'm just eating too much, that's all." But with a sinking heart she knew the real reason why she'd been feeling so strange and a little sick at times.

The dressmaker gave her a sharp, no-nonsense look. "I've seen more brides like you than I can count," she said with certainty. "You *are* going to have a child."

"Please don't tell anyone," Ondine said in panic, thinking of her parents.

"Of course not. We can drape some lace here, like an overskirt around your hips," the woman said, pinning the lace to show her, then sitting back on her heels and gazing at Ondine with a sympathy so rare that she nearly burst into tears. "Does Monsieur Renard know?" the dressmaker asked, looking doubtful, for no one could imagine the fastidious baker taking such advantage of his future bride.

"No!" Ondine cried out in anguish. The dressmaker's little black dog, who'd been asleep with his back against the stool, sprang up in alarm at her desperate outburst, then whimpered in sympathy.

"Is it Monsieur Renard's baby?" the dressmaker asked. Ondine's blush was her answer. "Does the father know?" the woman said in a low voice.

Ondine bit her lip, then shook her head. For weeks she'd bicycled to Picasso's villa in the hope that he would return. Yet he never did. The villa was rented to other summer people, and Ondine felt foolish, mournfully skulking about with strangers gazing back at her. She couldn't shake the feeling that Picasso had somehow taken her heart, mind and soul with him, leaving behind only a ghost of a girl.

Then one day she saw a newspaper photo of Picasso in St. Tropez— with that photographer Dora Maar by his side, looking triumphant. It seemed hopeless for the blonde mistress and her baby now; and so for Ondine as well. Picasso just boldly appeared anywhere he pleased without warning, then mysteriously vanished all over again. One thing was certain—he had definitely moved on. For weeks Ondine had felt like a sleepwalker, compliant to her parents as if she didn't care what happened to her.

The dressmaker rose to her feet and warned, "Forget about the baby's father. Let Monsieur Renard *think* it's his. It'll be better for both of you. I heard Renard say he wants to have two sons!"

It took Ondine a moment to comprehend that there was only one ridiculous way to convince the baker that he was a papa. *Now I have to seduce Monsieur Renard?* she thought disgustedly, wondering if she could even succeed because he was so proud and proper.

"If he feels he's compromised your virtue, he'll honor the promise he made to you and your family," the dressmaker said. "But stay away from other women; don't undress in front of them, don't let them see you getting sick in the morning. And don't let your friends tell you to 'get rid of it' by jumping off walls or drinking poison. Murder is messy, and it's often the mother who dies instead."

Ondine barely knew what "getting rid of it" meant. But she nodded dumbly, left the dressmaker's house and went for a long walk at the Parc de Vaugrenier in the special places where she and Luc used to stroll. There she threw herself down on a carpet of wildflowers and howled at the sky, rolling around and tearing out grass like a dog. When she turned onto her belly she thought she sensed a bump now— that little creature growing inside, greedily feeding off her.

"Who *asked* for you?" Ondine wailed savagely, wondering in a frenzied moment if she could just crush it and suffocate it, right here and now. But then, when her hot tears were spent, she lay on her back and sighed, and saw that the moon had already risen in the blue sky and was staring back at her.

It's the Virgin Mary watching, the nuns used to say. Ondine had the feeling that of all people, the Virgin would understand and forgive her. Wasn't this child inside Ondine like a heavy little moon revolving around her as if Ondine were the sun itself? She had to smile. The wind stirred the wild herbs and she breathed deeply, rhythmically, until one word filled her mind with peace.

"Mine," she whispered in wonder to herself, to the baby, to the moon. Nobody had ever belonged to her before. There was something so sweet about it that she wanted to run and tell someone.

But as she headed for home she couldn't imagine a single soul who'd be glad. "They won't let me keep the baby," she sighed. "They'll force me to give it up to an orphanage or a foster home. I'd never be able to sleep nights, knowing my child is out there without its mama."

When Ondine reached the Café Paradis she crept upstairs and sat on her bed, unable to go back to work today. "If it's the baby or Renard, I choose my baby," she decided resolutely. "But I'll have to do this quickly, before they find out what I'm up to." Now she knew why she'd kept her suitcase packed with her few pitiful treasures: a photo of Luc, her notebook from cooking for Picasso, a small coin purse and her favorite clothes. Like someone in a trance, she added a few more things to wear for when the weather changed.

After counting the coins in her purse Ondine concluded that she had enough money for a train fare to the convent. She would tell the nuns that she'd cooked for Picasso, and ask them to find her a suitable position cooking for someone else—but in a town far away from here, where she could pretend to be a widow, so she could have her baby there.

Carrying her coat and suitcase, Ondine slipped out of the café as stealthily as she came, hearing the clatter going on in the kitchen without her. Halfway down the street she saw a tramp coming in her direction. He looked like the kind of scoundrel who'd impudently go to the back of the café seeking a handout. Ondine automatically shrank from him, averting her eyes. Then the tramp lifted his weather-beaten face and saw her.

"Ondine!" he called out, hurrying toward her now. She eyed him warily until he said, "Don't you recognize your Luc?" Then she gasped and stopped short, afraid she must be imagining a ghost.

"Luc?" she exclaimed in shock. His clothes were worn and rumpled, his thick dark hair longer and wilder, his face covered with a beard. He was so very thin and brown and wiry and tough-looking.

"Ondine!" he shouted joyfully, dropping his own bundle on the road. At first his gaze was deep and searching and uncertain—until he saw something in her face that set his expression alight with joy, and then he couldn't hold back any longer. He scooped her up in his arms and swung her off her feet, then set her down to again gaze into her eyes. Ondine, gasping in amazement, could hardly take it all in.

He was taller than she remembered. He smelled like tobacco and fish and earth and musk—but underneath all that, he still smelled like Luc. The same intelligent dark eyes, that high forehead and the finely sculpted nose and jaw, the sensuous lips. He took her face into his two rough hands as if she were the most precious thing on earth, and then the kisses he covered her cheeks with were sweet and loving.

But when his lips found hers, he kissed her in a new way—seeking, giving, finding—and Ondine, shaking now, felt herself answering him with not just her kisses but her whole body. "Ondine!" he exclaimed again, as if it were she, and not he, who'd gone away for such a long time.

Off in the distance, a church bell clanged the hour. "We can't go to the café!" she warned him.

"Come on then, let's get out of here," he said promptly, and she recognized the healthy confidence in his beautiful voice, although it was lower and more resonant now, as if it were coming from the hold of a steady ship that had conquered the sea itself. The muscles in his neck and arms resembled ropes that had weathered many storms. He glanced at her suitcase, took it to carry for her and asked, "Where are you going? Or are you meeting someone?" For the first time he looked alarmed.

"The train station," she said instantly, still trembling with joy. "No, I'm not meeting anybody. I just don't want to stay here anymore." He didn't ask why. But as they walked, they kept staring at each other searchingly. "What happened to you?" Ondine asked. "Where have you been all this time?"

Luc explained that he'd caught typhoid in North Africa. "They had to put me ashore. They left me for dead in Tangiers—thinking they'd never have to pay me my last wages. No other ship would take me home or anywhere else." He'd lain ill in bed in a cheap rooming house, unable to move, barely able to think.

"I was down to skin and bones, more dead than alive." He told her that if not for the madam of the house, who'd fed and nursed him, he'd indeed have died. But when he recovered, she made him work to pay her back; so he'd been a kitchen porter in a restaurant called the Purple Parrot, which catered to the whorehouse girls and their seafaring clients.

Then Luc told her what he'd learned about what was happening now. "There *will* be another world war. Everybody pretends it isn't true, but there's no doubt the Nazis are coming; they're already sizing up our navy in Toulon. The cagey politicians and businessmen in Paris are ready to sacrifice France to the fascists, yet all they'll say to ordinary citizens is, 'Don't worry, the forts of the Maginot line will protect us.' But the line will not hold—ask any soldier who's drunk enough to tell the truth."

"Nobody here talks about war," Ondine said worriedly.

"Not to women," Luc said. "Not to children, or fools who wish to remain children."

Ondine suddenly saw her plan to go to the nuns as the lonely prospect it was. "I want to go and be a chef somewhere. Maybe Paris," she said, emboldened by his presence to dream a little bigger now.

He warned, "That's a bad idea. Paris won't be a good place to be when Hitler comes. If you don't believe me, read your history book. I did a lot of reading, first at sea, then when I was recovering. In our past wars the Parisians were surrounded by the enemy and reduced to eating rats—they even ate the animals in the zoo!"

Ondine tried to picture Picasso reduced to eating a giraffe. Well, he would surely do it. *You have to kill something every day, just to live,* he'd told her.

"The place to go is America," Luc said, his thin, dirty face alight. "That's where a man can make a fresh start." Ondine thought he might be mad. Her poor sweet man had returned looking half-starved, like a scarecrow; if her mother saw him approaching the café she'd chase him off with a broom.

Luc read her thoughts. "I may not look my best," he said defiantly. "*Bien sûr,* I could have stopped somewhere for a bath and a shave. But while I lay near death, I vowed to myself that if I ever got home again, I would let nothing—I tell you, *nothing*—stop me from seeing you as soon as my feet touched the earth of Juan-les-Pins." He stopped, put down the suitcase, reached into his pocket and pulled out a cloth sack with a drawstring, which he put in the palm of her hand. It was very, very heavy.

"It's all in gold," he said. "I made sure of that. Nobody knows which currency is going to count for anything in the days that come. I took dangerous work from anybody who'd pay high. Some of it was legal. Some of it wasn't. All I thought was, I'd like to see your father's face when he counts it!"

He stopped to kiss her again, and he held her while she actually swayed, still reeling with delight.

She could see that he had triumphed, after all. And he'd faithfully returned to Ondine, just as he'd promised, to share it with her. Gently he asked, "But, Ondine—why didn't you answer any of my letters?"

Now, as they kept walking, it was her turn to tell what had happened while he was gone. She explained how his letters had been kept hidden away, and why hers had never reached him. She told him about her father and Monsieur Renard's plans for her. Luc absorbed this information without comment, as if he were weighing the situation carefully.

"I'm so sorry, Luc. I can't believe my parents could be so cruel to you," Ondine said, ashamed.

But Luc just shook his head. "Parents are ordinary mortals, you know. And people do what they think they have to do to get what they want. I'm surprised to hear how much they really intended to keep us apart. But fate did not agree with them; for here I am, and here you are."

They had reached the station, where a few travellers awaited the last train. The stationmaster was just locking up his office to go home. Ondine and Luc sat close together on a bench on the far end of the platform so no one would notice them. He spoke very calmly, making it all seem so sensible and attainable. Ondine was listening in admiration, for he'd somehow taken the measure of the Great World, and his ambitions seemed rooted more deeply in the earth, no longer lost at sea.

"Well, Ondine, it's too bad about your parents but it's our choice now, not theirs. All we have is each other! All right, that's more than enough for me. Like anyone else, we have a right to do what we feel we must to take care of ourselves, just the two of us." Luc's face was so happy and trusting that Ondine burst into tears. "What's the matter?" he asked worriedly. "Don't you want to come with me?"

So, she told him about Picasso. Luc had always been a good listener. Even now, he listened as a horse would—patiently, without comment, but keenly attentive to every nuance in her voice as it rose and fell.

"I am going to have a baby," she said finally. She saw him absorb this. He was still holding her hand in his.

Quietly he asked, "Do you love this man?" As young as he was, Luc already possessed the kind of clarity and toughness that suffering sometimes produces; he exuded the intelligence of a man who knew that time must not be wasted on foolish grudges and things that should not matter.

Ondine knew the answer now, because she could feel, within her own flesh, how different love felt when it came from a young man who was brave enough to care about someone besides himself.

"No," she said in a low voice. "I'm not in love with Picasso." Luc smiled triumphantly.

"Then, never mind," he said decisively. "Nobody needs to know about it. I ask only two things."

"What do you want?" Ondine asked, her eyes misty as he kissed her again.

"That the child will always think of *me* as its father," Luc said. "And, if it's a girl, we name her after my mother. I promised her I'd do that, just before she died." Luc's mother had been a teacher who worked hard with him to make sure he learned everything he could in school. She'd died when he was only fourteen, and his face now revealed how deep the loss of her had been. Ondine, still crying, flung her arms around him, and pressed her wet face against his bearded one.

"Of course," she said. "If it's a girl we'll name her Julie."

They held each other for awhile. Then, very seriously, he said, "Some Americans told me about a place where you and I might be able to open a restaurant of our own. I learned a lot, working in one. Maybe there, you can be the great chef you say you want to be."

Ondine could hardly absorb what he was saying. "What is this place?" she asked, her eyes wide.

"It's called New Rochelle," he replied. "It's near New York, right by the sea. It was settled by the French, and named after La Rochelle. One day, we'll come back to France if you like. But now, this money will pay our fares to America and to start our own business. Come be with me, and be my wife."

All Ondine knew was that she loved the melody of his voice, the way it resonated in his chest, the warmth of his presence. It filled her heart with joy, and she had forgotten what this felt like. She did not want to ever forget again. The American town with the French name sounded lovely.

"But, Ondine, are you ready to leave home?" he asked tenderly.

Now that it was a reality, she had one last regret about no longer sitting in the garden under the Aleppo tree. She thought of the reassuring view of her mother's head in the kitchen window, calling out to her; and her father sitting in the front room, counting his money. But they would never let her marry Luc, nor keep this baby. She had been ready to run away alone. With Luc, she was ready to go anywhere.

The train pulled into the station. The conductors helped disembarking passengers to descend the metal steps. A familiar, well-dressed man alighted, mopping his brow with a handkerchief. Ondine's throat tightened when she saw Monsieur Renard. "Oh, Lord, it's him!" she cried. "He'll stop us!"

Luc squeezed her hand reassuringly. "Nothing will ever stop us again," he promised.

Monsieur Renard waved; he appeared to think Ondine was waiting for him, and she fleetingly felt sorry for him. Then he saw Luc, and his face hardened, and so did her heart as Renard came walking toward them with a stern expression. "What a scoundrel you are, Luc, showing up now!" he exclaimed. "Keep away from Ondine, or her father and I will have the police escort you out of town for good."

Luc never took his eyes off Ondine. "This is our train," he said steadily. "Are you ready to go?"

"Yes," she said, surprised at the strength in her own voice.

"You're coming home with *me,* young lady!" Monsieur Renard said sternly to Ondine, yanking her by the arm. This surprised her; she'd never seen him like this, but it was Luc he was staring at and talking to, and she could see it was male business that had nothing to do with her. And now she saw Luc stiffen, with a hard new glint of fearlessness in his eyes as he sized up his opponent.

Instinctively Ondine put a hand on Luc's chest. "Don't give them an excuse to put you in jail," she warned. She turned furiously to Monsieur Renard. She recalled the day he drove her home in his fancy auto and they saw Picasso out for a Sunday stroll with the blonde girl who was pushing a baby carriage. Monsieur Renard had sneered, *I could never take up with a woman who's had a child by another man.*

Now Ondine leaned forward and whispered in Renard's ear, "I'm going have a baby. What will your mother say? Do you really want me to marry you and then tell everyone it's not yours? Because I will, you know. I'll shout it from the rooftops! But if you let us go, your family name is safe."

Monsieur Renard gasped, then drew back in stunned horror, releasing her from his grasp.

Ondine took one last look at the world she was leaving behind. For some reason, all she could think about now was the cat and the dog, waiting for her in the backyard. She was still girlish enough to feel tears in her eyes for her beloved pets.

"Goodbye," Ondine whispered to the wind so that it would carry her message to the Aleppo tree, to tell the animals not to wait for her return. "Give them all my love."

She took Luc's arm, and hurried up onto the train.

21

Discovery: Céline in Mougins, 2014

I LEFT MONSIEUR CLÉMENT'S LAW OFFICE STILL FEELING STUNNED. To suddenly recast my mother's entire story of Grandmother Ondine's last days at Gil's *mas* instead of at the café presented mind-boggling new possibilities.

"I've been following in Grandma's footsteps all along, right there at the *mas*," I told myself, feeling goosebumps at the thought. *That* was where I needed to do my searching.

Standing in the labyrinthine center of the old town I realized that I had no way of getting back. I decided it was high time I got my own wheels. I lucked out at a nearby car rental; someone had just returned a pale blue Peugeot. Driving off, I felt a sense of independence and triumph.

Back at the *mas* I recalled that Gil arranged for my classmates to be out in the fields this afternoon. Aunt Matilda later told me they did a stint of farm work—milking wary cows, feeding nervous chickens and pigs, collecting eggs from indignant hens, picking the day's multitude of vegetables and fruit.

Maurice reminded me of this scheduled farm work while I was trying to creep past his concierge desk in the lobby. I mumbled something about having to first attend to "a personal matter" and I hurried up to my room to plan my next move. Searching for Grandma's Picasso here at the *mas* would be tricky; we had only three days left of the cooking course, and each was carefully mapped out; for instance, tomorrow was a trip to the museum.

So, with the whole class out in the fields this afternoon, this might be my best chance to snoop through my classmates' rooms. It wouldn't be my top priority to search the women's area, since Monsieur Clément said that Grandma Ondine had become unable to climb stairs and her bedroom was on the ground floor. But I wondered exactly where those older bedrooms were. Then I recalled that the desk in my room had a get-acquainted brochure about the *mas*.

I saw now that it contained a map of the buildings and grounds, which I could use to plot my search. The brochure described it all in glowing P.R. terms:

> *This typical Provençal farmhouse, built entirely of local stone, was made in the tradition of creating a completely self-contained entity producing everything its owners needed to live independently: vegetable and grain, meat and poultry, fruit orchards, a dairy, and even its own silkworm farm called a magnanerie.*
>
> *The "mas" or big main building is laid out in an L-shape facing south for maximum light and protection from the north winds. As you enter the lobby with its updated marble flooring, a spiral staircase takes you either upstairs to guest bedrooms; or downstairs to the bar, dining room and kitchen of Gil Halliwell's Michelin-starred restaurant, called "Pierrot". This large modern kitchen and dining area did not exist in the original mas; it was only a barn-like room where the animals were kept indoors in winter.*

THEREFORE, THE KITCHEN THAT MY class had been cooking in all this time wasn't Grandma Ondine's kitchen, I concluded, scrutinizing the map before continuing to read.

> *The other side of the mas—the shorter leg of the "L-shape"—was where the earlier owners spent their indoor hours, especially in winter. There were only two bedrooms and a farmhouse kitchen. In the summer, cook-*

ing was done in outdoor ovens, but in the winter months the owners cooked and ate in this original, large kitchen, using the big fireplace and its built-in ovens; so the room served as a combination kitchen-dining-and-living area. This section of the mas is currently undergoing expansion and reconstruction, as are the outbuildings, some of which were once used to grind and store grain, or to store fruit and vegetables. Our pool and spa are the first examples of our state-of-the-art renovations of the outbuildings.

So, I noted, the bedrooms on the shorter side of the "L" were where the men in our class slept. It appeared that they were both at ground level. I was willing to bet that one of them was Grandmother Ondine's bedroom—right near the old kitchen, where she might cook and take her meals. No stairs to climb.

The women in my class called that section the "boys' dorm" and everyone joked on the first night about how we'd been gender-segregated. Surely that was where I should search, and the sooner the better. Feeling inspired, I rummaged in my suitcase for any supplies I might find useful, and came up with an LED flashlight that I always take with me when I travel, and my nylon carry-on bag. I was optimistic enough to think that if I found the Picasso I could stash it inside. I hurried out of my room, moving quietly through the lobby. Maurice had gone back into his office, so he didn't see me.

I stole down the spiral staircase to the lower level, past *Pierrot*, Gil's restaurant, which had a cocktail area with a zinc bar and an enormous Art Deco mirror bearing needle-etched images of the legendary Pierrot and Harlequin clowns gaily chasing each other. I continued beyond the restaurant's empty dining area, elegantly designed in burgundy and pale rose. Tomorrow it would be buzzing with weekend customers; you had to make reservations weeks in advance even in the off-season, and whole months ahead in summer. The tables on the terrace were especially popular.

Next was Gil's shiny silver spit-spot-clean new kitchen where our class had been taking cooking lessons. I'd never gone beyond this modern kitchen because the other door was marked *Staff Only*. I opened it now, and stepped into a short vestibule leading to a heavy wooden door that appeared to be made of halved tree logs. Once I'd pushed past it, I found myself in the oldest section of the *mas*.

Shining my flashlight ahead, I could see that this long hallway eventually led to the old kitchen, now under construction. The site was like a big black pit with lots of treacherous scaffolding. But immediately to my left and right were two doors facing each other across the hallway.

"The old bedrooms!" I said, excited now as I squinted at my map. "So *this* is the boys' dorm."

The door on my left was ajar. I pushed inside. It was quite a large, elegantly decorated bedroom suite with a fireplace, and two alcoves containing beds. There was also a sizeable adjoining sitting room. The sitting room had a bed in it, too, so there was ample private space here for all three of my male classmates.

A pair of pajamas with a Texan flag on the breast pocket was draped on the sitting-room's bed; Joey's Chicago Cubs baseball cap lay on a table in one alcove; and, in the other alcove I spotted a British newspaper which surely belonged to Peter, the English wine steward who had become so chummy with Aunt Matilda.

I crossed the suite to a large closet and yanked open its door. I felt a stab of guilt, rummaging through my classmates' clothing that was folded on shelves and draped on hangers. Then I thought of my mother stuck in that awful nursing home, and I quickly stooped down to the floor where the men's empty suitcases were stacked. I hauled them out and examined the floorboards, which were slightly warped; and I noticed that, in the far right corner one particular plank wiggled like a loose tooth. Still, it took considerable work to pry it up. Once I finally got it out of there, I shined my flashlight and peered in.

I felt my pulse quicken, once again recalling what Mom had said about *a secret storage area under a closet floor, where during the wars Grandma's parents hid the café's best champagne from the German soldiers . . .*

The hollow space below was deep and wide enough to surely be such a storage area.

"Just like she told me!" I whispered, thrilled.

I had to lie down on the floor to really see into its corners. There I discovered only one item, tucked far in the back. Focusing my flashlight on it I reached in, gingerly at first, in case some mouse was nesting nearby. I hauled up the item and put it on the floor beside me.

"Whoa!" I exclaimed in disbelief. It was a cellophane cylinder, dry and brittle from being in its hiding place. I opened it and carefully slid the curled-up contents out: sheaves of large paper, heavy and linen-like. I could see that the interior side had vivid drawings done in strong black lines and bright colors—red and yellow and blue and green.

My fingers trembled a bit as I gently smoothed the paper which had clearly lain here for a very long time. At first it didn't want to uncurl. There were at least five or six sheets, all rolled together . . . Slowly, carefully, I flattened out the top one and gazed at the artwork in my lap . . .

"Wallpaper," I said aloud.

Scraps of sample wallpaper. With lots of clowns on it. And dogs and cats, also dressed in clown gear like ruffs and peaked caps. And believe me, the wallpaper artist may have been earnest, and even successful. But he definitely was no Picasso.

"Merde!" I growled. Dispirited, I rolled the pages back up, slid them into their cylinder, and deposited them in their burial chamber. I replaced the floorboard, stacked the suitcases on top, and, turning to the beds now, I cast the flashlight's beam to examine the flooring beneath them. Nothing.

Nice going, Céline, I thought, thoroughly disgusted.

I straightened up, replaced everything as I'd found it, and went across the hall to inspect a smaller bedroom—lo and behold, this was the one decorated with clown wallpaper. In spite of myself I had to laugh when I saw more of the fanciful, Art Deco masked clowns chasing each other across a black-and-white checkerboard. The bed and armoire were modern, inexpensive Scandinavian furniture. Nothing here could be from Grandmother Ondine's day. There were no clothes in the closet and nothing unusual about this room, which appeared un-occupied.

Maybe this wallpaper inspired Gil to name his restaurant *Pierrot*, I mused. It was such a modest-sized room, I wondered what Grandma used it for. A guest bedroom, no doubt. My parents might have stayed here when they visited. Well, if Dad had slept here, then this would be the *last* place that Grandma would hide a treasure that she didn't want him to know about!

But just to be sure, I dove under the bed and checked for any more loose floorboards. Then, as I came to my feet, I had the strange feeling that I was not alone. I turned around, and spotted a little boy standing in the doorway holding a suitcase, and wearing a polite, puzzled look on his face.

"Hullo," he said. "What are you doing in my room?" He had an English accent.

"Oh," I said. "Oh. Hi there." I had to smile; there was something innately sweet about him.

He studied me carefully. "You're snooping around for something, aren't you?" he asked. I could not answer. He grinned. "You're not supposed to be here, you know."

I recovered enough to say, "Well, who are *you* and what are you doing here?"

Very seriously he said, "This is my playroom now. My name is Martin, and my dad owns this place."

I absorbed his little speech. Could this kid actually belong to Gil? Of course he did. He was a pint-sized version of Gil: blond, curious, lots of intelligence in his eyes, and a touch of sadness. He was wearing black jeans and a black T-shirt, too, just like Gil. I guessed that he was about ten years old.

"I sleep in the dovecote," he said proudly. I had no idea what he meant.

"What's your name?" he asked.

"Look, can you keep a secret?" I said. "I lost something. So, I was just checking to see if I could find it. I didn't know you were staying here. I thought the room was empty."

Martin considered this. "Well, okay," he said doubtfully. "But what's your name?"

"Céline," I replied.

"Hi, Céline," he said, reaching out his small paw, offering to shake hands. I found this touching, and although his handshake was firm, his fingers were delicate. He struck me as fragile, somehow. Then I remembered what Aunt Matilda said, about Gil's wife committing suicide. The poor kid.

"Do you play cards?" Martin asked eagerly. "I have a brand-new deck of cards."

"Yes, I do," I said gently, "but I can't play now. I know some folks around here who love to play cards. I'll introduce them to you next time. But right now, I have to go."

"Oh," said Martin, failing to hide his disappointment. "Okay." He really was so sweet.

I left, determined to see this through for Mom's sake. I retraced my steps to Gil's new kitchen, then slipped outside beyond the terrace, and set off on the winding footpath that led away from the main house, weaving past terraced orchards with a view of the olive groves, vineyards and farmland beyond. Scattered along this path were smaller, freestanding stone outbuildings with terracotta-tiled roofs, looking like miniature versions of the main building, which gave them a sweet, playhouse appeal.

"I *suppose* a painting could be hidden in one of those," I muttered with waning conviction while eyeing the terrain. But whenever I paused to push a door open and peer inside, I saw that these were just rudimentary stone structures with earthen or cement floors; and while they may have provided useful winter storage for supplies or food, they were hardly the place to harbor a Picasso masterpiece.

I was now approaching a larger outbuilding which might be a good candidate—a barnlike structure near a small parking lot, with a dilapidated old picnic table in the grass nearby, where, judging from coffee stains and crumbs, the construction men had eaten their lunch. The men were gone, since they began their workdays at the crack of dawn; but they'd left a few construction vehicles parked nearby. I approached the building eagerly; yet as I reached the front path I heard the unmistakable vroom of a motorcycle approaching.

Sure enough, Gil came rumbling up on his Ducati and waved, so I couldn't duck out of sight. I waved back, hastily concocting a reason for being here as he parked and began eyeing me quizzically.

"Is everything all right? How did class go today?" he asked, walking up the front path. He looked to be in a much better mood than I'd seen him lately.

"Class was fine. Heather was great," I said brightly. "I never realized how many little storage buildings there are here! They're so cute, like dollhouses," I babbled on in an admiring tone. For some reason, acting a bit daft around men seems to work when you want to flatter or distract them.

Gil actually brightened with enthusiasm, like a boy who wants to show you his baseball card collection. "Over there is the old water mill that ground the grain they grew right here in our fields," he said, pointing off in the distance. He was so pleased by my interest that I felt a bit ashamed, but I continued acting fascinated and wide-eyed while he obligingly pointed to each outbuilding: "And there's the silo where they stored it. Beyond it is a henhouse, and a smokehouse . . ." His descriptions made me mentally cross each of them off the list as Grandma's likely hiding places. That left only this one.

"And what is *this* building we're standing in front of?" I asked, trying to sound casual. "A barn?"

"No, a *pigeonnier*," Gil said. He pointed to a row of tiny windows at the attic level, now closed up, but where, presumably, pigeons once flew in and out with wild abandon. "A dovecote," he explained.

"This whole building was all for pigeons?" I asked incredulously, while trying to assess whether Grandma Ondine would have raised pigeons. "Did people eat them, just like pheasants?"

"Sure, but pigeons were *really* prized for their excrement," he said.

When I made a face, he insisted, "Seriously—it made great fertilizer! *Pigeonniers* were status symbols ever since Roman times. When you totted up the value of a manor house, you included how much pigeon shit it produced! Anyway, we're converting this *pigeonnier* into a VIP guest villa. It won't be finished till next year, when we'll expand it and gussy it up. For now, I'm using it as my office. It'll give me some privacy from the guests in the high season."

I was thinking to myself, *Grandma would hardly park a Picasso among pigeon dung*. But just to be sure, I asked, "What was this *pigeonnier* originally like, inside? Did you have to change it much?"

"It *was* like a barn inside, actually," Gil said, reaching into his pocket for a set of jingling keys. "We had to install all the basics: windows, sliding doors, electric wiring, all the heat and air-conditioning; we're still working on the plumbing and bathrooms. It's nice now. Come see for yourself."

He let me in, smiling as if he were flattered that I'd chased him down to his private lair. It was big and open, like a huge loft with high ceilings and exposed beams. The floors had been painstakingly refinished, but the place was mostly empty, except for two modest beds, and a few provisional chairs around a table. One windowed alcove served as a study with a desk, lamp, and computer.

"Not much in the way of furniture for your VIP's," I teased.

"It's temporary, of course," Gil said, looking embarrassed. "There wasn't much to work with. The dairyman who sold me this *mas* left some old country-style stuff, which my business partner's got in storage. Some of it might work." Gil's mobile phone rang then, so he stepped away to take the call. I heard him say, "Yeah, Maurice, what's up?"

I wandered around inspecting the place carefully, but there was really nothing more to see, and I could find no possible trace of Grandmother Ondine.

"Rick was *here* today?" Gil exclaimed suddenly. "Why the fuck didn't he phone? What note? What does it say, then?" There was a pause, and he said in exasperation, "Yes, *read* it to me, now!"

I pictured Maurice quaking at his front desk as he recited the note Rick scribbled. Sure enough, Gil's expression became livid. He listened awhile longer, then hung up and turned to me, still glaring.

"Well, you're busy," I said hastily. "See you tomorrow."

"Hold on!" Gil said, looking at me intently now. "I've just heard from my staff that you've been sneaking all around my *mas*. I've got a fair idea of what you've been up to!"

For a wild moment I thought he'd somehow found out about the whole hidden Picasso thing. Then I realized how unlikely this was. "I don't know what you mean," I said warily. I wondered if his kid, Martin, had already tattled on me to the staff, just because I wouldn't play cards with him.

"What were you doing in the men's area?" Gil asked sharply.

Now I was sure that Martin ratted me out. "I took a wrong turn," I said, feeling defensive. "Your son Martin is very sweet but I just got lost, that's all."

The effect of hearing his son's name was immediate. It was as if Gil's tough-guy mask just fell away from his face, and he looked raw and vulnerable.

"You saw Martin?" he asked in a completely different tone.

"Yes," I said, realizing I'd blundered, because clearly it wasn't the kid who'd told him. "He looks just like you. You ought to introduce him to the class. They'd adore him."

"Yeah, I know," Gil muttered. "He's a good little guy." Then he recovered. "Look, you still haven't explained what you were doing there. We've got security cameras in the hallways near the construction site. Today you've had a starring role!" He was standing near his desk and he punched up his computer to show me. I peered at the screen, and there I was on the video, undeniably skulking in the corridors of the old section with my flashlight and duffel bag, looking like a cat-burglar.

"Who are you, really? Are you Rick Vandervass' girl?" Gil demanded. "Is that why you're collecting recipes and spying on local restaurants and sneaking around my *mas*?"

"Are you kidding?" I said, astonished yet relieved that he was so far off the scent. "I just met that guy in your lobby today!"

"Come on," Gil said, "people saw you go off with Rick and they said you looked pretty cozy. Are you his spy? This isn't my first time out at the rodeo. I've had bartenders who turned out to be bookies, waitresses who were food bloggers in disguise, and line cooks who stole my best recipes and sold them to the competition. So you can just tell *whoever* you're working for that he can kiss my ass."

"You must be joking! It so happens that I had a last-minute appointment in town today to see a lawyer about my grandmother's estate," I replied. "And I must say Maurice was no help at all at finding me a car. Rick offered to give me a lift. End of story. But quite frankly, even if I decide to go out with someone, it's still none of your business. You don't see me quizzing you about *your* girlfriend."

"What girlfriend?" he demanded, momentarily thrown.

"Heather, the pastry-slinger," I said. Then I was horrified with myself. Heather was perfectly nice. Why had I said that?

"Well, that would be well-nigh impossible," Gil said calmly, "since she doesn't fancy my type."

"Oh? What type is that?" I asked automatically.

"Males," he said. At my blank look he added, "Aw, for God's sake. Heather has lesbianic preferences, okay?" He watched with satisfaction as it sank in.

"Huh," I replied, resenting Gil for trapping me into this mortifying conversation. "Are all chefs as paranoid as you?"

"Yeah, pretty much," he admitted, more quietly now. It dawned on me that he must feel I'd made a fool of him, egging him on to chatter about his passion for this place, *pigeonnier* and all. He only wanted to know why. And after all, I *was* being cagey. "So—what did you and Rick talk about in the back of his car?" he asked, still looking suspicious, more about his partner than me at this point.

"He acted just like you—he asked me how long I've known you, and if you went off to meetings a lot, and how the construction was going, and if I thought you'd be ready to open in time," I said.

Gil asked instantly, "What did you tell him?"

"What *could* I tell him?" I retorted. "I said you've got a nice place, and business looks good."

"But—why did he pick *you* to chat up?" Gil wondered. I recalled the smirking chauffeur exchanging knowing looks in the rearview mirror with Rick.

"He thinks I'm your latest girlfriend," I said, feeling exasperated. "Perish the thought."

Gil actually blushed. "There are worse fates," he muttered. "But what gave him *that* idea?"

I didn't want to remind Gil of the fiasco at the Café Paradis with tourists snapping pictures of us being escorted out by police. So I shrugged. "You're up to no good, I can smell it," Gil said. "Your aunt told me you've got personal issues, but obviously there's more to it than she knows!"

Now it was my turn to be paranoid. "What exactly did my aunt tell you about me?" I demanded.

He said gently, "That you're here because your mum fell ill, so you're standing in for her. Which I guess explains why a woman who isn't particularly fond of cooking is taking my course."

I gave him my most enigmatic, Mona Lisa smile. He said, "Okay, I'll walk you back to the main building." We stepped outside and he locked the place up. Oddly enough, I found the walk quite restful; Gil, despite his boundless energy, was also capable of companionable silences. All we heard was the occasional hoot of those famous scops owls in the South of France, persistent in their lonely commentaries.

And just as we rounded a curved path leading to the front door, a whimsical little cloudburst caused soft rain to briefly shower through the branches of a tree, whose lovely pink blossoms were already drifting to the ground. I happened to be walking beneath the branches just as the rain made a cascade of pink petals come fluttering down, wetly and fragrantly, filling the air all around me.

All I could do was stop and catch my breath in childlike delight, turning my face up instead of trying to hide from it. The whole thing was over in seconds; but it was such an unexpected, sensual gift that I could only stand there, shocked, laughing and showered by the perfumed Mediterranean rain.

A moment later it was gone, and the sun peeped through the clouds.

COOKING FOR PICASSO / 225

Gil had stopped, too, but he was on the outer curve of the path, so he hadn't passed under the tree. Now he smiled.

"That was just incredible!" I gasped. Gil looked as if he were seeing me for the first time.

He moved closer, reaching out to pluck a few errant blossoms from my hair, saying quietly, "Beautiful." I must have automatically backed up, breaking the spell, because a look of comprehension crossed his face before he said lightly, "I must remember to add a flower-shower to the spa menu."

When we stepped inside the *mas* we parted at the lobby. I went up to my room to change clothes. Recalling the look on Gil's face, I felt strangely exposed; and out of habit I did a quick mental check to assess how much of myself I'd given away. It was like searching my pockets to see if I'd lost my house keys.

At least, when he interrogated me in that *pigeonnier,* I didn't blurt out anything about the lost Picasso painting. I found myself wishing my mother had kept her wild ideas to herself. The best thing I could do now was to stop sneaking around like a criminal, go back to being a normal person and finish this cooking class, I decided. Then, rather unwillingly, I recalled something Mom used to say while she sat there sewing in her kitchen in New York. *When you reach the end of your rope, make a knot and hold on.*

I sighed and went into the bathroom to towel my hair dry. My mother's stories, my grandmother's notebook—I'd been clutching at these straws as if they were a lifeline I just couldn't let go of; because on the other end of the line, I could see my small-but-indefatigably-optimistic mother—so far, far away—yet still hanging on.

22

Ondine in America (Part One), 1940

"HAVE YOU SEEN THE PICASSOS?"

Ondine's ears pricked up one wintry evening as she emerged from the kitchen of *Chez Ondine,* the pretty restaurant with a pink awning that she and Luc now owned in a seaside town called New Rochelle. Surviving in America hadn't been easy—in fact, the first three years had been quite overwhelming. Everything about this country was bigger, more spacious and spread out. There were more cars, more noise, more people who all seemed to know exactly where they were going in life.

When Luc and Ondine first arrived they went straight to an address he'd gotten from a shipmate for a rooming house not far from the harbor, so they could walk there and watch the fishing boats come and go on the Long Island Sound. They knew that their savings could dwindle to nothing quickly, so Luc, feeling perfectly at home with fishermen, worked with them whenever they needed extra help.

At first it was all Ondine could do just to learn the lay of the land, so she and Luc took long walks all over town to get a feeling for their new home. New Rochelle, though leafy and considered a suburb of Manhattan, was really a city itself, big and bustling. Although settled by French Protestants called the Huguenots, there was a Catholic girls' college that occupied a Gothic castle built by a hotelier in the 1800s. Nearby were large, beautiful houses nestled in their own enclaves where the captains of commerce lived.

"Look at the colors of the leaves on these oaks and maples!" Ondine marvelled when she and Luc walked past, hand-in-hand one Sunday, admiring the many shades of crimson and gold and orange and green. "Autumn here is much more colorful than it is back in France!"

From the fishermen Luc learned that there was a room-and-bath for rent in town above a florist's shop. It was small, but more private than the rooming house. And in the busy center of town, Ondine discovered vegetable and fruit markets bursting with an astonishing variety of apples that would be perfect for making *tarte Tatin*—a dessert that she discovered was "as American as apple pie".

The wholesale suppliers operated their business down by the railroad tracks where they had their own railcars packed full of foodstuffs. Even the produce in America was bigger—pears from Oregon; potatoes from Maine; oranges, lemons and grapes from exotic-sounding places like Florida and California; beef from Oklahoma and Texas. Trying to grasp the size of this country was mind-boggling, and every day on the street Ondine and Luc were jostled by throngs of people all pushing to get ahead.

But her husband was teaching her how to fight for a dream and win. Luc had dogged out the sale of a dilapidated but spacious old diner with a good-sized parking lot and a fine location, near the train and trolley lines, so he invested most of his money to repair it and turn it into a bistro. He knew how to bargain hard with his suppliers, and how to charm the city officials who helped him get a liquor license. Then he quickly assessed what kind of potential customers they might initially attract.

"We'll keep our prices low," he said, "because at first we'll be cooking mainly for the locals who work here in town during the day. They'll appreciate your *bonne femme* soups and stews, and they'll spread the word!" The modest profit they earned always went right back into the restaurant, to pay for a dishwasher and a waiter.

And along with the challenges of cooking, Ondine soon had a baby girl to look after, born just five months after their arrival in the States. The child, now nearly three years old, was named Julie, after Luc's mother. Ondine kept the baby by her side everywhere, even those Sundays when she and Luc struggled to learn English in the basement of a local church. The coziness between the three of them made her feel safer and more loved than she'd ever felt in her life.

However there'd been more than a few nights when Ondine lay awake worrying that perhaps they should have just put their money into a bank and gotten jobs, instead of seeking independence. But America was an exhilarating place, even, as Luc said, "while it's kicking you up the backside."

And Luc was right about many things, especially the wisdom of coming here to wait out the second world war. More and more refugees arrived at *Chez Ondine* claiming they'd escaped on "the last boat out": French governesses, German scientists, Polish musicians and Russian dancers. These newer, sophisticated customers worked in nearby universities and theatres, and discovered what the locals already knew— that Ondine's superb hot meals were delicious, comforting and reasonably priced.

TONIGHT, AN ELDERLY FRENCH PROFESSOR and his wife were just finishing up their beef *daube* when a younger, more glamorous American couple paused outside, peered in the window, spotted their neighbors and rapped on the glass excitedly. They came blowing in the front door, brushing snow off their shoulders and stomping their feet, delighted to join their friends.

They must have just come off the train, Ondine surmised. It was a week after New Year's, and the past months of holidays had nearly exhausted her meat and fish suppliers, starting with the bewildering festival of Thanksgiving in which the only thing people seemed to want to eat was turkey.

Luc quietly approached the American couple now with an apologetic gesture because the kitchen was closed. The dapper young fellow, handing off his silk top hat and silver-topped walking stick, responded with a breezy gesture as he sat down with his friends, saying, "Oh, don't worry, we've had our dinner. But—brrr! I wouldn't mind an espresso and a cognac just to thaw me out." When Luc nodded, the man said gracefully, "Yours is the only place with the lights still on at this hour. Lucky us!"

Ondine slipped behind the bar to make the coffee as Luc poured two glasses of cognac for the man and his slim, attractive wife, who wore a satin gown and a sable-trimmed cape. At first the two couples murmured companionably, but soon their conversation grew louder and livelier.

And it was just then that Ondine overheard them say the name Picasso.

"You mean you haven't seen his exhibit at the Museum of Modern Art?" The younger woman waved a hand glittering with diamonds. "We just came from there! It's called *Picasso: Forty Years of his Art*. But oh, what a pity—tonight was the last showing in New York! It's going to Chicago next. Look, I have the catalogue."

"Biggest display of his work this side of the Atlantic," her cheery husband explained to the elder French man. "Over three hundred pieces of art! Guess they're safer here than in Europe."

The men launched into a sober discussion of Hitler's army, the war's progress, and the perils of an artist like Picasso, whom the Nazis considered "degenerate", remaining in German-occupied Paris.

How will Picasso survive, much less paint? Ondine wondered, admiring his courage.

As the two couples rose to go, the young American woman swept her silver beaded purse from the table with a gloved hand, then paused to take a last appraising glance around the restaurant. "*Chez Ondine.* What a quaint little place! I didn't realize it changed hands. Wasn't it an awful old diner?"

"Not anymore! The new owners are French," the older woman assured her, glad to have news of her own to boast of. "Their cuisine is authentic Provençal, I assure you, and *très excellente*. And so reasonable. We eat here twice a week!"

"Hmm," said the young woman meaningfully to her husband on

their way out. "We'll have to come back here and see for ourselves. Isn't this a marvellous town?" They went out arm-in-arm, singing a Broadway tune about New Rochelle, *"Only forty-five minutes from Broadway, think of the changes it brings. . . ."*

The sleigh bells which Luc had put on the front door jingled as the two couples left. Ondine exchanged an amused glance with him and couldn't help saying, "Yes, New Rochelle has brought us many changes! Yet, it's not *so* different, for here I am, cooking in a café kitchen, just like *Maman*."

That ironic thought occurred to Ondine more than once, whenever she made a gesture like her mother, such as raising a flour-dusted arm to brush the hair from her face. She'd written to her parents asking if they were all right; but they would not answer a daughter who had disobeyed, eloped and abandoned them. This weighed on her heart, but she was not sorry that she'd left France, her parents, and even Picasso. Ondine understood that she had a family of her own now which must come first. She had a husband who treated her not as a servant, but as his business partner and the great love of his life as well. As they cleared up now she smiled gratefully at her tall, handsome man.

Luc beamed back at her. "Don't worry. This will be a good New Year for us," he promised. He took her into his arms and kissed her, and Ondine felt her own passionate love answering his in a way that still astonished her with its combination of ferocity and tenderness. For a moment, they just stayed there, embracing, kissing, feeling each other's heartbeat. Ondine nuzzled against his neck, sighing.

Finally, they broke apart, and companionably resumed their work. Luc stooped to retrieve something that had fallen to the floor, and handed it to her. "Look—they left this."

It was the catalogue from the Picasso exhibit. Ondine flipped through the pictures, pausing to gasp at one called *Guernica,* which captured the horrifying carnage after the fascists bombed a Spanish town. Yet with all the paintings, she could not find the portrait Picasso made of her, his *Girl-at-a-Window*.

Was it all just a dream? she wondered. But when they went across the street to sleep in their room above the florist's shop, the first thing

Ondine saw was indisputable proof that her adventures with Picasso were real. Little Julie, who lay drowsing in her cot in an alcove, popped her head up and held out her arms for a hug.

The child was still quite tiny for her age, and she had Picasso's inky dark eyes, making Ondine think of her as a sweet little black-eyed pea. Often, instead of playing with other children, Julie preferred to hide under her mama's kitchen table in the restaurant, busily absorbed in her coloring books and crayons. Sometimes Julie would just sit for hours staring dreamily into space, chuckling to herself.

"There's nothing wrong with her," a doctor assured Ondine. "She's just naturally introverted, and will always be smaller than other children her age. It's often inherited. Is anyone in her father's family like that, perhaps?" Ondine shrugged guiltily and did not relay this to Luc, who adored Julie.

"She's a daydreamer," Luc would say tenderly, kissing the girl on the top of her head, causing Julie to gaze up worshipfully at "Papa Luc" with utter adoration. At Christmastime Julie had been delighted with a little lighted crèche that Luc brought her, and she loved putting the infant Christ in his straw bed between the doting figures of Mary and Joseph.

"That's us, isn't it?" Julie had asked delightedly. "We're a Holy Family, too."

"Yes, *ma petite,*" Ondine replied, astounded at how her daughter's face struck a deep protective chord which she had scarcely imagined she possessed. The doctor had informed Ondine that the birth of this child made it impossible for her to have any more babies; but as Luc generously said, "We are blessed enough as we are."

A MONTH LATER, LUC CAME rushing into their bistro, triumphantly brandishing a New York newspaper. "We're in here!" he proclaimed. "The newsagent said it's a 'great review' and insisted I take it home." Ondine peered over his shoulder and recognized the photograph of the reviewer.

"It's that young man in the silk hat!" she reminded Luc. "With the wife who was chattering about Picasso at New Year's. They came back last week to eat here with all their friends, remember?"

"*Fabulous French Cuisine at Chez Ondine,*" Luc read the rhyming headline aloud. "It says, *I have dined in many of the world's best restaurants, yet I am astonished to find that the chef at Chez Ondine regularly spoons up a cuisine fine enough to match, and even rival, the very crème de la crème.*"

Luc looked up, his eyes shining with pride. Stunned, Ondine said, "We ought to say a prayer of thanks for the old monk Père Jacques who taught me his cooking secrets at the convent!"

"You'll soon see the power of a good review," Luc said, kissing her. "With luck, we'll get theatre and opera patrons from Manhattan, too. Things will be different from now on."

Yet Ondine could not say why such good news sent a strange, apprehensive shiver up her spine. Luc understood the ambivalent expression on her face, and he laughed and hugged her reassuringly. "Never mind what the old market ladies taught you in Juan-les-Pins! They feared good luck as well as bad. Too much superstition, with their talismans to ward off the evil eye of jealousy!"

It wasn't long before their parking lot swarmed with cars ferrying curious diners who drove not only from far-flung corners of the county, but from Connecticut and Manhattan and even New Jersey. This hubbub was easily observed by Luc's suppliers and by other restaurant owners who'd been in business for years but never managed to attract such a crowd.

"We got *too* successful," Ondine would say later, because the restaurant's profits did not go unnoticed by another very different sort of customer. Strange, predatory men with hardened faces began showing up at *Chez Ondine*. They sat at the bar drinking small cups of bitter coffee, sizing up Luc as they often did whenever a new immigrant grocer, shopkeeper, vegetable seller or baker began to prosper.

Ondine watched uneasily as Luc's business dealings—and the people he had to "play ball" with—became more complicated. With wifely concern she noted that after his nighttime "meetings" or Sunday card games with the men, Luc came home with a more tense and distracted expression. And just when she and Luc were earning enough to start a savings account, those strange, ominous-looking men began demanding a piece of the profits for "protection" against thieves, robbers and arsonists.

"What kind of nonsense is this?" Ondine asked when Luc first told her about the payoffs he was being forced to make every week. "We must pay those gangsters to protect us from *them*?"

"That's right," Luc replied calmly as they sat with the adding machine between them, counting the week's take. "Otherwise, some of our suppliers of wine and meat and fish would charge us more than they do—and sell us only their dregs! They're all connected. I'm told it's called 'the mob'."

"How is this possible? What about the police?" Ondine demanded. Luc just shook his head.

So they paid. Faced with a situation she couldn't control, Ondine resorted to slipping into church when it was empty. She'd go to the statue of the Virgin Mary, at whose feet stood an iron shelf with rows of small votive candles. Ondine deposited a coin in the metal box and, using a long, skinny wooden stick poking out of the ashes on a tray beneath the candles, she transferred a flame from one candle to her own, then closed her eyes and prayed fervently for a more benign form of protection.

23

Picasso in Paris, 1943

THE GESTAPO WERE MAKING A SURPRISE VISIT TO PICASSO'S STUDIO AGAIN. But as always, they were unsure of what to look for in the Minotaur's lair. A few years before the war, Picasso had moved into this elaborate apartment on the Rue des Grands-Augustins which Dora Maar had found for him, and its labyrinth of rooms suited his mysterious, secretive nature.

First you had to get past the Master's assistant, Sabartés, a suspicious-looking Spaniard who grudgingly allowed the German officers into the anteroom—an odd, rather chaotic reception area populated with a variety of caged birds and spiky exotic plants, and, on any given day, an assortment of fawning art dealers, collectors, magazine interviewers, would-be artists and anyone else who sought Picasso's favor.

"Why are non-Germans so badly organized?" the young blond officer asked his older, superior partner as they moved into the second room, which was narrower and cluttered with old furniture, tables of books, magazines, photographs, hats, men's suits, shoes, paintings, musical instruments, stones and shells and anything else that had once caught Picasso's fancy but now lay here, gathering dust.

A third room contained many large sculptures. It led to a winding staircase, which in turn took them to a second-floor studio where, finally, they discovered Picasso himself. Pablo liked to tell people that this was the studio which inspired Balzac's famed story about an artist whose painting came to life.

The two Gestapo officers did not know who Balzac was. But they noted it down. Then, affecting a stern and scornful manner, the elder one said, "Where is your friend Jacques Lipchitz? Was he here today?" This was a favorite question of the Gestapo that they asked whenever they visited.

And Picasso, his dark eyes watchful, would say the same thing he always said about this Jewish sculptor. "As far as I know, he's gone to America." If Picasso even knew the town's name where Lipchitz had gone, he didn't say so.

Besides, the Gestapo knew perfectly well that Lipchitz was long gone. Next they said tauntingly, "Well, how about you? You're Jewish, aren't you?"

"Non," Picasso answered curtly.

"Oh?" said the older, arrogant one. "Let's see your papers, then."

Despite Picasso's calm, disinterested manner, he always took care to have his papers in order. Then, inevitably, the search began. The German officers examined cupboards, opened closets, and stared at paintings.

Picasso had taken precautions. Many of his paintings were in vaults and other safe places. He had also hidden stockpiles of coal and firewood which was so scarce these days; and his emergency stashes of solid gold bars were wrapped up and mixed in with soaps from Marseilles in an old suitcase.

As for his women, Dora Maar lived in an apartment around the block, and Marie-Thérèse was ensconced in another one farther away but within visiting distance; yet neither woman was supposed to visit his studio unless invited. Of course, sometimes they broke this rule. But mostly, he could control them. He provided precious things like the coal for Marie-Thérèse so she could keep their daughter, Maya, warm during this period when everything of value was ruthlessly rationed.

Pablo considered himself lucky that the Gestapo came today, instead of one of those days when Spanish refugees or French resistance fighters showed up on his doorstep, needing money or whatever aid he could give.

"What's this supposed to be?" asked the young officer, staring at an abstract painting. He'd heard that Picasso was a great artist, yet also on the "degenerate" list, so his work was not allowed to be displayed in galleries. Picasso shrugged. Baffled, the man persisted, "Why do you paint like this?"

"I don't know," Picasso replied, playing the bohemian to the hilt. "Because it amuses me."

Light seemed to break across the young officer's face. "Ah! Then it's a fantasy, *ja*?"

The older officer, in no mood for cat-and-mouse games, picked up another canvas and said chillingly, "Is this painting yours?"

"Yes, but I didn't paint it," Picasso said. "I only own it. It's a Matisse."

"And this?" The elder officer moved into another narrow aisle stacked with pictures.

"It's a Renoir."

"And this, also, is a Renoir?"

"No, it's a Cézanne. You already inventoried that one."

"Did I? Are you sure?" The younger officer nervously checked his notes.

"Oh, yes," Picasso said disingenuously. "But you missed these over here."

On and on it went, as the older man peered into the bewildering stacks and directed the younger to write everything down. By now the officers were disoriented and confused, just as Picasso wanted them to be, while he continued telling them they'd seen this or missed that, until they were hopelessly lost amidst the clutter. When they asked what each painting was worth, Picasso invented modest prices. The officers believed him only because they were so out of their depth—they knew how to evaluate a chunk of gold from a Jew's tooth, or a gypsy's earring; they knew the sum total of the contents of every bank vault in Paris which they'd opened up as soon as they invaded the city; but modern art was a mystery that often eluded them.

Finally, at the end of Picasso's stacks of canvases, the young man's hand paused at an unusual portrait. This was unlike all the baffling modern paintings he'd seen today. It was a girl at a window, her face alight, her eyes gazing out at the world as if she alone could bring it to its knees. A curl of a smile lighted her young face.

"What's this one, then?" asked the junior officer, trying not to care personally. But something about that young woman made his heart yearn for home, and all the pretty girls he'd ever known.

Picasso's dark gaze followed his and rested on the portrait. For a moment he honestly could not remember when he'd painted it. Then he recalled his *ondine,* the girl from the sea, in a quieter time when privacy was a commodity easily attained; as opposed to now, when it was as rare as rubies. Unexpectedly Pablo felt deeply moved by this, for a moment wishing that he could transport himself back in time to that day in Juan-les-Pins, when France herself was almost as innocent as this radiant young lady.

"Oh, that," Picasso said as casually as possible. "That's just a girl I once knew."

The young man nodded sagely. "Yes," he said, his hand still on the canvas. "That's a good one."

Picasso felt strangely protective when, for a moment, it looked as if this callow German officer might tuck the portrait under his arm and take it with him. It wouldn't be the first time the victors took whatever spoils they wanted from Paris.

But the older man, whose heart could no longer be moved by love of anything pure and gentle, said curtly and importantly, "Yes, well, that's rather old-fashioned, isn't it? I imagine it's not worth as much as your fancier ones these days."

The younger man actually blushed scarlet, put down the picture and backed away.

"Ah, what painting *is* worth much these days?" Picasso said romantically. "Art can't warm your bathwater or feed your children."

*   *   *

LATER, WHEN THE OFFICERS HAD gone, Picasso went down to a nearby black-market café to calm his nerves with a glass of wine and supper. Dora Maar was there at his table, along with other friends.

"Have you heard about Cocteau?" Dora said to him *sotto voce*. "The Nazis beat him up on the Champs-Elysées, just because he refused to salute them." Picasso shook his head sadly; he'd heard far too many stories like this about people he knew. They all understood that the world they loved was vanishing, in ways large and small, every day.

So Pablo tried to lighten the atmosphere for his other friends at the café. The actress Simone Signoret listened intently as Picasso regaled his group around the table with what would become his most famous tale about the Gestapo inspecting his studio.

"Then one of the officers—the older one—he sees a photograph of my painting of the fascist bombing of *Guernica,* lying on the table," Pablo said. "This Nazi looks at all that carnage, and then he says to me, *Did you do this?* And so I said to him, *No, you did!*"

And along with his friends, Picasso laughed uproariously at how he'd forced the Nazis to confront the damage Hitler's army had done.

At that moment, Pablo spotted a young girl with dark-russet hair, sitting at another table with her girlfriend, accompanied by a man Picasso knew. Every time Pablo caught the eye of the russet-haired girl, she grinned back at him. So he kept telling more jokes and showing off, just to see that girl smile again. Finally, he rose from his table, leaving Dora Maar behind, and carrying a bowl of cherries.

"Well?" Picasso said to his friend who was sitting there with the young ladies. "Aren't you going to introduce me?"

He set down the bowl of cherries right in front of the russet-haired girl, then listened attentively as his friend made the rounds of introductions.

"And, this is Françoise Gilot," said the man. "She's been a law student at the Sorbonne, but now she thinks she'd rather be a painter."

Picasso laughed. "That's the funniest thing I've heard all day," he said. "Girls who look like *that* can't be painters."

But Françoise was no shrinking violet. She was the well-educated daughter of a very successful businessman who'd taught her how to think, debate and compete. So she jutted out her chin and informed Pablo that it just so happened that she and her girlfriend were not only painters, but this very week they were having a joint exhibition at a well-respected gallery. Perhaps Picasso ought to have a look. Then she smiled, and popped a cherry into her mouth.

"Is that so?" said Pablo. "Well, I am a painter, too. You must come to my studio and see some of *my* paintings."

"When?" asked Françoise. She was only twenty-one years old, but she knew how to heed the call of fate.

"Tomorrow. The next day. When you want to," Picasso replied.

Very seriously, Françoise and her best friend put their heads together and reviewed their schedule. "We can come next Monday," Françoise announced.

Picasso bowed. "As you wish." He shook hands with everyone; then he picked up his bowl of cherries and returned to his own table.

And Dora Maar wished, with all her heart, that they had picked a different café to have supper in that day.

24

Ondine in America (Part Two), 1952

By Julie's fifteenth birthday, *Chez Ondine* was so profitable that Ondine and Luc were able to enroll their daughter in a private well-regarded girls' high school. Ondine's little family had long since moved out of the room above the florist's shop, and they now rented a nice Victorian house with a wraparound porch, in an enclave by the sea called *Sans Souci*, where mute swans glided majestically along the shores with their fuzzy babies, hoping for tossed pieces of old bread.

In the summertime on their day off, Luc would take Ondine and Julie out in a little rowboat. They'd paddle across to Glen Island Park, an elegant public resort with nineteenth-century beachhouses, a colonnade and a casino. They'd picnic on the crescent-shaped beach and splash about in Long Island Sound until the sun went down. Then they'd sit on the seawall to hear big-band music wafting out from the casino, with Julie and Ondine watching to see what gowns the women wore.

One evening, on Ondine's thirty-third birthday, Luc surprised her by booking a table for two at the casino. They dined on "lobster casino with saffron rice" and sole *amandine*. Then they went into the enormous second-floor ballroom with French doors that opened onto private balconies overlooking the sea and sky, where a golden moon gazed down at its own rippling reflection in the darkened waves.

"See? Our stars are still there," Luc said, pointing, and taking her into his arms. She pressed her cheek against his as they listened to "Moonlight Sonata" and "Walkin' My Baby Back Home." Humming to each other they danced late into the night to their swing-time favorites.

"Where'd you learn these steps?" Luc demanded when Ondine tried a slightly new variation.

"Julie taught me," she said. "The girls do our dances a little differently now."

"Someday we'll go back to France with her, and show her to your parents," Luc promised.

It was a dream of theirs, even a plan, for although Ondine's letters home still went unanswered, Luc felt sure that Ondine's parents wouldn't be able to resist welcoming their only grandchild.

Julie was pretty, but she was still diminutive which made her seem younger than her age. Like other children of immigrants, she'd grown up speaking English in school but her parents' language at home—never quite knowing which language to think her own private thoughts in. Although her parents were full of love, they were secretive and given to certain dark and worried moods. She knew that their stress had to do with business, yet they never told her exactly why, so even on good days there was still a persistent, uneasy undercurrent, a lurking, unspeakable anxiety, beneath all their success.

But at school, as Julie gradually overcame her innate shyness and began making friends, her confidence grew. She began acting more like an American girl, imitating the optimistic exuberance of her friends. Ondine liked hearing Julie chattering with other girls her age when they came home from school in their identical wool blazers and pleated skirts, their arms full of books, their hair pulled back with bright ribbons or sparkling clips.

One Sunday afternoon when Luc was out at a card game, and Julie was in the backyard with her friends looking at fashion magazines, a well-dressed man in a suit came into the yard bearing a box of chocolates for Julie and a bouquet of flowers for her mother. He wore cologne and had a silky, elegant demeanor as he patted Julie's cheek and then went inside to speak to Ondine.

After he left, Julie asked, "Who was that nice man with the good manners?"

"He's not nice, and don't ever speak to him again. If you see him, tell your father immediately," Ondine retorted sharply. She'd been unnerved by the visitor, who had noiselessly let himself in the unlocked back door, walked through the house and appeared at the threshold of her parlor, like a phantom. His voice was so soft that at first, Ondine could not believe she'd heard him properly. She would never tell Julie what that man had said:

You have a lovely daughter. If you want her to live to see her own wedding, you'll pay what my men have been asking your husband for. If you don't, she might have a terrible accident and you'll find her bones scattered all over town.

"Tell your friends to go home," Ondine told Julie in a low voice. "And come inside at once."

"I can't just chase them away!" Julie objected.

"Find a nice way to do it, but do it," Ondine said more sharply than usual. Julie sighed, aggrieved, but obeyed. Once Julie was safely inside, Ondine locked all the doors and windows.

When Luc came home he was beaming with self-confidence, announcing, "I've found us a new fish supplier! He's just like the man I worked for in Juan-les-Pins—honest, no-nonsense, salt-of-the-earth. We can trust him." Ondine managed an encouraging nod before she described her visitor. Luc instantly knew who it was; the boss behind the men who came to collect the protection money.

Luc was furious. "That bastard actually came to our *house*?" he exclaimed, scowling. "He threatened our *child*? By God, I'll handle him!" He jutted out his chin with that dangerous look of pride and fearlessness, which Ondine had first seen at the train station with Monsieur Renard the day they left France, and which, lately, she was seeing more frequently. Luc had, as people here said, "a long fuse", but once aroused he could be a hothead. Yet he listened to Ondine whenever she intervened.

"What exactly does this man want from us?" she asked quietly as they went into their kitchen.

Luc shook his head with a dark look in his eyes. "That's just it. He says 'more'—always, 'more'! But he'll never really be satisfied until he gets it all. He runs a string of greasy diners and he's losing customers to people like us. He offered to buy us out for an insulting amount."

"You didn't tell me that," Ondine reproached him. Lately it had been difficult to tell the difference between Luc's allies and his foes; they were all tough men. Luc shrugged and sat down.

"I didn't want to worry you; it seemed like just big talk. But now that he sees he can't own us, he only wants to put us out of business. Well, there are bigger fish than him, in the Bronx. I met one today who can protect us from these puny local sharks. Enough is enough. I'll have to deal with this tonight."

Ondine gave Luc his dinner, which he ate calmly and methodically at their table that overlooked the tranquil Long Island Sound. "What will you do?" she asked, sitting beside him.

"We'll have to take on this Bronx boss as an 'investor' in our place; but that's okay," Luc said, as if he'd already been considering this for some time. "Because he's a real businessman. He can provide us with better suppliers for everything but the fish, and as I've said, I've got that taken care of now."

Ondine put a hand on his arm. "Don't go out tonight," she urged. "Wait until morning. It's safer to do things in the light of day." Luc's tense expression abated, and he nodded. When they went to bed she pressed close against his warm chest and he fell asleep quickly, exhausted. Ondine slept fitfully.

THE NEXT MORNING LUC LEFT early, first to see Julie safely off to school, and then he headed out for the Bronx. Ondine handled the lunchtime service, but when Luc didn't return in time to pick up Julie, she went to the schoolyard herself. Luc had told her to meet Julie if he was delayed.

"Oh, *Maman,* what is *wrong* with you and Papa today, escorting me to and fro like a child?" Julie groaned. "You're both embarrassing me in front of my friends."

Ondine and Luc had agreed not to frighten the girl by telling her of the kidnapping threat. So Ondine said only, "*Chère fille,* take your schoolbooks to Mrs. O'Malley's house and stay there, do your homework, until I come for you." Mrs. O'Malley was a kindly neighbor whose husband was a retired baseball coach. Ondine had told them about the threat to Julie and they'd agreed to keep a protective eye on her when Ondine was at work. The O'Malleys had two handsome sons, so Julie didn't object.

When Ondine returned to the restaurant to prepare for the dinner service, the telephone was ringing as she walked in. The caller was one of the waiters from the restaurant who often accompanied Luc to the freight yard to pick up fresh food supplies. And for the rest of her life Ondine would remember, word for word, what that man said: "Ondine, I'm so sorry. There's been a fight down here by the railroad tracks. A lotta men injured. But Luc . . . Luc is dead."

"No," Ondine said vehemently. "Not Luc. You must be mistaken. He didn't go down there today—he went to the Bronx."

"Yes, I know that. But then they all came here to a big meeting down by the railroad cars. I wasn't around when it happened, but I've talked to people who were. The rival gangs were supposed to come to terms, but there was a showdown of some kind and a fight broke out. I don't know if the bosses here were planning to kill your husband all along, or if he just got caught in the crossfire," the man said in a rush, as if to get it over with as quickly as he could. "They called a doctor who says that in Luc's case—it was a blow to the head."

"I'm coming there. I have to see him," Ondine said immediately, taking off her apron, still hoping it was all a mistake, as in Juan-les-Pins when everyone insisted that Luc was gone for good.

"Don't do that, Madame," the man warned with such conviction that she froze. "This is an ugly scene today, no place for a lady. Believe it or not, some people are trying to say the whole thing was just a terrible accident—that a tower of pallets packed with heavy boxes fell on the men standing below it. And the cops, well, some of them are in the pockets of the bosses. I'm handling it for you, believe me. You may get a call anyway from the police, but just tell them the truth—that you know nothing."

"I want to see Luc!" Ondine cried passionately.

"I know. I called the undertaker. The body is already on its way to the funeral parlor."

The telephone receiver slipped from Ondine's hands and clattered to the floor. She felt her body sag against the doorway. And even to her own ears, the cry that came from her throat sounded so much like a wounded animal that she pressed both hands to her mouth for fear of hearing it again.

THE UNDERTAKER SOLICITOUSLY USHERED ONDINE into the dimly lit room in the funeral parlor where Luc lay on a table. When the assistant pulled back the cloth, it was obvious that they'd worked carefully to make the body presentable. Luc's beautiful hair was combed perfectly with pomade—something he never used. And it was parted differently because, she later found out, they'd had to clip away the hair that was matted with blood from the mortal wound on his head. His face, strangely, betrayed no sign of duress; it was pale, but he still wore that determined expression which was so familiar—as if he'd been waiting for her and was about to speak in an ordinary way on an ordinary day.

"Luc," Ondine whispered, sinking into the chair beside him. "Don't leave me." She couldn't stop herself from thinking what she always did when faced with a problem: *I'll ask Luc about it when he comes home.* Her mind could not give up believing that they could overcome this difficulty as they always did—together, giving each other strength. She wanted to tell him what happened this awful afternoon after she got the phone call.

A police officer had indeed come to the restaurant and asked his perfunctory questions. How old was Luc? What business was he in? Was he a citizen? Ondine answered automatically. After he left she moved about like a sleepwalker and put up the *Closed* sign, turned off the lights, locked the doors.

Then she'd hurried off to Mrs. O'Malley's house, where Julie was waiting for her. The poor girl became so distraught when Ondine told her about Luc that Mrs. O'Malley had to call a doctor, who'd come and sedated Julie. She was sleeping now. So Ondine had gone to the funeral parlor alone.

Now, sitting in this darkened room beside her husband's body, she heard, through the numbing haze of her grief, a bell from a nearby church softly tolling the hours as if counting her sorrows. Ondine took Luc's cold hand in hers, and it was this awful chill that finally convinced her that she'd lost him. She felt as if she, too, were locked in a cold block of ice. Yet she wanted to remain here forever beside Luc in this silence—waiting, perhaps for him to awaken like a hero from an ancient myth who could somehow overcome even death.

But Luc lay still and silent. Ondine closed her eyes, too. She thought of that letter he'd sent her when he had been away at sea but then got sick with typhoid, and he'd written to her asking her to keep a small corner of her heart for his soul to come to rest there. "Yes, stay with me," she whispered.

But she could not let herself weep. Tears seemed like a luxury she could not risk, for she might just let herself drown in them. *Later, when this danger for my daughter is past, I'll go to pieces,* she thought.

The thought of Julie finally roused Ondine and brought her to her feet. But now there was a polite knock at the door, and the undertaker said she had a visitor who insisted on seeing her. "Do you know a man named Sal Miucci?" he asked.

"No," Ondine said, and yet the name sounded vaguely familiar.

The man was waiting at the back door. He was a tall, young fellow, holding his cap in his hands. "Can we speak in private?" he asked, eyeing the undertaker. "Outside, perhaps?"

"I'll be in my office if you need assistance," the mortician said meaningfully.

Ondine and the man stepped out into the parking lot behind the funeral home. "They call me Big Sal," he said, twisting his cap, his face full of sympathy. "Maybe your husband told you about me. I bring the fish on my boat. I'm based in Boston. Luc asked me to look out for you if anything happened to him."

Ondine said nothing, just listened to his voice for clues of which side he was truly on.

"Luc was afraid that without him here to protect you, the local toughs might try to scare you into giving them the money that he wouldn't let them have," the man continued. "He said it wouldn't be safe here for you and your daughter anymore—and he's right. He told me to get you out of town. He says you already know the emergency plan."

Ondine had been wary that this man was here to trick her into trusting him, but when he said "emergency plan" she now believed that Luc had confided in him. For, back when the gangsters first started demanding protection money, Luc sat her down at their kitchen table and said they must talk about exactly that—an "emergency plan".

With an unflinching gaze he'd looked deep into her eyes to make sure she was listening as he said firmly, *If anything happens to me, you know where our cash is. Take Julie away immediately—do you hear me, Ondine? Don't delay. Don't even go to the bank looking for more. Put the money you have in the lining of your coat, and don't pack anything more than you can carry in one bundle. Just go, tell no one where you're going, and don't look back.*

"I have a way to get you out of town, quick and quiet," Sal said. "I can take you on my boat to New York Harbor. From there, you can get a ship to France. Luc said you could get ready fast."

"I can't leave him," she whispered. She discovered now that she'd been trembling for some time and couldn't stop. She clasped her hands together to hold them still.

"Let's not give anybody time to kidnap Julie and try to shake you down," Sal was saying. "Tell the undertaker you don't want a funeral. Tell him to deal with me; I'll get Luc's ashes for you. Then go do whatever else you have to do to get ready. But don't sleep in your own house tonight. Do you have a neighbor you can stay with? Good. Early tomorrow morning, my boat sails."

Ondine did as Sal suggested and gave instructions to the undertaker. But before she left the funeral parlor, she returned to the back room and kissed Luc's cold lips once more. Looking at him now, she felt she knew what he would say if he could speak. *Follow the plan.*

Quickly, she slipped outside. Moving through the velvet darkness she went to the restaurant and entered by the back door, but she didn't dare turn on a light. She felt her way around the familiar kitchen as a blind woman might until she found the right spot. Crouching, she removed a cloth-wrapped bundle of money hidden beneath the false bottom of the pantry shelf. There was much more here than there had been the last time she'd checked it, only a few days ago.

"Luc must have just taken all this cash out of the bank for me!" Ondine whispered, tears now stinging her eyes. It looked like just about everything they'd saved. Trembling, she put all the packets of money in her coat's lining and roughly stitched it closed.

She was just finishing up when she heard the sound of shattered glass followed by a loud bang in the front room. The explosion shook the entire restaurant and she instinctively flung herself to the floor. Smoke and flames spread rapidly from the dining room. She knew what it was; she'd heard stories about these deadly "cocktail bottles" that gangsters threw to "torch" a place. Ondine, still on her belly, managed to crawl out the back door, then stumble to her feet and run home in the darkness.

Mr. O'Malley had already insisted that she and Julie stay in his house overnight. When she returned and told him what had happened, he listened grimly, then he assured her that his young sons would take turns that night, keeping watch for any strangers lurking.

THE NEXT MORNING ONDINE ROSE early and woke Julie, who had more questions now, but she was so upset she could barely comprehend the devastating answers that Ondine hurriedly blurted out to her: "Your father was killed last night by bad men who want his money. Don't ever speak of this to anyone. It's not safe for us here anymore. I promised your Papa I'd take you to France."

The shock was so supreme that Julie couldn't even muster the presence of mind to howl in protest. She followed her mother around as if afraid to let her out of her sight; as if Ondine, too, might suddenly vanish. After dressing and packing hastily, Julie was further stunned to discover how they were leaving town—sneaking out in the back of some fisherman's truck that was pulled right up to the garage door of Mr. O'Malley's house. His sons looked so serious when they said goodbye to Julie that for some reason this registered more than her mother's words.

Still numb from the sedatives, Julie followed her mother and they boarded the fisherman's rugged boat. As it chugged past the three small islands off the coast of New Rochelle, the screeching call of the seagulls grated on Ondine's nerves, and she covered her ears until Manhattan loomed in their view. From there, they were given third-class passage on one of the older vessels at the busy harbor.

The ship's cook had arranged to obtain these last-minute tickets and to help them get aboard in a hurry. He took Ondine's payment from her shaking hands, and escorted her to a small cabin. Julie trudged behind her like a sleepwalker who was only now beginning to awaken, just as the ship left the harbor and, with a mournful toot of its horn, it sailed for France.

25

Céline at the Museum, Antibes, 2014

AUNT MATILDA WAS LIKE A RACEHORSE CHAMPING AT THE BIT WHEN OUR cooking class assembled in the white van and went off to have our private tour of the Picasso exhibit.

"I can't believe they've got all these paintings in one place!" she chortled. "Do you realize how lucky we are to see this? It's a once-in-a-lifetime show."

The rest of us behaved like a bunch of school kids on a field trip as we arrived at the museum and descended from our minivan into the sparkling sunshine. Gil hadn't come with us; he was off on another one of his mysterious meetings. I couldn't imagine his restless persona in a museum.

Our guide, a slim, proper middle-aged French lady with wire-rimmed glasses and a decorous navy suit, was standing on the front steps of the museum to greet us. "This way, please," she said briskly, turning smartly on her chic, polished low-heeled shoes as if she would brook no lollygagging.

Aunt Matilda eyed her so warily that I stifled a giggle. We were going to have dueling art experts on this tour, I could sense it right away, as Aunt Matilda gazed at the exhibit's banner: *Picasso: Between the Wars and Between the Women*. "First of all," she muttered covertly from the side of her mouth, "there were no neat periods of this woman or that. There was a lot of overlap with Picasso's women—he kept them on the hook and played them against one another to make them jealous."

"Okay, Tilda, take it easy. Just go with the flow, all right?" Peter advised soothingly. The mild-mannered wine steward from London was turning out to be quite a companion to my aunt; she claimed that this genteel fellow was "a real beast at poker and bridge". She meant it as a compliment.

Our class shuffled with awe through the exhibit's rooms which were, indeed, arranged according to the women in Picasso's life. But I had my own timeline—Grandma Ondine's notebook. I was hoping that this excursion would provide me with answers about what was going on with Picasso while she was cooking for him. This morning I'd quickly flipped through her recipes and their dates; now, I was waiting impatiently for our tour to reach the period that really mattered to me: April and May, in 1936.

The first gallery we entered was earlier than that—it was called The Olga Period, with loving, dignified portraits of Picasso's Russian ballerina wife and their son. Then the images of his wife became uglier—she began to look like a miserable harridan, especially in *Large Nude in a Red Armchair*, a painting which caused the guide to comment, "Olga became highly nervous as her marriage fell apart. Here Picasso has reduced her to a naked, anguished, complaining heap of flesh. Picasso himself admitted that it must be painful for a woman to discover in a painting that she is 'on the way out'."

"Good God," Magda-from-Scotland grumbled as we looked at the mercilessly caricatured, amoeba-like creature splayed over a chair. "I always feel sorry for the wives of artists, don't you?"

"Next we have our Marie-Thérèse Period," the guide said, briskly leading us to a gallery of artwork that varied dramatically: from soft sweet schoolgirlish portraits in bluish-grey hues, to Amazonian giantesses thundering down the beach, to the erotic etchings of a Minotaur devouring his nude blonde mistress. There was another series that featured a cartoony girl with a penis-shaped head and body, to which my elderly classmates responded as if these were naughty schoolboy drawings.

"That's supposed to be a *woman?*" Lola drawled skeptically.

"Looks like a prick with eyes to me," Joey murmured to the other men, "but hey, I'm from Chicago, what do I know?"

"It's called the *femme-phallus,*" Aunt Matilda volunteered. "The girl and the penis become one."

"Whatever became of Marie-Thérèse?" Peter inquired in his polite English way.

"Not long after Picasso died, she hanged herself," the guide answered. There was a collective gasp of dismay among my classmates. "But that was many years after this period," she added hastily.

Lola asked rather knowingly, "What kind of lover was Picasso?"

Aunt Matilda announced breezily, "They say he took a perverse pleasure in denying women their orgasm." There was a collective clucking among the women.

Our guide primly pretended not to hear us. "And now, something different," she said hastily as she whisked us into another, adjunct room. "Here we have Picasso's mysterious interlude on our very own Côte d'Azur—in the spring of 1936." Aunt Matilda nudged me with those sharp elbows of hers.

"Picasso had stopped painting, perhaps because of distress over his personal life," the guide explained. She added proudly, "But then he retreated to the Riviera in great secrecy. And something in our little town of Juan-les-Pins provided the Master with the peace and inspiration he so desperately needed."

"What an odd series," Peter noted, peering at a wall covered with four pictures. "Hmm. These were *all* done the first week in April. See?" he said, craning his neck at the dates with scholarly interest.

"Wow, he was averaging about one a day!" Ben observed over my shoulder, impressed.

Eagerly I edged my way to the front of the group. I saw that Picasso had put the dates on each one in fierce black strokes, starting with: *2 Avril XXXVi.* The numbers instantly jogged my memory—this was the day that Grandmother Ondine cooked *bouillabaisse* for him! With a thrill of excitement I studied the picture. It was a pastel done in shades of charcoal-grey on a beige background, and at first it seemed hardly more than a doodle—of a face half in darkness and half in light, like tarot-card images of the moon—but the longer I gazed at it the more its magic worked on me, conveying a sublimely celestial yet warmly human quality, for the character even had a hat upon its surreal head.

I peered at the next ones which were dated April 3, 4 and 5. I recalled that in Grandmother Ondine's first week of cooking for Picasso she'd recorded in her notebook that she'd made him a beef *miroton,* a lamb *rissole* and a veal terrine.

"Love his sense of humor," Aunt Matilda murmured. "See how, in each successive canvas in this series, he re-imagines the face that was in that first pastel? Here it fragments into objects on a beach—a seashell, a cornucopia, a womb. An eye *here* becomes a clitoris in that one. A breast here, a hillside there. Picasso loved nature. Springtime blooming, animals mating, the stars, the sun—he embraces it all!"

Indeed, each successive canvas was bursting with color—dazzling Mediterranean blue and joyous Easter pastels of pink, yellow and green making a landscape of fecund breasts, hills, trees, and sea . . . as if Picasso were celebrating the entire earth's feminine powers of fertility and rebirth.

I wondered if Grandma ever saw these pictures. Could any of them even be the very painting he gave her? Or was there another one somewhere that was missing from this series?

"Character with a Seashell," Magda murmured, reading the title on a brass plate for the last painting in this series. "Looks like a face painted on a kite, right? I guess those gloves dangling at the bottom are the tail of the kite. At least, I *hope* they're gloves!" she added, staring at the lifeless pair of hands.

Joey grinned. "I like Picasso, but I have to admit, this dude is Jack the Ripper!"

"We must see these fragmented images in the context of twentieth-century history," Peter said quietly. "The speed of technological advances in science, medicine, psychology, travel—and warfare. Two terrible world wars that shattered cities, people and animals. We all saw things we wished we hadn't."

I glanced at Peter, so debonair-looking in his pale flannel suit and neatly trimmed white hair; but now I pictured him as a kid in London running for shelter during the "Blitz" bombings. There had always been an undercurrent of sadness in Peter's gentle nature, and now I could see why.

Across the room on another wall was a painting dated April 6. It was called *Minotaure tirant une charette*. Staring at this playful Minotaur pulling a wheelbarrow full of clutter, I quickly calculated that this was the day Grandma Ondine cooked a *cassoulet* for *a party of three*. Rather cryptically she'd noted, *P. and M. and C. were well pleased*. We drifted on to view more paintings from Picasso's Juan-les-Pins interlude; portraits of Marie-Thérèse, done in bright circus-like colors.

But then, at the last painting on this wall, our guide noted, "Here we have something different—a still life from this period."

A loaf of bread, a bowl of sensual fruit, a vase of wildly expressive yellow-orange flowers—

I stifled a gasp. There it was—an object so unmistakably familiar to me that it stopped me dead in my tracks. "Mom's pink-and-blue striped pitcher!" I said under my breath.

Aunt Matilda wore a shocked expression of recognition, too, and she raised her eyebrows at me. "Do you see what I see?" she whispered. I nodded, dumbstruck. Yes, although exaggerated, it was unmistakably that lovely Provençal pottery that Mom brought to America when she eloped. The same pitcher I'd seen all my life, which always had sentimental pride of place on a shelf in our kitchen—until Deirdre threw it away. Now here it was, triumphantly surviving for all eternity in Picasso land.

We stood there gaping until the guide spoke again. "And if you'll step this way, we have a very unusual pair of paintings, also from this mysterious period in Picasso's life," she announced, "which I feel form a bridge between the Marie-Thérèse Period and the Dora Maar Period." She moved us into a special alcove where two canvases were placed side by side because of their similar subject—a dark-haired girl in a blue dress, sitting on the floor and gazing into a mirror. Everyone clustered around the first painting, which was dated *30 avril XXXVi* and was so odd that you had to keep staring at it.

"Very strong, but strange, even for Picasso. Her neck looks like a can-opener," Lola said, gazing searchingly at the picture. "Which one of his sex slaves was *this* poor girl?"

"We do not know who the model was for this painting," the tour guide answered. "Some say the model must be Dora Maar, because of the dark hair," she continued. "Others say it is surely Marie-Thérèse, because of the curves and sensuality. Or perhaps this model was the dark-haired sister of Marie-Thérèse. We will never know for sure." I pressed forward to see it better.

And, as distorted as the model's face and body were, I felt goose-bumps at the sight of her. For there was something I recognized in the woman's graceful looks and attitude—and most strikingly in that long, dark curly hair flowing down her neck, which so distinctly resembled Grandmother Ondine's luxurious, poetic curls. In a strange way these paintings were telling me more about Grandma than her photograph did; and while I felt a poignant surge of admiration for the youthful sweetness of her draped limbs, I was also moved with pity for the tender vulnerability in her bowed head.

"Femme à la montre," Peter read the painting's title aloud from a brass plaque on the wall.

"Woman with a watch," Aunt Matilda translated, pointing to the wristwatch on the model's arm.

Could it truly be Grandma Ondine? I stared until I could almost hear the painted wristwatch ticking from its canvas. I noticed that Picasso, in his iconic, disjointed way, had painted a heart-shaped bottom visible through the skirt of the girl's blue checked dress, as if backlighting made the cloth translucent. I wondered why Mom didn't tell me that Grandma *posed* for Picasso—but maybe she hadn't known a thing about it.

"The second painting, *Femme dans un intérieur,* is the same model," the guide pointed out. I saw that it was dated *2 mai XXXVi*. She continued, "See how her mirror no longer has a reflection in it. But a ghostly 'double' sits on the floor opposite her—a *doppelgänger* with identical long dark curls."

Yes, that distinctive hair again. And if Grandma Ondine *was* the girl in these canvases, then it wasn't so farfetched that Picasso might really have rewarded her with the gift of a painting, after all.

"Was there a third study of this model?" I asked, trying to sound casual.

The guide shrugged. "Not that I know of," she replied, steering us into the next room. "But from time to time, unknown Picassos have turned up." We entered another gallery. "This brings us to the Dora Maar Period. She was an intelligent, artistic photographer. In early, more naturalistic portraits we observe her looking happy and spirited. Yet Picasso called her 'the weeping woman', and you can see that these later pictures indeed capture a look of utter despair and misery."

"Please God, don't tell me she killed herself," Magda said gloomily.

"No," Aunt Matilda piped up, "but they say Picasso sometimes beat Dora until she was practically unconscious. And she had a nervous breakdown after he dumped her."

My classmates groaned. We moved on to the exhibit's Postwar Coda. "The last two important women in Picasso's life were his mistress, the painter Françoise Gilot, who gave him two children, Paloma and Claude," the guide explained. "And Jacqueline, his second wife, who was twenty-five years old when she met the seventy-one-year-old Master. Jacqueline outlived Picasso—but not for long. She shot herself."

"Jeez," Joey commented. "Two suicides, two nervous breakdowns—not a good track record."

I'd felt proud that Grandma Ondine had achieved a place among the goddesses in this gallery. But now I found myself feeling uneasy for her. How had *she* survived her encounter with Picasso?

Our tour was ending as we reached the front door. "Any questions?" the guide asked.

"Did Picasso ever give away his paintings as gifts to people who, um, worked for him?" I asked.

"Why, yes," she replied. "Picasso could be extraordinarily generous when the mood struck him. It's said that he gave artwork to his chauffeur, doctor, housemaid—even his barber. But there were also court cases where other people who claimed to have received such gifts were accused of stealing them."

"How much is a Picasso worth these days?" asked Lola's brother Ben, ever the pragmatist.

"There was a recent sale at auction," our guide said carefully, "in which a single painting went for the price of a hundred seventy-nine point four million dollars." Joey whistled appreciatively.

"I don't care how rich and famous he was," Lola announced on our way out, "someone should have put up signs around him saying, *Ladies, beware of the dog!*"

As we stepped outside back into the brilliant midday sunlight, I felt reinvigorated by all I'd seen. When I recalled how the lawyer Clément had chortled over the notion that a little old lady like Ondine might have possessed a Picasso, I decided that I shouldn't have let him make me feel that I was on a fool's errand. Clearly there was a lot about Grandma that he—and my mother—knew nothing about.

Then suddenly I had an idea about a person I'd overlooked, who just might have some answers for me. So while my class was waiting for our bus to pull up to the curb, I sat down on a bench with my phone and tapped out a message asking Grandma's lawyer for the contact info I needed. Good old Clément was on vacation and might ignore this, but I flagged it as urgent, just the same:

Dear Monsieur Clément: My mother told me that on the day my Grandmother Ondine died, a neighbor had looked in on her and called for the doctor. Do you know who this neighbor was, and if so, please provide me with the name, address and telephone number. Any other information you have would be most helpful, as I feel it is extremely imperative that I make contact right away.

As we boarded the van that took us back to the *mas,* I glanced at Aunt Matilda, but she and Peter were deep in conversation about possible day trips they might take when our class was given its "free time" at the end of the course. I hadn't yet found the right moment to tell Aunt Matilda that the *mas* we were staying in had belonged to Grandma. When I'd returned from seeing Monsieur Clément, and Aunt Matilda asked me how it went with him, I told her only that he didn't seem to know about a lost Picasso painting. Since I'd already searched the *mas* and found nothing, there didn't seem to be any reason to burden the talkative Aunt Matilda with another one of Mom's little secrets.

When we arrived at the *mas* we were offered complimentary massages in the spa's open-air white tents that overlooked the lush fields and cerulean sky. As I lay there on my massage table I wondered what other family secrets Mom didn't know about. I'd just seen two paintings of a model with a mirror who I felt sure was Grandma Ondine. And even Aunt Matilda recognized that striped pitcher in a still life. I felt I was truly on the right path, but now I knew that my mother's ideas could only take me so far.

While sea breezes fluttered the spa curtains, an expert French masseuse gently kneaded my muscles with massage oils made of local lemon and almond. Beneath the sheet which I was lying on were crushed flower petals of violet, jasmine, rose and lavender, and I wondered fleetingly if this was a new addition inspired by my impromptu flower-shower. I smiled, recalling the look on Gil's face when he plucked the flowers out of my hair. A bit unsettled now, I closed my eyes and breathed deeply, surrendering to new impressions that came drifting in and out of my thoughts on the soft, scented air.

If I'm ever going to find that painting, I've got to stop thinking like Mom, I mused. I ought to think more like Grandmother Ondine in order to figure this all out.

Come to that, I might even have to learn—in whatever way possible—to think like Picasso.

26

Ondine and Julie in Juan-les-Pins, 1952

JULIE TOOK AN INSTANT DISLIKE TO FRANCE. EVEN WHEN ONDINE RE-minded her that they were in a country that had recently been torn apart by yet another world war, Julie was in no frame of mind to un-derstand why anyone would want to return here.

First, that awful sea voyage among a class of passengers comprised of wailing babies and their harried mothers, and rough men who drank too much and leered at her. And such unspeakable conditions for eat-ing, sleeping and *toilette*! Then, the horrible docking here on a cold, pitiless rainy night. Julie had never felt such biting rain, hurtling in from an Atlantic Ocean bearing absolutely no resemblance to *her* warm summery Atlantic that caressed the beaches of New York.

As if that weren't enough, they had to go through customs and be quizzed by a horrible man who smelled of fish and cigars, before they could be granted the privilege of boarding a third-class overnight train car, where awful Europeans chattering in every conceivable language crowded in with their bundles and elders and unkempt children—and all of *them* smelled as if they hadn't taken a bath in a hundred years.

This was France? This was the paradise that her parents always promised to show her one day? Her father Luc had worked and scrimped and saved and, ultimately, shed his blood for his wife and daughter—only to have them both end up *here*?

Poor Papa. Julie failed to accept, even now, that he was dead. Part of her believed he was hiding somewhere back in America. It was inconceivable that he'd been reduced to nothing but ashes confined in a small wooden box. And why should he have wanted his ashes scattered to the sea in a tiny provincial town called Juan-les-Pins?

Ondine felt apprehensive, too, as they finally arrived in her hometown. Everything seemed smaller, more compact than she remembered. And from the moment when they reached the Café Paradis, she instantly sensed that something was wrong. For one thing, the chairs were still stacked on top of the tables on the terrace, and it was nearly twelve-thirty in the afternoon. Did the café no longer serve lunch? Also, there was a very mangey cat sitting arrogantly right in the center of the terrace; this cat in no way resembled Ondine's girlhood pet.

Julie sensed her mother's hesitation. "This is where Grandma and Grandpa live? It *can't* be," Julie said tearfully. She was tired—bone-tired, soul-dead tired, in a way she'd never been in her life. With all her heart she wished they were back in New Rochelle.

Ondine was silent for a few minutes, then found her voice. "Yes, it is," she said rather sharply. "Don't whine. Be sweet and polite to your grandparents."

The truth was, Ondine had no idea whether her parents were going to greet her with open arms or hurl her right back into the streets. They hadn't answered any of her letters. But even if they still bore a grudge, they couldn't turn away poor Julie, their sweet grandchild. Could they?

"You're wrong, *Maman*," Julie whimpered. "See? Look at the sign above the door. It doesn't say *Café Paradis*. It says something else." She squinted, spelling it out. "It says *Café Renard*," she said, feeling vastly relieved that this grubby-looking hole-in-the-wall was not their ultimate destination.

"The awning. That's it! The awning is gone," Ondine said, startled. She put down her suitcase near the front door. Julie, always obedient, did the same with hers. The mangey cat got up, walked over to the suitcases, sniffed them imperiously, and then, with a slight shudder, returned to the center of the terrace. Ondine pushed the door open and went inside. Julie had no choice but to follow.

The dining room was unoccupied. Its floor had not been polished to its usual lustre; in fact, it looked quite scuffed. "Well, that's to be expected; after all, there was a war here," Ondine reminded the dubious Julie, who shrank from the stale smell of bygone meals. The white tablecloths were no longer spotless; they weren't even ironed properly. The cutlery and glasses were mismatched. The gilded mirror, once beautiful, looked downright smoky. And Rembrandt's *Girl at a Window* was gone.

"Allo!" Ondine called out boldly, moving toward the swinging doors in the back that led to the kitchen. Suddenly the doors were flung wide, and a plump man came out with a guarded, suspicious expression.

"Who's there?" he said loudly.

Ondine, blinking in the dim light, identified the voice before the face. "Good God. It *is* him. He's the baker who wanted to marry me," she told Julie in a horrified whisper. Earlier at the train station Ondine had recognized the stationmaster, and Rafaello the policeman, and other neighbors; but Monsieur Renard was the only person she'd met upon her return to France who'd gained weight since the war. It crossed her mind that people who'd been this well fed must have "played ball" as Luc would say, with the fascist invaders.

Julie was thoroughly disgusted now. "That awful fat man is the one Grandpa wanted you to marry instead of Papa?" she asked in disbelief, for Ondine had told her about it on the journey here.

"Shh! Yes," Ondine said. With the brightest smile she could muster, she greeted Renard.

"You are Ondine?" he repeated, searching her face for a clue before remembering to nod politely to Julie. But when Ondine asked for her mother, Monsieur Renard looked panicked at her ignorance and quickly explained that her parents—both of them—had not survived the war.

"The Occupation was too much for them. It was terrible. First the Italian soldiers, then the German ones—it all took a toll on your father's heart. He died before the war was over. Your poor mother carried on a few years after that, but she came down with flu, and like so many, she was already weakened by exhaustion. You can't imagine how hard we all worked, just to survive! There was no *real* food to serve our customers. We didn't even have fresh fish, because the Nazis wouldn't let us put our boats out to sea. Everything had to be obtained on the black market. Even so, your mother had to bake *tartes* and stews made of things we wouldn't have fed to the pigs before the war."

Julie noticed that the fat man had not even asked them to sit down, even though Ondine was now visibly teetering and pale, looking utterly exhausted by this devastating news. With an indignant glare at Monsieur Renard, Julie took her mother by the hand and led her to one of those tables with the stained cloth on it. She had to pull out two chairs before she could find one that was steady.

"Come and sit down, *Maman,*" she said pointedly.

Ondine, like a sleepwalker, followed her. Monsieur Renard, who'd seen the dirty look Julie gave him, pulled out another chair for Julie, then he sat down heavily on the rickety one.

"*Désolé!*" he murmured consolingly to Ondine. "I hate to be the bearer of this sad news!"

Julie didn't really think he was sorry. He didn't offer them anything to eat or drink, not even a glass of water. As if fearing that anyone returning from America looking this sad must be destitute and seeking a handout, Monsieur Renard hastily explained the current situation about the café to Ondine in no uncertain terms. He even went into his back office and returned with a stack of papers to show her that he had all the proper documents proving his sole ownership of her parents' café.

"We all lost some money during the war," Renard explained, "but your parents completely ran out of cash. So they had to sign over their half of the café to me. You can check with the judge who oversaw this. He'll tell you all about it."

The papers indeed made it clear there wasn't any money left to Ondine, and no share in the café.

Ondine listened to all this quietly, trying to ignore the rising panic she felt at the realization that she was officially being thrown out of her family's café—and her childhood home. When Renard finally stopped for breath, Ondine steeled herself, swallowed her pride and offered to become his new chef, hurriedly trying to tell him about the praise for her cooking and the success she'd had in America.

But Renard interrupted her and, not without a certain smugness, said proudly, "No, I don't need your help! I have a fine young man cooking in my kitchen. Come meet him."

Ondine rose shakily and followed him, glancing about doubtfully. Julie trailed behind, wondering if she could hold her nose and still not cause offense. For, if the café's dining room was a bit of a shambles, the rest of this place was worse, as Julie discovered when she hurriedly ducked past the kitchen, went to the lavatory and saw its leaky plumbing and other malodorous fixtures.

Meanwhile Ondine silently observed the dirty kitchen which to her emitted the smell of death—dead fish and meat bits that had undoubtedly fallen behind the stove and not been cleaned; decomposing rats and cockroaches probably entombed in the walls; rotting vegetables that should have been tossed into the compost but which lay in bushels waiting to be served to some unsuspecting diners.

The young chef was a blond, tousle-haired, handsome but slightly arrogant creature, and Ondine could see at a glance that his culinary skills were of the touristy, greasy-spoon variety. Yet Renard beamed happily as he gave Ondine a tour that ended by showing her out the door.

"Goodbye, goodbye!" Renard called out, waving his handkerchief as if he were on a dock and seeing them off to go right back on whatever boat had brought them here.

Witnessing all this, Julie found the whole scene unbearably humiliating. "Why did we have to come to France?" she whimpered as they were turned away.

It became a litany as soon as they boarded a train to the convent. "Nobody's been nice to us like they were in America when Papa was alive!" she pointed out. Ondine sighed and closed her eyes. The more their journey continued, the more Julie complained, while clinging to her suitcase as if it contained tangible precious memories of happier days in New Rochelle. She couldn't forgive her mother for making them leave America—and for what? To live with the nuns at the convent Ondine had attended as a girl?

It was nighttime when they arrived; pitch dark without a single light on. "Be grateful for their shelter, if they'll be kind enough to give it," Ondine whispered warningly as she knocked at the door. Her head and feet felt too heavy to make another move.

A young nun peeped out, and Ondine, feeling as if she had only one sentence left in her, explained who she was and that she would gladly pay to put Julie in school here, while perhaps Ondine could work to cook for the nuns.

But by now something too heavy to bear was overtaking Ondine; some tidal wave of grief that she'd forcefully pushed out of her mind during the entire voyage but could hold back no longer, as if it had finally breached the seawall of her resolve, engulfing her at last.

Luc. Sweet Luc. It felt wrong, like a betrayal, to have made it back to France without him. This should be his triumphant return. Suddenly, acutely, Ondine could feel his absence from her entire universe, as if a dangerous black undertow was dragging away everything and everyone she'd ever loved. Her parents were dead, too, and she'd never even guessed it. Now there would never be a chance to reconcile, nor to share Julie with them.

"Madame?" said the nun worriedly as she opened the convent door wider and stepped out.

Ondine moved her lips but she could no longer hear the sound of her own voice over the loud thudding in her eardrums; and right then and there, her resolve, her courage, and her legs finally gave way, and she felt as if she'd turned into a bundle of rags as she collapsed on the convent's stony front step.

27

Strangers in the Kitchen, Céline, 2014

"Can you believe this is our last day of cooking class?" I heard my group echo to one another. Everyone was getting sentimental, now that the end was nigh. But I was on the verge of a small panic, still trying to complete Mom's mission before the clock ran out on me.

I'd shamelessly rummaged around the women's bedrooms, even though I was pretty sure that Grandma Ondine hadn't slept up here. Nothing turned up. Now I'd have to find a spare moment either today or tomorrow to search for her Picasso in the last possible place it could be—the old kitchen of the *mas*. However, I could only do this at night when the construction workers weren't hammering and sawing. If I didn't find the painting there, I would be going home empty-handed.

"I'll do it tonight," I vowed to myself.

Meanwhile, Gil's son, Martin, had been given the entire run of the *mas,* and he apparently decided that all the nicely kept paths were a perfect runway for his skateboard, which he maneuvered with both surprising skill and yet frightful daring. Gil's serene French staff was being severely tested as Martin whizzed by and literally ran circles around them.

"C'mere, kid," Aunt Matilda said finally, catching Martin during one of his rare pauses to make him sit with her while we were waiting for Gil. She was shuffling a deck of cards like a pro.

"Céline told me about you. You like cards? Well, I'm going to teach you how to play 'Spit'. Pay attention if you want to win." Martin heard the voice of schoolteacher authority, so he sat down, meek and intrigued. Aunt Matilda said crisply, "Okay, podner, cut them cards."

Despite his hyperactive nature, Martin was, like most young kids, thrilled when adults paid him any attention. He had a sweetness and intelligence that made us all develop a soft spot for him; we enjoyed feeding him treats from the kitchen after we'd been cooking. Gil had taught his son discerning taste, so Martin let us know immediately if our efforts had resulted in good food or bad. And today, just before we left him to go to our last class, he even gave us a few tips about how to please Gil.

"Dad hates using parsley as a garnish," Martin told me, then added in his little grown-up way, "but I personally like parsley anywhere, even on the plate."

By now, miraculously, after days of feeling helpless and clumsy, my classmates found that Gil's rigorous teaching was finally paying off, and everyone was suddenly cooking competently and confidently.

All except me. Oh, I was improving, but I never quite seemed to acquire a knack for gauging just the right moment to stop whisking a sauce, or browning a cutlet, or sautéing a steak.

"You just don't have a red thumb," Gil finally admitted today.

"I do so!" I retorted, holding up a burnt finger. "Look at that blister," I said, aggrieved.

In reply, he held up his palm against mine. "Feel that?" he said, showing me a roughened hand that was a landscape of craters, cuts, blisters, scars, and black-and-blues under his broken nails. "You're a makeup artist. You deal with color and texture, wet and dry. That's what cooking is all about," he said, genuinely trying to be helpful. "You mingle your ingredients to create something new."

I returned to vigorously pounding garlic cloves with basil and olive oil for a Provençal specialty condiment called *pistou,* but he stopped me. "Most people misunderstand garlic," he said, taking the clove and holding it in his fingertips. "Treat it like a delicate flower. Crush gently. When I use garlic for salads, I only rub a whisper on the salad bowl and then I save the actual clove to throw in my stockpot. And I *never* fast-fry-brown the garlic on high heat. That is like rushed sex."

I glanced at my elder classmates but they were accustomed to Gil's sensual metaphors. They just chuckled to themselves, enjoying his provocative exuberance, because it was so evident that he passionately meant it when he exhorted them to handle chicken and fish cutlets "as if it were your lover's body". He really, truly loved to cook and was particularly smitten with Provençal cuisine, so I scored a few points today by letting him use one of Grandmother Ondine's recipes for our class, a *daube à l'orange*.

"*Daube* is thought to come from the Spanish word *dobar,* which means 'to braise' and that is exactly what we will do," Gil told the class. "We're following Céline's Grandma's recipe, which is to braise the beef in red wine with Provençal herbs (*not* lavender, thank you), tomatoes, onions, black olives, mushrooms, the special ingredient of orange peel—and this, a calf's foot."

"Oh, God," I said, actually feeling faint. "The poor thing."

Gil looked at me and said seriously, "Steady on! Yes, we cook and eat things that were once alive—be they vegetables or animals—in order to stoke the fire of life in us; but in return, we must keep our end of the bargain, which is to handle them humanely with great respect; and when it's our turn to die, we should do so gracefully and willingly, so that we, too, feed the fiery furnace of the earth's future plants and creatures. So today, let's celebrate life while we're alive and cooking, okay?"

A thoughtful hush fell over us as we continued working. Gil just had a knack for creating a sacred workspace. But just as we were getting lulled by the meditative atmosphere, we discovered that Gil had something else up his sleeve for this evening.

"Today, boys and girls, YOU are going to work in my restaurant. This is a comparatively quiet weekend, so you won't be subjected to the worst trial-by-fire. Each of you will pair up with one of my professionals, but remember, these people helped *Pierrot* win its first Michelin star—and we aim to win a second one this year! So my staff will brook no trouble from anyone. Do not argue. Do not ask *why* you are doing things. Just follow their instructions to the letter, and most importantly, keep your focus. Got it? Here are your assignments." He handed out strips of paper as if we'd drawn straws.

"Shoot, I thought you said we're having a party at the end of this boot camp," Lola's brother Ben objected. He looked so woeful standing there, a big Texan in an apron, that Gil had to smile.

"Tomorrow's your party. That will be your reward. But tonight you have to earn it," Gil replied. "Okay, I will now hand you over to my assistant, Lizbeth, and to our concierge, Maurice."

We discovered that Gil had given us the most improbable assignments for our personalities: the languorous Lola was to become a welcoming hostess; the buttoned-down Peter was tending bar; and the rough-and-tumble Joey and Magda were working in Heather's delicate bakery section.

"What about us?" Aunt Matilda asked, wide-eyed, as she and Ben and I remained there uncertainly.

"Ye also serve who wait on tables," Gil responded as he whizzed out of the room.

His restaurant team gave us uniforms and efficiently absorbed us into their impeccable routine. The morning of "prepping" flew by. Gil popped in and out of each station—watching, tasting, ever on the lookout for errors. Then suddenly, it was as if a flag had dropped.

"Ouvert!" cried the maître d'.

"What'd he say?" Magda hissed to me.

"We're open," I said, and I actually felt goosebumps on my skin.

The well-dressed diners for the first seating came strolling in, laughing and chattering in happy anticipation. Some paused for drinks at the bar, but many were seated immediately at the prized tables on the terrace, overlooking the fragrant gardens of the *mas* and the serene view of fields and vineyards.

"Céline, Table Two is yours. Tilda, Table Nine," said the French headwaiter, who spoke impeccable English and helped us with the other languages of the diners as well. He handed us the menus.

"Onward," he commanded.

"All in the valley of Death rode the six hundred," Aunt Matilda quoted under her breath.

Our first seating was mostly elegant French couples dining in groups of four and eight; they were amazingly quiet and dignified as they conversed in low murmurs. Even the black poodle who accompanied a party-of-eight behaved well, situating himself under a chair where he politely gnawed the biscuit his mistress had surreptitiously taken out of her Hermès handbag. There was also a scattering of British and American couples, middle-aged and decorous; and later, we seated some German and Russian families who each occupied an enormous round table headed by a proud silver-haired matriarch.

But then an overly made-up woman in a tight red dress and spike heels, loaded down with jewelry, walked into the bar and sloshed down a few drinks before teetering behind Maurice as he led her to her table-for-one. Even before she opened her mouth, I sensed the bad vibes building up in her.

As I handed her a menu, she looked up at me and asked, "So. Has Gil remarried yet?" I shook my head and she nodded sagely, smirking. When I returned to her table with her appetizers and wine, she asked how long had I been working for "the big maestro". Finally, she put her scarlet-polished, long talons on my arm and asked slurrily, "Where the fuck *is* Gil? Does he even *know* that I'm here?"

"He's in back of the house," I said automatically. "He'll be out front shortly."

She gave me a steady stare, though she swayed in her seat. "Do you know who I am? No? Well, let me enlighten you. Gil used to cook for *me* in *my* husband's restaurant," she said thickly. "But he *uses* people, you know. Women especially—oh, he likes the ladies. But he only dates the ones with money. His whole career was built on exploiting a long line of generous gals"—she walked her fingers across the surface of the table—"like a frog hopping from one lily pad to the next. And once he gets his chef's fingers on your money, well, honey, he's gone, baby, gone."

As her voice rose in volume, I shot the headwaiter a frantic look.

He hastily took over, soothing her with his French charm, helping her select the "best" main course, then telling the kitchen to rush her order; after which he escorted her to "Gil's private library" where, he later told me, Gil "personally served her a hazelnut caramel *crêpe,* then packed her off into a taxi."

Amid the hubbub of the guests' excited chatter, Aunt Matilda and I struggled to keep up with the waiters' shorthand:

"Seat that deuce at Table Five!"

"Where's the dupe for Table Three?"

"Bottled water *gazeuse*!"

"Jeepers, what's *gazeuse*?" Aunt Matilda wailed.

"Gas," said a waiter as he flashed by.

"Sparkling water," I translated.

Rushing back and forth from the serene terrace to the hot kitchen was like going from Dante's paradiso to his inferno, with an occasional stop at the purgatorio of the bar to pick up a tray of drinks. It was on one such run that Aunt Matilda, of all people, spotted a well-known food blogger who'd booked a table for three *incognito*. He was informally known as the Butcher of Bloggers because of his formidable influence. It was even said that he had some sway with Michelin judges, although this was never proven.

"Go tell Gil," Aunt Matilda whispered to me. "I'll keep the Butcher busy with cocktails."

I hurried into the kitchen, but at first I couldn't find Gil anywhere. Finally I spotted him, pacing back and forth in his walk-in freezer. The door was not quite shut; he must have rushed in there for privacy, yet even so, I could suddenly hear his raised, desperate voice as he spoke into his mobile phone.

"Fuck this, you tell Rick he must be joking!" he exclaimed vehemently. "On the eve of signing a contract, he's now going to dick around with it one more time? Have you read this shit? It gives him complete ownership of the entire *mas*—the new hotel *and* the restaurant. That makes me nothing more than a hired cook! Bloody hell, you're *my* lawyer, don't tell me about future net percentages as bonuses!"

Gil fell silent, listening for a moment. Then he burst out, "We've gone over this a hundred times. We've said 'yes' to every other ruddy revision he asked for. I don't *care* if his lawyer wants my bloody signature 'ASAP', I sure as shit will NOT sign *this* new draft!" Another pause. Then he exploded.

"DON'T bloody ask me if it's a 'deal-breaker'. You know this deal CANNOT be broken! Do you not understand what I'm telling you? Rick's *got* to wire six million euros to my bank before Gus sends his goons here on Thursday to collect the loan repayment. Don't ask me how you're going to get Rick to sign last week's draft, just GET it done to-NIGHT, damn it!"

He snapped his phone shut and burst out of the walk-in. Then he saw me hovering in a corner.

"Christ, Céline what are you doing here?" he said in a dead tone. I told him as quickly as I could about the famous food blogger. "Well, fuck me, that's just perfect," he said under his breath.

Aunt Matilda rushed in now, wide-eyed. "The Butcher is hungry as a vulture!" she announced, waving her order pad. "The rest of his party ordered from the menu, but *he* said, 'Ask Gil to send me his best—and please surprise me with something truly special for dessert.'"

I won't ever forget how quickly Gil's expression changed. He immediately put aside his troubles and snapped into gear. He made a quick check with his cooks to see which "mains" were still available, and they rattled off several dinner specials for him to choose from.

But when he asked about the desserts, someone whispered to him and he exclaimed, "What do you mean, you've run out of *gavotte au chocolat* already? Bloody hell! All right, dammit, here's what we're going to serve him: begin with the caviar-and-lobster *amuse-bouche,* then the *pistou* soup, followed by the spinach-and-ewes'-milk ravioli with Mediterranean honey, and for the main, Grandma Ondine's *daube a l'orange*. As for his bloody 'something special' for dessert, leave that to me."

"Yes, chef!" everyone shouted.

The whole thing was a blur after that. Fortunately for Aunt Matilda and me, all hands were on deck to help us serve, and the food just kept coming. The "Butcher" was a man with a fussy goatee and the alert eyes of a raptor, and at first his face steadfastly revealed nothing; but the excellent local wines and cuisine soon wore down his sphinx-like attitude, especially when Gil appeared, looking impeccable in his chef's whites, to serve a dramatic sweet *vol-au-vent* pastry filled with chocolate and caramel cream, served with a banana and armagnac sauce *flambé* that Gil personally, and with a showman's flourish, set fire to, before nonchalantly sliding it from the pan to the platter.

It was like a fireworks finale that got everyone in the restaurant on their feet, applauding. I heard one diner say breathlessly, "Can you believe that we were here tonight to *see* this?"

Gil accepted it all with great aplomb. And now I finally understood what it was that made him so special, even among other master chefs. He was like a man on a tightrope, fearless, and he had the perfect knack of knowing exactly when to go for it and give a moment everything he's got.

Aunt Matilda's friend Peter summed it all up. "Gil's like a great racehorse. The man's got *heart*."

After that, things wound down quickly, and although a few new diners trickled in, we knew the evening was pretty much done. Gil released my classmates from duty with great thanks for our support on such a challenging night, and he announced that sherry and a late-night supper had been laid out for us in the library. We all breathed a sigh of relief.

But Aunt Matilda caught me gazing off toward the construction site and she inquired, "You got something on your mind, Céline?" So I pulled her aside and dropped Monsieur Clément's bombshell about how Grandmother Ondine had owned this very *mas* that we'd been taking our cooking classes in.

"Ohhh!" she said, stunned. "*That's* why your mother was so keen to come here. *Now* it all makes sense!"

And, bless her, she didn't ask why I'd waited to tell her. I admitted I'd searched the bedrooms, then I said, "The construction site is the last possible place it can be. I've just *got* to find out tonight."

She said, "Well, go on, then. But be careful. I'll cover for you. You can tell me all about it later."

I smiled at the sight of Peter hovering in the doorway, waiting to escort her to the sherry in the library. Then I went to my room, grabbed my flashlight and slipped away.

I had done a little advance reconnaissance during the daytime and noticed that there weren't any security cameras on the construction site itself, so now I avoided the hotel corridors and instead went outside to approach the site from its far, open end.

The old kitchen looked pretty daunting in the dark of night. The floor was ripped open in various places where new plumbing and wiring were going in; and in some sections it was a sheer drop below to a black, cavernous abyss. I could see only as far as my flashlight's beam, so I stepped cautiously, fearful of tumbling into the darkness.

I tried to reassure myself that I was on the right track. After all, I reasoned, Grandma Ondine was a chef. She must have spent lots of time in this kitchen.

As my eyes adjusted to the sweep of my light, I saw that the kitchen had been an enormous, low-ceilinged room with rough stone walls painted egg-yolk yellow. It was big enough for cooking, dining and sitting in. The large fireplace was still intact, its firebox flanked by several small ovens built into the bricks, which the publicity brochure had said was for baking bread in wintertime. I checked them. Empty. Nearby, a series of built-in shelves were in various stages of being torn down.

A gaping hole in the ceiling testified to where a stovepipe might have been. I spotted an alcove that could have once been a pantry, but it, too, was in the process of being stripped and gutted. I searched where I could, but there really wasn't much else to check. It had begun to rain lightly, and the droplets were hitting the construction site with a monotonous plink-plink-*plonk*, plink-plink-*plonk* sound as they struck various spots on the site.

And right then and there, in this dark altar to the past, I realized that time may have finally consigned Grandmother Ondine's world to the dust heap. I had to conclude, at last, that the only sane response to this situation was to accept defeat. "Goodbye, Grandma," I said softly, a little surprised to feel truly mournful.

Disconsolately I turned away. But then I heard a commotion on the other end of the site, from the hallway leading back into the *mas*. I could not resist creeping closer and cautiously I peered in.

Three figures had come out of Gil's kitchen in an all-fired hurry, flinging open that heavy door made of halved logs, and pausing in the bright light of the hallway. I recognized Gil, who was followed by two big guys that gave off a menacing vibe—a pair of thick-looking creatures dressed in dark, heavy wool suits that were in stark contrast to the usual light, bright leisurely garb of the French Riviera.

"You should *not* have followed me into my kitchen," Gil told them testily. "This could have waited until I locked up." His tone was so ominous that I shrank further into the shadows.

"Gus sent us to make sure you understood the situation," one of them said. He was English, and spoke in such a low, soft voice that I was completely unprepared when his partner suddenly shoved Gil against the wall and held him there.

Yet, Gil's face under the light deliberately did not change expression. "Your presence in my restaurant is not only unnecessary," he said defiantly, "but rude."

The first man continued, "I'm not hearing what I ought to hear." Gil's eyes trained on one after the other, as if preparing to do whatever necessary to fight back.

The second man leaned closer and said helpfully, "Thursday. Know what Thursday is?"

"Of course. Gus knows perfectly well he'll get his money," Gil said contemptuously.

"All of it," the first man with the soft voice said. "Repeat after me. 'All of it by Thursday'."

And Gil, in his infinite wisdom, said, "Every last pound, on time. At which point you two can go fuck yourselves."

Well, the second guy hauled off and slugged him in the gut, then shoved him back against the wall so hard that I involuntarily did the only thing I could to interfere.

I let out a scream so loud that Gil and his escorts actually jumped in surprise. Fortunately, the rest of Gil's customers had already departed. But someone else heard my scream just as she came bursting into the hallway from the restaurant kitchen.

"Hullo, in there!" Aunt Matilda called out, peering down the hallway. Her hand was tucked in Peter's arm as if they were out for a casual evening stroll. She would later tell me that she'd immediately spotted this pair of thugs, who first came into the bar of *Pierrot* looking for Gil; and she watched them as they followed him down to the kitchen. And, being Aunt Matilda, she swung into action and rounded up her friends. Behind her were Ben and Lola, with Magda and Joey bringing up the rear.

"Hey, there, Gil!" Ben boomed in his rich Texas drawl. "Heard you might need a posse tonight."

Lola peered over her brother's shoulder. "You got yourself the A-Team here," she announced.

"Ben was just telling us that he's a retired FBI officer from Dallas," Magda said meaningfully.

Aunt Matilda's escort stepped forward. "Naval Intelligence Division, Great Britain," Peter said, squaring his shoulders.

"United States Air Force commando," Joey said from the other side. He pretended he was seeing the intruders for the first time. "Is there a problem here, gentlemen?"

The two thugs were already looking around warily for the nearest exit. Gil had managed to recover from their rough treatment, and he had an oddly triumphant look on his face.

"Did I mention," he said now, "that there are security cameras in these corridors?"

And then another door opened, from the room with the clown wallpaper. Out came Martin, carrying a slingshot. "Dad?" he asked, in his most grown-up manner. "Need a hand?"

It was the sight of Martin that finally clinched it.

"The exit is this way, gentlemen," Peter said firmly, and his group parted to clear a path. The two thugs quickly took it, but the first guy could not resist saying once more to Gil, "Thursday."

Nobody else said a word, but we all went outside and watched the two men get into a car and drive off with a sputtering of gravel.

Then Gil hoisted Martin in his arms and said protectively, "Come on, son, time for bed."

Martin turned to the rest of us and said excitedly, "Dad and I sleep in the dovecote!"

"You're in France, it's called a *pigeonnier,*" Gil said, but as he turned to go he said to my classmates, "Many, many thanks, folks. Bedtime for everybody, yes? Show's over tonight."

28

Ondine and Julie in Vallauris, 1952–1953

ONDINE ONLY VAGUELY REMEMBERED THE MOTHER SUPERIOR AT THE CON-
vent summoning a doctor, who observed that she'd finally succumbed
to a severe pneumonia which she no doubt contracted on the voyage
over from America. The doctor quickly packed her off to a sanitarium
in the mountains, and Ondine, weakened by too much grief, took time
convalescing. The money she'd saved went quickly after that, to pay
for her care and for Julie's board at the convent school.

Once Ondine's savings were completely gone, the nuns placed Julie
with a foster family—a farmer and his wife who needed "a little help".
What they really wanted was an unpaid servant who'd rise early, feed
the chickens, milk the cows and shovel out the pigpen.

The farmer had a fearsome temper, especially when in a drunken
rage. Julie had never been around a violent man like that, but she soon
understood why the farmer's wife was relieved to have someone else in
the house to become her husband's scapegoat.

His shouting was bad enough; but on nights when he was drunk,
Julie quickly learned where every conceivable hiding place existed—
behind bales of hay in the barn loft; on the hardened earth underneath
the porch; in the small space behind the furnace. But one night, he
came into her bedroom when she was asleep. He yanked her to her

feet, then pushed her down on her knees, unzipped his pants and thrust himself into her mouth. The utter shock of it caused her to freeze, which ultimately pleased him. Gagging, she crept away, back into her bed, cowering beneath the covers, praying she might die. But it was only the beginning of a hundred humiliations to come.

"If you tell anyone," he threatened after each incident, "I'll give you worse next time."

When Ondine's health finally improved and she found out that Julie had been given away to a foster family, Ondine struggled to her feet, determined to go back to cooking so that she could earn a steady enough income to reclaim her daughter. The Mother Superior helped her find a job as a cook for an old widower lawyer near the pottery town of Vallauris, not far from Cannes and Antibes.

"It's going to be all right now," Ondine promised Julie. But the truth was, she barely recognized her own daughter. Julie's hair had been cut haphazardly; she had lost a lot of weight, and her skin had a terrible pallor, but worse than that was the mousy way she hung her head, as if afraid to raise her gaze and look anybody in the eye. She never spoke unless asked to; and even then, she mumbled in a submissive way that irritated people and inadvertently invited them to be sharp with her. Yet Julie flatly refused to talk to her mother about what her life had been like in foster care.

When they settled in at Ondine's new job at the lawyer's house, Ondine was profoundly grateful, and for awhile it seemed as if they'd found a safe haven where they might recover from the string of recent shocks they'd endured. But after only a few months, the elderly lawyer's housekeeper delivered some bad news.

"The old coot's getting married again! And his new bride is bringing her own servants from Bordeaux, so she's kicking out all of *us* with only a month's pay. You'll have to find a new place to cook, Ondine."

It was amidst this servants' chatter that Ondine once again heard the name Picasso. He'd left his mark in the most unlikely places. In 1946 he'd returned to Antibes and set up shop in the Château Grimaldi— the very spot he'd visited with Ondine on that last day in the donkey cart, when local urchins had invited him to explore the old castle which had become a museum.

Upon his return there Picasso, undaunted by postwar shortages of paint and canvas, resorted to using boat paint to create his exuberant artwork upon the very walls of the castle; and he'd even painted over some old pictures he found there.

Then, in that mysterious way of his, Picasso had gone off in search of other inspiration. Ondine learned that he'd taken a house right here in Vallauris and became intrigued with the local pottery. Inspired, he began making his own fantastic creations, and in so doing he'd single-handedly rescued the town's dwindling pottery industry, causing business to boom once again.

Ondine heard all this from the housekeeper where she worked, who showed her various magazine stories about it all. Ondine found herself scrutinizing one photograph in particular, of Picasso on a beach, pretending to be a slave while holding a parasol over his mistress who strode proudly ahead of him—a beautiful woman named Françoise. The article noted that she'd been a student at the Sorbonne when she met Pablo in Paris during the war. There was another photo of the two children they'd had together.

They both have Picasso's eyes! Ondine observed. She read that he now had four kids—a son by his Russian wife, a daughter by the blonde Marie-Thérèse, and these two elegant little creatures.

"But rumor has it that this mistress and Picasso aren't getting along so well anymore," the housekeeper said in a low, knowing voice.

Ondine could not resist asking, "Where is Picasso's house?"

The housekeeper replied, "Not far at all. It's called Villa La Galloise."

29

Picasso in Vallauris, September 1953

PABLO PICASSO HAD NEVER BEEN SO INSULTED IN HIS LIFE. HE SAT IN A dark room alone, smoking. He had come to the conclusion that women simply weren't human, after all. You gave them everything—your love, your children, a fine house—so why did they make a man feel guilty for just being a man?

"They're all impossible," he thought, reviewing his grudges. Take Olga. She remained his wife—and still went by the name of Madame Picasso—and she'd won a tidy share of his assets, but that wasn't good enough for her; she went about following his mistresses, shouting at them, pinching them, telling them that they had no business being with Picasso.

As for Marie-Thérèse, she now needed constant reassurance, so Pablo kept writing her letters swearing that she was the only woman he'd ever really loved; but lately, on his twice-weekly visits to see their child, Marie-Thérèse kept urging him to finally make good on his vague promises to marry her.

And poor Dora Maar, well, some of Picasso's friends actually blamed him for her breakdown, saying he'd crushed her spirit with jealousy, manipulating her by parading other women before her, egging her on and then rejecting her yet again. Friends found her wandering the streets of Paris, talking incoherently. Picasso had to call a doctor who carted Dora off to a rest home and gave her electroshock treatments. The vivacious, intellectual brunette was never quite the same after that; she "found" religion, and when Pablo saw her in Paris, she shouted at him that God would make him pay for his sins if he didn't kneel down right now and beg the Lord's forgiveness.

"It's not my fault that women are so weak!" Pablo protested to his friends. After all, God kept rewarding him with more money and success—and a new young mistress; so Pablo thought it would be different this time with Françoise. The Parisian girl with flowing, dark-russet hair was the young artist to whom he'd brought a bowl of cherries at the café, when the Gestapo were still running Paris; and after the war she'd defied her wealthy father and even her benevolent grandmother, to come and live with Picasso here in Vallauris.

"I allowed her to share my life, my time, my talent for a whole decade," Pablo fumed, "and now, what thanks do I get? What does the lovely Françoise say to me?" Picasso repeated the words incredulously. *"I am sorry, Pablo, but I want to live with people of my own generation and the problems of MY time."*

And, she'd told him that she simply was no longer happy with their relationship.

He'd thundered back in outrage, "Your job is to remain by my side, to devote yourself to me and the children. Whether it makes you happy or unhappy is no concern of mine."

But he'd failed to notice that the worshipful girl had turned into an elegant woman with a mind of her own; after all, she was in her thirties now—and he was in his seventies.

"She makes me feel like an old goat," he thought savagely; and now his canvases were filled with nude young models indifferent to the pathetic dwarfs and clowns who sought to make love to them.

Still, Françoise didn't leave right away, so Pablo didn't really believe she meant it. He tried to make a brave joke of it to his friends. "Françoise's going to leave me soon," he'd announce. "Maybe today. Maybe tomorrow." *Poor me,* he was saying. *I am a man without love.* For a while it seemed to work; friends rushed up to Françoise and begged her not to do such a cruel thing to the Master.

And soon the word leaked out to the press, who hovered on doorsteps to ask Françoise if the rumors were true. She would flee to Paris, only to return to Pablo in the South of France.

"No woman leaves a man like me," Picasso assured himself. The truth was, he really didn't know what to do in a situation like this with an independent-minded, modern younger woman.

So, when the moment finally came, Pablo was not emotionally prepared. On this otherwise beautiful September day, Françoise packed her suitcases, picked up her handbag, took their son and daughter by the hand and led them into a waiting auto. The driver seized their suitcases and deposited them in the trunk while the children piled into the car, then peered out the back window, their inky dark eyes dancing in the mischief of the moment, as if they were off on a dangerous but intriguing adventure.

"You'll be back," Picasso had told Françoise with a shrug, pretending not to care. But just as she and the children settled into the car, he charged down the stairs like an enraged bull. By the time he caught up with them, the car was already in motion.

Pablo glared into the window as if to command his mistress to stop. She gazed back at him, defiant and resolute. The driver slowed uncertainly.

"Go!" Françoise ordered. The driver floored the accelerator, making the tires spin in the gravel. The car drove on.

"*Merde!*" Picasso bellowed, brandishing his fist at the disappearing auto. He followed it for a few paces with a cigarette between his fingers, watching with an expression of utter outrage and betrayal.

In the deafening silence, he took a long, furious drag before he hurled the cigarette into the dust and stepped on it, as if to extinguish something more than just its glowing, ashy tip.

Then Picasso turned, went back into the house and slammed the door behind him.

THE NEXT DAY, HE AWOKE shortly before noon. The house was dark and shuttered, silent. He was alone. He would have to get up sooner or later, call a friend or servant in Paris, get them to help him make a change, make a move, do something. Pablo had refused to learn how to drive, fearing that it would affect and even injure his hands. He hated operating modern machines, even talking on the telephone, but today he did so, summoning the son he'd had with Olga to come and get him.

Picasso was not a man who was meant to be alone. Still, he lay there in his darkened room, smoking. Then he thought he heard a noise outside the house. Did he imagine it? It was too soon for his son to be here. He strained to listen to the light and lilting sound.

What could it be—human voices, or just birdsong? Warily he sighed, got up and went to the window, parted the curtain and peeped out.

There were two figures approaching the house. Pablo ducked out of sight from the window. Through sheer habit he waited for someone else to resolve this, then reminded himself that there was not a mistress nor a servant nor a friend in this house to send to the front door to investigate.

He would have to handle this for himself today. Or else ignore it.

The irresistible lure of his own insatiable curiosity tugged at him. He thrust his feet into his sandals and went down the stairs as noiselessly as possible. He paused on his side of the front door and waited there, feeling like a spy, listening to the voices as they finally reached the house. Female voices, light, sweet and pleasant.

Even so, his nerves were startled when he heard the sharp rap of the door knocker resonating through his front door while he remained right there on the other side of it.

Picasso held his breath, trying to decide, torturously, what to do.

Then he made up his mind.

30

Ondine in Vallauris, September 1953

AT FIRST, ONDINE WASN'T ENTIRELY SURE SHE HAD THE RIGHT HOUSE FOR Picasso. She and Julie had paused momentarily at the foot of a long, steep flight of wide stone steps, flanked on both sides by a free-spirited garden that was arranged in terraced layers on a hill, all leading up to a rather modest villa perched at the top.

"*Maman,* do I really have to climb all these steps with this basket on my arm?" Julie exclaimed.

"Yes," Ondine had answered, gazing upward.

"Must I go looking like Little Red Riding Hood?" Julie whimpered. "I'm sixteen, after all!"

She's nearly the same age I was when I met Picasso, Ondine thought to herself.

"Who is this man we're visiting?" Julie had asked. "Why is he so important?"

"I knew him back in Juan-les-Pins. He's very rich, and he might be able to help us," Ondine answered carefully, mindful of her promise to Luc that she would never tell Julie about Picasso.

But I never said I wouldn't tell Picasso about Julie! Ondine thought determinedly.

"Well, if he's *your* friend, why do *I* have to be the one to give him this basket?" Julie fretted.

"Because he prefers young women," Ondine said, more to herself. She'd examined her reflection in the mirror only this morning; she was thirty-four now, and the face that looked back at her possessed a brave radiance. But life had toughened her up, and her eyes were those of a woman unafraid to look the truth square in the face. *Let's see if Picasso can do the same,* she thought.

Tenderly she smoothed out the shoulder seams of Julie's dress and gave a sharp tug to adjust her hair ribbon, saying, "Remember to call him *Patron* when you address him. And be sure to smile and curtsey. You look too gloomy when you fail to smile."

Julie misunderstood and pouted. *My own mother thinks I'm not pretty enough,* she reasoned with a queer little feeling of hurt. In truth, she had a lovely face, with warm dark eyes and lustrous auburn hair, but nobody seemed to notice the shy little creature who kept her head down.

Obedience was the only weapon of survival that Julie had managed to make her own. She lowered her lashes resentfully but said, "Yes, *Maman*."

Ondine saw her daughter's pout and wasn't fooled one bit. Everyone thought of Julie as pleasantly compliant, but the girl had a reticence which sometimes amounted to passive mutiny.

She blames me for everything that's gone wrong since Luc died, Ondine reminded herself.

As they climbed the steep stone staircase to Picasso's house they could hear bees humming busily in the tall grass of the terraced gardens they passed. It was a hot day for September. Ondine thought she saw a curtain twitch in the window as she moved forward resolutely toward the house.

"Maybe your friend's not even home today," Julie said hopefully, lagging behind. The hamper was heavy and she wished they could just leave it on the front stoop and run away. She couldn't imagine knocking on that door, curtseying and offering this basket to a total stranger.

Ondine had cooked a *lapin à tomates, les olives et la moutarde*—rabbit stewed with onions, mustard, tomatoes, white wine, black olives, capers and herbs. She led Julie right up to the front door. They had to knock on it twice before they heard a man's heavy tread at the other side of the door. After a long pause, the door creaked open a bit more, and the Minotaur peeped out, his dark eyes glowering.

"Who is it?" Picasso demanded, shading his eyes from the sun's glare with his hand. "Come closer, I can't see you," he said, sounding irritated. He had a folded newspaper tucked under his arm.

She stepped forward courageously and said, "*Bonjour, Patron.* I am Ondine, your chef from many years ago, from the Café Paradis in Juan-les-Pins. My daughter has a gift for you."

Picasso stared at Ondine, then opened the door a bit wider. Julie saw a short, leathery-looking, powerfully built man, dressed in shorts and a short-sleeved shirt that hung open to reveal his broad chest. He was tanned all over to the color of bronze, even his balding head. He wore a furious scowl with those smoldering black eyes. But this man, although he appeared strong and fit, looked more like a grandfather.

"He's so *old*! Not at all like you told me," Julie whispered from behind, for Ondine had described this "friend" as a virile, dark-haired *Patron,* not a man in his seventies.

"Shh," Ondine whispered back. Julie, terrified, stepped forward and mutely handed Picasso the picnic hamper. He looked astounded, but could not resist peering inside, sniffing. The scent of the food appealed to him just as Ondine knew it would. *No man can resist being pampered,* she saw in satisfaction, stealing a better look at him. He was even shorter than she remembered. His dark hair had turned white and was almost all gone now—yet her heart responded to his familiar, magnetic presence.

Picasso glanced from mother to daughter, as if Julie's youthful face was balm to his wounded pride. "Well, why not?" he exclaimed, stepping out and closing the door behind him. "No one else has thought to feed me a meal like this today! I'll eat in the garden. Want to see it, young lady?"

Julie beamed at him in relief, finding this change of tone encouraging. They followed Picasso around the side of the house to a sitting area where he deposited himself in a wrought-iron chair, placing the hamper on a matching table. Ondine swiftly unpacked the delicate rabbit stew that was so tender you could cut it with a fork. As she laid out the meal for him, he sat like an emperor allowing his attendants to wait on him. Then Picasso ate hungrily, looking pleased all the while.

Ondine nodded to Julie, who, on cue, did what she'd been told to do: leave the adults to have their private conversation among old friends. As Julie tactfully wandered off into the garden to look at the flowers, Picasso's gaze followed the girl, then returned curiously to Ondine.

"Tell me—how exactly do I know you?" he asked, as if stirred by only a distant memory—one so monumental to Ondine, but, she noted, hardly more than a footnote in this man's mind.

Trying not to be wounded by this she said quickly, "It was 1936 in Juan-les-Pins. I used to bring your lunch to you on a bicycle. I posed for you, in a blue dress, wearing your wristwatch. I am Ondine, your *Femme à la montre*." She watched for any sign of the interest he'd once taken in her.

"Ah! Ondine," he repeated in wonder, like a man waking from a dream. "Yes, yes! The one with the hair like the waves of the sea! Still cooking in that café? Or did you marry some local hero?"

So he did remember. There was even a fond note in his voice. Ondine found herself blushing. Absurd, at her age. "I *did* marry," she said carefully, "and went to America, where we had our own café in a town called New Rochelle. Important people from Manhattan lined up at my door just to taste my *bouillabaisse*," she said proudly.

"*Bon!* I only like to be around winners, not losers," Picasso proclaimed. He tore off a corner of his bread roll to mop up his sauce. "And what kind of man is your husband?"

"A good one. But, he died," she said quietly.

Picasso, apparently not wishing to indulge in chatter about death, especially of someone he didn't know, said rather curtly, "So—what are *you* doing here in Vallauris?"

"I am a private chef now. When I heard you were my neighbor I had to pay a call." Tentatively she said, "My boss is changing his living arrangements. Could you perhaps use my services as a cook?"

He shook his head firmly, speaking more to himself in a bitter tone. "No, I've got my cook coming down from Paris. But I won't stay in this house for long. Why should I? It's time to move on!"

Ondine said softly, "I've thought of you often, ever since that day when I cycled to your villa in Juan-les-Pins, only to find the house empty. You left so suddenly. How I missed you! And I looked everywhere for the portrait you made for me, yet that was gone, too. But, you left me a precious gift from our love. I thought you ought to know. Your daughter has your eyes, as you can see."

There was a long silence, punctuated only by the chirping of birds and the drone of insects in the grass. Picasso's gaze narrowed. "You come to me now, after all this time? That seems unlikely."

Ondine was determined not to back down. "Julie is yours, but my husband loved her and cared for her as his own. So I promised him I'd never tell her about you, and I never will," she said, so that he would understand that she was not going to make unreasonable demands.

"That's wise," he said firmly, removing his napkin from where he'd tucked it under his chin to wipe his mouth. "These days, people usually want either of two things from me. Some wish me to immortalize them in a painting. The others—complete strangers—knock on my door and ask for money. Can you imagine? What do they think I am, a bank? I have four children now, and I give to them whatever and whenever it pleases me. But they know better than to ask for more."

She heard his bullish tone and absorbed his warning. He was scowling again. Her heart sank but, sensing Julie still moving about in the garden, picking flowers, Ondine thought, *I must not fail her*.

Picasso studied her face. "Well, Ondine, what do *you* want?" he asked with some asperity.

She didn't dare say, *I want you to love and provide for this daughter of yours!* Obviously he'd sized her up as an unprotected woman without powerful male relatives to demand justice for her and Julie. So she tried to conjure an acceptable reply to Picasso's question, as if he were a genie who might grant her only one wish. Her thoughts landed on it as delicately as a butterfly on the grass.

"I want the special portrait you made of me after our night of love," she said quietly. "We talked of Rembrandt, and you had me pose as your *Girl-at-a-Window*. You promised I could have it."

Did he remember? Did he even still possess the portrait? His face remained inscrutable. She plunged on. "You said the picture was mine to keep. And I know you are a man of your word. It's important because now that painting will serve as your daughter's dowry," she added earnestly.

"I'll have to think about that. When a decision is made, someone wins, someone loses. So there is always blood on the floor." He looked as if such a dilemma already perplexed him. After a pause he wagged a finger at her, saying, "But you see, if I *did* give you that painting, it would be as a gift. And you must never sell a gift." He wore a cunning look now; Ondine wondered if he was just playing cat-and-mouse. For all she knew he may have sold the picture, long ago. Clearly he was testing her.

She said carefully, "I believe I won't have to sell it. Just owning it will be enough to impress a suitor's family. I want our daughter to marry well, and have a decent start in life."

Picasso said sternly, "If I give it to you, will that be an end to this?" His unsentimental eyes told her what the only answer could be.

Ondine sized up the situation and saw that she must take this offer before he withdrew it. "Yes."

From the road came a noise of gravel as a car climbed up the hill. Picasso heard it, and he rose abruptly. Ondine rose, too, and Picasso swept his hand toward the villa as if throwing down a gauntlet.

"Who knows where that painting is? The house is bursting with artwork; I can't keep track anymore. People keep trying to 'organize' me. I paint, I draw, I sculpt—then I have to buy bigger houses just to find room to hold it all! Some of my pictures were sent here from my apartment in Paris. Some I sold. Some I gave away. Maybe I gave away that *Girl-at-a-Window*? I don't have time to look for it now. But if I come across it, I'll let you know. Goodbye." His tone was final.

Ondine glanced up and realized that Julie must have wandered down the terraced garden steps; for now she returned, blushingly self-conscious, followed by a handsome red-haired man who appeared to be about six feet tall. He'd just arrived and, from the looks on both their faces, had been flirting with Julie.

"That's my eldest son," Picasso said. "Since he has no gainful employment at the moment, he's working for me, as my chauffeur."

At first, Ondine thought it must be a joke. This tall redhead the son of the short, dark Picasso? Ondine made a fast calculation and decided that this must be the child of Picasso's Russian wife.

"Your car's ready," the tall fellow said.

Picasso was now eyeing Julie, who came toward him and remembered to curtsey before presenting him with a bouquet of flowers. For a moment he looked touched, even proud, almost in spite of himself. Ondine held her breath as the two black-eyed creatures gazed at each other.

"Yes, yes, very nice," he said somewhat gruffly as he accepted her flowers, but then turned away and followed his son. Ondine had packed up the food hamper, and now she handed it to Julie. Picasso climbed inside his fancy car without a backward glance.

"Are we going home now?" Julie asked. Ondine nodded, but as they set off, her feet dragged. Picasso's car soon overtook them and roared ahead, kicking up dust as it disappeared beyond the bend.

As they walked past cicadas making their mind-numbing chatter in the tall grass, Ondine glanced at Julie. And suddenly the sight of her daughter, panting and staggering under the weight of a hamper full of Picasso's dirty dishes, was too much to bear. This must not be her fate.

"Julie, I forgot something," Ondine said decisively. "You go on home ahead of me."

Julie gave a long-suffering sigh and trudged ahead. Ondine hurried back to the villa, alert for any servant who might spy her and call the police. But the place was as silent as a tomb. She stole up the house's stone steps. The big French windows were locked, some even shuttered. She searched determinedly until she saw a smaller, high kitchen window that was left open to relieve the heat.

Ondine hoisted herself up, scraping her palms in the process. She squirmed through the window and landed on a kitchen counter. Tiptoeing around, she peered into shuttered rooms until she found a likely candidate—a room devoid of furniture but completely stuffed with art. Row after row of paintings were kept in groups, some arranged by size, others haphazardly tied with string, or piled on tables, or in stacks simply propped up on the floor. There must be hundreds here.

"I'd better move fast," Ondine told herself, switching on a small light. She knelt down and attacked each group. They were stretched canvases on wood bars. She worked systematically and swiftly, trying not to get distracted by the strange beauty of the pictures, all full of life and energy. Some had dates painted on them; some did not. Some were grouped by a particular year or subject; some weren't.

So many pictures of that elegant woman whom Ondine recognized as the pretty mistress from the magazine photos. Sorting through the canvases Ondine felt her hopes diminishing, even as the artwork seemed to be going back in time, with pictures Picasso had made in the 1940s, perhaps to celebrate the end of the second world war—joyous images of frolicking goats and horses, cavorting nymphs and fauns and other mythological creatures.

As she dug deeper the stacks grew dustier; these batches even had spiderwebs wrapped around them, with a scattering of long-dead flies trapped forever. Ondine wrinkled her nose as she put her hand through the webs. These older paintings were more surreal and harder to fathom.

But then she saw a familiar face—the one that looked like a kite. "Ah!" she cried at another and another in those pastel Easter colors, all from the first week she'd met him. Paintings she remembered, but time had forgotten.

But the Minotaur with the wheelbarrow was gone. So was the still life with the striped pitcher. She reached for a last, smaller canvas, propped in a corner, its front turned away like a bad student forced to stand at the back of a classroom and face the wall. When she turned the painting around she let out a small cry—for it was like looking into an enchanted mirror that transported her back in time. The *Girl-at-a-*

Window gazed right back, full of hope and triumph, her lips slightly parted as if about to speak.

"Was that really me?" Ondine murmured, barely able to recall what it felt like to be a creature who believes in her own unquenchable power. She sat back on her heels, remaining quietly in communion with her lost self. Then she heard the sound of a car approaching.

Ondine gasped. She'd never stolen anything in her life, not even small schoolgirlish thefts. But she reminded herself, "When he made this painting, Picasso said it was *mine*. He can't go back on his word. It's the least he can do for Julie. He just said now, *When a decision is made, someone wins, someone loses*. Well, I'm tired of losing." The picture wasn't large, only about half a meter high and even less wide; she could carry it. Hastily she wrapped it in some old newspapers that lay beneath the canvases.

She realized in a panic that she'd have to go out on the other side of the house. She hurried into one room after another, each with its windows shuttered. She mustn't make a noise that might draw attention. Finally she found a window at the back of the house that opened quietly. She lowered the canvas out first, depositing it onto the grass below. She could hear the car coming closer to the house as she slipped out. She crept around the corner, then peered out cautiously.

It wasn't Picasso's car. It was a gardener, unloading his truck. Watching him walk back and forth several times, Ondine timed his moves until she knew when his back would be turned; then she ran out and ducked into the tall grass beyond the house. She inched her way down each terrace, lowering the painting ahead of her until she finally reached the road.

As soon as she got home, Ondine hid the painting under her clothes in a large drawer. For a few days she waited nervously, but soon she believed that her painting *was* bringing her good luck. For one thing, Picasso evidently didn't miss it because no policeman showed up to arrest her.

Then, not long afterwards, while she was still desperate to find a job, she heard that the Café Paradis—or the Café Renard, as she must call it now—was in serious trouble. She decided to go there and see for herself, but when she arrived, the front window bore a sign saying *CLOSED*.

She shaded her eyes and peered inside, spotting the portly baker sitting alone in a crumpled heap at a corner table. He unlocked the door, listlessly allowing her to follow him inside. And—she couldn't believe it, but there were tears running down his face.

"What's happened to you?" she exclaimed.

"He left me!" Renard cried, sitting down heavily. "My chef has run off to Rome with an Italian aristocrat! To think I neglected my own business to give him everything I had to spend—everything, I tell you!" he blurted out, searching his pockets for a handkerchief. "He didn't even leave a note. Just slipped away early one morning like a thief! I had to hear about it from the stationmaster."

Suddenly the whole thing was clear to Ondine, and she thought she understood why Renard had been an elusive bachelor all these years, only willing to marry when it suited his business plans.

Why, the poor man has at last fallen in love—with that ungrateful boy! she realized. She was touched, but she also saw an opening. So for the first time, she spoke to Renard as if they were friends. "You know, Fabius," she said gently, sitting next to him as he resurrected his handkerchief and wiped his eyes, "be glad that you have some good memories of love. But it's a mistake to try to hold on to happiness forever. It makes you miss the opportunities that are right here in front of you, right now."

Renard had grown quiet, lulled by her soothing, maternal voice and the fact that she addressed him by his first name. "What opportunities?" he muttered interestedly, blowing his nose.

"For one thing, that boy was costing you too much money," Ondine answered. "He wasn't a good cook, and you let him make a mess of this place. Now don't argue—you know it's true. He's lost you a lot of customers. You said yourself that your business is a shambles."

"Yes," Renard admitted sadly.

"I think fate sent me to you today," she went on. "It's time you and

I put our talents together." When Renard looked faintly alarmed, she assured him, "I'm not speaking of marriage. We both have hearts that have not mended. But you are a good baker, and I can cook. I know this café and its local and seasonal clientele like the back of my hand. Together we can make it successful again."

"It will take years—and all our profits—to fix up the café as it was before the war," he warned. "But you're right, no one cooked like you and your mother. You surely *would* bring in more customers."

Ondine said carefully, "Yes, I will cook here, but not as a hired chef. I want to be a partner, just as my father was." Renard gasped, but she plunged on. "Do you still own the *mas* in Mougins?"

"Yes, but it, too, has seen better days," he admitted.

"Ah. Well, I will help you build up the farm as well," Ondine continued boldly. Luc had, after all, taught her a thing or two about bargaining and taking advantages of every single opportunity.

"Why should you do that?" the baker asked, astonished.

"Because that *mas* is the lifeblood of this café, and you are not using it well," she said frankly. "I will put all my body and soul into making both businesses a success. But I'm not going to be a hired hand. I'll be your legal partner, or nothing."

"But what does that mean, exactly?" Renard demanded.

"It means that we share the profits equally, and if you die, the entire business will go to me, just as if I were your wife," Ondine replied firmly. "People will think we're a couple, but you're free to love whomever you please, so long as you do so quietly, without jeopardizing my claim on the café and *mas*. You won't ask any spousal duties of me but we'll be kind to each other. Agreed?"

She showed him her review clippings from America which she'd brought today to convince him to hire her. This time she made him read them. He studied each one, pausing now and again to eye her speculatively. Ondine had grown from an unpredictable, defiant girl into an intelligent, ambitious businesswoman. Renard, too, had a nose for a good deal, no matter whom it came from. At last he nodded decisively, looking both awed and relieved.

Ondine said, "I'll ask the lawyer I've been cooking for to draw up the papers. And one more thing. I want my daughter, Julie, to be employed as a waitress in our café. She needs to be around people, to cure her of her shyness."

"Oh, all right," Renard said. "Can you start right away?"

Ondine made another discovery that day, when she rolled up her sleeves and cleared out the café's kitchen and basement. Down in a jumble of old boxes she found her mother's pink-and-blue pitcher that had been intended for Ondine's wedding trousseau. "It's a sign that Julie *will* marry," she decided, removing it to show to Julie so that she, too, would believe in a happy future.

But Ondine wasn't ready to tell anyone about her portrait. When she and Julie moved into the larger bedroom above the café, she waited until the girl was taking her bath, and only then did Ondine unpack the painting. It was lying at the bottom of her suitcase, face-up, protected by her clothes.

"Picasso was right to tell me not to sell you," Ondine whispered to the *Girl-at-a-Window*. "You've brought me good luck." Carefully she wrapped it in a clean pillowcase, laid it in a drawer of the armoire under her clothes, and locked it. Not until later did she realize that, this time, she'd put the painting face-down.

And shortly thereafter, her luck changed again.

31

Céline and the Soothsayer, Vence 2014

"CÉLINE DARLING," AUNT MATILDA SAID BREEZILY TO ME, "I NEED YOUR skills as an Oscar-nominated makeup artist." Our cooking class was having a class photo taken down by the pool, and Aunt Matilda commanded me to do her face for it.

"But don't make me a monster," she warned. So I took out my brushes and pots of paint, highlighting her cheekbones, contouring her jawline, brightening her eyes and "sculpting" her nose. When I held up a mirror, she peered at her image in astonishment. "Ooh, I like what you do with the color white!" she marvelled, admiring herself. "I look so glamorous—and I feel ten years younger!"

We went down to the pool to join our classmates, who'd run out of gossip about the fate of Gil and his *mas,* so they were now happily talking about their own plans for the free days we had left.

Maurice snapped the pictures as Lizbeth informed our class, "For the rest of the afternoon you'll have the pool all to yourselves; and tonight you'll be served a champagne dinner at the pergola here."

So now everyone was gleefully climbing into their bathing suits, determined to kick back and have fun. But my phone buzzed just then, with an e-mail from Grandmother Ondine's lawyer:

Chère Céline: In answer to your recent inquiry, I have arranged for you to meet Madame Sylvie, the neighbor of your Grandmother Ondine, who was with her just before she died. Madame Sylvie is believed to have the "second sight" and she has consented to read your fortune at two o'clock today if that meets with your convenience. You may telephone her directly at the number below. In any case, please let her know if you cannot attend, as she is in great demand and normally does not give appointments to first-time clients until the end of the year. Sincerely, Monsieur Clément

"Good Lord," I grumbled, "I didn't ask to have my fortune told. Now I guess I'll have to pay her for this visit!" But I still had my rental car, and I had nothing to lose.

"Want to come and get your fortune told?" I asked Aunt Matilda after telling her where I was headed. She glanced across the pool and observed that the men were deeply engrossed in a game of *boules* in a nearby pit.

"It's like a cross between horseshoes and croquet," she observed, sounding bored. "They'll be at it for hours. Sure, I'm game."

Madame Sylvie lived in Vence, high up in the hills above Nice. We got lost in the outskirts several times, and once found ourselves trapped in the dead end of a street so narrow that I couldn't turn the car around; I had to back up, inch by inch, on a road that was really just the perilous edge of a cliff. At the end was an old graveyard.

"Bet it's filled with dead Victorian tourists who fell off this cliff," Aunt Matilda said, terrified.

Finally, we found my soothsayer. She lived in the center of town, in a building wedged among many others, with pretty window boxes full of geraniums. Her narrow front door squeaked as we entered a small, dark front parlor where she met with her clients. When she greeted us I had to stop myself from saying, *You don't look like a fortune-teller!* No wild gypsy scarves here.

Madame Sylvie had only been in her twenties the year that Grandma

Ondine died, so now she was in her late fifties. She was still slender, with straw-colored hair and green eyes, impeccably dressed in a well-tailored beige suit and matching pumps. I introduced her to Aunt Matilda, then we sat down before a small, round table with a black marble top. A deck of gilt-edged cards lay upon it.

"A pleasure to meet Ondine's grand-daughter. But why have you sought me out?" Madame Sylvie said. Her fingers were long and nimble as she dealt the cards out in three neat rows of seven cards each. Aunt Matilda watched, wary and fascinated, since she loved playing card games.

Unable to resist a subversive urge to test Madame Sylvie, I said, "Maybe you can 'see' what's on my mind?"

I half-expected her to betray some guilt—a flicker of the eyelid, a tightening of the mouth—to reveal that she'd been the one who pilfered Grandma's Picasso. Instead she continued to study the cards, then answered serenely, "Yes, I understand that you wish to protect your mother. But I also see that *she* did not defend *you* from the first man in your life. By forcing you to take on the role of her protector—against the father who should have guarded you both—your mother robbed you of the delight of being the younger one, the innocent one. So, now you have come to France to reclaim your right to be cherished as a woman. Your mother has her own destiny; she only wants you to find yours."

Aunt Matilda nodded meaningfully at me. I caught my breath in shock, experiencing a peculiar feeling, as if my entire face were in peril of slipping right off like a mask. "Look," I said abruptly, "I'm not really here to have my fortune told. I came because I heard that you were the last person to see my grandmother alive, and I just need to know what happened that day."

"What happened is that you were born early," Madame Sylvie said with a kindly smile. "Your mother and father had already gone off to the hospital when I stopped by to visit Ondine. We had some tea, and she was excited about *you* and your destiny! But then, God took her that day." She paused, and looked at me keenly. "Now you are seeking to learn Ondine's secrets. Why?"

"I need to know one thing especially, just to set my mother's mind at ease," I said. "Did my Grandmother Ondine ever own a Picasso?"

There was a moment of silence. "This is possible," Madame Sylvie said finally.

If this woman stole the painting, would she dare say that? I wondered. *Sure, why not?* It could even be upstairs hanging in her bedroom right now; although I doubted it, based on nothing more than when a trail feels hot or cold. I supposed that Grandma might simply have put the damned thing into a safe-deposit vault and died before she got the chance to tell Mom where it was.

Tentatively I asked, "I mean, have you actually seen the painting? Not in a vision. For *real*."

"*Non*. But Ondine said Picasso gave her a valuable 'gift'. She was worried about protecting it."

"So, what happened to it?" Aunt Matilda interjected eagerly.

Madame Sylvie's expression remained calm and benign. "I do not know. She didn't say any more about it. I don't think dear Ondine expected to die that day," she added softly, turning to me. "Even someone as practical as your grandmother always believes she'll live just one more day."

Then, gazing meditatively off into the distance, Madame Sylvie said admiringly, "Ondine didn't do anything in the usual way. She was fearless about trying the unexpected, putting this-with-that. It not only made her a great chef; it made her a *femme très formidable*."

"Can't you—predict—where the painting is?" I asked. I was surprised at how pleading I sounded. Madame Sylvie obligingly closed her eyes, breathed deeply and became so still and quiet that I could hear a lizard scurrying on the path outside beneath her open window.

"She put it in a—*placard*—" She paused, searching for the English word, miming opening a door.

"A cupboard," I supplied, startled.

"It's painted blue," she added, opening her eyes now.

"Oh, my God," I said, remembering the photo of Grandmother Ondine in the café's kitchen, with a bright blue cupboard in the background. "But that cupboard isn't at the Café Paradis anymore," I said, feeling panicked that it must have been sold off to some antiques market.

She nodded her head vigorously. "Yes, I see it at the *mas*." That made sense to me; Grandma could have brought the cupboard with her to Mougins when she stopped living in Juan-les-Pins. And, I thought cynically, my fortune-teller might have actually seen it there and was just now remembering.

Madame Sylvie collected and swept away all the cards. I felt I wouldn't be able to hold her much longer, so I cut to the chase. "But I haven't seen that cupboard at the *mas,* either. So exactly where is it now?" I demanded.

Madame Sylvie passed her palm in front of her face from top to bottom. *"Il s'est déplacé."*

"It moved?" I pressed her. "The painting? Or the cupboard, or both?" At this point, in spite of myself, I was hoping that her so-called psychic powers were operating like a GPS tracking system.

Now she only shook her head. "That's all I can tell you. I see nothing more."

She was dealing out the cards again, but this time when she studied them, she gave Aunt Matilda a quick, sympathetic look. I didn't catch on right away. Madame Sylvie returned her gaze to the cards, not so much to study them as to avoid having to speak.

"I haven't got very long, have I?" Aunt Matilda said dryly.

"It all depends," Madame Sylvie said gently. "You must learn not to worry. If your heart is more at peace, you may live a lot longer than you'd expect."

I WAS IMMENSELY GLAD TO leave Madame Sylvie's dark parlor after that. Deeply unsettled by everything she'd said, I was only too ready to shake off the dust of that strange woman's house, which seemed to have enveloped me with an unwanted air of inevitability. I couldn't believe what had just transpired with Aunt Matilda.

"What was *that* all about?" I demanded as soon as we got into the car.

Aunt Matilda took a deep breath, then said, "You heard her. It's my heart. Doctor said the same thing about stress."

"What stress?" I prodded. I'd always assumed her life was as peaceful as it appeared.

"Money," she said shortly. I suddenly remembered what she'd said when she learned of what my father did with all the money in his will. Aunt Matilda had commented, *No surprise there. My father did the same thing to my mom and me.*

"But all these vacations you take—you always seemed not to have a care in the world," I said.

She smiled wryly. "Oh, it was fine while I was still teaching. And for awhile the pension held out. But then the medical bills kicked in, and I took out a reverse mortgage on the house. Frankly, I'm already living longer than everyone told me I would. So when your mother asked me to go with her, I knew she needed a friend. And I figured, what the hell? Might as well go out with a bang."

I leaned over and gave her a big hug, then and there in the car. She allowed this for a moment, then said, "Oh, go on! Start driving." And the farther away we drove from Vence, the more we felt the sun and the salty air reviving us, bringing us out of the dead past and into the lively present.

"At least the painting *did* exist and made it as far as the *mas,*" Aunt Matilda said encouragingly.

"So Madame Sylvie says! But if I find it, Aunt Matilda, we'll have enough money to help Mom *and* to keep you sitting pretty in that house of yours!" I said resolutely, determined to keep her alive and kicking.

She said, "Great. I'll take it." Then she added meaningfully, "But you know, there's somebody else you ought to take into consideration. Gil. You saw those gorillas he's dealing with."

I had been afraid all along that someone might suggest Gil had proprietary rights to anything found at the *mas,* and therefore owned the Picasso. "It belonged to Grandma," I said with a stab of anxiety. "If it's there, it's Mom's. Not mine, and not Gil's. If he finds out about the portrait, he might want to keep it all to himself—he wouldn't care about my mother."

Aunt Matilda eyed me speculatively. "Listen, that Madame What-sis who just read your fortune may have been right—maybe it's more important for you to find yourself, not just that painting."

"Yeah, yeah," I muttered, feeling embarrassed by today's discussion of my psyche.

"I think what you're really looking for is somebody you can trust," Aunt Matilda remarked.

"I have you," I answered.

"And as you heard, I won't be around forever! You know, Céline, people don't necessarily have to *earn* your trust. In the end, trust is a choice we make. We decide, 'I choose to trust this one'. Sometimes, you just have to roll the dice."

WHEN WE ARRIVED BACK AT the *mas* Aunt Matilda said, "I for one could use a swim and a cocktail."

I smiled, knowing that she was eager to see Peter. "Go ahead," I said, dropping her off in front. "I'll park this buggy and catch up."

I drove on and pulled into a good space in the parking lot. I was thinking that if Grandma Ondine died before she could tell Mom that her Picasso was hidden in her blue cupboard, then either the dairyman who bought the *mas* found the painting in the cupboard and sold it; or, the painting was still hidden somewhere in that cupboard. But where was the cupboard now?

It wasn't until I arrived back at the front door of the *mas* and spotted Rick walking out that I recalled what Gil said: *The dairyman who sold me this mas left some old country-style stuff, which my business partner's got in storage.*

"Then Rick probably has it!" I reasoned. As I got closer I noticed that he was looking supremely pleased with himself, and I wondered if he'd convinced Gil to sign his contract.

"Hi, there, Rick," I said in the most charming way I could manage.

He glanced up quickly, with the look of surprised pleasure that a guy gets when a woman who's been inaccessible suddenly becomes nice to him. "Hi, yourself," he said. "What are you up to today?"

"I'm hoping to convince Gil to decorate the *pigeonnier* with some of that lovely country furniture from here that you guys put into storage," I said blithely. "But you know Gil. He's *so* stubborn."

"*That* he most definitely is," Rick said knowingly.

"I'm thinking I should *show* Gil, rather than *tell* him," I went on recklessly. "You know, just pick out a few good pieces and bring them back here to convince him. I think he said you put them in a storage vault for him? Are they kept very far away?"

For a moment he had to think about it. "Oh, *that* stuff. It's in Monaco," Rick said easily. "Forty-five minutes, if the traffic's not too bad. I can't take you there today; I've got meetings. Tomorrow afternoon, okay?" His voice was low and sexy now, as if he'd just asked me for a date.

"Okay," I said. Then I found myself adding in a conspiratorial hush, "But look, please don't mention this to Gil. I want to surprise him."

Rick laughed as his driver arrived with his car. "Your secret's safe with me, babe," he said.

When I went into the lobby Maurice was engrossed in his computer until I greeted him directly. Then he glanced up distractedly and said, "The farewell dinner is being served down by the pool."

"Maurice—what's happening with Gil today? Is everything—okay?" I said in a low voice.

He answered carefully, "We are fortunate. The blog review for the restaurant was *très bien*."

"But Rick was just here. Does that mean he and Gil have come to terms?" I asked. After all, Gil would have to repay his loan by Thursday. Today was Sunday.

Maurice glanced around first to make sure no one was listening. "The game is not yet finished," he murmured, as if the whole thing was too much of a burden to bear silently. "But I think we have reached *la crise*."

Crisis time. Not just for Gil, either, because this was surely my last chance to find that Picasso.

* * *

I CHANGED INTO MY BATHING suit and went down to the pool to join the others. The poolside bar had opened and everyone was getting a little high-spirited, even frisky. Joey, Magda, Lola and Ben were all lying on inflatable floats, which had armrests with circles for holding their drinks. Aunt Matilda and Peter sat under the pergola, side by side on matching *chaises longues,* nibbling canapés and sipping champagne. And Martin was skateboarding all around the pool, performing more and more daring stunts, egged on by the applause he was getting from his elders.

"Gil was here for a bit, but he's gone off somewhere again," Aunt Matilda told me. "I take it things aren't going swimmingly for him?" I nodded. I kept getting distracted by Martin, who'd disappear around a bend and then come wheeling back from a completely different direction.

This time he was heading directly toward the pool. Even placid Aunt Matilda sat up alert.

"He's not going to try to vault across the water, is he?" she asked in trepidation.

But that was exactly what Martin intended. Apparently, as he told us later, he'd done it successfully before; but there hadn't been any people in the pool then. The distraction of those paddlers must have thrown him slightly off his expert timing, because this time Martin leapt up into the air, skateboard and all, and came down just a bit too short. With a yell, he smashed right into the water, plunging deeply and then, on the way up, he got conked on the head by his own skateboard.

Nobody else in the pool was hurt, because they'd all scrambled to the other side. Aunt Matilda sprang to her feet, but I had already dived in, stroking rapidly over to Martin. He'd been so stunned by the blow that he began to sink. I fished him out, scooped him in my arms and dragged him to the side. Joey, Ben and Peter all helped me pull Martin out and lay him on the ground like a beached baby seal.

"Anyone know CPR?" Ben asked worriedly, checking the boy's pulse. "He doesn't seem to be breathing."

I summoned up my first-aid training and bent down to Martin's little face. Gently as I could, I pushed on his chest again and again, then, seeing that he really wasn't breathing yet, I pinched his nose, covered his mouth with mine and breathed into his until I saw his chest rise. I had to do this several times. The whole thing was one of those incidents that just seem suspended in time.

At last, Martin choked, gurgled and gasped. He opened his eyes, but it took him awhile to realize where he was. Then, his first words were, "Don't tell Dad."

"Bollocks," said a familiar voice behind me. Someone had telephoned Gil and he'd rushed over here. His voice was shaky with high emotion, but what he said to his son was, "You're bloody lucky you're alive, you little shit."

32

Céline and Gil: A Gamble in Mougins

THE NEXT DAY WAS A FREE-FOR-ALL, WITH EVERYONE ARRANGING OUTINGS and day trips, now that the working part of our class was over. Lola and Ben were taking off to make various stops along the coast, ending up in St. Tropez, so they weren't coming back. Magda, Joey and Peter invited Aunt Matilda to join them on the ferry to Corsica for an overnight trip.

"Want to come?" Aunt Matilda asked. I told her about my little rendezvous with Rick.

"Hmm," she said. "Ordinarily I might hang around in case you needed a chaperone. But if I don't go with the others, Magda will put the moves on Peter," she said with all seriousness. I couldn't believe that at their age, the dynamics of courtship were the same as in high school. As if reading my thoughts she said, "It only gets more immature as you get older, because everybody has less time."

I kissed her and said, "Have a great trip!"

A little while later, when I went downstairs, I found the lobby uncharacteristically silent. Rick didn't show up, so I had no idea if he intended to honor his promise to take me to Monaco, and I had no way to reach him without arousing suspicion. Even the front desk was unattended.

I stepped outside for a breath of air, trying to regroup. To my surprise I came upon Gil sitting on the stone wall near the entrance, slumped and defeated-looking, his coffee cup in his hands, staring into space while talking on his mobile. As I drew nearer I saw that he hadn't shaved, and this gave him a slightly derelict look. He ended his call just as I came out.

"How's Martin?" I asked. The French doctor who'd been summoned had insisted on keeping Martin under observation overnight at the hospital, just in case he'd had a concussion or retained any water in his lungs.

"He's fine," Gil said, with that vulnerable look crossing his face again. "I get to bring him home tonight." He paused. "Look, I really want to thank you for springing into action as you did. That dumb kid. He owes you. Well, *I* owe you one."

"You already thanked me yesterday," I said, "and you don't owe me anything."

There was something else bothering him, though. I could hear it in his reserved tone. I sat down beside him and asked in dread, "What's the matter? Is it about the *mas*?"

"Why don't you ask your boyfriend?" Gil could not resist saying. I shot him a puzzled look.

"You know who I'm talking about," he said bitterly. I immediately wondered if Rick had blabbed about my interest in the furniture storage.

I felt myself flushing guiltily, but I said, "What are you talking about?"

"He told me he had a nice conversation with you yesterday, and he thinks you'd make an excellent hostess for the hotel. Yep, he definitely sees a future for *you* in his new operation." Gil smirked as if daring me to deny it. But it didn't appear that Rick had said anything about taking me to Monaco.

So all I said was, "*His* new operation?"

"That's right," Gil replied in a self-mocking tone. "As of Thursday, if I sign his ruddy contract, Rick will own this entire place—lock, stock and barrel. So you picked the right horse to back."

"What happened, Gil?" I asked. "Aren't you guys partners any-more?"

"Partners?" Gil said with a hollow laugh. "As it turns out, we were *never* going to be partners. He knew how to play me, though. Back then, money was tight with all the banks, so the only way I could raise enough to cover the renovation costs for the *mas* was to borrow from the loan sharks. I only did it because I had Rick's assurances that if I made him my partner, he'd sell off some of his other properties in time to raise the cash so I could repay my loan to—"

"Those thugs!" I exclaimed in alarm.

"To their boss, Gus," he corrected. "Who absolutely will not extend the loan period no matter what I say. So, after months of back-and-forth with Rick's lawyer and mine just 'ironing out the details' of our 'good-faith' agreement—suddenly, at the eleventh hour, Rick tells me he can't come up with the promised cash to pay back my loan—UNLESS we modify our contract with his new clause to satisfy his bankers. Now I find out that, all along, he only wanted to take over my beautiful, newly renovated *mas* and simply add it to his hotel chain. It will be, as he put it, 'another diamond in the tiara'."

"And what happens to you?" I asked in disbelief.

"Hah!" Gil said hollowly. "He wants me to stay on and 'cook for him'. He bloody well wants to use my chef's brand for his own profits, and keep me on as an indentured servant, basically. Or, as he puts it, 'You just be creative, Gil, and leave the business end to me.'"

"Well, that's preposterous!" I spluttered. "You don't have to take a rotten deal like that."

"In fact, I do," Gil said heavily. "Because those are the only terms under which Rick will go to his bank and transfer enough funds to cover my reconstruction loan. I have to sign his deal tomorrow, in order to pay off the bad boys on Thursday. Otherwise I sleep with the fishes. And if I don't take Rick's deal, then the loan shark will own the *mas*. Either way, I lose it. Thing is, this place will soon be worth so much more than what I owe! Well, maybe I *should* just let Gus have it!" he scowled.

"Can't you get any other backers to take Rick's place?" I asked. Gil gave me a withering look.

"What do you think I've been trying to do ever since I got wind of the fact that Rick has no intention of honoring our original deal? But this is too short a window for most investors, and I don't blame them. I was, in retrospect, a raving idiot to believe that Rick has been negotiating in good faith, just 'tweaking' the damned contract here and there to appease his investors. The bloody bastard had this trick in mind all the time; he was just stringing me along with the promise of good terms to make sure I didn't make a better deal with anybody else. Well, more fool me, for believing it was in the bag."

I realized that Rick was a well-dressed thug, no better than the loan shark—worse, really, for betraying Gil's trust. A little voice inside my head—sounding an awful lot like Aunt Matilda—was telling me that if I had to deal with Rick instead of Gil, I could just kiss that Picasso goodbye.

"NO!" I cried. "Don't sign it! You *can't* sell this place!" Gil was taken aback.

"Why should *you* care so much?" He stared at me keenly. "Are you ever going to tell me what you've really been up to in France? All I want is some truth. From somebody! Rick's gone to London and left me in the shit unless I sign to his demands."

"Rick's gone to London?" I echoed. "But—when's he coming back here?"

"Never; unless I sign his wretched contract," Gil said flatly.

"But—but," I stuttered. "Are you sure he's gone?"

"Of course I'm sure," Gil said, sounding irritable again. Then he recovered and said, "Hey, this isn't your problem. Thanks for asking, though."

I figured it was a pretty good bet that Rick had no intention of returning here today just to honor his promise to take me to the storage area, because why would he care about decorating the *mas* now that Gil was resisting signing his contract? So how was I going to find the blue cupboard before this takeover happened? I knew I'd reached the point of no return. I could either get Gil on board right now, or go home and forget the whole thing.

"I just *might* have a better backer for you," I said carefully. "It's a long shot, but you'll have to promise that no matter what happens, the deal is, the ownership of the *mas* will be divided fifty–fifty."

Gil looked dubious. "An equal split with someone I don't know? Just who've you got in mind?"

"Me," I said with more boldness than I felt.

Gil eyed me speculatively. "Well, you *have* been casing out this place ever since you got off the plane. So it's been business all along, eh? With most people, it's *always* about the money. But for some reason I got the idea that you had higher priorities, and the money was secondary."

"It was—but I can't afford to think that way anymore," I said. "If I turn up the money you need, no matter how I do it, then fifty percent of *everything* at the *mas* is mine, right?"

"Are you going to rob the bank of Monte Carlo or something?" he asked.

"You don't need the details," I answered.

"Are you using legal means to obtain this money?" Gil pursued.

"Mostly," I said. "So you have to swear that you'll honor this agreement, even-Steven."

Gil looked as if it occurred to him for the first time that I might actually be serious. The desperate expression on his face abated, and I detected a faint glint in his eyes. "If you can really come up with the money before Thursday, it's a deal," he said suddenly, offering his hand for me to shake.

"You can't welch on it like Rick did," I said, before letting him take my hand. I was watching his face more closely than I've ever looked at anyone's face in my entire life.

"I won't welch," he promised with his most winning, convincing smile. "Swear to God."

"Write it on a napkin," I said, and he actually did scribble out our impromptu deal on his coffee napkin and he signed it.

But he couldn't resist asking, "Are you going to sell off a yacht or a string of pearls?"

"Something like that," I replied. "If you want the money you'll have to help me get my hands on it." He gave me a deeply suspicious look. I plunged on. "Do you know where Rick's storage facility is?"

"Yeah, sure," Gil said, bewildered. "It's in Monaco. Why?"

"Do you have a key to the place?" I asked.

"It's not a key. It's got a code," he answered. "I think we can get in. Why?"

I had to tell him now. "Rick's got something that belongs to my mother in there," I blurted out.

Gil said in surprise, "As far as I know, all he's got is the dairyman's old furniture from the *mas*. What's that got to do with your mum?"

There must be something about Monte Carlo that brings out the gambler in people. I knew what my lawyer would say if he had any idea of the risk I was about to take. But lawyers, I've discovered, know nothing about life. As Aunt Matilda said, *Sometimes, you just have to roll the dice*.

"Brace yourself, Gil. And don't freak out. That dairyman that you bought the *mas* from?" I said. "Well, *he* bought this place from my grandmother."

Gil looked stunned, but then the light broke across his face as if it all made sense to him at last.

"So, *that's* it! No wonder you've been hanging about here. I knew it couldn't be your love of cooking, that's for sure. But what good's the old furniture? Is one of them some rare antique?"

I shook my head. "I've got reason to believe that my grandmother left something extremely valuable in it for my mom, which she desperately needs," I said softly. "Grandma didn't want my dad or anyone else to get hold of it. I think it's hidden in a blue cupboard. Does a piece like that ring a bell?"

Gil glanced at me as if he now feared for my sanity, and said with some confusion, "But, I'm pretty sure all that stuff was empty when I took possession of it."

I paused, remembering what my mother had told me about Grandmother Ondine: *She did have her little hiding places* ...

I told Gil this. "So I really have to see it for myself," I insisted. "Otherwise I'll be haunted by it for the rest of my life, just like my mother was." I explained to him that I was facing a custody battle with siblings. "If I *do* find this item, I might be able to sell it, for a *lot* more than what you need, and then I can pay my lawyer to fight for Mom."

"Oh," he said gently. Then he added doubtfully, "And *that's* how you're going to raise the money to save this *mas* as well? On this slim chance of finding some family heirloom?"

"Yes," I said. "Laugh if you want to. Just get me into that storage area, right now."

Gil said under his breath, "Well, fuck me, this is just about what I deserve."

"What other chance have you got?" I pointed out.

Gil pondered this for several seconds, then said, "Not a one. Let's go."

33

A Surprise from Picasso: Ondine, 1967

At first, Ondine kept her Picasso portrait hidden in her bedroom and never showed it to anyone. She focused all her time and energy on making a success of the café and Renard's *mas* in Mougins, which were both starting to look like a good gamble. Because now there were more tourists on the Riviera than ever before, thanks to an actress named Brigitte Bardot, who frolicked on the beach in a scandalous bikini to promote a movie; and Grace Kelly, who married Prince Rainier of Monaco in a glorious, fairy-tale ceremony that was filmed and shown around the world. And so, as the café and *mas* began to flourish, Ondine continued to think of her *Girl-at-a-Window* as a sound investment which, if left alone, would accrue in value and serve as Julie's dowry.

But Julie's prospects for marriage were rapidly diminishing. First, the poor girl fell in love with a local boy who ultimately broke her heart by running off to Toulouse with another woman. If Julie had the confidence of most young ladies in the sassy 1960s, she might have shrugged it off and picked a new boyfriend; but, Ondine observed, Julie seemed to fall in love with being miserable by insistently mourning the boy who got away, and stubbornly avoiding having her heart broken again.

Worse yet, that spring Julie fell ill with a fever of 104 degrees after swimming in a nearby stream. Her condition was so severe that the priest was called in to give her the last rites, and even though she eventually recovered, she lost some of her hair. It came out in sad clumps and took many months to grow back into something that looked presentable.

"She's had so much trauma as it is, and now this," Ondine worried.

During that time, no boy came courting, and Julie would not have wanted anyone to see her that way. She couldn't wait on tables, so she kept out of sight in the back of the house, helping out in the kitchen. Julie felt that she was doing some kind of penance for a sin she couldn't remember committing. She got so accustomed to hanging her head in shame that even when her new hair grew in and she began to wait on tables again, she forgot to lift her face and smile at people.

And that's how things remained, until one day when a party of businessmen came into the café. Two were German, two French, one English, and one American. The New York accent caught Julie's attention; it shot her right back to her happier childhood days in New Rochelle.

"Bone-jour, ma'am-zelle!" the handsome American called out to her. With his sandy hair, laughing Irish eyes, and astonishingly perfect, small white teeth, he reminded her of those easygoing Hollywood movie stars who were so brave and breezy and cheerful. When Julie leaned over to translate the menu for him, he looked up at her with such gratitude that she felt a warm flush of pleasure. He made a good-natured joke about his bad pronunciation, then he asked her name, and introduced himself: Arthur, a lawyer meeting his colleagues here "in the Frenchie branch" of his firm.

"Say, Julie, wouldja like to go to the movies with me tonight?" he asked. He added coaxingly, "I saw a poster for a great John Wayne film!"

When Julie told her mother where she was going, the girl looked so happy to finally have an escort that Ondine almost wept with relief. Yet at the same time, she felt a peculiar twinge of misgiving.

It was a gentle night, and after the movie Arthur and Julie went for a walk through town where he bought her ice cream. He told her all about his boyhood, and how, for awhile, he'd thought seriously about becoming a priest. When he spoke of his deceased wife, he cast himself as a brave martyr. "But I have two kids, and I think the good Lord wants me to have a new wife to complete my family," he said, as if he believed that his life was of particularly high value to the Almighty.

He must be a very pious man, Julie thought admiringly, basking in the warmth of his gaze.

After their first date he showed up every evening at the café to take her out. He was genuinely fond of Julie, and touchingly vulnerable, as if he feared she'd grow tired of him and stop wanting to see him. Every time he called on her he wore a searching, eager look; and he confided that Julie's soft, reassuring touch made him feel truly "connected" with someone for the first time in his life.

There was only one problem for Julie—her mother.

Ondine tried to like Arthur, but she had learned never to ignore reality no matter how much she wished to avert her eyes.

"He's the kind of man who can't bear to hear the sound of any voice but his own," she told Renard after observing that whenever someone else told a story or a joke, Arthur drummed his fingers on the table, impatiently waiting for his turn to speak again, like a bad actor looking for his next cue. And, the jokes he told were often at someone else's expense—even Julie's. "A man like that would make *any* woman miserable, but for Julie, who'll never fight back, he'd be a disaster for a husband!"

"Oh, let her have some fun," Renard advised. "It's just a flirtation; this fellow will be gone in a week and she'll have a happy memory, and some confidence! Whereas if you forbid her to see him, she'll imagine you ruined her life, and she'll hold it against you forever." Ondine could see the wisdom in this.

But one afternoon in the café, Ondine overheard Arthur having dinner with some American colleagues. Julie was dealing with another customer, so one of the busboys who didn't speak English came to deliver the check. Ondine, still unnoticed behind the bar, watched as Arthur broke into an enormous fake smile when he handed the money to the French busboy and said in English, "Here you go, why don't you take this and shove it up your ass?"

The busboy, reacting only to the smile without comprehending the insulting words, nodded and said, *"Merci."* Arthur howled with laughter while his friends just shook their heads.

"Here comes my girlfriend," Arthur boasted to them as Julie approached him now. "She's French, too, but I've already got her obedience-trained." To Julie he called out, "Grab your hat and coat, honey. We're going dancing tonight. Hurry!" Julie quickly removed her apron and went to get her coat.

Ondine said sharply, "Julie, I need to talk to you."

But Julie sensed from her mother's tone that it was something she didn't want to hear, and for the first time in her entire life, the meek little mouse put her foot down. "We're late for the dance, *Maman,*" she called out cheerfully as she put on her hat. "Let's talk when I get home." Her newfound stubbornness felt like strength, and she flounced defiantly out of the café, giddy with her own daring.

Watching them go, Ondine had a queer feeling; and sure enough, when Julie and Arthur returned to the café later that night, Arthur dramatically announced that Julie had agreed to become his wife. Beaming, Julie held out her left hand, so everyone could admire the sizeable diamond ring there.

The staff and diners applauded—even tightfisted Monsieur Renard poured champagne to toast Julie and her fiancé. Ondine couldn't believe how foolishly sentimental Renard was, knowing how she felt. Perhaps it was a displaced fatherly urge; and, he seemed intimidated by this aggressive American.

Arthur was a sly one, she thought, announcing his proposal so publicly, just to make it difficult for Ondine to object without humiliating Julie in front of everyone she knew. *He wouldn't dare use this tactic if Luc were alive. Well, he'll marry Julie over my dead body!* she decided.

When Arthur finally left, and Julie climbed the stairs to the bedroom she shared with her mother, Ondine said firmly, "Julie. This egoist is not the man for you."

Fearful that her mother would put a stop to it, Julie shrieked, "You don't know him as I do!"

For Arthur had confided many things to her. He'd confessed that he was not such a popular man with the ladies back home; his first wife, he felt sure, had been more interested in his money and success than in making him happy. "People can be rotten," he'd said, adding that he'd "just about given up hope" until he met Julie. And when he proposed to her, he'd actually had tears in his eyes.

He'd taken her hand and held it against his cheek, adding in all sincerity, "You're the sweetest human being I've ever met, and I'll raise heaven and earth to make sure you live the good life, because you deserve so much more than this life you've had."

It had been such a personal moment that Julie couldn't explain it to her mother. And Ondine, although she knew that this was a troubled man, also sensed that there might be something genuine between her daughter and Arthur. So now Ondine asked, "How is he when you are alone? Does he ever ask what *you* want? Is he gentle? Has he said you're beautiful, and that he loves you, *ma chérie*?"

Julie was momentarily thrown by her mother's prescience, for although Arthur had been affectionate, holding hands, smiling at her indulgently, eager to see her again, she could not honestly quote him saying anything about love. Surely he had, once? But some men didn't like to have to say the actual word. Then she thought she understood what her mother really wanted to know.

"Oh, don't worry, he only kissed me. Nothing more." Julie gaily waved her sparkling engagement ring. "He wouldn't ask to marry me if he didn't love me! Arthur is just like Papa Luc, only richer," she boasted. "He says no wife of his will *ever* have to work!"

Ondine said carefully, "I'm glad he's good with money. But a woman should earn and handle money, too. If you rely entirely on him, you will be forever at his mercy. Even when a husband is loving, you don't want him to know that he has so much power over you. Not that much."

But Julie felt only a strange thrill at the idea of total surrender to a husband. After all, that was what all the movies and fairy tales and operas said love was all about. Like throwing yourself off a cliff, trusting that the sea below would catch you—and ready to die if it didn't.

That night, as Ondine lay awake listening to her slumbering daughter's measured breathing, she suddenly knew what she must do. She crept out of bed to retrieve her portrait from the wardrobe drawer, and tiptoed into the kitchen to lay it on the table.

"Maybe it was a mistake to hold on to my Picasso! If I'd sold it, we could have moved away from Juan-les-Pins and sent Julie to university. Then she'd never have met this awful man," Ondine fretted. "Well, I could *still* sell it and use the money to travel with Julie, so she'll meet someone better."

Guiltily she thought of what Picasso said about never selling a gift. But why should he care if she sold one painting? He had so many more than he could count, sitting up there like a king in his castle.

"It's easy for Picasso to talk about not selling it—when was the last time he had to work for peanuts to keep from starving? He's forgotten how hard it can be," Ondine reasoned. "I wonder how much it's worth," she mused, staring at her *Girl-at-a-Window*. "But what if Picasso told all the dealers that this painting is stolen goods? If I try to sell it, they'll catch me and put me in jail!" Well, that was a chance she'd just have to take. She recalled that the elderly lawyer she'd cooked for in Vallauris had a nephew who'd just recently opened an art gallery in Antibes. "I'll get him to appraise it for me tomorrow," she decided, wrapping it in brown paper and string, and replacing it in the armoire.

She rose early the next morning to do all her cooking for the café, so she could leave Julie in charge of the breakfast and lunch service. Then, under the pretext of going to the market, Ondine slipped out while everyone at the café was too busy to notice the package under her arm. She paid for a taxi to carry her precious cargo to the gallery.

"Picasso?" said Pierre, the dealer, who had the face of a cherub. Carefully but doubtfully he examined the painting. Then he called out to his assistant. "André! Come take a look at this, will you?"

His assistant was finishing up with another client, and presently he joined them. "Look here, and tell me what you see," Pierre commanded. Ondine stood by, holding her breath. What was wrong?

André peered at the painting. "Hmm," he said thoughtfully.

"Who painted it?" Pierre demanded.

André frowned. "I don't know," he admitted. "It hasn't been signed by the painter."

Ondine had never noticed this. But now that she was looking closely, she saw that Picasso had not put a date on it, either, as he often did in those distinctive Roman numerals.

"Well, who do you *think* painted it?" Pierre persisted. André shrugged, and named a few artists that Ondine had never heard of. "You left out Picasso," Pierre said.

André shook his head. "No, not at all," he said firmly.

"Thank you, André," Pierre said. André nodded and went into the back room.

"You see?" Pierre said in a low voice. "It's just as I thought. It's beautiful but it's not what people think of as a Picasso. Who told you it was his work? I'd be careful about making such a claim!"

"I was his model!" Ondine exclaimed indignantly. "I cooked for him and he made it as a gift."

Pierre looked from Ondine to the painting, considering this possibility. "Did he give you a letter or a receipt of some sort?" he asked hopefully. Ondine shook her head. He shrugged. "Without his signature, I can't really sell it. Picasso surely knows that."

Ondine gasped. Had Picasso outfoxed her somehow? Were the gods punishing her for taking it? "But—there must be *someone* who'd like to buy it!" she protested.

Pierre warned, "People will question its authenticity, just as I did. So you'd better go back and ask him to sign it. But I warn you," he added in a low voice, "Picasso can be very touchy. I heard of a woman who asked him to sign an older work, and he said he wouldn't put today's signature on a painting he'd done twenty years ago. Another time with another request, he signed it, all right—he painted his name all over it so many times that he effectively defaced it and ruined it!"

Ondine declared, "He wouldn't do such a thing to *this* painting."

But her heart was hammering with guilt now. Heaven knew what Picasso would do with a thief like Ondine, especially if she were audacious enough to ask him to sign it.

"Picasso might even say this painting was never 'finished'," Pierre went on. "Or, he could say it was an inferior work, not up to his usual standards and *that* was why he didn't sign it, because he intended to destroy it. He's a powerful man, and nobody in the art world wants to displease the great Picasso. If he should 'disown' your picture in this way, well . . ." Pierre's voice trailed off.

"What then?" Ondine asked in dread.

"The painting would surely lose its market value," Pierre said formally. "I'm so sorry, Madame."

34

Céline and Gil in Monaco, 2014

"Picasso!" Gil exclaimed as we drove along the highway to Monaco in the white minivan from the *mas,* since we couldn't very well take a painting on a motorcycle, and I'd already returned my rental car. "*That's* who your grandmother cooked for?" he asked.

"Yes," I said, reaching into my bag and pulling out Grandma Ondine's notebook. I opened it up to the flyleaf and showed him. "See? *P* for Picasso. Every single recipe in this book was for him."

"Incredible," Gil said, stunned. "No wonder she kept that notebook all her life."

"Mom said Picasso gave Grandma one of his paintings as a gift. So I'm telling you, she must have kept *that* all her life, too," I insisted. "I don't believe she sold it. She just didn't want my father to find it, because it would be worth a lot of money. I think she went to great pains to hide it."

Gil absorbed this in awe. "And you really think you've tracked it down?"

"Right," I said, showing him the photo of Grandma Ondine in front of the blue cupboard.

But I was glad that the heavy, unpredictable traffic distracted Gil, because I didn't want to tell him that it was a fortune-teller who gave me the "hot tip" that put me on this trail.

When we reached the bustling city of Monte Carlo, Gil drove right past the casino, past the fancy Hôtel de Paris, past the pricey, blingy shops and the deceptively plain-looking buildings that housed some of the world's most expensive apartments. Toward the outskirts of town he steered past a heliport, and beyond that, a very large, unassuming structure that looked like a gigantic warehouse. When he pulled into the parking lot behind it, I glanced up at him questioningly.

"What's this?" I asked. "A private airplane hangar?"

"Hardly," he said. "You are looking at one of the most exclusive storage facilities in the world. Inside those walls are priceless everythings: artwork—antique furniture—rare jewels—prized Persian carpets—multimillion-dollar vintage wine collections—ancient sculptures—elephant ivory—and God knows what else."

"Are you serious?" I said. "In a garage?"

"This 'garage' is a state-of-the-art fortress," Gil said as he shut off the motor. "Every vault is climate-controlled and big enough to hold whatever you fancy. Yet each vault can, if necessary, be put on a giant freight elevator and moved down to the showroom level, where there are special meeting rooms for you to privately exhibit whatever items you wish to sell to the select buyers you invite here. Or, you can just come here on your own, sit there in your box and stare at your haul," he added as we got out and approached the building.

"Looks pretty drab and nondescript," I observed.

"Discretion, my dear," Gil said with a knowing look. "So nobody knows the extraordinary value of what's inside. A collector can quietly show up and pack his treasures quickly to move them to, say, a similar vault in Switzerland, South Africa or Dubai."

I finally caught on. "Sounds like some of the clientele got their collectibles in questionable ways? Looting an archeological site, taking artwork the Nazis stole—or buying it off the back of a truck?"

"Quiet, the guards will hear you," Gil warned. "Act as though you belong here. Just leave this to me, okay?"

As we approached the front doors they automatically opened, and as soon as we stepped into a foyer they instantly closed behind us with an aggressive whoosh. Three burly security guards stood at the ready. Gil signed in at the reception desk, where a fourth man kept watch. The foyer was as cool as a wine cellar, but it had the scent of money the way banks do. It was all steel, chrome and glass.

Across from the reception desk were two elevators. One door was very narrow. The other was very wide. Gil chose the narrow one and we stepped in.

"Tight squeeze," I commented. "What was wrong with the bigger elevator?"

"Freight elevator," Gil said out of the side of his mouth.

"How come you didn't have to tell them where you're going?" I asked.

"They have my information on their computer. They know," Gil said, still *sotto voce*.

"Hey, there aren't any buttons for the floor numbers in here," I said, feeling slightly panicked.

"Front desk. Remote control," Gil said shortly.

Silently I counted the floors as we rose past them. One, two, three, four. Then, rather eerily, the elevator stopped of its own accord and opened onto another reception area with low lighting. This was more glamorous than downstairs. It looked like the lobby of a very posh auction house, with plush red leather chairs, golden glass-topped tables, and expensive carpeting.

"This way, please." A woman in a severe black pantsuit, with her pale brown hair pulled back into a tightly braided ponytail, appeared out of nowhere and seemed to know exactly where to lead us. She walked ramrod-straight with both hands held rigidly behind her at the small of her back, and with her elbows out, military-style. I suppressed a mad desire to giggle.

We followed her noiselessly down the carpeted corridor. More security guards floated past us, wearing visible guns in leather holsters. I waggled my eyebrows at Gil. Occasionally other collectors and their clients wafted down the corridor, so light-footed and silent as they vanished beyond the doors of their own vaults that they seemed more like ghosts who'd melted right into the walls.

Our escort stopped suddenly in front of a door marked with three brass numbers. Just then the walkie-talkie in her jacket coughed the way police radios do, and she stepped away to murmur into it.

Gil moved up to our vault's entrance where, instead of a doorknob, there was a keypad on which to enter a security code. He punched in some numbers. The keypad's light flashed red in response.

"Shit," Gil whispered. "Rick must have changed the code, dammit."

I noticed that our ponytailed guide was now standing with two security guards who'd wandered over to her. The three of them were conferring in hushed tones. Were they discussing us? Had someone downstairs alerted them?

Desperately I turned to Gil and hissed, "Well, you'd better figure out what the *new* code is, before Brunhilde over there has us arrested."

"It was the last four digits of his phone—the one he keeps in his car," Gil said, trying again in case he'd punched it in wrong. The light flashed red once more. I thought of the day Rick gave me a ride in his fancy car.

"His phone," I repeated. "The one with the diamond and emerald horseshoe on it?"

"Haven't seen that model," Gil said. "Maybe he upgraded when his racehorse won the Derby. He was ecstatic and he still won't stop talking about it."

"What was the name of the horse?" I suggested.

"Fancy-Dancer," Gil said. "Too many letters for this code box."

"What was the date that he won the Derby?" I prodded.

Gil looked skyward, trying to remember. I nudged him to hurry as one of the guards approached us. Gil drew in his breath and punched new numbers.

The keypad absorbed this information thoughtfully.

Then, just as Brunhilde moved toward us, the keypad's little light turned green.

A second later, the door to the vault quietly slid open on its tracks.

35

Céline and Gil in Monte Carlo

"WOW. RICK'S GOT A LOT OF STUFF STASHED AWAY IN HERE," I WHISPERED to Gil, feeling worried.

"But all we're looking for is a blue cupboard, right?" Gil replied as we searched for Grandma's furniture that he'd sent here from the *mas*. I followed him past Rick's enormous, mysterious crates marked *Africa Safari* and *Ming, China* and *Grand Hotel auction, Sweden*. There were also polo mallets and antique horse saddles, and a hand-carved ivory chess set sealed in a glass box.

"Here!" Gil said triumphantly, pointing to a more modest cluster of brightly painted, Provençal furniture: a red rocking chair, a yellow chest of drawers, a blue-and-white dining table surrounded by a set of six white dining chairs with bright blue tufted cushions.

"This is definitely the stuff that came from the *mas* when I bought it," he said positively. "Rick and I just threw 'em into the van and he carted it off here. I remember this box of pots and pans."

I wandered behind the yellow chest of drawers. "Look!" I exclaimed, having landed face-to-face with the blue cupboard. "It's identical to the one in the photo of Grandma," I said, getting excited now.

"Okay, great. Check it out. Better hurry," Gil warned.

I studied the cupboard carefully. I knocked on its door with the funny wooden knob before I opened it up. Then I checked out the interior with its four shelves, and searched for hidden drawers or compartments. I tapped its walls to see if a painting could have been sealed up in there, or sequestered in a false bottom. Nothing. No sign even that it had ever belonged to Grandmother Ondine. It was just a nice, country-style oak cupboard painted a bright blue.

"It's empty," Gil said, feeling it necessary to state the obvious. "You sure it isn't in some other piece of furniture?"

I was sure of nothing now, except that if I could ever get my hands on Madame Sylvie again I'd cheerfully wring her neck for giving me false hope with this fool's errand.

"I guess we'd better check them all," I said, feeling gloomy now.

Gil obligingly helped me ransack the other furnishings that had been trucked over here from the *mas*. We had to work quickly, but it was soon obvious that there was absolutely no Picasso hidden in their midst. I dusted off my hands, unable to look Gil in the eye after having completely misled him with false hopes. But he was busy sorting through boxes of copper pots and pans and other cookware that he'd gotten with the *mas*. He now put all the things he thought he could use in one box.

"At least we're not leaving here totally empty-handed," he said wryly.

We retraced our steps, yet when we reached the door of the vault, I noticed for the first time that it didn't have a handle on the inside.

"How do we get out of this cracker box?" I asked. But as I moved closer to the door, its automatic sensors responded, and it obligingly, eerily slid open. We glided down the carpeted hallway just like all the other visitors, never uttering a word even when we rode down in the freight elevator to the lobby. I held my breath as the guard stopped Gil, but the box from the *mas* was bar-coded under his name, so Gil signed out his pots and pans and we sailed on. He hoisted the box into the van and climbed into the driver's seat, looking singularly unimpressed by this whole episode.

"Go ahead and say it—you think I'm a crazy fool," I said morosely.

"No, you're just desperate to help your mum," Gil said resignedly, as if now, out in the stark reality of daylight, he was adjusting his expectations. "Let's face it—maybe your Gran cooked for Picasso, but it just doesn't look like she ever got one of his paintings."

"I absolutely believe she had it," I insisted. "I still *feel* that she did."

"Well, then how come you can't *feel* wherever the hell it is?" Gil asked a bit testily. I thought of Madame Sylvie again, and decided that Gil was right; relying on intuition at this point seemed just plain delusional.

For the rest of the trip home he remained moodily silent, staring straight ahead as he drove, lost in his own thoughts and no doubt returning to the stark fact that he was going to have to swallow Rick's deal or surrender his restaurant to the loan shark.

When we entered the *mas* we found Maurice looking frantic, telling Gil he had a ton of messages. I slipped upstairs to my room and threw my handbag on the chair.

"Well, Grandma," I said aloud, "looks like my goose is cooked."

I knew I should stop talking to my dead grandmother. And I knew I should stop obsessing about that Picasso. And yet . . . and yet . . .

"Damn it, I *know* that was Mom's striped pitcher in the still life," I muttered. "I *know* that was Grandma's long curly hair in those other two paintings. And I *know* she cooked those fabulous meals for him. So why would she bother to tell Mom that she owned a Picasso if she'd already sold it or given it away or lost it? Come on, Grandma. *Where* did you put it?"

And then my mind landed on a terrible thought; one that had been lurking in the shadows all along, but which I had resolutely pushed away until now.

Dad had been staying at Grandma Ondine's house when she died, I realized with a chill. What if it was Dad who found the painting, after all?

36

Ondine at Notre Dame de Vie, Mougins, 1967

"*Ah bon?* Then I've got to go see Picasso and get him to sign my portrait!" Ondine declared as the art dealer rewrapped the picture. Urgently she asked him, "Pierre, where is Picasso living now?"

"Hmm, he changes house as often as he changes women!" Pierre commented. "I heard that his Russian wife died, so he was free to marry a woman who worked in the pottery studio; and they live in Mougins, near a church called *Notre Dame de Vie*."

Pierre took a pencil and drew a rudimentary map. Picasso's villa wasn't very far from Monsieur Renard's *mas*, where Ondine went every day to check on the farm. This time, when she finished her rounds at the *mas,* she packed up a small gift basket for Picasso, containing a wheel of *Banon* cheese wrapped in chestnut leaves, along with a jar of fig-and-star-anise preserves freshly made from the fruit of the *mas*. Then she set off for Picasso's place on foot, carrying the wrapped-up painting under one arm and her basket in the other.

But tracking the Minotaur to the center of his labyrinth wasn't so simple. Using Pierre's crude map, she followed a single, unassuming road. At first she wasn't even sure she had the right path, until a truck came rumbling along and an electrical repairman who was driving it called out to inquire if she was lost. She hesitantly asked for the house of Picasso.

"Straight ahead. I'm going there myself to do some work on the place," the electrician said, then added curiously, "What's your business there?"

Ondine thought quickly. "I am his new cook."

The man said, "Ah! Come, then, I'll give you a ride." Ondine sized up his open, honest face and agreed to join him. When they approached the imposing, secluded villa set high among terraced layers of olive and cypress trees, she saw that it was protected by a very tall, forbidding-looking fence, and the driveway was barred by a fancy electronic gate. The repairman pulled up close enough so that he could now lean over to press a button.

"Who goes there?" growled an unfamiliar voice over an intercom.

The repairman said to Ondine in a low, knowing tone, "That's the gardener. He watches out for Picasso." He leaned toward the intercom and shouted his own name. Slowly, the gates creaked open.

"Not many people get into this place," the man commented as he drove in and the gate swung shut behind them. "Workers like us—no problem. But to his children and grandchildren, his gardener says, 'Sorry, Picasso is too busy' and 'No, he won't have any time for you to-morrow'."

Ondine wasn't sure whether this was idle gossip, or a warning from the gods. "Why won't he see his own kids?" she asked apprehensively, not sure she wanted to know the answer.

The man shrugged. "They're young, and he's eighty-six years old! He doesn't like to be reminded of that. Besides, his wife, Jacqueline—she's less than half his age, you know—she's very protective."

He parked the truck expertly among other cars. The villa was a big, elegant white house with arched doorways and wide windows with pink shutters. When they entered the bright interior, the repair-man set off in one direction but nodded toward another, saying, "The kitchen is through there."

Ondine pretended to go that way, but as soon as the man was out of sight she turned back, not wanting to collide with kitchen staff. She needed to find Picasso's studio. She hesitated, then boldly went up an elegant staircase. At the landing she spotted an open door and cautiously peered inside.

An old dog was curled up on a chair, snoring. He smelled quite bad and did not look particularly friendly. The bed was made, but someone was letting water out of the tub and moving about in the nearby bathroom.

Ondine backed away from the dog and bumped into a chest of drawers. She saw that on its lace-covered surface lay two scissors, a small one for fingernails and a longer one for hair. Nearby lay tissue-paper packets, both neatly dated today, their contents labelled—one for Picasso's hair clippings, and one for his nail clippings—which, instead of being discarded, had been reverentially saved.

"*Dieu!*" Ondine exclaimed, recoiling. Why would he want to keep such things? Then she recalled an old superstition that if such personal effects left your possession, they could fall into the hands of an enemy or evil spirit who would then use a lock of your hair, for instance, to cast spells and make you sicken and even die. Was Picasso actually bedeviled by such superstitious fears?

The bathroom door opened now and a maid came out with an armful of rumpled towels. Ondine said hurriedly, "Where is Picasso's studio? He said I must personally deliver this picture to him."

The maid said indifferently, "He works downstairs. Follow me."

They went down to the lower level again and along a corridor. When they reached the end, the maid pointed to an enclosed area that was originally an outdoor terrace, but had been turned into a workroom, filled with canvases, easels and tables crammed with paint pots and bottles of brushes.

The artistic clutter was immediately familiar to Ondine, and now she knew she was moving closer to the heart of the Minotaur's labyrinth. But at first she hardly recognized the little shriveled, stooped figure when he emerged from behind an easel, hunched over his canvas, his back to her.

"Bonjour, Patron," Ondine said softly; then, when she realized that he had not heard her, she raised her voice when repeating her greeting. He turned his head and peered at her through large black-framed eyeglasses.

"Maman, is that you?" he asked in a tone that was loud enough to indicate he was perhaps a bit hard of hearing. "Why weren't you back from shopping when I woke from my nap? You promised you would be here for my bath and my haircut!" he said as plaintively as a child, peering through those big eyeglasses. Then he paused reflectively. "You are not my wife," he observed, puzzled.

"I am Ondine from Juan-les-Pins," she said, setting down the wrapped painting.

The old man shuffled forward, looking wary and confused as his gaze searchingly took her in, almost a fragment at a time. She wondered if he'd become senile. But when he saw the food basket she'd brought, a childlike smile of delight spread across his face. "Did you bring me something good to eat?" he asked eagerly. Ondine was uncertain that he really knew who she was.

"Cheese and fruit *confit* fresh from my farm, which you can eat whenever you please," she said.

He nodded approvingly. "That's good. I had some stomach surgery, did you hear?" he said regretfully, patting his belly. "They gave me quite a goring. I've got a scar as big as a bullfighter's. I checked into the hospital under the name of Monsieur Ruiz. You remember that fellow Ruiz, don't you?" he joked. Ondine smiled indulgently as Picasso continued, "I had to use that name again just to throw the reporters off the scent. Otherwise they'd have stood over me waiting to hear my famous last words. To hell with them, I'm still here! But I don't eat as much as I used to," he said sadly. "They won't even let me smoke my cigarettes anymore!"

Did he really know her? She still couldn't be sure.

"And yet you are painting as much as ever, I see!" Ondine said encouragingly.

"I've got a house full of paintings. They breed like rabbits," he commented mischievously, with a broad sweep of his arm; and she saw that his skin hung in wrinkled folds, as deeply tanned as leather, but fitting him like a suit of clothes that was too big for his frail frame now.

"My wife got a special deal on sixty canvases at a closeout sale. Now I have to fill them all up! Go ahead, have a look," he said, gesturing.

Ondine tried to steady her nerves as she took a brief tour of the colorful paintings. The subjects were all men in seventeenth-century garb with white ruffs and jaunty broad-brimmed hats. They had long noses, twirling black moustaches and pointy beards, and romantically long curly black hair; and they brandished their antiquated swords in endlessly quixotic ways. It was all so utterly playful, done chiefly in primary colors of red and yellow.

As Picasso opened Ondine's basket he explained, "While recuperating from my surgery, I was reading Dumas in the hospital—have you read Dumas?"

"The Three Musketeers," Ondine said. She could not help admiring his indomitable verve and zest for life; the Minotaur had put her under his spell, once again.

He nodded. "Dumas' musketeers reminded me of Rembrandt's soldiers. Then I came home and began painting my own, and they just keep coming and coming!"

"They're beautiful," she said with a smile of comprehension, for perhaps this was Picasso's private army of mythological bodyguards bravely attempting to help him fend off Death. "They look like the soldiers a boy conjures in his head when he fights his imaginary foes," she observed.

"Ah, yes. It took me four years to paint like Raphael, but a lifetime to paint like a child," Picasso said, nibbling on the food like an old bird. He smacked his lips in satisfaction, then nodded at the brown-wrapped package she had set down. "Well, why have you brought a painting to show me? Don't tell me that *you* paint pictures now!"

He may be old and doddering but he still doesn't miss a trick, Ondine thought, awakening from the enchantment and steeling herself now. Determinedly she unwrapped it and went ahead with her prepared speech. "It's the portrait you made for me, your *Girl-at-a-Window.*" She kept her face as neutral as possible, dreading that he'd finally recall he'd never actually handed it over to her. She searched his face, looking for clues but finding none. The only way to pull this off was to plunge ahead.

"But, nobody believes you painted this portrait of me, because you forgot to sign it!" she said as casually as possible.

"Did I?" he said vaguely, perhaps a shade too innocently. "Well, let's see, is it worth signing?"

Ondine held her breath as Picasso peered at the picture through those big glasses. Thoughtfully he pursed his lips. "Hmm," he said slyly, "not bad, my *Fille-à-la-Fenêtre*. Not bad at all, really. But I don't know if I *feel* like signing pictures today," he added with an impish, challenging look.

How much *did* he remember? Ondine stared at this diminutive old man in his shorts and slippers. Refusing to take the bait, she said calmly, "Now, now! This is for our daughter, and it's important to keep the promises we give to the young."

Picasso gave her a sharper look now, but she kept a steady smile. He looked grudgingly impressed by her resolve, then commented, "Well, I signed for Tony Curtis—you know that actor? American. He bought one of my unsigned ones and came here asking me to mark it. Gary Cooper visited me. Famous people and movie stars, you know. They're hard to resist."

Ondine understood that Julie was neither a movie star nor an international celebrity, but she rallied, and now it was she who put on an innocent expression to play her last card. "I have friends who are art experts, but when they saw this picture, they said, 'No, Picasso couldn't have painted *this*! It's too beautiful. Why, this is as good as a Rembrandt.'"

"Hah! That just shows you how much the 'experts' know," Picasso snorted indignantly. He stared at the painting, then made up his mind. Agitation had given him a sudden burst of energy, and he strode over to his worktable to make a great show of selecting just the right brush. This he dipped in just the right pot of paint. "Well, come on, bring it over here," he said, looking determined now.

Carefully, as if it were the first time in his life that he'd ever written his signature, the great man leaned over the canvas, his hand trembling slightly; and in his inimitable, expert flourish, he painted a single word at the bottom with unmistakable lettering.

Picasso.

"I don't remember the date that I painted this," he said, pausing. "Then again, I don't even remember today's date. Do you recall?"

"Yes, I remember," Ondine said softly, for just this morning she'd looked at her leather-bound notebook with all the meals she'd cooked. Now she told Picasso the date he'd created it and he leaned forward again, concentrating like an earnest schoolboy in a way she found unexpectedly touching.

He painted *7 mai XXXVi*. When he was done, he straightened up, looking satisfied, and patted the top of the painting as if it were a pet or a child. "If you want it that badly, Ondine, you may as well have it," he said, looking at her cunningly. "One cannot resist courage."

She caught her breath. He knew she'd taken it! How long had he known? Was he playing with her the entire time, or did it just dawn on him?

But then there was a sudden slam of a door in another part of the house, and a woman's voice called out in a strange, shrill birdlike trill. "*Monseigneur,* where are you?" she cooed.

Picasso had the face of a schoolboy caught with the cookies. "Jacqueline won't like this," he warned. "She'll try to stop you. If you want to keep this painting, go out that side door!"

Ondine picked it up carefully, for his signature was still wet. Unsentimentally, Picasso looked her straight in the eye now and said, "It will be worth more when I'm dead, you know."

It was unlike him to mention death, yet he did so with courage, like a warrior prepared to confront the inevitable battle ahead. "May God grant that day to be far away," Ondine said tenderly; and just before leaving him, something compelled her to kiss him on his warm, leathery cheek.

"*Adieu,*" she said softly, then added, "*A Dios.*" He raised a gnarled hand to her cheek, as if carving her from clay—a gesture she remembered, but today he made it new, one more time.

"Yes, yes." Picasso's face had become very gentle, almost mournful. "Now, go!" he admonished.

Indeed, the new wife's sharp footsteps were tap-tapping on the hall floor indicating that she was coming closer. Ondine hurried to the side exit, but cast one last look over her shoulder at the small man, still standing before his easel, surrounded by the paintings that he simply could not stop making.

Picasso had picked up his brush again, and with it, he waved good-bye.

WALKING BACK TO THE *MAS,* Ondine felt as if she were encased in a soft, sacred glow, like having been in the presence of a holy man who'd finally, at long last, given her his blessing.

And for once, she could provide her daughter with a much better future, she reflected happily. She took a ride with the farm's delivery boy, whose truck was making its last run of the day from the *mas* to the café. Ondine burst inside the café, excited to show the painting to Julie.

But she found only Monsieur Renard waiting for her in the kitchen, wringing his hands. "Julie is *gone*! She sneaked out without a word to anyone. Can you believe it, she eloped with that Arthur! She left us only this very short note."

Ondine's breath came out in one hard gasp. She sat down at the kitchen table and allowed Renard to read it to her—a brief, hasty goodbye from Julie, who'd obviously written exactly what Arthur had dictated, assuring them in somewhat legalistic language that she was perfectly certain about marrying him and going to live in America, and asking them only to be happy for her.

At first, Ondine did not believe it. Her fingers had turned to icicles and even her heart seemed frozen, for she could not feel anything. Only when she raised her eyes to the blue cupboard did she realize that something else was missing—the pink-and-blue striped pitcher which she'd kept atop it for Julie's bridal trousseau. Julie must have taken it with her, and now Ondine comprehended that her little daughter really was gone for good.

Like a sleepwalker, Ondine rose and went upstairs to the bedroom they'd shared. Her fingers were still clamped onto the wrapped painting which she'd carried up here with her. She laid it out on the bed as if it were a corpse.

"What does this matter now?" she said bitterly as she walked over to her window and gazed out, overcome with grief that was flowing through her blood. "What good is this painting to me? I may just as well throw it into the sea!"

37

Céline at the Mas, 2014

On Tuesday I awoke with the rueful certainty that I'd finally exhausted every single idea I had about finding the lost Picasso. It was time for me to accept that wherever this phantom painting was, it was going to stay there.

Aunt Matilda and her friend Peter were due back this afternoon, but all the other guests were gone. I went downstairs and discovered that, even though I was the sole lodger today, the French staff was as courteous to their one guest as they'd be to a full house. They'd laid out a small but elegant buffet breakfast on the terrace for Gil and me.

I didn't really expect to see him, but there he was, at a table beneath a plane tree, talking into his phone. His profile was sober-looking but betrayed no sentimentality; it was as if he'd made up his mind to face the music with all the dignity he could muster.

I wished I could be like him, but just the thought of my mother nodding in her wheelchair out in that Nevada nursing home—which now seemed farther away than ever, as if she were in another galaxy and completely out of reach—brought such despair into my throat that it almost choked me.

When Gil looked up, he gestured for me to join him at his table, and a waiter quietly brought a new pot of coffee. "Look at what the world has already been up to," Gil said, handing off the day's news-paper to me. "Bombings. Floods. War and pestilence. Death and de-struction. I'd say there are far worse things that could happen to a bloke than losing control of his restaurant."

"Are you going to London today to see Rick?" I asked in dread.

Gil shook his head. "The contracts are at my lawyer's office in Cannes. Apparently Rick wants to make sure I don't perish in a train or plane wreck en route to London before he gets my signature on it. But the good news is, he's put the money I need into an escrow account, so when I sign today I'll be able to pay off the loan shark on time."

I glanced out at the sweeping property of the *mas,* but I found every beautiful garden view and every breathtaking farmland vista too heart-breakingly painful to look at now, so I averted my eyes rather than imagine it all in Rick's greedy hands. If this was how I felt about the loss of Grandma's *mas,* how could Gil endure it?

As if reading my mind, he said, "Your life and work have to be more important than one battle."

"Why do the bad guys always win?" I grumbled.

Unexpectedly, Gil reached out and patted my arm so gently that I had to fight off the impulse to cry, even before he said softly, "Céline, you'll find another way to rescue your mum."

I didn't trust myself to speak. He was being so understanding today.

"Why don't you take it easy, have a swim and a massage at the spa?" Gil suggested. "I'll tell my staff that everything's on the house while it's still mine! Lunch and drinks included."

It crossed my mind that he was behaving like someone who's just sold his house and is determined to throw a party and use up every-thing before handing it over to a stranger. I pictured myself doing what he suggested and wandering around the spa in one of those fluffy bath-robes, looking ridiculous. Then I thought about sitting by the pool and ordering enough drinks to get good and snockered. Why the hell not?

"Well, I'm on my way," Gil said rather abruptly now, as he rose to do the inevitable.

"Good luck," I said. He nodded but didn't look back once. I decided that if he could endure the signing away of his beloved *mas,* I should be stoic, too.

Determinedly, I went up to my room, changed into my swimsuit, and walked along the garden paths, where the grass and plantings were still glistening with their early-morning watering. Inquisitive bees and butterflies flitted about their business. I stalked onward, to the hilltop infinity pool and its beautiful view of the valleys and the wide-open sky.

Among the neat rows of *chaises longues,* two had been discreetly set up with plush towels. I put down my things, walked to the pool and dipped in a toe. The water, undulating gently against the sides of the pool, was still cool from last night's air. But the sun was hot upon my back. I took the plunge.

I swam, listening to the rippling splashes coming from me, the lone swimmer. Back and forth I went, wanting to exhaust myself so I could turn off my worries about Mom. Then I remembered a sad story I'd heard about a polar bear in a New York zoo who went a little batty from captivity and kept madly swimming back and forth until he dropped dead.

I glanced up and saw a small figure hesitating by the side of the pool. It was Martin, dressed in a swimsuit but looking nervous about going anywhere near a pool, ever again. Lizbeth was with him, saying encouragingly, "See? The water's nice today."

I opened my arms to Martin. "Come on, pal, if I can do it, you can. I'll watch out for you."

Martin steeled himself, then came into the pool via the steps, gradually, until he reached my open arms, and he put his arms around my neck as if I were a lifesaver.

Lizbeth said in relief, "Give me a call when he's ready to shower up. Lunch is at twelve-thirty."

She went off, and I held Martin up as he began to paddle tentatively. He'd been taught to swim, evidently, because it all came back to him. He just needed to know that someone was watching over him and wouldn't let him drown.

Eventually we climbed out and flopped down on the sun beds. The wind was rustling through the trees, whispering like a conspirator with vital clues. For awhile, I closed my eyes, lying very still, with an odd, unsettled feeling, as if someone had cast a fishing line and was slowly reeling me back in. Martin lay beside me, gazing up at the clouds and telling me about their funny shapes.

When a church bell tolled the noon hour, I said, "Well, we'd better get going, so we're not late for lunch." I sent a message to Lizbeth that we were on our way.

"Can we go by the construction guys?" Martin asked eagerly. He took my hand and led me back by a different route, skirting along the older area where renovations were still proceeding apace. We paused to peer in and view the progress. Many of the workmen knew Martin and waved to him.

They were busily scraping off the old, peeling paint in Grandma's kitchen. I stood there, hypnotized by the rhythmic, up-and-down motions of the workers.

I found myself wondering if Grandma cooked for Mom and Dad when they visited her at the *mas*. But maybe they just ate in the café in Juan-les-Pins.

"What are you looking for?" Martin asked, perceptive lad that he was.

I smiled and admitted, "Hidden treasure. It was supposed to be in a blue cupboard."

Being a kid, Martin didn't think this was at all strange. Immediately he scanned the area, trying to help. I shaded my eyes because the glare of the midday sun was reflecting off something with blinding intensity, the way it can bounce off metal such as on the hoods of cars in a parking lot on a hot day. Which was odd, I thought, since the site was made of wood and stone.

Gazing at the old kitchen I recalled the night I'd gone down there in the dark to investigate, and then it had begun to rain. The sound of that patter struck me afresh now: plink-plink-*plonk*, plink-plink-*plonk*. I recalled how the *plonk* had been a jarring note compared to the gentler first two notes. It occurred to me now that the rain might have occasionally struck metal instead of wood and stone. Perhaps a worker had left something metal there? I drew closer to get a better look.

Martin plucked at my sleeve. "That cupboard used to be blue," he offered, pointing to the same area I was staring at, where a crewman was working on one of the built-in cupboards that had apparently been sealed off and painted over. The man was stripping away its white paint . . . revealing the original blue paint beneath it. And at the top of the cupboard there was that bright gleam of sunlight reflecting off something metal, as if it had a chimney cap on it.

Lizbeth arrived just then and steered Martin away. "See you at lunch," he said to me, waving.

I nodded, but I remained rooted to the spot, squinting intently. Whatever this was, I had to check it out. So I abandoned all restraint and rushed right onto the work site to inspect it up close.

The foreman was none too happy to see me there. But when I asked him about the cupboard, he told me something that made me hastily dig into my pocket for my phone. I had to ring Gil three times—twice getting his recorded message—before he finally picked up.

"Gil!" I cried out.

"Céline?" he said in disbelief. "What's wrong?"

"Nothing's *wrong*!" I bellowed. "Listen, have you signed that contract yet?"

"No." He sounded annoyed. "My lawyer insists we read every word. He doesn't trust Rick."

"Well, STOP! Whatever you do, do NOT sign it yet!" I shouted, not caring that the construction workers were gaping at me as I stood there with my big fat bathrobe hanging open, revealing my still-damp bathing suit. "Just put them off a little longer," I continued vehemently.

"Céline, what the fuck?" Gil shouted back.

"Listen," I exclaimed, "I think I found the REAL blue cupboard. It was built right into the kitchen of the *mas*! But we might have to bust into it or tear it out of the wall if necessary. Is that okay?"

"Céline, please, there's no more time for fun and games and treasure hunts. Rick's going to inspect the place tonight," Gil warned. "So don't do anything stupid on your own."

"Then, damn it, drop everything and get your ass back to the *mas* right now, so we can do something stupid together!" I commanded, exasperated.

"Jesus," Gil said worriedly, "I'm on my way."

38

Reunion: Ondine and Julie in Mougins, Summer 1983

ON THE MORNING THAT JULIE WAS FINALLY COMING HOME TO FRANCE FOR a visit, Ondine awoke early in her bedroom in Mougins feeling oddly apprehensive.

After all these many years, she'd just had a dream about Picasso. His ghost was right here at the *mas,* wandering into her kitchen, looking hungry and alert, yet wearing only a long nightshirt, and barefooted, which she found disturbing. And when he spoke to her, his voice was oddly thin.

"Where is my painting, Ondine?" he asked, looking bewildered. "Did you put it in a safe place? There are lots of thieves around the Riviera, you know."

She awakened with the strong feeling of Picasso's physical presence in her house. But that was impossible, for he'd died ten years ago. She'd been startled and sorry when she heard it on the radio; somehow she thought he'd go on living and painting forever like Zeus on his mountaintop, unseen but very much alive. Predictably his art was now fetching prices that were sailing into the stratosphere.

Yet in all this time Ondine could not bring herself to show her portrait to anyone. She'd kept it under wraps at the café, until Monsieur Renard died, and then she moved all her possessions to set up house here at the *mas*—on doctor's orders, because he would not permit Ondine to continue living above the café and climbing those stairs to the bedroom every night.

"It's your heart," the doctor said. "You must learn to listen to it. You've had a small attack already."

Ever since then, the Picasso portrait was Ondine's secret companion, propped up atop a chest of drawers in her bedroom. She'd never had it framed; Picasso once told her that nothing kills a painting like a frame. Nobody was permitted to come into this room, so no one else knew it was here.

Today, as she snapped on her light and peered across her bedroom, she was relieved to see that, despite the warning in her dream from Picasso's ghost, the painting was still here. These days, at sixty-four years old, she preferred waking to this image of her younger self, full of confidence and hope and flush with love, rather than peering into a mirror and scrutinizing her face for further evidence of age.

Ondine reached for her cane, got out of bed and dressed carefully. She went into the kitchen and drank her coffee standing up while making plans for the day. There was so much to do, now that Julie was at last coming home!

"I must make it clear to her that I am no longer angry," Ondine reminded herself. She *had* been resentful at first; in all these years since Julie and Arthur eloped they hadn't once returned to France, nor even invited Ondine to visit them in America. All she got were the annual Christmas cards they sent everyone else—professionally printed with a proud family photograph showing the twins' progress.

Ondine kept all her photos in an album in her bedside table. Strangely, Luc's image from so many years ago seemed more alive than Julie's most recent Christmas photo. Year after year, standing amidst the aggressive-looking Arthur and his children, whom Ondine had never met, poor Julie seemed to be fading away, growing more pale and ghostly, her mouth forced into a smile for the camera while her unfocused eyes gazed off in the distance, appearing all the more sad to anyone who cared to notice.

"A well-loved woman doesn't look like that," Ondine fretted each time she saw another photo. She was not the kind of mother who felt smug about accurately predicting an unhappy marriage; on the contrary, she heartily wished she'd been wrong about Arthur.

Then came the joyous news that Julie was pregnant. And, just as gratifying, Julie longed to be near her mother, and wrote that she was accompanying Arthur on his business convention in Cannes, so they would finally come to visit.

When Ondine got the letter she surprised herself by bursting into tears.

"I'm going to get my daughter back! And, soon I'll be a grandmother," she boasted to the ladies in the market and at church, who'd always patronizingly pitied Ondine for not having any family in town, nor any grandchildren.

This morning she hummed to herself as she prepared for her visitors. But, busy as she was, she paused to telephone that nice young Madame Sylvie, who was so gifted at reading one's fortune, and had become such a considerate, dear friend.

"You've got to come and tell me what you see," Ondine said excitedly. "My daughter arrives today with that husband of hers. I need to know what will come of this."

"I can't do it this morning," Madame Sylvie said pragmatically. "Perhaps tomorrow?"

"No, this can't wait," Ondine insisted. "Julie will be so anxious to hear what you think about the future."

"She's going to have a healthy girl," Madame Sylvie said patiently. "I told you that last week!"

"Yes, of course," Ondine replied, "but, there's something else on my mind. I've had a dream. I saw Picasso. You know I cooked for him. He was warning me to protect a treasure he gave me."

"Ah! Well, perhaps I'll manage to stop by this afternoon, then," Madame Sylvie conceded, sounding curious now.

When Ondine got off the telephone she felt better. She'd hired a new chef at the café who was eager to please her, so she'd instructed him to prepare a nice feast tonight for Julie and Arthur, and send it up to the *mas* with a waiter to serve.

"The sun is bright today, yet the weather might be too windy to dine on the terrace up here," Ondine mused. "We may have to eat indoors, but that will be all right."

She'd created separate cooking, dining and sitting areas in the spacious farmhouse kitchen, all elegantly decorated with Provençal ceramics and fresh flowers from her own gardens; and upon the yellow walls she'd hung paintings done by local artists who'd assembled here at the *mas* one autumn for a retreat she sponsored. They had wandered the fields and orchards, painting landscapes of the many lovely views. And like their Riviera forebears, they'd paid for their dinner by giving the proprietor some pictures.

"It feels like a real home, even though it's just me living here," Ondine observed, glancing around approvingly.

Within a few hours she heard a knock at the door, and when she opened it, there was little Julie, already looking much happier than her photos, her modest face lit with an unusual expression of joy, as if a candle glowed from within her. She stood there shyly, almost tentatively, touchingly uncertain of whether she'd be truly welcomed by the mother she'd abandoned so many years ago.

She forgets that I, too, ran away from home when I was a girl, Ondine thought, amused. She opened her arms wide with a cry of *"Bienvenue, chère fille!"*

"Dear sweet *Maman!*" Julie cried, rushing to hug her. Arthur waited politely, looking grudgingly relieved that his wife was happy. Ondine quickly invited them both inside, surprised by how very pregnant Julie looked. Ondine had lost track of the months.

"This is my miracle baby!" Julie declared, her eyes bright with joyful tears.

Ondine took them to the terrace so they could assess whether to dine indoors or out. For awhile, mother and daughter sat companionably on the *chaises longues,* chatting animatedly. Ondine had decided to be gracious and welcoming to Arthur, but this only seemed to make him wary. He remained standing at the edge of the terrace with his hands in his pockets, jingling his loose coins and hardly seeming to notice the impressive property. It was clear that he had not wished to take this detour from Cannes, and now he roamed restlessly around the terrace as if plotting his escape.

He knows I detest him, as he does me, Ondine thought ruefully. *I guess it can't be helped.*

When prompted by Julie to participate in their conversation about France, Arthur announced rather belligerently that he thought the French were politically ungrateful to America. Julie shushed him and he sulked, finally sitting in a chair to bury his nose in an English financial newspaper he'd brought.

I should have invited my young lawyer, Gerard Clément, so Arthur would have a man to talk to, Ondine realized. Aloud she told Julie, "Madame Sylvie says your baby will definitely be a girl!"

Julie squealed with delight, but her husband snorted. "Arthur wants a son named after him," she explained. "But if it's a girl, what shall we call her?"

Ondine had already given this some thought, lying awake last night under a full moon. So she said, "You should name her Céline, after the moon goddess Selene."

"Céline," Julie repeated as if tasting the name on her tongue. "That's pretty, *Maman*. I like it."

She looked so confident about this pregnancy, as if it had restored her faith in the future. "I'm redecorating our house for *le bébé*," Julie confided. "Now you'll *have* to come see it. We'll take little Céline down to the beach in New Rochelle as you did with me, remember, *Maman*? Oh, we'll all be so happy again!"

Ondine could see that Arthur's prosperity had made it possible for Julie to have a comfortable domestic life; and now this coming child was giving Julie another chance to love and be loved, to carve out a happier existence for herself. *Well, at least she has this pleasure in her life,* Ondine observed gratefully.

Arthur was still hiding behind his newspaper as if it were a brick wall, so Ondine gave up on him, and brought Julie into the kitchen to show her how she'd decorated it. And as it turned out, this was Ondine's only moment alone with her daughter.

"I wish I'd paid more attention to your cooking!" Julie said, gazing admiringly at the impressive array of copper pots and specialty cooking pans. "Won't you share some of your recipes with me now?"

Ondine hesitated, then pulled down the old leather-bound notebook that she'd kept all these years on her kitchen shelf. They sat together at the table, and when Julie turned the pages she exclaimed with delight over the recipes. "I must copy these down before I go home," she said, her eyes shining with pride in her mother's work.

"You can keep the notebook," Ondine said, feeling the familiar, protective instinct she always had around Julie. "But take good care of it. Then one day you must hand it down to *your* daughter."

Julie had become thoroughly absorbed in the pages. "All right. But which patron was all this for?" she asked, fascinated. Ondine paused, made Julie promise not to tell a soul, even Arthur, and then began explaining to the stunned Julie about how she'd cooked for Picasso as a girl in Juan-les-Pins, and that he had even given her a painting of his.

Despite her promise to Luc, Ondine felt herself on the brink of saying, *Do you remember that man we visited together in Vallauris? That was Picasso, and he was your father!* But before she could utter these words, Arthur called out for his wife in an irritated tone, and Julie jumped guiltily to her feet.

"We must talk more about Picasso later. But I'd better go see what Arthur wants," Julie said, going out dutifully. A moment later she reappeared with her husband at her side, her arm tucked in his.

"Doesn't *Maman* have such a pretty place here?" she said, nudging him. He allowed a nod.

Ondine opened a bottle of sparkling water, and she and Julie settled into chairs in the sitting area near the fireplace. Arthur refused a glass and remained standing. When Julie told him about all her mother's hard work to make the *mas* and the café a success, he obligingly gave the big room an appraising glance. Something seemed to dawn on him, but all he said was, "So—you are the sole owner of the café and this entire *mas*?"

Ondine chose to ignore his social *faux pas* of asking a pointed question about her finances, but Julie answered earnestly, "Yes, but these days *Maman* doesn't do all the cooking anymore!"

"How is your health, Mother Ondine?" he asked with a look on his face that Ondine didn't like.

"It's perfect," she answered, trying not to sound annoyed. Arthur's gaze travelled to the cane propped against her chair which Ondine carried with her since her heart attack.

"Next time we'll bring the twins here to visit you," Julie offered. "Perhaps for Christmas. We just couldn't tear them away from their friends in the summertime." She glanced anxiously again at Arthur because he was glowering at her for making holiday promises he had no intention of keeping.

Ondine patted Julie's hand reassuringly, but their chatter remained tinged with nervousness as they waited for Arthur to settle down somewhere; yet he continued to wander around the room. He now seemed unduly interested in his surroundings, Ondine thought, as his travelling gaze occasionally rested on a prized silver vase or a valuable piece of china.

Why, he's assessing their worth! As if he's got an adding machine in his head, she thought indignantly. *It's like having a vulture circling around, just waiting for me to drop to the ground. I'm only sixty-four years old. These days, that's not exactly ancient!*

"Interesting paintings," Arthur said abruptly as he stopped his pacing before the wall of framed pictures in the dining area. "Are these artists anyone I'd have heard of?"

"I doubt it," Ondine said dryly, outraged by his audacity.

"So when do we get the royal tour of the *mas*?" he asked, acting friendly now. "We've hardly seen much of it." Ondine was glad to hear the delivery truck from the café pull up in the driveway.

"That will be our dinner," she said firmly. She reached for her cane and rose to her feet.

"Let me help you," Julie offered, rising quickly.

"The wind is dying down, after all. Let's dine on the terrace. Why don't you two take these things outside and set the table, all right?" Ondine said, filling their arms with trays of linen, china and silver. She saw the gleam of the flatware catch Arthur's eye. Really, it was intolerable to watch.

Ondine opened a side door to let in the waiter who'd come to serve the meal. She gave him his instructions, then slipped out of the kitchen and went into her bedroom. The nagging feeling she'd had all day had become a full-blown presentiment. The painting was still here, but now Ondine didn't need Madame Sylvie to interpret Picasso's warning in her dream.

She knew what she must do. With one decisive gesture Ondine yanked her portrait off the chest of drawers. "Oh, where can I hide it so that awful Arthur will never look?" she whispered, her heart fluttering worriedly in her chest. "Him and his 'royal tour', indeed! If he tells Julie to peek in my bedroom closets and drawers for anything valuable, she might just obey him. I must find a place he'll never think of."

Ondine carried the painting back with her into the kitchen. The waiter had gone outside and was consulting with Julie and Arthur. Ondine went into the pantry, assessing it for a potential hiding place.

But then she heard her guests' voices returning to the house. The pantry shelves were useless; they were too narrow. Ondine glanced around her own familiar kitchen, overcome by an uncharacteristic panic inspired by Arthur. Wildly, she searched for a temporary solution.

"*Maman?*" Julie called out, her voice closer still. "Dinner is served. Where are you?"

Ondine's desperate gaze fell on the dumbwaiter. It was big enough, and it could ferry the painting down into the old wine cellar which she no longer used. A stack of old crates were piled up against the door of the dumbwaiter down below, so Arthur wouldn't even know it was there. The cellar was just an empty, uninviting cave with an unfinished earth floor and lots of spiderwebs.

"I'll get it back later, when Arthur is off to one of his business meetings in Cannes," Ondine decided hastily, opening the dumbwaiter's door. She reached inside it and deposited the painting in its temporary hiding place within. Closing the door of the dumbwaiter, she pressed the button, and listened to its reassuring rumble, waiting until she heard the soft thud of its landing.

A moment later, Arthur walked in.

39

Céline and Gil in the Kitchen, Mougins 2014

GIL CAME ROARING UP ON HIS DUCATI, NOT STOPPING WHEN HE REACHED the gravel parking lot. He rode right across the impeccable grassy lawns and headed straight for the renovation site of the *mas*.

The effect on the workmen was immediate. They were so astonished that they simply stopped what they'd been doing, and we all watched, dumbfounded, unable to take our eyes off Gil as he madly vroomed right up to the construction site, then careened to an abrupt stop right where we were standing.

Meanwhile, Aunt Matilda and Peter had arrived back at the *mas,* hungry for lunch. They discovered Martin on the terrace, who told them where I was. The three of them came over to fetch me to lunch, and I hastily took Aunt Matilda aside to tell her what I'd discovered—maybe.

But now I experienced a familiar pang of doubt—*Lord, what if I'm completely wrong about this?* My batting average so far had been spectacularly bad. Then as Gil jumped off the bike and hurried toward us, I felt a strange, defiant sense of confidence. Something that Madame Sylvie had told me now popped back into my head: *Ondine didn't do anything in the usual way. She was fearless about trying the unexpected, putting this-with-that. It not only made her a great chef; it made her a "femme très formidable".*

"Céline," Gil said, sounding both alarmed and yet impressed by the sheer audacity of the situation, "what the hell? We're going to break into a wall because—why?"

"Look at this cupboard. Your workman say it's unusual, because although it's made of wood, its interior seems to be lined with aluminum. They discovered this when they ripped off some old wood at the very top—the 'roof' of it, so to speak—which was badly deteriorated. That's when they found the aluminum lining beneath it." This, I'd realized, explained why the rain made music when it struck the exposed metal; and now the sunlight was reflecting off it.

"Odd," Gil agreed.

"And look," Martin piped up, scratching with his fingernail to flick off a chunk of white paint. "There's blue paint underneath! Céline says she's been looking for hidden treasure in a blue cupboard."

Now I was embarrassed, but I soldiered on, saying, "Well, the point is, the whole thing is very intriguing. See right here—somebody sealed up the door of this cupboard ages ago with cement or something, the way you close up an old fireplace. So it hasn't been used in years. Gil, I've just *got* to see what's inside!"

But the foreman of the crew exhibited his displeasure by rapping sharply on the cupboard so that Gil could hear the hollow, empty sound behind it. "*Rien*. Nothing's in there!" the man objected.

Gil looked from him to me, then made up his mind to get this over with quickly, so he crisply ordered the foreman, "Break it open." The workman raised his eyebrows, but Gil nodded firmly.

"Carefully!" I warned. "Don't let them just hack into it and hurt what's inside!"

"*Très doucement,*" Gil told the workman who'd picked up his tools to force it open.

Seeing the resolute look on Gil's face, the man began to carefully chip away at the sealed edges of the cupboard's outer frame where it met the door. I watched as the wood trim splintered and gave way. Then there was some discussion about whether the men ought to break off the hinges of the door or just try to swing them open. But while they were deciding, one of the workers discovered that the wooden door was already crumbling away from the hinges, so he was able to pry it off with his crowbar.

We all stared at the interior of the cupboard, which indeed appeared to be an aluminum shaft. It didn't really look like a cupboard at all, because it had no shelves.

"*C'est vide,*" the foreman said in a tone of perplexed satisfaction.

Empty, yes. No pots and pans. No leftover canisters of salt and pepper. No mops and brooms.

And no Picasso.

Gil grabbed a flashlight from a workman and shone it at the interior. I glimpsed some ropes and pulleys, until Gil suddenly blocked the whole thing with his body as he stuck his head right into the cupboard and flashed his light down it. When he spoke, his voice sounded muffled.

"*Ceci n'est pas* a cupboard," he said positively. "It's a professional, restaurant-sized dumbwaiter."

"A dumbwaiter!" I echoed.

He withdrew his head and scanned the exterior again; then, he ran his fingers along the frame until he found what he was looking for—an embedded stainless-steel square button that had also been painted over. He pressed the button and paused expectantly, like a man waiting for an elevator.

Nothing happened. "An early electric model," he said, sticking his head back in it, shining his flashlight below. "Nicely insulated, though."

"If that thing starts moving now, you'll get guillotined," I warned.

Gil remained where he was. "It's stuck down there. The dumbwaiter goes all the way down to the old wine and root cellar. I can see the cab sitting there at the bottom of the shaft," he reported.

"*Il s'est déplacé!*" Aunt Matilda said suddenly to me. "That's what Madame Sylvie told you. Maybe, when she passed her hand over her face and said those words, it wasn't that a 'cupboard' had 'moved' away from the premises, as we thought. Maybe it was a dumbwaiter that had simply moved on its track, from up here in the old kitchen, down to the unfinished cellar below," she added, nodding sagely.

"Who the hell is Madame Sylvie?" Gil pulled his head out of the dumbwaiter shaft and now stared at the two of us as if we'd completely lost our minds. I shrugged off his question.

"Never mind. We've got to get down there and check it out!" I insisted. *"Now."*

With all the construction going on, the cellar below was a formidable, gaping black pit. The foreman warned, "The old staircase, it is not safe for you to walk on."

"Then we'll use that ladder over there," Gil said decisively.

The crowd of workers parted as we reached the ladder. All the while, perhaps because of their skeptical faces, a voice in my head kept warning me, "But why would Grandmother Ondine have thrown a priceless Picasso down *there?*"

40

Céline and Gil in Mougins

GIL GALLANTLY CLIMBED DOWN THE LADDER FIRST, INTO THE CAVERNOUS pit that had once been Grandmother Ondine's old wine cellar. Then he held the ladder as I followed cautiously. When I reached the bottom I stepped gingerly on the irregular floor that had patches of muddy dirt, rock, sawdust. Gil took my arm to steady me and he shined his flashlight ahead so we could dodge old wooden wine racks, empty green bottles and broken glass shards. We picked our way carefully toward the area where we calculated that the cab of the dumbwaiter should be.

We were faced with a tower of heavy, decrepit, wooden crates that looked as though they'd been there forever and had to be removed one by one. My hands were quickly covered with dust from the splintered wood. But our efforts were rewarded, for behind it we found the bottom part of the dumbwaiter. Gil had brought some tools with him, and now he carefully pried open its door.

The cab was sitting right there in its tracks. Gil crouched down and aimed his flashlight in every corner. Impatiently I peered over his shoulder but couldn't see much. Finally he straightened up, stepped aside and dusted off his hands.

"Nothing inside there," he announced, sounding irritated now. "It's empty."

I moved closer and squatted beside it, running my fingers along each corner of the interior space, fruitlessly searching, as if my hands themselves could not accept the truth.

Gil turned to the two construction men who'd followed us down here. "Back to work," he said tersely. They mumbled what was probably the French version of *We told you so—why do you listen to this crazy woman?* But the look in Gil's eyes brought a swift end to their grousing. The silence that followed was, in a way, worse.

"Let's go, Céline. We're just in their way now," he said. He was starting to look truly pissed off. I didn't care.

"She did have her little hiding places," I repeated aloud, more to myself. I heard Gil's exasperated sigh as he walked away. My fingers were still idly exploring the floor of the cab, feeling the cool, dusty surface. I murmured a plea to Grandma Ondine, whose face I could conjure up clearly, thanks to that photo; and now her image in my mind was so sharp that I felt as if she were about to speak to me.

That was when my index finger found a hard bump on the floor of the cab. It was like a dried-out pea sitting in the far left corner. I pressed harder to see what it was. A little button.

Immediately the dumbwaiter responded just as if I'd said, *Open sesame,* for the floor of the cab slid aside on its spring, revealing an insulated compartment. I dipped my hand inside and brushed it against something with a slightly rough surface. My fingertips seemed to know what it was even before my mind could catch up, because my skin thrilled to the touch.

"Gil," I gasped, then halted. I tried again. "Give me your flashlight!"

He'd stepped aside to check his phone for messages, but now he came hurrying back and handed me the light. I pointed the beam inside the dumbwaiter's secret compartment.

The image of a woman's face stared right back at me. "She's in there!" I exclaimed, suddenly light-headed. My hands were trembling so much that I stood up, backed away and had to steady myself against the wall.

"Who's in there?" Gil asked in astonishment. "The painting?"

"I'm afraid to yank it out and damage it," I whispered, awed. Behind him I saw the startled, wary faces of the workmen who were now frozen in place, not knowing what to do.

Gil moved closer. "Let me do it," he suggested. I watched as he diligently worked to ease the painting from its hiding place. I remained rooted to the spot, like an awestruck explorer who'd made a climb to the North Pole and was now frozen in time at the top of a silent world.

"Got it," Gil said softly as he carefully lifted the canvas out of the dumbwaiter. The renovation crew, still unsure about the significance of this, understood that something lost had been found, and they broke into spontaneous applause.

Gil said in a low voice, "Come on, let's get this upstairs where we can really see it."

I snapped to, and scrambled up the ladder. He followed, reverentially carrying the portrait into Grandmother Ondine's old kitchen. But, mindful of the sawdust and plaster all around us he said, "Let's take this over to the *pigeonnier* where you can have a quiet look at your grandmother's painting."

The whole thing was so—well, surreal—that my feet seemed scarcely to touch the path, and I felt I was walking in another dimension. Aunt Matilda, Peter and Martin traipsed behind us. Gil unlocked the door of the *pigeonnier* and propped the painting on a chair as if it were on an easel. Then he stepped back so we could all look at it.

A stretched canvas on wood, unframed, about eighteen by fifteen inches. The painted surface, with its masterly strokes, was just as thrilling to touch now as when my fingers first made contact with it. The subject was a girl leaning out a window with her arms resting on the windowsill; but the composition was such that she was also facing toward us, as if simultaneously peering out into the world below her, yet watching us, too, with those big, intelligent eyes that were so alive and observant.

"That's *her*. My Grandmother Ondine!" I exclaimed.

"She's beautiful," Peter observed.

"Yes," I said, mesmerized. The model's cheeks were flushed with good health, her mouth soft with happiness, her entire expression one of triumph and verve, as if she had conquered the world. I felt a share in her triumph welling up in my chest. Picasso had made something more than just a likeness; he'd captured in paint the very archetypal joy and tragedy of all hopeful young girls.

"You look like her," little Martin said to me, wide-eyed. Gil nodded, looking surprised, as if he were seeing something new about me.

Aunt Matilda had been giving the painting an appraising look with a professional eye. Now she said in an awed voice, "Céline. Look at this." She pointed.

Sunlight was streaming in the window, filtered through the branches of nearby trees, and as the wind stirred the leaves, the light fell in shifting ribbons across the painting. At that moment, one bright shaft of light illuminated a series of words and numbers, painted with a forceful black flourish that told me exactly what I needed to know:

Picasso in one corner, and *7 mai XXXVi* in another.

"God, it's him," I said, peering at the signature. Gil stared at it, too, and I saw a fleeting glint of lust in his eyes as he registered what that signature was worth, especially to him in his current dire straits.

Then he recovered. "You were right, all along," he said, looking impressed.

Aunt Matilda by now had sized up the situation in her inimitable way, and exchanged a knowing glance with Peter, who seemed to understand. "Come on, Martin," Aunt Matilda said briskly. "It's well past your lunchtime, and mine, too. I'm starved, aren't you?"

"I could eat a bear!" Martin proclaimed. "A whole one!"

Aunt Matilda turned to Gil and me and said, "You guys take as long as you like. Peter and I are going to teach Martin how to play a card game called 'Go Fish'."

I scarcely heard her. I just couldn't take my eyes off that painting. Gil and I walked around the canvas in amazement, saying inane but jubilant things like, "Can you imagine Picasso painting these strokes? Can you just see Grandmother Ondine sitting for this? What did they say to each other? When did he decide to give it to her? Why would she put it in a dumbwaiter and just leave it there? What would she have told my mom if they'd had more time together that last day?"

At the thought of my mother, I exclaimed, "Do you understand what this means? She was right, all along. She's *not* deluded, she's healthy and smart and she's . . . *free* now!"

I nearly choked on that last word, *free,* and after that I couldn't say anything except "Huh!" My dazed euphoria was finally lifting, and I could sense the beginnings of an emotion I'd been holding back for such a long time. It came rolling toward me now with terrifying force.

Gil looked up, alerted by my change of tone. "Maybe it means *you're* free now," he said astutely.

But I was like a warrior who's been on a long slog and has suddenly been told the war's over. I found myself trembling uncontrollably, even shivering, on such a warm day. My eyes were stinging with tears of relief. The surprised look on Gil's face changed to utter comprehension.

"Hey!" he said softly, moving toward me, tentatively at first, then taking me by the shoulders. "It's okay. It's okay," he kept saying soothingly, over and over, drawing me to his warm and reassuring embrace. Dimly I felt him kissing the top of my head, and then my face, as his lips found mine.

Normally, I might have hesitated. But this time I just couldn't help stepping right into his arms and resting my head against his chest until the shaking stopped.

"Céline," Gil murmured quietly, tenderly. "Sweet Céline."

When he stroked my neck and face with his chef's toughened fingers, so bruised and scarred, it somehow felt healing to my own invisible scars, and reawakened in my flesh a long-lost sensation of being alive and hungry; and our initially tentative kisses were the kind that kept feeding each other's hunger all the more.

With all the tumult of emotion I was already feeling, this was one more cascade of delight on such an incredible day of surprises. I think we even laughed at ourselves while we kept kissing each other as we were finding our way to the bed. Some warm and vital river had resumed flowing through my veins, as if I'd been a half-frozen Alpine trekker all my life, and had now come upon a cabin with a warm fire where I could begin, at last, to feel human again.

* * *

WHEN I AWOKE, AT FIRST I couldn't remember where I was. I felt sated and relaxed as I shook off the sleepiness. Then suddenly I sat up, trying to grasp something new and awful. Gil was gone. I jumped up wildly, my danger-instinct kicking in. I pulled off the sheet, gathered it round me and ran into the other room, searching.

The chair where the painting had stood was there. But the *Girl-at-a-Window* was not.

"Gil!" I shouted. Silence.

Then he came in from the kitchen door, having stepped outside the *pigeonnier,* holding his phone.

"What's the matter?" he asked. I was still standing there wrapped in a sheet.

"Where's the painting?" I asked sharply.

He looked embarrassed. "The sun was shining on it, full stop, so I moved it to a safe place." He opened a closet which had several wide drawers. In one of them, the painting lay safely nestled on some clean towels. "I was afraid it would just disintegrate right before my eyes," he confessed. "Silly, isn't it?"

I sighed in relief, but I felt a strong premonition urging me not to put down my sword just yet. At first I couldn't make sense of it. When I saw the angle of the sun in the sky, I thought I knew why.

"Gil, it's late!" I said. "Don't you have to deal with Rick? That means we've got to—"

"Take it easy," he said firmly. "I've made some calls to hold him off a few hours. Consider your options. I can still sign Rick's contract. I can just go back to Cannes and do the deed."

"You certainly can *not*! Give away my grandmother's *mas* to that bastard? Are you crazy?" I said indignantly, going into action mode and looking around for my cast-off clothes. "No way. I'm your partner now, remember? But how are we going to get the cash in time to pay off the loan shark?"

"Don't be daft. You just got possession of a Picasso! You need time to think things through, in case you decide you want to keep it." Gil was acting reasonable, like a parent with a hyperactive kid.

I hesitated only a moment, then thought of my mother and my whole reason for being here.

"Look, I can rescue Mom *and* Grandma's *mas*—or I can keep the painting. I know what I have to do!" I insisted. "I just don't know how to sell artwork really quickly, do you?"

"If you wait to put it up for auction, you can surely get a much higher price than if you simply make some quick sale," Gil pointed out carefully, as if struggling to be straight with me.

"Oh, sure," I countered, "and give Danny and Deirdre time to find out? Imagine the pair of them wanting to make a claim on it? That's all I need! A legal battle could drag on for years. You don't know those two. There's nothing they wouldn't stoop to. No, I can never go public with this. We've got to find somebody who'd just buy it, right now, no questions asked." I paused for breath.

"Don't you know anybody with lots of money and no scruples?" I asked dramatically.

Gil fell silent for a moment, then said thoughtfully, "Well, actually, I know a guy who'd kill to get his hands on it. He's obsessed with Picasso."

"Great! Who is he?" I demanded.

"Paul. He's the guy who hired me to cook on his yacht," he said slowly, a gleam in his eye now.

"The one you went off to work for when you had your nervous breakdown?" I blurted out.

Gil said quickly, "Look, I never had an *actual* breakdown. Not really. That was just the press."

"For God's sake, Gil," I said in exasperation, "pick up the damned phone and call him, now!"

I must have seemed a bit manic, because he then looked me in the eye rather sternly, as if to extract a promise that I would not recant later. "Céline, this is your legacy from your grandmother. So, take the time right now to look at the painting and see how you *feel*. I want to know for sure that you can give it up and never see it again."

"Can't you get this Paul-guy to invite us on his yacht once in awhile, as part of the bargain?" I said. "So I can visit my painting?" But I thought I understood what he was trying to say, so I did as he asked. I padded across the room and for several intense moments I stood in front of that extraordinary portrait. This Picasso seemed too monumental for any one mortal to possess, and I told Gil so. I gazed into the girl's eyes for awhile longer, thinking, *Grandma, if you don't want me to sell, then please, send me a sign!*

But she only looked back at me as if to say, *Don't bother me, it's your life now.*

And since no tree fell on my head and lightning didn't strike me dead, I turned away more resolved than ever. "I don't think Grandma Ondine was terribly sentimental. If *she* was in this situation and needed it to help Mom and to keep the *mas,* I know she'd do what she must," I said briskly.

Then I heard my phone buzzing with an incoming message. I fished it out of my pile of clothes.

"What's the matter?" Gil said when I went pale after seeing the name of the caller. Now I understood my earlier instinct, summoning me back to battle. I put the phone on speaker mode so we could hear the voicemail message. It was from the hairdresser at the care home in Nevada:

Céline, your mother's had an attack of some kind. They've taken her to the hospital as "only a precaution", but you might want to be here. The good news is, this week your mother began speaking again and she asked where you were. I asked the ambulance driver which hospital they were taking her to. Here's the name and address. But I heard your brother tell the hospital not to put through any phone calls or messages to your mom, nor to allow any visitors.

"DAMN IT!" I SAID UNDER my breath, struggling shakily to climb into my clothes. "Those siblings of mine are going to be rotten, right to the very end. But this time I'm going to *really* fight for her."

"Céline, you ought to call your lawyer," Gil suggested. "You shouldn't have to face those people without him. Tell me who to call and I'll do it for you."

I looked at him through a blur of tears. "You want to help me? Get me money. Lots of it, so I can finally defend my mom. Sell the painting, Gil. Do it now, wire me my share and pay off your thugs to save our *mas*. But first—please get Maurice to change my flight to Nevada, tonight!"

Gil gave me a hug, then stroked my cheek soothingly. What I saw in his eyes was lovely and I felt a joyous urge to savor it; in fact, it made me tremble, but I was already steeling myself for the battle ahead and he seemed to understand that.

"I'll take care of everything," he promised, picking up the phone. "Just leave it to me."

I was too worried about my mother to even give it a second thought.

41

Ondine and Madame Sylvie in Mougins, 1983

"BABY CÉLINE *EST ARRIVÉE!*" ONDINE EXCLAIMED JUBILANTLY WHEN MADAME Sylvie came to her front door that afternoon. Breathlessly Ondine explained that, just as she was about to sit down to dinner with her daughter, Julie had gone into labor right here at the *mas,* and Arthur had to rush her off to the hospital. Ondine had been waiting at home for hours, so anxious for news.

"But just now I finally heard from the doctor!" Ondine continued, clearly ecstatic. "Julie's baby *is* a girl, and she's healthy and beautiful."

Madame Sylvie smiled indulgently. "Well, you don't need me, then," she said.

Ondine took her by the arm and pulled her inside. *"Au contraire!"* she exclaimed. "Let's go out to the terrace and have tea, and then you can read the tea leaves and the cards."

"For you or for Julie?" Madame Sylvie inquired.

"I don't want to hear about *me* or Julie!" Ondine said with an airy wave of her hand. "The die has already been cast for us. Now it is the baby's fortune you must tell me!" As the two ladies sat down to tea and an almond *gâteau* with cream and peaches, Ondine remarked, "Poor Julie never had a chance to eat her dinner. Well, tomorrow I'll take her some nice roast chicken from the café, and I'll bring her a cherry *tarte*, too. All right, now, please tell me—what kind of future do you see for baby Céline?"

Madame Sylvie poured tea into a special tiny ceramic cup trimmed in gold which she'd brought as a gift, and Ondine obligingly drank this thimbleful of tea for the infant. Then Madame Sylvie peered at the leaves left behind in the cup. Instantly she tried to suppress a frown, but Ondine was quick to demand, "What's wrong? Tell me quickly, don't hold back."

Madame Sylvie assured her, "No, it's all right. The girl will be healthy and strong, and intelligent and gifted. And girls today are smarter—they have careers of their own!"

Ondine agreed with this. But she was nobody's fool. "What else can you see?" she prompted.

Madame Sylvie dealt the cards now. She studied them closely, then said forthrightly, "It's only that it won't be easy for Céline. She will struggle to attain the true destiny that was meant for her."

"It's because of her father, isn't it?" Ondine said worriedly, leaning forward.

Madame Sylvie said hesitantly, "Yes, he's an impediment. He will be exactly the opposite of what a parent should be—an adversary rather than an ally. And—I'm afraid Céline won't get much help from her mother, either. Julie will not protect her from him, which will drive the girl away from home."

Ondine sighed deeply. "Then—what are my grand-daughter's real chances?" she asked. "Will she succumb to the obstacles life presents her, or will she triumph?"

Madame Sylvie looked at her reproachfully. "You know I can't tell you that, since I can't yet see so far ahead as to how chance and luck will enter her life. I can only say, the girl will sink or swim depending solely upon her own strengths and her will to survive."

Ondine did not like this one bit. A baby, after all, should come into the world with nothing but hope. She felt the old protective instincts surging in her heart, making it beat worriedly. Some part of her wished she hadn't summoned Madame Sylvie here today at all. "Will she find love?" she demanded.

"Ah!" Madame Sylvie responded. "I see men in her life. Can she choose wisely? That all depends on the path she follows. You can only find love where you are brave enough to see the truth."

After Madame Sylvie left, Ondine carried her mail into her kitchen, temporarily distracted from her worries while sorting over her affairs, taking comfort in resuming the routine of her life after all this disruptive excitement.

"I haven't done so badly, after all," she commented as she paid a few bills and consulted her ledger. "One has to be organized, that's the key."

Ondine enjoyed having money, chiefly for the security of going to bed at night knowing that there was a tidy sum in her bank account as a bulwark against hard times, war, the economy, and anything else those thieves in government and commerce got up to. She liked being in control of her own business; the *mas* was thriving and the café functioned like a well-tended clock, although she had to keep a sharp eye on those rascals in her kitchen.

Ondine stuck stamps on a few pieces of mail, then put them aside with a sigh of satisfaction. At the end of the week, her handsome young lawyer, Gerard Clément, would stop by the café to review her documents and eat his lunch, which he'd done, as a friend, twice a month, for years. But nowadays, he and Ondine no longer discreetly sneaked off together to her bedroom above the café. Still, the passionate trysts they'd had for a few fine months were memorable enough.

"What a surprise that delightful Clément turned out to be!" she recalled with a smile. She'd been in her fifties when he took over the law practice of the elder lawyer that she once cooked for. Gerard Clément, like many young Frenchmen, had chosen a woman nearer his mother's age for his first great love affair.

"Would he have found me so attractive if I didn't have money?" Ondine said with a chuckle. "Yes, frankly, I think he would. But who cares, anyway? Joy is joy. How charmingly ardent he was. Oh, yes, that was fun!" Nowadays her heart wouldn't be able to endure climbing those stairs—not to mention the other exertions that once awaited her in that bedroom!

She sighed and picked up her cane. "All in all, it's a good life." She glanced at the fine golden sunlight pouring into the room, beckoning her to come back outside.

She stopped by her bedroom to get a scarf, and out of habit her gaze darted to the spot where the Picasso portrait used to be. At first it gave her a jolt to see only the empty space atop the chest of drawers. Then she remembered.

"Oh, yes, I put the painting in the dumbwaiter! All because of Arthur. What a poor little fool Julie was to marry that man!" she exclaimed. "He's not satisfied unless he can control everything he touches. Well, at least Arthur never laid his greedy eyes on my Picasso. And, by God, he never will!"

It was too bad that Ondine had not regained an opportunity to speak to Julie alone, as she'd hoped she might do after dinner. But, *alors!* The baby Céline had insisted on interrupting them to be born.

But perhaps that, too, was an omen, she mused. She'd already set up enough money in trust for Julie financially. She didn't need the painting for a dowry anymore. It was Céline's turn to have *her* dowry. Did girls even have dowries these days? Well, this grand-daughter would!

Ondine went into the kitchen to retrieve her portrait from its hiding place. She pressed the button, but the dumbwaiter, like a stubborn beast, refused to budge, only making an alarming electronic groan before the motor died out completely. Ondine peered down the shaft.

"How annoying that I can't go downstairs and get that painting myself!" she said, exasperated. "Well, I'll just tell Clément about it tomorrow, and ask him to go and retrieve it for me."

She had never shown Clément the Picasso, nor even told him about it, chiefly because Ondine didn't want her lover to see how much younger her face looked in that portrait.

"Ah, I can't be so vain any longer," she decided. She'd get him to draw up the proper legal papers so everybody would understand that Picasso's *Girl-at-a-Window* belonged to Céline. Clément was an honest, discreet fellow; he would do whatever she asked.

Thinking of the eager young man who loved to please her, Ondine smiled again.

She felt much better now, having resolved this weighty issue in her mind. When she glanced up, she saw her face mirrored in a window. Drawing nearer she thought stoutly that, while young faces were nice, even at their best there was something a little blank about them because they were only halfway-there to becoming themselves.

Somehow today, for once, Ondine was able to assess her reflection with enough detachment so that she could indeed see something worth capturing—not merely to illuminate who she was, but to express so much about life itself in all its bittersweetness. "Imagine what a portrait of me would look like now! But how would Picasso see it?" Contemplating this, she concluded sagely, "Women should paint. The human face is far too important to leave solely to the eyes of men!"

She gathered her basket and gloves, but then another thought occurred to her that made her pause. A good organizer, after all, knows when there is still a loose thread somewhere in the tapestry.

42

Céline in America, 2014

My flight was halfway across the Atlantic Ocean when I over-heard two women in a row behind me, high on champagne, having an animated conversation about what a bad idea it was to trust men.

"You did *what*?" one of them asked the other incredulously. "You let him manage your finances *before* the wedding? So what if he's a hedge fund genius? Don't *ever* give a guy control of your money! Okay, don't cry. My brother's a lawyer. He'll help you."

I closed my eyes, willing them to shut up. But their loud chatter continued unabated, making it clear that a boyfriend had run off with his fiancée's money *and* his secretary, and the gullible woman here on the plane was left with some terrible financial "exposure" to his shady dealings.

Thanks to those chatterboxes I suddenly imagined how horrified Sam, my lawyer, would be if he learned that the minute I got my hands on a Picasso I turned it over to a man I hardly knew. I'd left Mougins in such a blur. Aunt Matilda helped me pack my bags; then she wisely took Martin away for a two-day visit to one of Gil's friends in Cannes, so Gil could deal with the painting—and his loan shark.

Just leave it to me, Gil had said. But now, I pictured him running off with my painting, making a quick, dirty deal with his art-collector

friend, pocketing the change, paying off his loan shark, and never looking back. I had no proof of ownership. I wouldn't be able to do a thing.
I recalled the night at the restaurant when the tipsy lady-in-red—the
one he'd had an affair with—said, *Once he gets his chef's fingers on your
money, well, honey, he's gone, baby, gone . . .*

"Oh, God," I said now. Well, I had no choice but to hope for the
best. I determinedly tore open a packet from the airline containing an
eyeshade and slipper-socks, and earplugs that I quickly stuck in my
ears. I drank the glass of wine the stewardess offered, hoping that it
would blot out my fears about my mother, too. I put my seat back,
pulled up my blanket and shut my eyes.

When I arrived in the States I needed to change planes in New
York, with an hour's layover, which was bad enough, but then came the
news that my flight to Nevada was delayed because of "a weather
event". I sat in a café in the terminal anxiously fiddling with my phone,
firing off messages to Gil asking for an update on the sale of the painting, but I got absolutely no response from him.

At last I boarded my flight to Nevada, only to have the plane sit on
the tarmac in an interminable queue of delayed flights. The final straw
was when the airline announced that our plane was experiencing mechanical problems and we would have to disembark and wait for another flight.

The airline personnel were sympathetic when I told them my
mother was seriously ill, and they tried mightily to find me a quicker
alternative, allowing me to wait in a private lounge normally reserved
for VIPs. All this time I continued sending messages to Gil, spilling my
woes about being unable to get to Nevada. I even checked my bank account, but found that no money had been wired to it yet even though
Gil had asked for the number before I left. Not a single word from
him.

At this point I started muttering to myself. "Nice going, Céline.
You have never trusted a man with your life and your money before, so
what do you do? You pick *this time* to take up with some crazy chef,
and after one sexual encounter, you just hand him your Grandma's
long-lost Picasso. Terrific."

Meanwhile, my mother was all alone in Nevada with those jackals. I was dissolving into tears of frustration in a public place, when out of the corner of my eye I saw a tall, purposeful figure come loping across the lounge, aggressively cutting through the crowd. He was wearing a hat and sunglasses.

"Céline? Come with me," Gil said authoritatively, and he picked up my carry-on bag.

"What are *you* doing here?" I gasped. Then I found myself saying, "Where's the painting?"

"With my lawyer," Gil answered. "He's holding it in his safe, pending the sale. As soon as you left I knew I had to come after you. Matilda had already told me in no uncertain terms to go help you! But first, I did as promised—I got hold of my friend Paul. He jumped at it! He made an offer, and if you are okay with it, my lawyer will handle the sale, and Paul will wire the money to us. But right now, let's get you on a plane."

"There *is* no flight," I said sourly. "Didn't you read any of my messages?"

"Yes, yes. I've had quite a few fucking balls in the air to juggle! Follow me," Gil said briskly, steering me through a discreet airport corridor reserved for political and celebrity clientele.

"Where are we going?" I asked. He was walking so fast that I could hardly keep up.

"I told Paul that *you* would be the one to accept or reject his offer, so when I mentioned that you needed to get to your mum, he didn't mind sweetening the pot by putting his private jet at my disposal, so I could get here fast, and then fly you to Nevada," Gil explained with a sly grin, as the airport personnel nodded deferentially to us and stepped aside to let us through.

And that's how I ended up on a billionaire's airplane. I kept staring at Gil in disbelief as we stretched out on the cushy black-leather seats that were more like sofa-beds. Our plane was cleared for takeoff, and a short while later we were airborne.

"Paul's standing by on his yacht in St. Tropez, waiting to hear your answer," Gil announced, looking enormously satisfied with the results of all his efforts.

Still breathless from rushing across the terminal, I couldn't help but ask, "So. How much?"

"Well, keep in mind that this painting is not well known, hasn't been verified as a genuine Picasso, nor have you presented proof of ownership along with the painting's provenance," he cautioned. "Paul wants an expert he often uses to look it over, so we've got him on standby, too."

"That painting is real, all right," I said, feeling feisty now.

"Yes, but even so, remember that Paul's taking a big risk believing that your grandmother—and you—are the true owners."

"Yeah, yeah. How *much*?" I repeated.

"Fifty-five million," Gil said calmly.

"Dollars?" I squeaked idiotically.

Gil nodded. "He wants his pre-empt to be high enough so you don't take it to auction," he explained. "Plus, I got him to agree that if you sell it to him, he'll let you come visit the painting once in awhile. I also told him you wanted the *Girl-at-a-Window* to ultimately end up in a place where everyone has a chance to see it. He seemed to understand that. Said he'd arrange right now for the painting to be bequeathed to a public museum upon his death. He's eccentric, but he's honorable."

For awhile we said absolutely nothing. Finally Gil said gently, "It's your decision, Céline. I figure we've got a couple hours of keeping Paul on the string, but frankly he's met all our demands, so I wouldn't give him too much time to reconsider this deal. He's a shark, and sharks move on."

For the first time, the whole thing was real to me; and I let myself feel the pang of regret that I seemed to be losing my Grandmother Ondine almost as soon as I'd found her.

Gil was saying, "If you decide to sell, I'd like my lawyer to handle it today so he can pay off my loan and get Gus to call off his dogs. As it was, those meatheads were hanging around the *mas* again—I literally had to sneak out in the laundry truck to board this jet. Still, as I said, you can take all the time in the world, and even put it up for auction, if you want to. I'll stand behind whatever you decide."

I thought of Grandma's *mas* in peril of those thugs *and* Rick; and my mother in the hospital, waiting for me. I took a deep breath. Then I said firmly, "Sell!"

WHEN WE LANDED IN NEVADA, the town car that Gil had hired was already waiting for us. It took us straight to the hospital, and the driver would continue to wait for us there.

"Where's your lawyer?" Gil asked worriedly as the car pulled to a stop. I checked my phone.

"Sam's in some meeting but left me a message," I muttered. "Says the twins gave explicit orders not to let *any* visitors in to see Mom, 'not even other family members'. That means me, of course."

"Can they do that?" Gil asked. "What the bloody hell are they afraid of?"

"Money, as always. Sam says they're worried Mom will 'fully revive and alter her will'," I explained. "He told me not to try to get into the hospital without him, because the twins might call the cops and make the whole thing very unpleasant. He says it's better to fight them in court. But my mother can't wait for him and his dumb meeting, and neither can I."

My telephone rang then. It was a private detective my lawyer had hired to keep an eye on Mom's hospital room for me until I arrived, and he was sending me an update.

"Deirdre has just left," he said. "So your mother is alone now. No change in her condition. I have two visitors' passes that I will hand you as I go by your car. Don't give your mother's name when they ask who you're visiting. I have another patient's name; at least it will get you past the downstairs reception desk. Upstairs, you're on your own. Your mom's room is 243; third left past the elevator."

I told Gil this, and we watched in fascination as the P.I. strolled by our rolled-down window, dropped the passes in my lap and continued walking, having made no outward sign of even stopping, much less interacting with us. "I've got an idea about getting past the upstairs nurses," Gil said.

He and I went inside the hospital. The night crew was coming on, so during the changing of the guard they only glanced distractedly at our passes and nodded. But if we showed these passes upstairs we'd be directed to another patient's room. So when the elevator landed on Mom's floor, Gil said, "I'll cover for you. Ready to rock and roll?" I nodded, ducked into the ladies' room and counted to fifty.

Then I returned to the hallway and cautiously inched toward my mother's room. Gil was parked at the nurse's station, where all the nurses on duty were gathered in a curious cluster around him while he regaled them in his irresistible English accent with a tall tale about Prince Harry. His broad back was facing me and he'd carefully squared his shoulders to block the nurses' view, as he indulgently answered their questions with great charm. Inwardly I blessed him as I slipped unnoticed into my mother's room.

She lay there, asleep in the bed, with tubes in her nose. Several bags of I-V drip were hanging beside her, with tubing connected to her hand by needles. The first thing that struck me was that she looked incredibly small, making the bed seem bigger than it actually was. They had stopped coloring her hair, so instead of her usual auburn, she was more grey-haired now. Her skin, though very pale, was still youthful-looking for her age. I noticed that Mom's lips were dry and chapped. A cup of water stood on a table beside the bed—just out of reach.

I sat down gently on the bed and tentatively took her hand—the one without the I-V needle in it. Her fingers were soft and warm and delicate, as I remembered from childhood, but it seemed as if now she was down to just skin and bones. She had her usual trusting, hopeful expression on her face. Overwhelming love for her welled up in my chest, making it feel as if my heart were about to burst.

She opened her eyes. For a moment, she didn't seem able to focus, but stirred sleepily and then squinted to see who had taken her hand. I put the water to her lips and she drank. When she finally spoke, it was in such a faint whisper that I had to put my head close to her to hear it.

"Who's there?" she asked; then, as if she had sensed rather than seen me, said, "Céline, is that you?" Now she gazed directly at me with surprise and that pure delight of hers.

"Yes, Mom," I said quickly, kissing her forehead. "I love you." She smiled sweetly and lifted her hand to stroke my face—first one cheek, then the other. Then she took my hand and squeezed it.

Filled with emotion I said, "I've come to take you home."

"Home?" she said wonderingly. "Really, home?" I nodded, not trusting myself to speak. Then she said softly, "I love *you,* my brave Céline. Always my sweet one." She sighed. "Where did you come from?" she asked with sudden clarity, sounding just like her old self, lucid and curious. "California?"

"No, Mom, I've been to France. I found Grandma's *mas,*" I began. Her eyes widened, but then her eyelids fluttered and I feared she was falling back into a druggy sleep. "Mom, I found Grandma's painting. From Picasso," I said more urgently. She murmured something unintelligible. "Mom?" I said. "Can you hear me? Everything's going to be all right now. I went to France and I found what you wanted there. You were right. Picasso *did* give Grandma a painting!"

I didn't realize that Gil had come to the doorway and was standing behind me now. I tried again. "Mom, did you hear me? Grandma's painting from Picasso. Mom, I found it!"

She opened her eyes once more, as if it took an extreme effort to do so. But this time, she didn't look at me. Her gaze went beyond me, toward the doorway where Gil was standing.

She stared at him for a time, then smiled knowingly and looked back at me again, just as I was saying to her, "I found it!" She must have heard the last word differently, as she looked from Gil to me.

"I'm so glad you found *him,*" she whispered conspiratorially, squeezing my hand once more. And just before she sank back to sleep she added, "He looks as if he loves you very much."

DANNY AND DEIRDRE NEVER KNEW that I'd gotten in to see Mom. I slipped out just as my P.I. warned me that Danny was on his way up. Gil and I took the private jet to Los Angeles so I could pick up a few things from my apartment before returning to Nevada. While Gil camped out with his computer in my living room to handle the money transfers from the sale of the painting, I worked with my lawyer via phone on the emergency court order so I could go back to see Mom without being harassed by my step-siblings.

But in the early hours of the next morning, my mother passed away peacefully in her sleep. I heard about it from my P.I., who was still keeping an eye on her for me. After he delivered this devastating news, I sank onto my sofa and just sat there, quiet and immobilized for the rest of the day.

Deirdre waited another twenty-four hours before she got around to officially notifying me. "Mom just died in her sleep," she lied as we spoke on the phone. "There won't be a wake. Her body's been flown to New York to be buried with Dad's. It's the way she and Dad wanted it."

For all the world she sounded like a murderer hastily trying to bury the evidence. As far as Deirdre knew, I hadn't seen Mom since she'd had her stroke, yet Deirdre never once asked if I wanted to sit with my mother's body to say goodbye to her. My sister's smug tone told me she was enormously pleased to be the one in charge, as if that conferred some sort of superiority on her. She continued ticking things off on her to-do list, sounding more as if she were planning a party instead of presiding over a death.

"One more thing. Danny says to let you know—don't expect much from Dad's estate. The expenses for Mom's care were very steep," she recited in a parrot-like way, which told me she was reading a rehearsed speech she'd composed with her lawyer. "Céline?" she inquired, having noticed for the first time that I'd said nothing throughout the entire phone call.

"Goodbye, Deirdre," I said, and we hung up.

Gil emerged from the next room. He told me that his lawyer had arranged the transfer of my share of the money from the sale of the painting to a new bank account for me in France. Just by the skin of our teeth we wired Gil's repayment of his loan in time. But there were still a few documents we had to sign in person in France.

"Ready when you are," Gil said simply. When I told him what Deirdre said, he paused. "Céline. Let's talk about this. Do you want to stop in New York for the burial?" I shook my head, but I finally burst into tears. He came to me swiftly and held me as we sat there, until I just couldn't cry anymore. I clung to the warmth and strength of his chest. He kept making soothing sounds and kissed the top of my head. I raised my tear-streaked face and nuzzled it to his cheek.

Later, sitting dry-eyed at my table while we ate the supper he'd cooked, I told him, "I swear to God, I don't know who these people are that I grew up with. I loved them because I thought of them as family. But they never loved Mom. So, they were never my family. How *could* they not love her? I wanted to rescue her. And now she's gone. God, what's the point of everything I've just been doing?"

"You made sure your mother knew that she at least had *your* love," Gil said simply. "Right up to the end, you were there for her. So, no justification needed."

"My love didn't stop her from being a victim," I said bitterly. "It's as if everything that I thought was important in life is now all up for grabs. I really don't even know who I am anymore."

"I know where you can go to find out," Gil said quietly. "But it's up to you."

The look in his eyes gave me the strength I needed. My suitcases were already packed.

So that night, we boarded the private jet once more, and we headed back to France.

43

Ondine in the Garden, Mougins, 1983

Ondine was sitting at her kitchen table in the *mas* when the telephone rang again.

It was Arthur, calling from the maternity ward. "Julie's fine. She wants me to stay with her a little longer, but I'll come back to the *mas* to sleep tonight. Then I have early meetings first thing tomorrow, but I'll pick you up at noon to go see the baby," he said firmly, clearly determined to control Ondine's exposure to his wife. He sounded irritated, as if the baby's earlier-than-expected arrival was a deliberate plot to keep Julie in France longer than he'd scheduled.

Ondine politely pretended to accept his plan. But after they hung up, she decided that as soon as Arthur left in the morning, she'd get Monsieur Clément to drop her off at the hospital; she couldn't wait to see Julie and dear little Céline, and she wanted to be certain that they were both really all right.

The more Ondine thought about it, the more she believed that it would be wrong to break her promise to Luc by telling Julie about Picasso being her father. But a nagging feeling persisted, and finally she understood why.

"*Somebody* in this family ought to know the whole story about me and Picasso and Luc and Julie. I never promised Luc I wouldn't tell

Picasso's *grand*-daughter who she really is! It might help Céline to choose wisely and find her true destiny. But, will I still be alive when she is old enough to listen? When she grows up, will she ever come to visit me? Or will Arthur poison her against me? I wish I could tell her now—but how can you whisper a secret to a baby?"

Then, inspired, Ondine reached for her pen. As she wrote, the kitchen echoed with the sound of her pen scratching its way across the last of the *Café Paradis* stationery she'd kept from the old days:

> *Cher Céline,*
> *I am entrusting you with a secret I have told no one, not even your mother. I feel it is important for you to know exactly who you really are, but I hope that after you have read everything I have to say, in the end you'll understand that it's really up to you to decide who you wish to become, and to find a path to the life you truly want . . .*

WHEN AT LAST SHE GOT to the end, Ondine uttered a satisfied, "Hah!" and signed it, *Your loving grandmother, Ondine.* She folded the letter into its envelope and sealed it.

"But how do you mail a letter to a baby?" she brooded. She decided she would entrust it to Monsieur Clément, so he could keep it with the painting in a safe place. And yet, it wouldn't be wise to leave this letter lying around here even for one night, while Arthur was still sleeping over.

She pondered this quietly for awhile; then she came up with a temporary hiding place where Arthur would never look. At least her letter would be safe from prying eyes until she could meet up with Clément tomorrow to give it to him, so he could lock it up with the painting in his safe.

Ondine felt much better as she picked up her basket and went outside. The sun was still hot, scenting the flower fields; and a light wind mingled its fragrance with that of the salty sea.

"Such a bright, happy day!" Ondine sighed as she dragged a small stepladder over to the cherry tree at the far end of the terrace. The cherries hung there like dark rubies, and quite soon she'd picked enough to fill her basket for the fresh *tarte* she would bake for Julie.

When she finished she was panting with pleasure, and, feeling a bit short of breath, she left the stepladder as it was. Peering up into the tree in the heat of this day had made her light-headed. Turning now in the direction of the terrace, she felt dizzy, then experienced a queer little pain in her chest.

The next thing she knew, she'd fallen into the soft grass under the tree, just like a ripe fruit. There seemed to be a brief flash of time and consciousness, as if she'd clicked the shutter of an old-fashioned camera and her view had disappeared and gone black momentarily, before re-appearing.

"Now what should I do?" Ondine asked herself, perplexed. The sun was setting and there was a chill in the air; but when the wind stirred in the grass, she thought she heard a familiar voice whispering to her, like the swish of the sea with its rushing sound, as if someone were holding a seashell to her ear. Someone who loved her, and would guide her soul home with his sheltering, soothing voice.

"Luc?" Ondine said wonderingly. "I thought you'd been gone all these years, *mon cher,* but it turns out that you've been here all along, out in the garden the whole time, watching over me!"

She was still lying on her back and gazing at the darkening blue sky, where the moon was already hanging like a lustrous pearl.

"Ah," Ondine sighed, "what a good day to be born."

Not far from Ondine's house, Madame Sylvie had stopped at a road-side farmstand to pick up a few fresh things for dinner and to chat with friends before heading home. Then she continued down the long, dusty road, until a sudden, strong impulse made her halt right there in her tracks like a horse.

"Ondine!" she cried aloud, startling the birds in the trees and the rabbits in the grass. From somewhere overhead, an owl hooted.

Madame Sylvie did not hesitate. She turned right around, and hurried back to Ondine's house.

44

Céline in France, 2014–2016

THE GRAND OPENING OF *LE MAS ONDINE* WAS STIMULATING ENOUGH TO assuage some of my grief. Now that I was a full partner in the *mas,* I was less inclined to brood about the past or worry about the future. I was taking that one step at a time, even though it was a terrifying thrill to be hurtling through life's challenges with Gil. Every time I saw his face, after being apart for even just a few hours, I felt my entire being flooded with joy. And because I saw this exuberance mirrored in his gaze as well, I threw away the inhibitions that had once served as my armor, and I put my faith in the strength of being unarmed.

When I wasn't working with Gil on the menus and bookings, I was busy with makeup jobs on movie shoots in Europe. I could afford to be selective about assignments now, and I took an apartment in Cannes as my new business base, since so many Hollywood companies were filming abroad these days. Meanwhile Gil won his second Michelin star for our restaurant, *Pierrot.* And things looked promising for the future of the newly opened hotel, too. But the competition at this level was more fierce than any I'd ever known, and it kept us on our toes.

"We're booked up for most of next year," Gil reported one bright morning at the *mas*. While he spoke, the postman came zooming up in his little car to deliver the mail. When he saw us standing in the doorway he deposited the letters in Gil's hands with a brisk *Bonjour!* then tipped his cap and drove on.

"This one's for you," Gil said, sorting through the envelopes and handing one to me. It was from the twins' lawyer. A check was enclosed representing my share of my parents' estate. Gil watched as I read the amount aloud for his amusement.

"Two thousand five hundred dollars," I said, showing it to him. If I had ever considered sharing some of my good fortune with Danny and Deirdre, this final fillip from them clinched my resolve to never have anything to do with them again.

Gil shook his head. "The bandits!"

"I think I'll donate it to that little church nearby," I said, recalling how the sweet sound of its old-fashioned bells pealing gently on Sunday had comforted me when I returned from America.

Months passed before Deirdre saw a restaurant review and got wind of the fact that Gil and I were "an item". This prompted her to send a Christmas card signed with an uncharacteristic, *So, what's new with you??!!* But she and Danny never found out about the painting; my entire Picasso escapade remained a secret among Gil, me, our lawyers and Gil's friend Paul who bought the *Girl-at-a-Window*.

And, of course, dear Aunt Matilda. Gil unexpectedly insisted that we share the good fortune from the sale of the painting with her in order to help her hold on to her house in Connecticut. He said, "Thanks to you, Céline, we're going to make much more money now that we've got the *mas* in full swing again. That's enough for me. So, use whatever you need from my share of the painting's sale to help your aunt, and anything else you feel you need to do. Of course, she and her friend Peter are welcome to stay at the *mas* as our guests any time they like."

"Yes, I do want to help out Aunt Matilda," I agreed. "But I'm also going to set aside enough money so that we never, ever again have to go to a loan shark to hold on to *Le Mas Ondine*!"

I didn't really think there could be any more big surprises in store for me. I was wrong.

EPILOGUE

Port Vauban, 2016

IT'S BEEN TWO YEARS SINCE I SOLD THE PAINTING, AND THE BUYER HAD promised to let me approve its new home once he found a place for *Girl-at-a-Window*. But as soon as Paul got his hands on it, he was not an easy man to pin down, and I began to have doubts about the deal I'd made.

That's why, when I finally got a message from Paul saying I could come visit before he "cast off", I hurried off to Billionaires' Quay in Port Vauban for this impromptu meeting on his grand yacht, *Le Troubadour*.

And now, while I'm sitting here in the ship's library, waiting on a bench that resembles a church pew, right before my eyes one of the bookcases begins to move—swinging open like the secret door that it is.

A blonde woman in a bright white linen suit and a dazzling necklace made of violet diamonds emerges from this inner sanctum and introduces herself as Cheryl, Paul's wife. Smiling, she says softly, "You can come in now."

I follow her into what turns out to be Grandma Ondine's cabin. Amid sumptuous Louis XVI sofas, a pair of nineteenth-century *bergère* armchairs and some tiny Giacometti and Rodin sculptures, there is a walnut alcove, like an altar, where Picasso's *Girl-at-a-Window* reigns supreme. She's flanked by two slim, carefully placed windows that let in a glimpse of the sky and the splashing sea. As my hostess hands me a glass of champagne she explains that Grandma's portrait spends spring and summer here on the Riviera, making stops at all the best hot spots where it is admired by esteemed guests. Then the *Girl-at-a-Window* gets a Grand Tour of the world, wintering in Palm Beach, the Caribbean isles and even Patagonia.

"And," Cheryl says reassuringly, "Paul wants you to know that he's made a special arrangement with the Louvre in Paris. They've picked out a wonderful spot for the painting there, once they get it as our bequest. So," she concedes with a nod, "your grandmother will live on long after you and I are gone. Well, enjoy your visit with her." Then she thoughtfully leaves the room so I can have some private time.

"Bonjour, Grand-mère," I whisper. I stand there before her, listening to the distant cry of the gulls and feeling the occasional nudge of the tide. The youthful Ondine, gazing back at me, looks like a princess presiding over her new, opulent surroundings and she seems to be smiling down at me in triumph; after all, she has indeed, in her own invincible way, achieved a kind of immortality.

"Superbe," I say softly. I perch at the end of a *bergère* chair, and fall into a brief reverie, recalling all that's happened to get us here. And in this tranquil hush, I even feel my mother's presence today, like a breeze that lightly, consolingly touches my shoulder.

"Merci, Maman," I say, my eyes misty now.

For it's as if Mom and Grandmother Ondine conspired to give me a new family to care about—not only Gil and sweet little Martin, but Aunt Matilda and her friend Peter, too. Among all these people I love, I feel more at home than I ever have in my life.

The ship's horn toots. All ashore that's going ashore. Reluctantly, I turn to leave, just as Paul enters the room. He's a strange guy—quiet, short, bald, preoccupied-looking; and there is an eerie stillness to him, a peculiar serenity that is somehow a bit scary.

But then this man—a god in the world of merciless killer investors—pauses reverently before the painting as if it's something holy. "She's a beauty," he says with a besotted look on his face. After a few moments he turns to me and says gently, "We'll keep her safe. Come visit her again sometime."

Now that the movie I've been working on has wrapped up production, I'll soon be focusing my attention on the *mas*. It's the same every year—we always brace ourselves for the juggernaut of the Grand Prix auto race in Monaco which officially launches the new season on the Riviera, and the real onslaught of tourists begins. Between Gil's work and mine I know that soon we won't have an hour we can call our own. And this year I'm doing the makeup for actresses at the Cannes Film Festival.

But just this morning Gil, already busy training new kitchen and hotel staff, advised me, "You should take a few days off before you plunge into that circus. Enjoy some time to yourself while you can get it!"

So as I return to my car in the parking lot, I see that, already, more yachts from around the world are returning to the Mediterranean, their white sails fluttering gently as they glide into view. They inspire me to do something I haven't done in a long time—put aside my makeup brushes, and pick up my old paint box and portable easel, which I'd shipped over here from my apartment in L.A. and threw into the trunk of my car.

Ever since school I've painted, but only intermittently, usually on holidays. Now when I set up my easel in the park by the harbor at Port Vauban I finally, literally, begin to see the light—that bewitching combination of brightness and softness reflecting off the Mediterranean Sea which has held so many painters spellbound over the centuries. I scramble with palette and paint tubes, squishing out fat blobs of color in a delirious frenzy to capture what I see, starting with a horizon layered in every conceivable shade of blue—deep cobalt and French ultramarine and cerulean and azure and turquoise.

At noon in the marketplace, the sun ignites everything it touches to its eye-dazzling essence—cadmium yellow and scarlet and chrome green for the stalls bursting with spring vegetables, fruit, flowers and wheels of cheese so fresh that they are still warm when the *fromagère* hands them to me. And at day's end, the departing light leaves a burnished monochrome trail somewhere between rose and ochre and umber, that washes over the sphinx-like faces of those old village men at picnic tables who play cards as seriously as if they are saying their prayers. I paint in a frenzy of inspiration which requires so much concentration that I manage, if not to forget the past, then at least to leave it there.

When I return to the *mas* I go straight to the *pigeonnier* to unpack the mouth-watering groceries I've brought home from the market. Gil and I often end up here at the end of the day to make drinks and supper. The light and shadows in the kitchen garden today are so striking that I can't resist setting up my easel right there.

And as I work, Gil literally walks right into the scene I'm trying to capture. He's carrying a box that he sets down with a thump on the old picnic table, which neither one of us could bear to throw away. "What's that?" I ask absently as I begin to paint an image of him into my scenario.

"Old pots and pans," he says enthusiastically. "They were in that box we took out of storage from Monaco when we were chasing down your wretched blue cupboard, remember? This cookware is great. And look, here's an old-fashioned knife roll full of kitchen knives!" He places the rolled-up leather on the table and undoes the straps that are like narrow belt buckles.

"They're beauties!" Gil proclaims, admiring each knife sheathed inside its own special felt-lined leather pocket. "Made in France. Vintage Opinel," he muses, examining them one by one. "It's a complete chef's line. Huh." He suddenly falls silent.

I am so absorbed in my painting that I don't grasp what's happening until he rises from the table and comes nearer, wearing an odd look on his face. He stops right in front of me, holding out an envelope. "It's for you," he says.

"What's up?" I ask, putting down my brush and wiping paint off my hands.

"This looks personal. You might say it came special-delivery," he replies, intrigued. "It was stuffed in one of those knife pockets. Apparently these kitchen things belonged to your grandmother. You know, a chef never goes anywhere without her knife roll." Bewildered, I take the envelope and study the handwriting, which has become so familiar to both of us from Grandmother Ondine's notebook, since we are using some of her recipes this season.

The front of the envelope reads: *For Céline, on the day of her birth*.

"Oh, my God," I say, staring at it long and hard before I open it, so very carefully. I unfold the page that was inside, letting Gil read over my shoulder. I have to read it again and again, stunned by astonishing words like *Picasso's legacy* and *your mother's heritage* and *your grandfather*. Finally we look at each other, flabbergasted. Yet even then, I still can't completely comprehend it.

"Picasso—and Ondine—so, my mother was *his*? But—what does it all mean?" I finally stammer.

Gil, looking genuinely awed, gestures at my riotous array of paint tubes and brushes.

"I think, my darling," he says gently, "it means that, all along, your grandmother's long-lost Picasso was really . . . *you*."

THE END

ACKNOWLEDGMENTS

I wish to thank all the people who were helpful to me: To Rosamond Bernier, who, during her tenure as a lecturer at the Metropolitan Museum of Art, was so generous with her anecdotes and research about Picasso and Matisse when I interviewed her for a newspaper story. I also thank the Pelham Arts Center, who introduced me to collectors and critics of twentieth-century art when I worked on their publicity. And I will always be grateful to the painter Alexander Rutsch, friend of Picasso, who made me his Girl-at-a-Window in his sketches during our train commute together.

I'd like to thank all my friends in France, especially Jean-Jacques Poulet and Giuseppe Cosmai. And Christophe Prosper, and Michelin-starred chefs Didier Aniès and David Chauvac for teaching me about Provençal cuisine. Also, I thank all the people at the Musée Picasso (Château Grimaldi) in Antibes for their kind consideration.

I give many thanks to Ruth G. Koizim, senior lector and language program director in French at Yale University. And to the researchers at the French Institute Alliance Française in Manhattan, particularly Yann Carmona. I thank Brandon Collura of the Lauderdale Yacht Club for his thoughts on all things nautical. And I appreciate Jaime Gant Dittus and Elizabeth Corradino for their wise counsel.

At Writers House, my fond thanks to Susan Golomb for her warmth, understanding and advice; and all her colleagues, especially the generous Amy Berkower, and also Genevieve Gagne-Hawes, Maja Nikolic and Scott Cohen.

At Random House, special thanks to Gina Centrello and Jennifer Hershey for their early and continued support. And how can I ever thank Susanna Porter, for her unstinting encouragement, intuitive wisdom, her patience and sense of humor and her fine, sensitive editing. Thanks also to Kim Hovey, Mark Tavani, Libby McGuire, Sheila Kay, Susan Corcoran, Melanie DeNardo, Robbin Schiff, Kathy Lord, and Priyanka Krishnan.

My very special thanks to Margaret Atwood, for the years of advice, encouragement, friendship, tea and "wilderness tips". Finally, all my love and gratitude to my husband, Ray, for his never-failing faith, editorial advice, intelligence and on-the-road camaraderie as we trawl the far corners of France together in search of good stories, good swimming and good food.

COOKING
FOR
PICASSO

———

CAMILLE AUBRAY

A Reader's Guide

A CONVERSATION WITH CAMILLE AUBRAY

THE FIRST QUESTION MOST PEOPLE ASK ME ABOUT MY NOVEL *COOKING FOR Picasso* is usually, "Where did you get the idea for this story?" And I can't help thinking, "The inspiration was right there on the French Riviera just waiting to be noticed, so perhaps *it* found *me*!"

It all began in Antibes. While traveling along the bright blue Mediterranean coast with its glittering sea, I glanced up at an enormous image of a face on a museum banner, staring back at me with dark, compelling eyes. It was Pablo Picasso, and the museum banner was for the famed Château Grimaldi. I learned that, shortly after the Second World War ended, when paint and canvases were in short supply, Picasso had painted murals upon those very walls and whatever other surfaces he could find. Now this castle is called the Musée Picasso.

"Who are you looking for?" his challenging gaze seemed to ask. And soon enough my answer was, "You!"

For, in researching Picasso's many years of residence on the Côte d'Azur, I discovered a true but little-known fact: in 1936, Pablo's life in Paris was in such utter turmoil that he'd actually stopped painting. His wife, Olga, the Russian ballerina, discovered that Picasso's young mistress, Marie-Thérèse, had given birth to a daughter. Olga began separation proceedings, and once the lawyers got involved, the endless legal wrangling was just too much for anybody, let alone a highly sensitive soul like Picasso; because, perhaps more than other artists, for him the personal life and the professional life were indelibly intertwined. Stressed out and desperate for relief, Pablo secretly slipped out of Paris by train. The surname of Picasso is actually his mother's family name; so now he traveled under his father's surname, Ruiz, as a way to remain anonymous. The mysterious Monsieur Ruiz rented a villa in the seaside town of Juan-les-Pins during the less-touristy season of spring. No one knows for sure what happened during this reclusive interlude—but whatever it was, it enabled him to pick up his brush and begin painting again. Within a year he would produce his masterpiece, *Guernica*.

That little biographical tidbit was enough to set my imagination on fire. Furthermore, as I delved into the unusual artwork that Picasso created during this interval, I learned another intriguing detail: he'd made a pair of paintings of a dark-haired, unidentified woman. People still wonder today—who was she? Because of her hair color, some say she was the photographer Dora Maar who was soon to become Pablo's new mistress and muse. Others say it was the brunette sister of Marie-Thérèse. But I knew exactly who that enigmatic model was—my heroine, for I now felt free to invent a fictional character.

Surrounded by the irresistible cuisine of the South of France, with its prodigious food markets and its lively cafés, I asked myself one key question: Who fed Pablo Picasso? If he was in hiding, he'd be careful about dining out too often and being recognized. So, who cooked for him?

As I roamed the village of Juan-les-Pins and its cafés, I envisioned a local girl, Ondine, riding a bicycle with a hamper of food, pedalling to the beautiful surrounding villas, with their high stone walls spilling over with flowers—and secrets. I imagined that my young heroine's Provençal cuisine and her very presence would be the flame that reignited Picasso's creative fervor; and that he, with his brilliance, forceful personality and absolute dedication to his work, would in turn inspire Ondine to greater risks and heights. *Bouillabaisse, bourride, tapenade, pissaladière, tartines, daube de boeuf à la provençale . . .*

these iconic dishes all found their way into my novel at key moments in the story. Meanwhile my readers would meet some of the Côte d'Azur's most famous residents: Henri Matisse, Jean Cocteau, and of course, Picasso's women.

For, as one of the characters in my novel says, "Picasso changed houses as often as he changed women." Going up and down the coast of the French Riviera and its hilltop villages, you can pick out multiple towns where Picasso lived for various periods—with various ladies. My research took me from the beaches and cafés of Antibes and the fishing town of Juan-les-Pins, to the food markets and museums of Nice, Ménerbes, Golfe-Juan, Cannes. And, of course, to the pottery town of Vallauris, where Pablo lived with his mistress, the artist Françoise Gilot. It was all so intriguing, for, as another of my characters in *Cooking for Picasso* says, "There was a lot of overlap with Picasso's women—he kept them on the hook and played them against one another."

In writing about my heroine Ondine, I wondered, how would *she* survive her intense encounter with Picasso? I knew the impact would be life-changing, so I decided to follow her—and Picasso—through the years, revealing other crucial moments that helped Ondine to mature into a courageous adult whose ambitions intersected with Picasso at times that were also greatly significant in his life. And, in following Ondine's lifetime, it was natural for me to think about how her adventures with Picasso might also affect her daughter, Julie, and even her American grand-daughter, Céline. This finally led me to the hilltop village of Mougins, where Picasso lived with his second (and last) wife, Jacqueline, in a house they called Notre Dame de Vie. Here the great artist died in 1973. Mougins has for decades been a center of gastronomie, so it was a perfect locale for my novel.

Drawing on my experiences writing and producing for film and TV, I envisioned Ondine's modern-day grand-daughter as a freelance Hollywood makeup artist who feels compelled to find out what happened when her Grandmother Ondine crossed paths with Pablo Picasso. So Céline enrolls in a cooking-class-travel-package deal, held at a *mas* hotel in Mougins, run by a fictional, attractive but temperamental British chef. Unlike her Grandmother Ondine, Céline has no natural talent for cooking, and this will sorely try the patience of her Michelin-starred chef. But Céline and Gil find other reasons to overcome their mutual wariness and to help each other.

For my research about the subtleties of French and Provençal cuisine, I sought out several French chefs on the Riviera who graciously invited me into their kitchens, as well as the generous Jacques Pépin, onetime chef to Charles de Gaulle and now a revered television personality—who told me that my novel made him homesick for his mother's *coq au vin*. I found these brilliant artists of cuisine to be more soulful, modest and practical than popular culture imagines great chefs to be.

All of the artwork that I describe in my novel was really made by Picasso, except for one that I invented—the portrait of Ondine, the *Girl-at-a-Window*. But this was indeed based on the painting that Rembrandt made in 1645 with the same name. Picasso was often inspired to do his own versions of the masters, especially Rembrandt.

Following in Picasso's footsteps on the Côte d'Azur led me to richer experiences than I could possibly have imagined when I first began my journey. To this day there are enduring signs of his vitality, his art and his verve, in the many statues, paintings, pottery and murals he bequeathed to the various towns and their museums. All you have to do, as the French author and Riviera resident Colette once advised, is, *"Regarde!"* Yes, just "Look!" Readers have already begun to tell me, "I took your book along with me, as a travel guide speaking in the voice of a trusted friend."

And so *merci,* Picasso, for helping me to connect with all these kindred souls who, like me, can't resist the lure of *la joie de vivre* on the French Riviera.

QUESTIONS AND TOPICS FOR DISCUSSION

1. In the early chapters of *Cooking for Picasso,* long before we actually see Pablo Picasso, we hear a lot about him when the heroine Ondine talks to her parents. What does she observe later from his eating habits, the letter he wrote to his friend in Paris, and the note he left for Ondine on the table? What do you remember most from that moment when Ondine actually meets Picasso for the first time?

2. When you learned of Picasso's childhood through his eyes, did this change your view of him? What made him feel guilty about his ambition and dedication to his art? What is causing him the stress that made him stop painting?

3. How would you describe the different personalities of Ondine, Julie and Céline? What are the roots of the family's tensions? What legal and financial complications make it impossible for Céline to help her mother?

4. When Céline and her Aunt Matilda begin their cooking class in Mougins, what causes Céline to immediately get off on the wrong foot with Chef Gilby Hallliwell? Why is secrecy necessary for Céline's quest? Why do Céline and Gil have trouble trusting each other? What draws them together in spite of their wariness?

5. Ondine's life takes an unexpected turn just when she is getting more confident about Picasso. What were your feelings about Luc? Did you feel relief or apprehension about what impact he might have on Ondine's life? Did you later feel that your instincts were correct?

6. Céline's visit to a French lawyer results in a startling revelation about her Grandmother Ondine's death. How does what Céline learns from Monsieur Clément change everything for her? And what does this revelation tell the reader about Ondine's fate?

7. Try making a list of all the paintings mentioned in the novel and looking them up on the Internet. (The only fictional painting in the novel is Picasso's portrait of Ondine called *Girl-at-a-Window*.) What do you feel about the artwork that Picasso produced during this mysterious interlude?

8. Discuss the impact of Ondine's return to France on her daughter Julie. How does seeing familiar things and people feel different to the reader when we view it all through Julie's eyes?

9. After the Second World War, Picasso comes back into Ondine's life. What has happened to them both with the passage of time? How does this encounter strengthen Ondine's resolve to do something to help Julie?

10. What makes Céline finally open up to her Aunt Matilda and bring her along to visit the fortune-telling neighbor Madame Sylvie? How did you feel about Madame Sylvie's revelations?

11. How does Céline's quest collide with Gil's business problems? What makes her finally decide to take Gil into her confidence? Why is it now possible for them to begin to trust each other?

12. What gives Ondine the courage to seek out Picasso again after so many years? Do you think he planned to help her all along, or do you think he made a sudden decision to do so?

13. What do we learn about Céline's father, Arthur, in the chapters when he was courting Céline's mother, Julie? When Arthur and Julie come to visit Ondine years later, why does the birth of Céline impact Ondine so deeply? What significance can be found in Ondine's dream about being visited by Picasso after his death?

14. What did you feel about the final revelation at the end of the novel? How does Gil help Céline understand its significance?

CAMILLE AUBRAY is an Edward Albee Foundation Fellowship winner. A writer-in-residence at the Karolyi Foundation in the South of France, she was a finalist for the Pushcart Press Editors' Book Award and the Eugene O'Neill National Playwrights Conference. She studied writing at the University of London with David Hare, Tom Stoppard, and Fay Weldon; and with her mentor Margaret Atwood at the Humber College School of Creative Writing Workshop in Toronto. Aubray has been a staff writer for the daytime dramas *One Life to Live* and *Capitol,* has taught writing at New York University, and has written and produced for ABC News, PBS, and A&E. The author divides her time between Connecticut and the South of France. Visit her at her website: camilleaubray.com.

ABOUT THE TYPE

This book was set in Granjon, a modern recutting of a typeface produced under the direction of George W. Jones (1860–1942), who based Granjon's design upon the letterforms of Claude Garamond (1480–1561). The name was given to the typeface as a tribute to the typographic designer Robert Granjon (1513–89).

Chat.
Comment.
Connect.

Visit our online book club community at
Facebook.com/RHReadersCircle

Chat
Meet fellow book lovers and discuss what you're reading.

Comment
Post reviews of books, ask—and answer—thought-provoking
questions, or give and receive book club ideas.

Connect
Find an author on tour, visit our author blog, or invite one of
our 150 available authors to chat with your group on the phone.

Explore
Also visit our site for discussion questions, excerpts, author
interviews, videos, free books, news on the latest releases,
and more.

Books are better with buddies.
Facebook.com/RHReadersCircle

RANDOM HOUSE READER'S CIRCLE ®

RANDOM  HOUSE